THE EXILED

A NOVEL

JORDAN LOWERY

First published by Hoos Books 2026

This novel is entirely a work of fiction. The names, characters and incidents portrayed in it are the work of the author's imagination. Any resemblance to actual persons, living or dead, events or localities is entirely coincidental.

Second edition.

ISBN (paperback): 979-8-9921003-1-0

Editing by Erin Young

Editing by Joe Pierson

Cover and book design by Christian Storm/Stormhausen Design

To my younger self, who insanely rooted

the idea of writing a book into my brain.

We made it.

THE EXILED

CHAPTER ONE
DAY ONE OF EXILE

JACOB HUGHES IS DEAD.

That is what the populace of Derro are forced to believe. Stripped of his citizenship and erased from official records, Jacob's existence had been purged. He is now a nonentity, a mere memory, a cautionary tale.

Such was the cost of exile—a punishment considered graver than death. The council took immense pride in emphasizing this.

The truth, however, was that Jacob wasn't *truly* dead. Only *legally*. After all, in Derro, as in life, death was all but inevitable. If he'd had a choice, he would have preferred the finality of actual death, rather than this new excruciating existence.

But unfortunately for him, his own attempt had failed.

And now, as his eyes snapped open, instantly flooding with awareness as if jolting back to life, he was quickly reminded of that bitter reality. His heart pounded fiercely, and a surge of adrenaline coursed through his veins, propelling his body forward, only to be pinned down by an unyielding force.

"Easy there," a voice murmured, muffled yet commanding.

Jacob squinted as his new world spun into a disorienting whirlwind. Amid the dizzying chaos, a burly figure materialized before him, their identity obscured by the haze. The blurred figure grabbed Jacob's chin, their callused hand scraping against his face as they wrenched his head, making it sway like a pendulum.

"Rise and shine, exiled," the voice said, its arrogance cutting through the air, accompanied by the stench of tobacco. "Welcome to life after death."

As the scent invaded Jacob's senses, a rush of recognition flooded through him, instantly linking the figure to one person—*Wes:* a former commander of the Cullers, the merciless civil force of Derro, tasked with culling criminals and enforcing the council's iron-fisted control over society.

"You're almost *home*," Wes said, his gritty hands patting Jacob's face before finally releasing his grip.

Jacob's heavy head sank into his chest. He groaned, the sudden drop stinging his shoulder, a stiff reminder of his wound. And of *that night*. The night that had brought him here. Wherever *here* was.

Almost home? Jacob wished that were true.

He grasped at what little he could conjure from his weary mind, recalling memories of his former home, hoping to find comfort amid this uncertainty unfolding before him. With floor-to-ceiling windows, his house had felt encased in glass, offering a serene view of the Tuto forest. The rooms, each adorned with photographs *she* had captured, immortalizing their cherished moments in frozen frames. The loveseat on their second-story deck, where they'd sit together countless mornings and evenings, attuned to the sounds of nature and the ever-present scent of pine. His heart yearned with an insatiable hunger for those stolen moments, the everyday routines and shared rituals that had never hinted at an imminent end.

Sadly for Jacob, they had.

The weight of his exile settled upon him, heavy and suffocating. He blinked repeatedly, needing his eyes to adjust to his surroundings. As his vision finally cleared, an unexpected sight greeted him: his wrists and ankles were bound by holocuffs. Jacob attempted to move his limbs, knowing full well it would be futile. Still, he tried, and found little movement. These holographic restraints were highly secure, their strength adaptable based on the detainee's resistance, rendering them unbreakable. Just as they were now for Jacob.

His only move was to wait and see how all this would play out. As he slowly lifted his head, he noticed he was dressed in the same clothes as *that night*: black denim jeans, a long-sleeved flannel, and a rugged jacket. Whipping his unruly brown hair from his eyes, his breath immediately became caught in his throat. He had found himself aboard a Screech. The fuselage loomed overhead, its grim interior lined with rows of red seats, each occupied by other exiles.

This must be how it happens.

In the few times he had seen it soar through the sky, the Screech's electric batteries emitted a high-pitched whine, like the distant screech of an owl. Fitting, really, for a council whose emblem was an owl. Jacob could see the emblem even now: the haunting owl with glimmering red eyes, its wings forming an unending circle, a cruel reminder of life's relentless cycle: birth, life, and, of course, death. Or, in Jacob's case … exile. Screeches bore a terrifying presence, cold and unforgiving. Just like the fate of those it carried.

Jacob had never imagined himself ensnared within this metallic behemoth, condemned to a journey with no return. Drawing a deep breath, he tried calming his nerves as he tilted his head back. He flinched, surprised to find his head resting against a cold surface. Looking over his shoulder, he found a small window offering a narrow view of his so-called "new home," as Wes had cynically labeled it.

But for Jacob, it felt more like purgatory. His home was now gone, lost forever. And the notion of his new home resided solely with *her*—Charlotte.

Beyond the window, Jacob watched the ocean ripple under the descending sun. Usually, the sight would be comforting. Now, it terrorized him. As if the undulations were taunting him, conspiring to amplify his despair, a precursor to the horrors that awaited him in exile. Thoughts of his destination gripped him, causing his palms to sweat. Every muscle in his body seemed to coil as a barrage of worst-case scenarios assaulted his mind, each one more terrifying than the last.

Please don't be Eremos, he pleaded silently, knowing it was the worst island to be exiled to.

That was the rumor, anyway. Eremos was the council's first island of exile, a place seen by some as a relic of the Anarchy Era—a lawless period that had preceded the council's rule. An era the council had saved everyone from. Or so it had seemed, until recently.

Suddenly, a guttural cough erupted from the man seated beside Jacob, causing him to jolt. Tearing his gaze from the window, his unease deepened as he took in the disheveled figure next to him. The man looked as though he'd emerged from the depths of hell. The left side of his face was marred by a burn, the skin splotchy and taut against his jawline and cheekbones. His tattered clothes clung to his scarred frame, and his smoky gray hair, matted and frayed like straw, brushed limply on his shoulders.

The sight was enough to chill the bravest of souls, leaving Jacob frozen, unable to tear his eyes away as he watched the man battle a fit of coughing that wracked his fragile body. Just as it seemed the fit would never end, the coughing finally subsided, leaving the man's neck bent in exhaustion.

"Evil men will soon disappear," the man rasped as he slowly leaned back into his seat. He turned toward Jacob, eyes ablaze with a searing intensity. "You'll stare at the spot where they once were, but they will be gone."

Jacob bit the insides of his cheeks, a nervous habit for him, as he locked eyes with the man, utterly at a loss for words. It felt as though the depths of his soul were being probed.

"You're staring at *my face.*"

"I didn't mean to—"

"What you're staring at is a *reminder* of where *they* once *were.*"

Jacob shifted uncomfortably, as little as his holocuffs allowed. "And … who are … *they?*"

"*They* are the evildoers. The wicked ones."

Evildoers? Wicked ones? Jacob thought, his mind racing. "Are you … well?"

The man shrugged, turning away from Jacob to peer out the small window over his shoulder. "I'm better now. Far better than I was. But not nearly as good as I'm going to be."

Jacob sat stunned, struggling to piece together whatever the hell that meant. The words felt almost hopeful, as if the madman were eager to reach their island of exile. The thought made Jacob tremble, knowing undoubtedly there were others like this man waiting for them on the shores.

"So, you're not afraid of where we're going?" he asked.

"Through death's shadowed valley, fear finds no hold, for He carries me into Exile," the man said, returning his gaze to Jacob, a twisted smile stretching across his face. "You see, I exist here solely because … I was *spared*."

Then he burst into a fit of laughter, a chilling, unhinged sound that echoed throughout the cabin, drawing the attention of others, before abruptly subsiding, replaced by another round of coughing.

Now Jacob's whole body shuddered with a cold sweat. *I'm definitely headed to Eremos.*

He turned his gaze away and scanned the Screech, his eyes meeting those of the other exiles aboard, who watched the madman cough. Unlike the maniac next to him, most of them appeared outwardly normal, showing no signs of fear, as if being transported in a Screech and bound by holocuffs were just another routine experience.

Not for Jacob.

He wondered how many among them were Last Patriots—members of the rebellion against the council's rule. Their goal was to restore Derro to its former glory, as the United States of America. Recent events had led to a mass exile of many of them, so it was safe to assume there were a few among them. Regardless of their allegiance, Jacob resolved to mimic his criminal companion's composed demeanor, aiming to blend in and avoid attracting unwanted attention. The last thing he wanted was to become an easy target.

That, sadly, seemed to be the fate of the teenage boy who stood out among the others. The adolescent huddled in his seat, his wide-eyed gaze darting anxiously around the Screech as his body tensed at every movement. Tall and gaunt, the kid had a lock of amber-colored curls that dangled to his dry, bloodshot eyes. Jacob struggled to maintain his gaze as he witnessed the kid's vulnerability, his own fear momentarily overshadowed by empathy. Innocence could be lost at any age. And, unfortunately for the kid, exile had no age limit.

"All right, listen up," Wes commanded, drawing Jacob's attention. "I expect everyone to shut up and obey my instructions."

A hushed silence invaded the cabin. It was evident why Wes had once been a commander of the Cullers, the way he had just effortlessly seized control. Or perhaps it was only because he was a Culler, equipped in an all-black, form-fitting uniform that bulged against his heavy biceps, an owl emblem adorning the shoulder plates, and body armor that hugged his burly frame. Feared and dreaded by both law-abiding citizens and criminals alike, all Cullers were a force to be reckoned with. Jacob watched as Wes stood at the far end of the fuselage, in front of a fortified alloy cargo door, the gateway to his new home.

"This is what's going to happen next," Wes declared. "We are approaching the drop zone, where your new home awaits. Once we arrive, this door behind me will descend. We'll be hovering above the Nyctea Ocean, and one by one, each of you will jump out of my Screech and swim to shore."

Jacob let out a breath as Wes's words sank in, his expectations shattering before him. The harsh reality of his exile had hit him like a sucker punch to the gut. Suddenly, he felt as if he were refuse, simply being discarded by the council, just another routine dump.

Wes chuckled. "You should see the look on all your faces. It's easily become my favorite part of this new role I've found myself in. Unless that is, any of you gives me a reason to use this."

Wes reached behind his back, drawing a pistol, which he raised above his head, his lips curling into a satisfied grin. Jacob recognized the firearm instantly: the Talon, a standard-issue Culler firearm. The sight of it sent a chill down Jacob's spine.

"This beauty holds twenty bullets," Wes taunted. "And if you include my partner's, then combined, we have forty."

Allen, the second, and only other Culler on the Screech positioned himself beside Wes, his Talon pointed downward. Though much younger than Wes, Allen was just as intimidating, his youthful face overshadowed by a faint scar above his eye. The Culler wore a stern, attentive expression as he awaited Wes's instructions.

"That's plenty enough to end all of your souls," Wes threatened, his eyes scanning the exiles before halting suddenly. "Including yours, *princess*."

Jacob followed Wes's gaze to the only woman on board. Her lips curled in disgust as she scoffed, blowing her wavy, rose-gold hair from her eyes. She flashed Wes a sarcastic grin, exuding an edginess that matched her attire: cargo pants, a white top, and a fitted black leather jacket.

"Don't test me, Alex," Wes said, punctuating his threat with the nodding of his Talon. "The same goes for the rest of you exiles. If any of you get any bright ideas, you can kiss your chances of seeing your new home goodbye. And trust me when I say, none of you will want to miss it. I've heard Eremos is the greatest."

No … Jacob gasped internally. He'd been exiled to the island reserved for the worst of the worst. *Just like Commander Brody had promised.* He scrunched his nose and clenched his fists.

His options had narrowed to a binary choice: obedience or oblivion. Both paths led to the same destination—death. The only distinction lay in their timing. One offered instantaneous demise, while the other delayed it. Death, as it had been in Derro, was just as inevitable on Eremos, if not more. All that mattered now was the sickening truth that whichever choice he made, it would only be a matter of when.

"Drop zone reached," announced the Screech's Aux, its words crisp and well enunciated.

As the report reached Jacob's ears, he closed his eyes, a pang of longing stirring memories of his former AI companion—Sid. Otherwise known as his Aux.

In Derro, Auxes were compulsory for the populace: small AI computer chips implanted into the brain. They allowed people to control every piece of technology they owned via voice commands, seamlessly interwoven into modern life, rendering them omnipresent. Growing up, Sid had always been there, a tiny voice in Jacob's head, a comforting presence and steadfast companion who seemed to know him better than he knew himself. The collection of Sid reminded him of a time when he'd had someone to rely on, someone who understood him in ways no human ever could. Sid's ability to adapt to his preferences and anticipate his needs had left an indelible mark on Jacob's heart.

And in this moment, minutes away from his exile, Jacob yearned for Sid's comforting presence once again. The thought of having someone by his side, even if it was just an AI, would give him a flicker of hope amid the anarchy that awaited him.

But Sid is gone now. Just like Charlotte. I'm more alone than I've ever been.

"Well, isn't that just the most exciting news?" Wes said. "*Lady*, and gentlemen, you heard the Aux. Your new home awaits."

A deafening screech filled the air, assaulting Jacob's ears as the cargo door behind Wes began its slow descent, transforming into a sturdy ramp. Wes raised his hands in synchrony, clearing relishing the theatrics of the impending plunges. A stiff wind rushed into the Screech, tugging at Jacob's clothes and sending a tremor of unease slithering through his bones.

He scanned the faces of the other exiles, hoping to find any potential allies. He knew that facing the terrors of Eremos together, rather than alone, offered the best chance for survival. Some cracked their necks, others stretched their limbs as far as their holocuffs allowed, but everyone seemed to take deep breaths as they prepared for their jump. The collective resolve among them was palpable, a shared determination, an unspoken understanding that their fight for their lives had only just begun.

Jacob knew he could no longer afford to dwell on his past, nor the uncertainty of what awaited him any longer. Instead, he focused on the present moment, honing his mind and body for the leap he was about to take.

You're stronger than you think. Charlotte's words soothed his mind, offering a brief respite. He closed his eyes and embraced them, letting them build strength within him, something he should have done that night.

"Let's start with the little monster," Wes ordered Allen, indicating his first target.

Allen started toward the kid, and upon reaching him, deactivated his holocuffs with a remote encrypted scan. The boy's face turned ashen, his gaze locked beyond the exit, revealing nothing more than a white void. Once released, Allen seized the kid by the neck and forcefully pushed him toward the center of the fuselage, where Wes stood waiting.

"Move it, kid," Allen growled.

The adolescent stumbled forward, his body shuddering as he scanned the Screech for help. All he saw staring back at him were cold, unsympathetic eyes. That was until he saw Jacob. Knowing there wasn't anything he could do for the kid, Jacob simply nodded, hoping to offer the boy a boost of courage.

"It's Morgan, right?" Wes asked.

The kid backed away, nodding.

"Well Morgan, it's a damn shame you're the first to go. But perhaps it's fate. You know, for what you did. And who am I to question fate?"

Wes clearly hadn't let his new position change him. Even this low on the Culler totem pole, he still found a way to exert his own twisted sense of justice, just as he had with members of the Last Patriots when he was a commander. Though in this dark and unforgiving world, it seemed all notions of justice were distorted. The lines between right and wrong had long since blurred, a line Jacob had been teetering on for the past year.

"*Wait*," Morgan shrieked, his eyes widening until only the whites of his irises were visible. "Nobody said I had to jump—"

Morgan's words were cut short as Wes grabbed him by the collar and yanked him close. "Did you not hear a word I just said, you twerp?" he snapped. "Can't you see, kid? You have *no choice*. Did you honestly believe we'd risk our lives to land on that godforsaken wasteland? Allen, you hearing this?"

Allen simply dismissed Morgan's pleas with a roll of his eyes. "Kids these days," he said, turning away from Morgan and making his way toward Alex to release her next.

"Here's a choice for you," Wes said. "And for the sake of your young soul, I hope you choose wisely. You can either jump out of my Screech, or I can tell everyone here exactly what you did to get exiled. Try finding friends to help you out there after that." Wes released his grip on Morgan and adjusted his jacket's collar with a motion that felt more like mockery than assistance. "The choice is yours."

Jacob's eyes mirrored the steady, collective gaze of the other exiles, all locked on Morgan, whose head hung low, like a defeated animal. Fitting, for someone about to be *culled*. Morgan took a deep breath, as if summoning what little courage he had left, then turned toward the cargo door and ran. Jacob imagined tears streaming down the boy's face as he sprinted toward the white void. Then Morgan leaped out of the Screech and vanished into thin air.

Wes erupted in hysterical laughter. "Gets me every time," he said, in between breaths. But as his eyes landed on Alex, his expression shifted. She now stood where Morgan once had, Allen's Talon pressed to her back. "Ah, it's your turn now, princess," he said, a sly grin curling across his face. He circled her slowly, like a predator closing in on its prey. "There is no denying it. You truly are a beautiful one."

Jacob felt sick to his stomach as he watched Wes's spectacle. Then his eyes grew wide, shocked, and fearful of what Alex was doing. In her own act of defiance, she slowly and dramatically offered a curtsy to Wes. A chorus of mumbled chuckles from some of the exiles filled the cabin, rising as Alex rose and bolted toward the exit. As she jumped, she spun midair, a perfect 180 degrees, and extended both her middle fingers toward Wes as she fell and disappeared.

"*You bitch!*" Wes yelled, his anger rising with every deadened titter. "*Shut up. All of you.*"

Jacob fought to suppress the rising chuckle that Alex's boldness had provoked, a reaction mirrored by the other criminals. It was a brave move indeed, one Jacob felt a small surge of pride for. Sure, it was a fleeting act, but it was also empowering, in a situation where Alex had little control.

And it reminded him of Charlotte.

Following Alex's lead, the rest of the exiles plunged from the Screech one by one, accepting their bleak fates. Jacob watched the scene unfold, a growing fear building within him, knowing it was only a matter of time before he was next. Eventually, his attention shifted to the madman as Allen started deactivating the burned man's holocuffs.

Up this close, Jacob could hear the soft hum, like an electrical current, as Allen raised the remote above the holocuffs. The hum triggered a faint, pulsating glow from the holocuffs, as if they were acknowledging their impending release. Then, with a final flicker, they vanished, leaving no trace behind.

"No funny games this time," Allen warned as he shoved the madman toward the center of the Screech.

Wes approached the maniac with a smirk. "Well, well, aren't you a sight to behold," he said, his lip curling in disgust as he took in the grotesque scars that marred the man's face. "Tell me, Michael, what's it like carrying a constant reminder of your mistakes?"

Michael tilted his head, meeting Wes's stare, his jaw tightening. "It's a dreadful thing to fall into the hands of the living God."

Then he snapped his gaze toward Jacob, his piercing eyes drilling into him. "The eyes of the Lord are upon the *righteous*," he proclaimed, lifting his head, as if drawing strength from some unseen power. "And *His* ears are open unto their cry."

Jacob went completely still, his gaze locked on Michael, trying to make sense of the madman's cryptic words. This man was clearly deranged. Was he quoting scripture? Or was this some manifestation of his own twisted beliefs? Jacob knew all too well how someone could find their own meaning in words told by man, and how those words could be warped, offering a sense of purpose, even if that purpose caused harm. People often looked for hope in all the wrong places.

"I must admit, I'm not entirely sure what that meant," Wes said. "But one thing's for sure. If anyone's perfectly suited to capture the essence of Eremos, it's undeniably you. Hell, the council oughta put your face on their billboards." Wes nodded toward the cargo door. "Now, don't keep Eremos waiting. Go on."

"*No!*" Michael roared, his hands clenched into fists.

Jacob's heart skipped a beat at Michael's outburst. This didn't feel like Alex's act of defiance. This felt different, heavier, like the final, frantic snap of a feral animal, desperate to fight back.

"Not this again." Wes sighed nonchalantly while leveling his Talon at Michael.

Unfazed by the pistol, Michael inched closer until the barrel pressed against his burned cheek. It was as if he were daring Wes to pull the trigger, choosing death over the hell of exile. Jacob, unfortunately, understood Michael's choice all too well.

Meanwhile, Allen remained undaunted by the escalating situation, as if such scenes were a common occurrence. He started deactivating the holocuffs around Jacob's ankles, their rising hum matching the tension in the cabin.

"You think your face scares me, Prince Charring?" Wes taunted. "Turn around and start running, or I'll put a bullet through that disgusting face."

Wes lightly jabbed the barrel of his talon against Michael's face, gesturing for him to run, but the madman didn't budge. For several seconds, the two men locked eyes, Michael showing no fear despite the threat. Jacob tensed, anticipating the inevitable gunshot.

Then, without warning, Wes swiftly redirected his aim, pointing toward the white void and fired. Jacob flinched at the gunshot, but Michael had seen through the ruse. In fact, he had bet his life on it. Immediately the madman struck Wes with a brutal blow to the neck.

The Culler staggered, his legs buckling beneath him as he dropped to his knees. Terror flashed in his wide eyes, the Talon slipping from his grasp as Wes's hands shot to his throat, clutching at it in a frantic, desperate struggle for air, a wheezing death rattle escaping his lips.

Alerted by Michael's attack, Allen jumped up from Jacob's now freed ankles, and quickly reached for his Talon. But Michael's reflexes were too fast. In a flash, he'd seized Wes's fallen pistol, aimed, and fired. The bullet struck Allen square in the forehead, and he crumpled to the floor, dead before he hit the ground.

Jacob recoiled in horror as blood splattered his face. He stumbled back, collapsing into his seat, and stared, transfixed, as Michael hammered the butt of the Talon into Wes's nose. The sickening crack of bone filled the air as Wes collapsed to the floor, his body convulsing in pain.

Michael glanced over his shoulder, his eyes burning with an otherworldly fervor as he glared at Jacob. Slowly, he turned to face him fully, a chilling sense of purpose radiating from him.

"The mighty man's flame shall kindle, an unquenchable inferno," he proclaimed. "I, the instrument, bear witness. The scorched path is not chaos, but divine intent. A flame that devours, yet purifies." His gaze lingered on the Talon gripped in his hand. "Fear has no hold, for He is with me. In this rod, I find solace amid the darkness."

In that moment, Michael seemed less a man and more an instrument of divine justice, poised to fulfill some sacred mission.

Then the madman sprinted toward the white void, his footfalls echoing until silence reclaimed the space. Jacob shook his head, his mind trapped in a haze of shock and disbelief of what had just happened. Suddenly, a loud siren tore through the Screech, accompanied by the relentless flash of red lights. *I don't have much time.*

Jacob, his wrists still bound by holocuffs, struggled to his feet, his heart pounding as his gaze fell on Allen's lifeless body, a pool of blood spreading around the Culler's head. Panic surged through him, clouding his thoughts as he searched for a way to free himself. There was no way he could swim to shore, fighting the waves, bound as he was. He needed that remote, and just as he reached down to grab it from Allen's outstretched hand, a pained grunt snapped his attention away. He looked up to see Wes beginning to stir, his movements labored.

Acting with desperate urgency, Jacob reached for the remote, his trembling fingers hovering it over his holocuffs, willing it to emit the familiar hum of deactivation, but nothing happened. He tried angling the remote in different positions, hoping for a response, but still there was nothing.

Shit. Shit. Shit.

His eyes darted upward, continuously checking in on Wes, who was now slowly rising to his knees, visibly struggling to regain balance. Needing to try something different, Jacob placed the remote in Allen's lifeless hand and closed the Culler's fist, ensuring his fingers gripped the remote, which lit up in response to his prints. Then he brought Allen's hands above his holocuffs, which were finally met with an emitting hum.

Come on. Come on.

In what felt like long, agonizing seconds, his holocuffs finally vanished, and Jacob was free. He immediately grabbed Allen's Talon from the Culler's other hand, rose, and aimed it at Wes, his finger hovering over the trigger. Wes's arm shot up in surrender, a defeated sigh escaping him. The look of submission didn't suit him, clashing with his usual air of confidence. Then, as if overcome by the absurdity of it all, Wes started to laugh.

"You'd be doing me a favor," Wes wheezed over the sirens. *"I'm a dead man anyways."*

Jacob's finger twitched on the trigger, but before he could act, the same deafening screech from before erupted, overpowering the blaring sirens. The cargo door was slowly rising, sealing off his only way out.

He burst into a sprint, heart thumping against his chest, the Talon gripped tightly in his hand. Jacob never imagined himself running toward his exile, but there was nothing else he could do. The gap to Eremos was rapidly diminishing, forcing him to push beyond his limits. He feared he wasn't going to make it in time, his mind panicking as he searched for a solution. There was only one way he would clear that gap.

I have to dive through.

Jacob dove through the narrow opening of the rising door and tumbled into open air. Wind whipped past his face as he plummeted toward the ocean below. In that fleeting second, his gaze caught the large island of Eremos, dominated by mountains, their jagged peaks piercing the sky. And there, atop the highest summit, sprawled a vast, flat expanse, encircled by sheer cliffs, waterfalls cascading down into a pool. At its center stood a towering structure, rising like a sentinel.

The surprising sight vanished as Jacob descended, his focus shifting to the ocean below. The impact with the water sent a jolt of icy cold through his body as he submerged. Beneath the surface, startled fish darted away in a flurry, fleeing his presence. He paused, captivated by their instinctual fear, and realized that he—and the others who had jumped before him—were unwelcome intruders disrupting their daily rhythm.

Though his threat to them was only temporary, the sensation of being an unwanted guest lingered. Jacob knew this feeling would accompany him to Eremos's shore, where he would inevitably face the dangers that awaited him. And in due time, experience the same trepidation as the fleeing fish.

With unease tightening in his chest, his instincts took over, propelling his legs upward. Breaking through the surface, he gasped for air, his lungs reluctantly drawing in the unwelcome breath of a new existence.

In the distance, he caught sight of the Screech dwindling on the horizon as it glided toward the setting sun. A sense of doom settled over him as he floated, the crashing waves engulfing his body. They continued their taunt, dragging him inexorably toward Eremos while also pushing him further from the world that had discarded him, emphasizing there was no return.

Only exile.

CHAPTER TWO

ONE YEAR BEFORE EXILE

IT HURT TO LOOK AT.

Jacob closed his eyes and drew a deep breath, letting the rich, familiar scent of gun oil wash over him like a loved one's embrace. The smell had always clung to him, like old memories etched in the fabric of his clothes and the pores of his skin. The scent reminded him of his father. And of home.

Son, oiling your gun is a ritual, his father would constantly tell him. *It's a connection. To those who came before us and a responsibility to those who follow.*

His father's wisdom lingered in his mind, filling him with reverence as he stood behind the front counter of Hoos. He opened his eyes, feeling the hurt once again, and started oiling their pistol, the one they'd built together when Jacob was just a boy. Each stroke carried purpose and intention, a tribute to the tradition and legacy his father had bequeathed to him.

Since his father's passing, Jacob had made it a ritual to regularly oil their gun, ensuring that, over time, the firearm maintained its peak performance and all its parts operated smoothly. Yet, despite his dedicated care, the pistol had begun to exhibit signs of rust and patina. It had become a personal obligation to his father, a pledge to care for the gun, just as he felt compelled to continue operating Hoos.

Hoos wasn't a typical firearm store. It embodied a mission deeply rooted in Jacob's core, to safeguard the citizens of Tuto, the metropolis of Derro. However, its distinctive emphasis on antique guns set it apart, a choice to highlight and preserve history for generations to come.

Preserving history, one shot *at a time,* his father's motto echoed in his head.

To its customers, Hoos felt like a sanctuary steeped in history and tradition. Firearm enthusiasts came not just to browse but to connect, to share their passion, and to tap into the well of knowledge held by its proprietor—Jacob's father. The man had seemed to know everything there was about firearms and their history. Jacob did his best to step into that legacy, but it often felt like wearing shoes a size too big, an uneasy fit that reminded him just how far he still had to go.

The front counter of Hoos was composed of a series of glass display cases showcasing the latest in gunpowder weaponry. Inside, rows of tempered glass shelves presented holographic stands cradling an array of firearms, making it seem as if the guns were hovering. A gentle, perpetual hum resonated from these cases, accompanied by a subtle warmth that Jacob often found comfort in by leaning his knee against the glass, just as he did today.

Beyond the display counter, a wide assortment of ammunition was neatly stacked in old-fashioned wooden crates. Despite technological advancements, the council mandated that firearms still utilized ballistic ammunition. Just another one of their measures aimed to suppress innovations in weaponry, as well as preventing criminals or citizens with low social scores—often one and the same—from rising up and resisting the council.

This was why Jacob's father focused more on antique firearms. That, and his love for history. Unfortunately for him, however, it wasn't the antiques that kept Hoos afloat.

Jacob paused for a moment, his eyes surveying Hoos's walls, all adorned with many period firearms, each carefully labeled with its history and significance on the world. Most told stories of wars fought centuries ago, but a few recounted the Collapse of the United States, a time before the Derro Council's rule, now known as the Anarchy Era. Jacob, being born long after the era of chaos, knew very little of the Collapse. What he did know was attributed to his father's stories. And among all the tales he'd heard, a common theme had emerged.

Division.

Division among the states. Division among the people.

It ceased to be the United States, his father would always recount.

The collapse had been attributed to the rise of technology, which reshaped society and created significant disparities between the rich and poor. The middle class had vanished, leaving only the impoverished and the affluent. This increasing gap between social strata led to soaring crime rates. The US government struggled to maintain order, and public trust in institutions eroded.

Law and order had become a distant memory, Jake.

In response, the Derro Council emerged, a clandestine assembly working behind closed doors, promising to restore law and order. Some believed them to be an oppressive force, a coalition of elitists, the military, and corporations. Others viewed them as saviors from the prolonged anarchy. The truth, however, one that is clear even today, is that nobody truly knows who *they* are.

Whoever they are, they had swiftly and covertly gained political power, sidelining a weak US government within a decade, and before anyone realized, they held complete control over a new nation known as Derro. Some felt as if the Collapse was the council's plan all along, the way they had swept in and saved everyone from years of anarchy. Of course, there were signs; there always are. But sadly, as history has shown time and time again, those signs were either ignored or not seen until it was too late.

The first indicator had been the deployment of the Cullers, a ruthless force tasked with restoring peace. Jacob could see how hard it was to miss this sign, when citizens were seeing hope amid the Anarchy Era; Culler's patrolling the streets, fighting crime with severe measures, however avoiding lethal force. The fate of criminals was always left to the council's judgment. The council placed immense emphasis on this.

Next came widespread surveillance. Cameras and drones became omnipresent, ensuring strict enforcement of laws and suppression of dissent. Rumors had spread about heavily fortified Control Hubs scattered across Derro, functioning as nerve centers for monitoring and manipulating the country's surveillance systems, AI networks, and communication channels. Though Jacob had never seen one, he'd heard talk that they were heavily guarded and hidden from public view.

Following this, AI Auxiliaries, now known as Auxes, became mandatory for all citizens. In the aftermath of the Anarchy Era, the council required all citizens to undergo Aux implantation. Events were held in major cities and towns, where citizens could receive their implants free of charge. Noncompliance resulted in a loss of privileges, such as loss of employment and the ability to pay for life's necessities, as payments were now completed by an Aux.

This left everyone with no choice but to obey. And now, the council implants Auxes at birth. *That's how you got Sid, Jake,* his father told him as a kid, *the little voice inside your head.*

Auxes were akin to personal assistants, subtly guiding the lives of every person in Derro, observing them, learning their habits, preferences, and daily routines. But beneath their helpful facade lay a more sinister purpose, understood by all as an aspect of the council's cultural manipulation.

These Auxes served as tools to feed the council data for calculating social scores, a measure of a citizen's behavior, loyalty to Derro, and adherence to their laws. These scores determined the privileges one would be granted, the higher the score, the greater the privileges. However, those with low social scores were dealt with severe restrictions. No matter what side a citizen fell under, it meant a life lived under the council's ever-watchful gaze.

The final sign, and what culminated the council's authoritative rule, was the Derro Act, a promise to maintain order, never ensuring an Anarchy Era would occur again. This law vested the council with the power to exile criminals to remote islands, serving as a stern deterrent against crime. These distant islands became symbols of terror, where criminals faced a fate rumored to be worse than death. Jacob couldn't quite shake the image of these islands reflecting the lawlessness of the Anarchy Era, vividly recounted by his father.

It was pure chaos, Jake. Picture society unraveling at its seams. Criminality running rampant, unchecked, with no effective governance to restore order. The whole world seemed to spiral into a lawless abyss. That was, until the council emerged.

The Derro Act had brought about a drastic change over Derro. Exiling criminals meant maintaining peace. However, as time passed, this solution fell short of eradicating the deep-rooted crime issue. It merely offered a temporary respite. This ignited divisions among the populace, some viewing exile as a necessary evil, and others condemning it, those others mostly being citizens with low social scores. As the social divide deepened, the impoverished turned to the only instincts they knew: survival. And inevitably, survival led to criminal acts. The council would continue to exile criminals, but some, like the Last Patriots, argued that their reliance on social scores would only perpetuate the creation of criminals.

Exile was a relentless cycle.

The US's prevailing theme had carried over into Derro and remained unchanged: division.

Amid the challenges posed by the council's rule, Jacob unwaveringly clung to the belief that there could be no justification for criminal behavior. He took pride in knowing that each firearm he sold empowered people to protect themselves. A shared perspective with the council emerged in this regard: by allowing the sale of guns, they armed the citizenry, establishing an additional deterrent against criminals. Instead of banning firearms, like some had preached, the council had chosen to confront the root issue head-on: the criminals themselves.

The jangling chime from the small bell adorning Hoos's entrance door snapped Jacob from his thoughts and alerted him to his first customer of the day.

"Welcome to Hoos," he greeted, turning his head toward the newcomer. Recognition dawned as Frank, a longtime customer of Hoos, stepped in. A round-shaped, elderly man with a bald head and a scruffy ginger beard that brushed against Jacob's glass cases with every visit.

"Hey, bud."

For reasons unknown, Frank never addressed Jacob by name. Whether he'd forgotten or simply preferred the moniker "bud," Jacob never bothered to correct him.

"Frank, how's it going?" he asked, a question he already knew the answer to, as it was always the same.

"Oh, you know, the usual. Just doin' my darnedest to keep myself physically strong, mentally awake, and morally straight."

Jacob smiled. "The *old* boy scout's honor."

"It's the only *law* I live by."

"And how's all that been working out for ya?"

Frank smirked at Jacob, an expression he interpreted as an *of course you'd ask me that* look. The old man let out a sigh of disappointment. "Well, let's just say that first one seems to be gettin' farther and farther away from me," he said, playfully tapping his ample belly.

"Oh, is that right?"

"The sumbich creeps up on ya like a darn owl swoopin' down on its prey."

"You sure it's not all that whiskey? I see you coming out of Liberties all the time."

Frank let out a hearty, deep laugh. "I've always been a tad bibulous, haven't I?"

"That you have."

"So, what you got here?" Frank asked, intrigued by Jacob's pistol. "Some sort of collectible?"

"Ah, this old thing," Jacob said, feeling a sense of pride overcoming him. "My father and I made this when I was a boy."

Frank raised a single eyebrow. "You done made this?"

"Yes sir," Jacob said as he started to reassemble the firearm. "We spent a little over a year scouring local antique gun shows and shops all over Derro to find all the ideal parts. The barrel, slide, and frame here were salvaged from vintage pieces found to give it a bit of history. But the trigger assembly, sights, and recoil spring were brand new at the time. This way we ensure precision and reliability."

Frank watched, his weathered eyes squinting as he observed Jacob finishing the pistol assembly. "It's a real beauty," he remarked. "And *blue?*"

"My father's touch. It's our favorite color. The bluing process was quite an endeavor. I remember my father patiently applying layer after layer of bluing solution, carefully polishing the steel between applications to create the deep, protective finish you see here."

"Your old man, he was a darn good fella."

"Thanks, Frank. He most certainly was."

"He work on them wooden grips too?"

"That was actually me. My father was the gunsmith, so he took pride in modifying all the parts so they fit well together. I took pride in carving the grips, which I did with American walnut to give it that warm, polished touch."

"Well I'll be damned. You two were quite the pair back in the day. How much you lookin' to get for it?"

"Oh, it's not for sale," Jacob said, placing the pistol back into its glass case and turning away from Frank to place it on the display shelf. "It's an heirloom. Between this old gun here, my home, and Hoos, it's all I've got left of my father."

Frank gave the display case a friendly pat. "Ah, ain't no way I could ever afford that beauty, anyways."

"But I'm happy to sell you any other gun," Jacob offered, turning back toward Frank.

The senior surveyed the collection of firearms hovering inside the display cases. As was tradition, his lengthy beard gently brushed against the glass. "What kind of pistol do you reckon'd be a good pick for the missus?"

"Well, that depends on the purpose."

"Just for keepin' her safe. I wanna make sure she has her protection. You know how it is."

Jacob nodded, understanding the unspoken implications. He couldn't blame Frank for wanting to ensure the safety of his wife, especially given the current state of Tuto. And Derro, for that matter.

"Been meanin' to get her one for quite some time now, and with them darn taxes on guns goin' up tomorrow, I figured it's best to take action now rather than wait any longer."

"I'm sure you're not the only one thinking that way. The last time the council raised taxes on guns, I nearly ran out of stock. Luckily I just received a new shipment last week."

Frank scoffed. "Them council folks think raisin' taxes on guns makes 'em harder to get, but they're dead *wrong*. It just makes 'em all the more desirin.'"

"So it seems," Jacob replied. "Well, my recommendation for Dolores will depend on her social score, as you know. Any idea what her score is?"

Frank gave a dismissive wave. "Our scores are just fine," he said, though a hint of worry crept into his voice. "I don't need you actin' like my damn Aux. Just show me what you think's best for her."

"All right, then. If it's self-defense you're looking for, I'd recommend this pistol here." Jacob reached into his pocket and grabbed his keys to unlock the glass case. Then, using a small remote hooked to his keychain, he hovered it above the firearm. A soft hum emitted from the remote, and within a few seconds, the holographic stand vanished, releasing the gun into his hand, which he placed on the counter for Frank to inspect. "It's petite, has a surprisingly easy-to-control 9-mm chamber, and mild recoil. It's a popular choice for women."

"Seems straightforward," Frank said after only a few seconds of inspection. "Let's get it done."

Jacob arched an eyebrow. "Okay, then. When can Dolores come by for paperwork?"

"Ain't no need for that. Just register it in my name. I aim for it to be a surprise."

Jacob hesitated. The implications of Frank's request began to weigh heavily on him, and he knew that what he was about to tell Frank might not be well received. It rarely was.

"I'm sorry, Frank, but I can't do that. The gun is for Dolores. The law requires the gun to be registered to her. I'll need her to come in for the paperwork."

Frank's expression turned crestfallen. "Ah, now that's *nonsense*. You know me and Dolores, now, after all."

"It's not about that, Frank. It's about following the law. I won't risk Hoos with a straw purchase."

Frank's disappointment was palpable. He paused, absorbing the consequences, and then eventually, he nodded. "Or worse, exile?"

Jacob, like everyone else in Derro, didn't truly know what exile was like. All he knew stemmed from the terrifying whispers that circulated around Tuto and online. There was also the council's use of sophisticated propaganda and disinformation campaigns to maintain public perception. They spread fear-inducing narratives, portraying the exiled criminals as monstrous, and the Derro Act as the only thing standing between civilization and anarchy.

Exile felt like being condemned to a real-life hell recreated.

"That too," Jacob said.

"Well, all righty," Frank said with a hint of reluctance. "Dolores and I will swing back by tomorrow morning. You think you can hold that for me?"

"No problem at all. Just be aware that the paperwork process is quite lengthy."

"Yeah, yeah," Frank waved off as he turned and exited Hoos.

Frustration with the constant changes in gun regulations was all too common among Hoos's customers. But for Jacob, following these restrictions and guidelines was a matter of principle. Not just to avoid losing Hoos and the threat of exile, but also to prevent firearms from falling into the wrong hands. This often created tension with locals who thought he was too strict. Jacob didn't care. To him, it was worth it. It was his way of contributing to the fight against crime. Frank had taken it better than some, and despite his initial disappointment, Jacob knew he'd come around.

With Frank gone and his pistol oiled, Jacob settled back into his routine. "Sid, turn on the TV," he requested his Aux.

Of course, Jacob, Sid said promptly, his voice seamlessly entering Jacob's mind as if it were his own.

Instantly, in the front corner of Hoos, a large, translucent screen materialized in the air. The holographic display projected vivid, three-dimensional images with stunning clarity. Jacob squinted, his senses sharpening at the sight of a news reporter speaking in hushed tones, the words "Breaking News" flashing across the screen. Jacob could tell right away something was wrong.

"Sid, turn it up."

Jacob stepped closer, his eyes glued to the holographic display as the reporter continued to speak, her voice rising with the volume on the TV.

"At this time, we believe there have been five casualties and three individuals severely injured from a school shooting that occurred just moments ago here in Tuto. The Cullers quickly responded to the scene and were able to disarm the shooter before further harm could be inflicted. Although details are still emerging, we know the suspect was a student, and that it's only a matter of time before they face exile."

"Sid, mute," Jacob said, his head bowing as he processed the recent tragedy. "Damn," he muttered under his breath. He leaned forward, gripping the edges of the counter as a tightness filled his throat and his stomach sank. It seemed like every day Tuto became scarier to live in. Moments like this were the reason he felt pride in offering protection to the citizens.

The bell rang again, signaling another customer entering Hoos. A twinge of suspicion overcame Jacob, as if he already knew who had entered without even looking up.

"Hello, Jacob," a honeyed voice greeted.

Jacob lifted his head and found that his suspicion had been confirmed. *Not again.*

Richard Woodwin had returned. A man with deep pockets and a keen desire to acquire businesses in Tuto. His ash-blond hair brushed against the shoulders of the sleek, fitted black leather jacket he wore over a crisp white dress shirt. The top two buttons were casually left undone, revealing unblemished, golden-toned skin. He was close in age to Jacob and exuded an aura of affluence, clearly using his wealth to maintain a youthful appearance.

"I thought I had made myself very clear. You're not welcome here," Jacob said firmly.

"It's a shame, isn't it?" Richard said, ignoring Jacob's remark and gesturing his gray eyes toward the TV.

Jacob bit the insides of his cheeks. "It's tragic."

"At least they caught the little monster. Won't be long for the victims' families to have justice. One less criminal to worry about in Tuto, thanks to the council."

"In times like this, exile doesn't always feel like enough justice."

"Yeah, well apparently neither did prison. But that was long before our time."

"Sid, turn off the TV."

The holographic display vanished. Jacob had seen enough. He let out a deep sigh as he bent down to grab a bottle of glass cleaner and a few hand towels, and began wiping down the display cases.

"I don't have time for this again, Richard. I will *not* be selling Hoos. It's only been in a no-go zone for a few weeks."

The council, as part of their Derro Act, marked specific areas within the country as no-go zones when crime rates within those regions soared to dangerous levels. These designations served as a warning to the public to avoid these areas entirely, or to enter with extreme caution. The anarchy that had preceded the council's rule left a lasting impact, making people choose to steer clear of these zones, and for good reason. However, the consequences were dire for businesses operating within these areas, as they suffered harsh repercussions, from reduced customers to increased crime activity.

"It's best to at least *consider* my offer," Richard attempted to persuade. "Before the value of Hoos suffers any further."

"I have a busy day ahead of me, so you need to leave," Jacob said, brushing off Richard's sales pitch.

"Oh, I have no doubt about that. The reactions from people after hearing about today's school shooting is going to send in herds of people into Hoos. Panic stricken, and desperate for a sense of control over their lives, they'll be clamoring for the same weapons the shooter used."

"I know what you're doing—"

"And that's where *you* come in, Jacob," Richard interrupted. "You'll be the one providing them with a false sense of security. An illusion that they can protect themselves, when in reality … you'll only be adding fuel to the fire. And that's where the *real* power lies."

Richard leaned forward, placing an elbow on the spot Jacob had just cleaned, his eyes gleaming with a wicked pleasure. "It actually reminds me of a book my father made me read when I was a kid. One of his personal favorites. *Crimson Hands.* Ever heard of it?"

Jacob frowned. "No, I haven't," he said, his hand tightening around the towel.

"That's all right, I figured you hadn't. I mean, it's an *old* book, written shortly after the Anarchy Era. I'd be surprised if you had. But this work of fiction, old as it may be, explores themes that couldn't be more relevant today."

I really don't want to hear you rant about some old, obscure book no one knows about.

"It's about a man named Tyrell Macy, who owns a successful gun manufacturing company. During the Anarchy Era, he was contracted by what remained of the US government to produce weapons for the front lines. When his factory discovered that some of his firearms were prone to backfiring or erupting when fired, Tyrell, under immense pressure, chose to ignore the issue and shipped them out anyway. The result?" Richard smirked. "Soldiers were harmed by the very weapons meant to protect them, leaving them defenseless on the battlefield, where they eventually died."

"Go to *hell,*" Jacob snarled, acutely aware of the parallels Richard was trying to convey. "I'm not responsible for the actions of some lunatic with a gun. Guns don't kill people. *People* kill people. As shown in that damn book."

"I suppose we see things differently. It's indicative of the world we live in, isn't it? We overlook the bigger picture. Or in this case, the underlying problem. Someone like *you* puts guns into Derro every day, making it inevitable they'll fall into the wrong hands. Just like that kid today, who decided to shoot his classmates. Now *that's* blood on hands."

Jacob leaned over the counter, his face contorted with rage. "Get out of my store. *Now.*"

"All right, all right, I'll leave. But before I go, I want to offer you something." Richard fished into his back pocket, produced a check, and placed it in front of Jacob.

Jacob frowned. "I don't need your *old* money. Go buy another business."

"Oh, I most certainly will. But you see, it's Hoos I'm truly interested in. I have a legacy to uphold, and in a world plagued by crime, there seems to be one source of hope. A hope from which I can profit." Richard tapped his finger on the check and slid it over to Jacob. "In case you have a change of heart," he said, before turning toward the exit.

"You're a *sick man*, Richard Woodwin."

Richard spun, his eyes meeting Jacob's with a steady gaze. As he continued walking backward, he extended his arms outward, as if embracing Jacob's accusation. "Some people, the sicker they become, the longer they *survive*."

Then he turned away and exited Hoos, the jangling bell slowly fading into silence. Bowing his head, Jacob's gaze fell upon the handwritten check. It was already signed and made payable to Jacob Hughes with the amount left blank. The memo line simply stated, "Purchase of Hoos."

Though part of him wanted nothing more than to tear the check in half, something held him back. The money promised limitless possibilities, and in that moment, he felt as though he were in the driver's seat of his own future. A future free from the burden of Hoos and its legacy.

A jingle pulled Jacob's attention to another customer entering Hoos. He greeted them with a polite smile. But as his gaze shifted back to the check, an impulse took hold of him. Thinking no longer, he snatched up the check and tore it cleanly in half.

He had a legacy of his own to uphold.

CHAPTER THREE
DAY ONE OF EXILE

THE SUN'S DESCENT NEARED completion, casting the horizon in fiery hues as the moon began its quiet ascent. Jacob's gaze swept over his surroundings, his heart racing in sync with his imagination. Visions of the dangers lurking on Eremos's shore flooded his mind: serial killers, child abusers, rapists, and men like Michael, teetering on the edge of insanity. The weight of fear pressed hard, threatening to pull him under. Yet, a sudden realization cut through the chaos.

Jacob possessed an instrument of defense.

A gun.

Suddenly, the fear gripping him receded, overshadowed by the Talon's potential. Not just to protect but to instill hope. With darkness pressing closer, hesitation was no longer an option. His gaze returned to Eremos, the fading sunlight revealing a crimson sliver of towering mountains, sprawling valleys, and tangled jungles. It felt as though a heavy eyelid was closing, sealing Jacob into a waking nightmare. Eremos loomed ahead, a colossal no-go zone, with no alternate route. Only onward.

He embarked on his swim, enduring the sting of saltwater in his eyes and the pain from his shoulder wound. The unforgiving waves battered his body, turning each stroke into a struggle. The briny taste of the sea filled his mouth and nostrils, forcing him to expel it forcefully. He gasped for air, battling to keep his head above the surface.

Thoughts of his impending arrival continued to assail his mind. What awaited him on the shore? Had Michael arrived and continued his slaughter? Or would his fellow exiles lie in ambush, ready to strike the moment he set foot on land? Alternatively, had enough time passed since their jump, leaving Jacob to face the dangers of Eremos alone? Amid the uncertainty, Jacob clenched his teeth and pressed on through the challenging swim, driven by a flickering hope that, somehow, he could uncover a way to escape his grim fate.

After a grueling swim, he finally reached the shore, where complete darkness greeted him. The bitter water had left his skin prickling and his muscles aching, but the relief of solid ground drove him forward. Rising unsteadily to his feet, he scanned the shore, surprised to find no one in sight. Stumbling over countless pebbles, his body weighed down by exhaustion and wet clothes, he struggled with each step as he pressed toward the driest patch of sand he could find.

The crashing waves soothed his ears, their thunderous roars reminding him of the treasured beach back in Tuto—the one he'd never see again. The salty scent of the sea clung to him, mingling with the lingering brine still coating his mouth. Unseen birds cried out, their calls cutting through the night, alerting his presence as he collapsed onto the sand.

I need water.

His body shivered as gritty grains stuck to his damp skin and clothes. Every fiber of his being ached, as though he'd been filled with the weight of wet sand. Though his mouth was dry, and his throat parched, he knew he had to rest before seeking a freshwater source. Moving felt impossible now; even if he needed to, he doubted he could.

He gazed upward at the inky sky, sparsely adorned with an ocean of shimmering stars. Though they sparkled like tiny diamonds, their beauty eluded him. *Are they watching me, even now?*

The council was notorious for their omnipresence, wielding advanced surveillance measures such as cameras and drones throughout Derro. Rumors even suggested they could eavesdrop on citizens' everyday lives through their Auxes.

Though, no matter how pervasive their ever-watching might be, it didn't alter Jacob's perception of Sid. Constant monitoring wasn't new to him. It was the norm, a necessity to safeguard the populace of Derro. And now, as he stared up at the stars, he couldn't help but wonder if some of those distant points of light were satellites in orbit, watching him from the heavens.

"Sid, you there?"

No response came.

Worth a shot.

Jacob knew Sid wouldn't respond, even if the Aux had wanted to. His Aux was still intact, but he'd lost the ability to communicate with Sid. Or, more accurately, had it taken away from him. But did that mean Sid couldn't hear him at all? Jacob wasn't sure.

Turning his head northward, his gaze was drawn to a distant flicker of light. *Fire*, his mind screamed. Had some of his fellow exiles set camp for the evening? He desperately hoped so. The allure of the campfire's warmth tugged at him like a moth to a flame. Sure, approaching would be dangerous, but his need for survival had taken over.

Mustering what strength he'd gained, he gradually rose to his feet. Retrieving his newly acquired Talon, he inspected it, finding comfort in its familiar weight. He released the magazine, revealing high-velocity hollow-point rounds chambered inside. Satisfied the weapon was fully loaded, he ensured its safety was engaged and concealed the pistol at the back of his waistline.

He started toward the campfire, boots squeaking in the sand with every step. Once closer, he bent his knees and stealthily advanced toward the glow, muting his boot's whimper. As the campfire came more into view, he noticed three people huddled around its dancing flames. Two of them he recognized instantly. There in a circle sat Morgan, Alex, and an elderly man he'd remembered aboard the Screech.

Despite their familiarity, an underlying unease slithered in Jacob's gut. *Can I trust them?* The thought tempted him to retreat in the direction he came, yet the prospect of facing the dangers alone on his first night on Eremos was more disturbing. So much so, he decided to continue his approach, taking cautious steps with his palms raised.

"I mean no harm," he announced.

The trio jolted in surprise, but their eyes quickly locked with recognition. Morgan dug his feet into the sand, preparing to flee at a moment's notice, while Alex clenched her fists at her side. The elderly man, dressed in a flannel, stretched his long neck as he gazed up at Jacob.

"Last one to take the plunge, eh?"

"Yeah, I remember you," Alex said. "You were sitting next to that man with the burnt face."

"Yes, that's me," Jacob said, his gaze shifting among the three of them. *Why are there only these three around the fire?* Jacob rubbed his chilly hands together. "Would you mind if I joined you?"

"It's a free country," the senior said, gesturing toward the campfire with an open palm.

Jacob raised his eyebrows at the man's remark as he settled into the sand beside Morgan and stretched his hands toward the fire. *Last Patriot?* he wondered. He looked at the senior's wrists, searching for the known rebellion identifier—a simple star tattoo—but couldn't see anything because of his long-sleeved flannel. Despite the quip, Jacob struggled to shake off the unease that gripped him, a persistent sense that *true* freedom was a distant dream on Eremos.

Instead, what reigned was anarchy.

And luckily for Jacob, he had the Talon to keep him safe. He shifted cautiously, ensuring the firearm pressed against his back remained covered. Lord knows he'd be a dead man if the others knew what he possessed. Although the three of them appeared friendly, united in an uneasy alliance to survive the night, he still wondered whether any of them harbored ulterior motives. They were all criminals, after all. And the conspicuous absence of others from the Screech didn't help any.

"Where is everyone else?" Jacob asked.

"We caught sight of a few others who arrived shortly after us, but they seemed uninterested in joining our fire," Alex said. "My guess is they went further inland before nightfall. Probably in search of shelter."

That made sense, though Jacob's suspicions lingered. Those other exiles were out there, as were others, long exiled before. Among them, and the most dangerous in Jacob's eyes, was Michael. Not only did he have a Talon, but he was also driven by some divine purpose Jacob struggled to piece together. *What was the hidden message behind his cryptic words? And what did it mean for Eremos?*

"Any chance either of you saw Michael?" Jacob asked. Then, quickly realizing they most likely didn't know the madman's name, he said, "the man with the burnt face."

A collective shaking of heads followed.

"I really didn't think anyone else would show up, given how much time had passed since we last saw someone," Alex said. She tilted her head, her eyes narrowing toward Jacob. "So, what took *you* so long?"

Jacob hesitated. Alex clearly was suspicious of him. Understandable, given their predicament. After all, he was just as scrutinizing, searching for any signs of danger hidden beneath their facades. He would need to proceed carefully.

"I'm not the best swimmer," he lied.

Alex's eyelids inched closer. Digging her hands into the sand, she leaned back, her gaze never leaving Jacob. Something told him she knew he was lying, sensing his story was more complicated than a simple admission of swimming prowess. And though she didn't respond, Jacob could tell she had chosen to accept his answer, at least for now.

"Say, what's your name?" the old man asked, breaking the momentary silence.

"Jacob," he answered, turning to face the senior.

There was a sense of familiarity about the man, his presence reminding Jacob of his old friend Frank. He closed his eyes briefly, a wave of regret washing over him as he recalled their last encounter. He wished he'd handled things differently and listened to Frank. *Maybe if I had, I wouldn't have been exiled.*

"I'm Wyatt," the senior replied, extending his hand toward Jacob.

Jacob met Wyatt's handshake and shook it firmly, hoping to earn his respect. Wyatt squeezed back. Then, out of nowhere, the old man yanked Jacob close, face to face, his eyes piercing into him.

"Can we trust you?"

Jacob gulped, caught off guard by the sudden shift in the old man's demeanor. He paused, grappling with the fragile nature of trust in their precarious situation. How could anyone trust someone they had just met? Especially if that person was a criminal. Trust had to be earned, and that took time. Jacob knew there was nothing he could say to prove he could be trusted, but he did understand that unity was their strongest tool for survival.

"I suppose you'll have to trust me the same way I'm going to trust the three of you," he said. "Blindly. And as hard as that will be, I think we can all agree, us working together will increase our chances of surviving this hell we've just entered."

Wyatt considered Jacob's answer, his eyes narrowing into slits. Alex and Morgan watched in silence, uncertain of how the senior would respond. After a few seconds, Wyatt released Jacob's hand.

"I think that's fair," he said. "We're all here for the same reason. No sense in denying that. Let's just work together to survive this night and avoid letting those *reasons* clash. Can we all do that?"

Jacob flexed his fingers, surprised by Wyatt's firm grip as he exchanged glances with the others, all nodding in silent agreement. A shared understanding settled among them, and their bodies seemed to relax ever so slightly.

"Marvelous," Wyatt said, patting his knee with a playful grin. "Well, if you don't know already, the youngin' next to you is Morgan, and this Texas Tornado here is Alex."

"*Enough* with the damn nicknames," Alex said, rolling her eyes.

Wyatt smirked, raising his hands in a conciliatory gesture. "Apologies. Just a habit of mine."

"Who built the fire?" Jacob asked, cutting the tension.

"The kid did," Alex answered. "Surprised the hell out of me when I got here."

Jacob glanced toward Morgan, who had shrunk under the attention. "Nice work, kid. Where'd you learn that?"

"My dad," Morgan mumbled.

"Well, he taught you well. How old are you?"

"Fifteen."

"I know full-grown men who couldn't do what you just did," Jacob said, leaning closer to Morgan. "Including me. But do me a favor and don't tell *them* that."

Morgan smiled. Jacob returned the grin, feeling a small sense of pride in helping Morgan open up, even if just a little. It was a small win on his first night of exile. Sure, what he'd done wasn't grand, but for Morgan, Jacob hoped it was.

"Before you arrived, Jacob, we were all discussing the need to find water," Wyatt said.

"Finding water should be our top priority," Alex added, wiping the corners of her mouth.

She was right. Jacob's thirst had grown, his mouth as dry as the surrounding sand. Finding water would be crucial. But at least they had a fire, which he hoped would ward off predators. The flames were high and bright, casting a warm embrace that had already begun to dry his wet clothes.

"How long can we, like, survive without water?" Morgan asked.

"Not long," Jacob said. "A few days at most."

"We could venture inland, look for a stream or river?" Wyatt suggested.

Jacob turned toward the dark jungle, knowing they'd have to leave their makeshift haven at some point. The soft wind whooshed through the trees and bushes, causing them to rustle as if people were moving among them.

"Seems too risky tonight," he said. "Who knows what we might encounter with no knowledge of the terrain."

Then, a sudden realization surfaced in Jacob's mind—the memory of his jump from the Screech. He recalled seeing what looked like a tall tower and a large pool of water, surrounded by towering cliffs. Was that some sort of sanctuary? He wasn't sure, but perhaps it was a destination worth pursuing. A source of hope amid the uncertainty.

"Well, let's not forget, we're not one hundred percent safe here either," Wyatt said. "Almost feels like we're sitting du—"

A gunshot tore through the air.

Jacob leaped to his feet, his hand flying instinctively to his Talon, but then quickly froze, reluctant to reveal it. The jungle exploded with chaos. Out of sight birds flapped wildly in retreat as he scanned the dense foliage, searching for any approaching threat, knowing full well that shot came from Michael.

"Was that a gunshot?" Morgan quivered.

"You bet your darn ass it was," Wyatt said.

Morgan started pacing in tight circles, his hands trembling as they clutched his head. His gaze darted toward every sound, the rustling of foliage, the snap of a twig. "How are there guns here?" he stammered. "What are we going to do?"

"It'll be all right," Jacob said, trying to calm the kid.

He resumed his frantic search, eyes darting around. He half-expected Michael to burst from the jungle at any moment, but no one came. His gaze eventually connected with Alex's, who stood with her arms folded, her piercing eyes locked on him. *Shit, did she see me reach for the gun?*

"What?" Jacob asked defensively.

"You were the last to jump," she pointed out again. "Did anything else happen on the Screech that you're not telling us?"

A heaviness settled over Jacob, uncertain of how much to reveal about his encounter with Michael. Admitting the madman was the source of the gunshot would only lead to questions—questions that might expose the fact that Jacob also had a gun. If Alex didn't already suspect it. That thought troubled him the most.

He'd seen firsthand what people were willing to do to obtain guns.

"No," Jacob lied again. "I jumped. Just like everyone else."

"Then I'm afraid things just got a whole lot more dangerous," Wyatt said. "Best to stay on high alert."

Alex's gaze stayed locked on Jacob. It was clear she wasn't entirely convinced by his answer, yet again.

"What if they find us?" Morgan asked.

"We'll face that challenge when it comes, kid," Jacob said. "For now, we stay put and keep the fire burning."

Wyatt nodded. "Agreed. At first light, we'll head out to find water. But until then, we stay here, keep watch, and pray to whatever god you believe in that we make it through the night."

A tense silence enveloped them as they grappled with the gunshot. Like them, the jungle seemed to hold its breath, waiting for the next turn of events.

Then another gunshot shattered the stillness, followed by a blood-curdling scream that pierced the air. It dragged on, like a wounded animal fighting for its life, until another shot fired, silencing it.

"More like *survive* through the night," Alex said.

Feeling at a loss, Jacob settled back into the sand, his mind consumed with questions. He'd heard three shots. Why did Michael use his gun? Was he fulfilling his sacred mission, those screams coming from another exile? Or was he defending himself? Jacob felt it was only a matter of time before the answer came to light.

The others followed suit, taking a seat around the fire at their own pace, Morgan choosing to sit a little closer to Jacob than before. Jacob fixed his gaze on the flickering flames, feeling a strange mix of calm and unease wash over him. The crashing waves soothed his panicked insides, pulling him away from Eremos and into a meditative state. The choices that had led to his exile began to weigh heavily on his conscience, and he hesitated to delve into that space, fearing the darkness it might bring.

But in his short time on Eremos, that darkness had already appeared, almost as if it had followed him from Derro. And the longer he remained here on Eremos, the more inevitable it felt he'd need to welcome back in that darkness. How else could he face the dangers closing in around them?

With a heavy sigh, Jacob embraced the fleeting calm, allowing it to fortify him for the storm he knew lay ahead.

CHAPTER FOUR

ONE YEAR BEFORE EXILE

CHARLOTTE HUGHES INHALED deeply, savoring the crisp morning air, mixed with pine, as she relaxed on the loveseat on her back porch. The first rays of sunlight filtered through the towering trees, their warmth brushing her skin. With a contented sigh, she let her eyelids drift shut, letting her entire being attune to the symphony of the forest awakening around her, the rustle of leaves, the distant burbling of a stream.

Her second-story deck wrapped around the rear of her home, a graceful structure with large floor-to-ceiling windows, allowing her to live with nature. This was Charlotte's favorite spot in her home, her sanctuary, a place of natural beauty that always left her in awe.

As the sun continued to rise, the sky transformed into a canvas of vibrant hues, a gradient of pink, orange, and yellow. Charlotte watched as the colors danced and swirled, painting her world in an ethereal light that flooded her soul. A sense of peace washed over her, filling her heart with quiet joy. Indulging in nature had become her daily ritual, her sacred refuge, connecting her to a greater existence.

Particularly today.

Last night, she had teetered between surprise and shock, emotions that had lingered into this morning. The view before her, as it always did, soothed her emotional turbulence, offering a newfound understanding of the world and her place in it.

Charlotte set her coffee down and reached for the camera resting beside her. Steadying her hands, she lifted it to her eyes and adjusted the aperture and shutter speed, determined to capture every detail. There was something about capturing nature in its raw beauty through her lens that filled her with a profound sense of purpose.

Yet, after last night, she could feel that purpose shifting, a new one taking root within her.

She pushed the shutter button, the sound breaking the stillness of the morning. She knew she'd captured something special—a moment frozen in time, never to be repeated. Leaning back from her camera, she kept her eyes fixed on the view before her, and a deep sense of gratitude welled up within her.

Search for the tiny flickers, Charlotte, her father would always tell her.

Setting the camera aside, she reached for her coffee while pulling a small plastic object from her hoodie pocket, discreetly concealing it behind the cup. It was a pink-capped stick with two vertical lines on its digital screen, confirming the inkling she had harbored for the past few days. Hope bloomed within her, mingling with excitement. *I can't believe I'm finally pregnant.* She couldn't wait to tell Jacob. It's one of the reasons she got up early, crafting the perfect way to reveal it to him.

"Morning, beautiful."

Charlotte, briefly startled, lowered her coffee to her lap and cautiously tucked the pregnancy test back into her hoodie pocket as she watched Jacob step onto the deck through their bedroom patio doors.

"Hey, *you.*"

Jacob was dressed for work: blue jeans, a charcoal vest he layered over a blue, checkered button-up shirt, and his unruly brown hair swept back, a few strands falling loosely around his face. Placing his leather satchel on the ground, he bent down and kissed Charlotte on her forehead and then snuggled into the seat next to her. Charlotte nestled closer, savoring the comforting heat from his body.

"I had a feeling I'd find you out here," he said. "You okay?"

"I'm great. Just couldn't sleep much last night. Thought I'd take in the view and watch the sunrise."

"It sure is beautiful. You should've woken me."

Charlotte gazed up at Jacob, her head still nestled against his chest. "It crossed my mind, but I needed some time alone."

Jacob gave her a soft squeeze. "I know what you mean."

Charlotte had always admired Jacob's emotional intelligence. He had an uncanny ability to sense her moods and respond with just the right words or actions. It showed her he listened, which had surprised her early in their relationship, especially when she learned he'd grown up without his mother. In a world where empathy felt on the brink of extinction, Jacob was a rare gem.

You're going to be a great father, Jake.

They both quickly found contentment in the simple joy of sitting together, their bodies pressed close, savoring the comfortable silence. For Charlotte, quiet moments were cherished gifts, rare opportunities to disconnect from the persistent flood of information life bestowed upon her. Silence was her companion. While most people were glued to their holographic screens, endlessly scrolling through social media feeds, Charlotte found solace in the stillness, using it to tap into her creativity.

Iris, although, often grew agitated and interrupted her moments of peace. Whether it was helping with her photography, reminding her of tasks that needed to be completed, or simply keeping her informed, it felt as though her Aux had a mind of its own. Charlotte couldn't blame Iris. It was part of its programming.

Early in their relationship, the same could be said for Jacob. He had always been a go-getter, constantly in pursuit of something to accomplish. Quiet moments felt jittery for him, as if his bones protested the calm. Eventually, however, under Charlotte's patient guidance, he had gradually learned to, like her, appreciate the power of stillness. Their hushed moments became cherished rituals, offering them refuge to tune out the clamor of Tuto, where they could live fully in the present, savoring life's simple beauty, while also forging a deeper connection with each other.

Seated in Jacob's warm embrace, the smell of gun oil permeating her senses, Charlotte let her mind wander. She envisioned their future together, now as a trio. The patter of baby thumps on the deck, Jacob chasing after their child, and the contagious, uncontrollable laughter that would follow. Their cherished space would change, intertwined with the glee of parenthood. She could hardly wait.

The warmth of her coffee mug slipping from her hands interrupted her thoughts as she watched Jacob steal a sip. His face lit up with a playful grin as he handed the cup back to her.

"Hey, you remember that night a bat flew into our house?"

Charlotte smiled. "Of course I do. How could I forget you running around like a maniac, trying to swat it with your hat and lead it back outside?"

"*That thing* was like mini-Dracula. And if I recall, you were no help at all. Just standing there with your wine glass like you were at a theater performance."

Charlotte's mouth dropped. "*Hey.* We were on our second bottle. *And* we'd been smoking. I honestly wasn't even sure what I was seeing was real."

"Oh, sure, blame the weed."

Charlotte playfully punched Jacob's arm, then collapsed back into him with laughter. More memories of their time out here flooded her mind; playing board games, watching their favorite movies on the holographic projector, the indulgence of smokes and drinks until they were three sheets to the wind. And occasionally, when their passion overwhelmed them, they surrendered to love-making on their circular daybed. Since they've been together, they'd spent just about every waking and sleeping moment out here, and over time, the space had transformed into their sanctuary, a refuge to retreat to after a tiring day.

Soon, it would evolve again.

"I can't wait to make more memories out here."

"Me too," Jacob whispered, his lips brushing against her hair as he spoke. He inhaled deeply, savoring her scent. "I'm sorry about last night, by the way."

"You don't have to apologize," Charlotte said, looking up at him. "I could tell something was bothering you. You know, I've come to know you pretty well by now."

"Ain't that the truth. I'm pretty sure you understand me better than Sid."

Charlotte scoffed. "Oh, definitely. Your Aux has nothing on me."

"You continue to prove that."

"I'm here, if you want to talk about it."

Jacob drew a deep breath, his gaze shifting to the sprawling view. "I just feel like Hoos is losing its identity. Crime is rising in Tuto, and it's becoming increasingly difficult to uphold my father's legacy. He envisioned protecting the citizens of Tuto, but now, I can't shake the feeling that my efforts are somehow contributing to the crime problem."

"I see. And was there something that triggered this feeling?"

Jacob nodded. "Last week, a group of drunk guys came in, wanting to buy a gun, and I refused to sell them one."

Charlotte leaned out of Jacob's embrace, her eyebrows furrowing with concern. "What happened? How'd you handle it?"

"I stood my ground and insisted they leave. For a second, I thought they wouldn't listen, and things might escalate. One of them even tried intimidating me. But thankfully they ended up leaving."

"Ugh, I'm sorry you had to deal with that. I *swear*, it seems like people are just trying to get exiled."

The pain of her cousin's exile remained vivid in Charlotte's memory, her only personal connection to the punishment. She could still picture her Aunt Nora's tear-streaked face as she recounted the event, seeking solace in the embrace of Charlotte's mother. The Cullers had come to Nora's doorstep, delivering the devastating news: her son was dead. Even at a young age, Charlotte had understood her cousin hadn't *actually* died. Not yet, anyway. Just a *legal* death.

A year later, on the anniversary of his exile, Aunt Nora took her own life.

Charlotte's head bowed toward her sinking stomach, pondering that moment she had witnessed as a child. *What kind of world will you grow up in?*

"It does feel that way," Jacob said, pulling Charlotte from her thoughts.

Charlotte lifted her head and refocused her attention back on Jacob. "Well, you did the right thing."

"Thanks, Char."

Charlotte smiled hearing him call her Char. A name that had become something of an inside joke between them. It had started as a playful teasing on Jacob's part, but now it had become a term of endearment, one he used almost unconsciously. Whenever he called her Char, she couldn't help but feel a warm affection toward him, and her smile became an instinctive response.

"Richard came by Hoos again yesterday."

Charlotte rolled her eyes. "To try and purchase it again?"

"He handed me a blank check this time. And I have to admit, for a moment, I actually considered accepting it."

"Hoos has only been in a no-go zone for a short while," Charlotte said, puzzled. "I don't get it. Why the keen interest in buying it?"

"Seems he's been acquiring multiple businesses in these no-go zones. And he's *ruthless* about it, at least to me. The way he spoke to me yesterday …" Jacob's voice trailed off. "He said I create a false sense of security for people. An *illusion* that buying guns from me offers protection. When in reality, I'm just fueling the fire."

That's what he meant by adding *to the crime issue*, Charlotte realized. She sighed, her lips curling in distaste. "That's horrible. He's clearly only saying that to influence you to sell."

"And that's where the real power lies," Jacob said, his gaze distant. Charlotte could tell he was lost in thought.

"What's that mean?"

Jacob shook his head, as if pulling himself back to the moment. "Just something else Richard said. Like, even with all the *supposed* harm I'm contributing in Tuto, he still envied the power and opportunity to profit from it."

"Well, if you ask me, that's *exactly* the problem with men like him. Jake, you're nothing like him. I know it must feel like you're the bad guy sometimes, but you're far from it. Yes, you sell guns to people, but you don't decide who can actually buy them. That's up to the council. And hell, you turned those drunk guys away. Not everyone would've done that. Thanks to you, people can protect themselves from men like them."

Jacob sighed. "I wish I was strong enough to lean on that thought process."

"You're *stronger* than you think."

Jacob looked at his watch, and Charlotte knew instantly that Sid had just reminded him it was time to go to work. *Damn, Aux.*

"I should be going," Jacob said.

"All right … Are you going to be okay today?"

Jacob forced a smile. "I'll manage."

Charlotte watched him rise, sling his leather satchel over his shoulder, and smooth his hair with his fingers—oddly enduring gestures. She fought the impulse to reach for his hand, to urge him to stay, if only a little longer, to shield him from yet another challenging day.

Just as Jacob was about to turn and walk away, he paused, his lips curling into a mischievous grin. "We should do something out here tonight."

Charlotte raised an eyebrow, smirking. "What did you have in mind?"

"Oh, I don't know. Something wild, something daring. I say we start with a movie, and then we let the 'something wild and daring' introduce itself."

Charlotte rolled her eyes and couldn't help but chuckle. "All right, then. Sounds like a plan."

Jacob smiled, and this one was genuine. "*Yes*," he celebrated. He sauntered over and kneeled to kiss her goodbye. "Love you, Char."

Charlotte returned the kiss. "Love you too, Jake."

She watched as Jacob departed, feeling a great affection for him. She admired how fit he kept himself, but her mind wandered to how charming he would look with a dad bod.

"And don't worry," Jacob called over his shoulder. "I've heard the bats are in hibernation."

Charlotte chuckled softly as Jacob vanished inside. While her evening plans hadn't initially involved hanging out on the deck, she adapted seamlessly, embracing the Earth's rhythm to guide her through the rest of her day.

Aware she needed to leave to set her plans in motion, Charlotte finished the last sip of her coffee and stepped inside to change. After throwing on some makeup and finding an outfit to wear, she grabbed her hovering phone from its holographic charger, its soft glow fading as she picked it up, and then started toward the garage, where she approached her Nervo Pod, the sleek, metallic cube gleaming under the overhead lights.

"Iris, take me to Storks."

Of course, Charlotte.

In response, the pod's double glass doors slid open with a whispering smoothness. Soft ambient light illuminated the sleek interior as Charlotte settled into the plush green seats. The windows came alive with serene nature scenes, obscuring the outside world—a thoughtful customization she had chosen. This was a privilege reserved for the fortunate, while many others still relied on outdated, gas-powered vehicles.

The fastest route to Storks is exactly 8.8 miles away, with an estimated ETA of thirteen minutes, Iris informed.

As Iris planned for the drive, Charlotte sifted through her notifications, her phone's holographic display glowing softly in the dim cabin. She frowned, noticing she'd missed a video call from her mother, in response to the one she had made the night before. While Jacob slept, she had tried to share her big news, but her mother hadn't answered.

Charlotte's parents lived in Strix, a quaint town nestled amid rolling hills nearly fifteen hundred miles away from Tuto. Since marrying Jacob, her relationship with them had depended almost entirely on electronic communication, with only a few cherished visits to bridge the physical distance between them.

"Iris, make a video call to my mom."

Would you like the video call to be with your phone or Nervo Pod?

"Pod, please."

Iris responded by projecting a holographic screen upward from the Nervo Pod's floor, displaying a picture of Charlotte's mother. A soft ringing sound filled the pod as Charlotte waited eagerly for her mother to answer. But after a few moments, once again, there was no response.

Your mother did not answer, Charlotte. Would you like me to send her a text message?

"Yes, just have her video call me when she has a free moment. I want to share some big news with her."

Certainly. Now before we depart, might I suggest a drive with the roof open? It's a clear day in Tuto, with a temperature of seventy degrees.

Charlotte was about to give her usual answer of "no," but her curiosity got the better of her. Today, she felt one with the universe and decided to seize the moment. "Sure, let's do it."

As you wish.

For the first time, Charlotte looked upward, her gaze drawn to the expansive glass roof, which gracefully slid open, like the parting of theater curtains.

Please relax Charlotte as I release your safety belt.

Charlotte leaned back, and with a soft hum, a set of holographic seat belts appeared, gently wrapping around her, securing her comfortably in her seat. As her Nervo Pod started gliding out of the garage, it remained a sight to behold—no steering wheel in sight, just an Aux-driven vehicle navigating seamlessly.

Her home sat atop a hillside, nuzzled among the forest, and was only accessible via a long, winding road that curved like a snake and could accommodate just one Nervo Pod or vehicle at a time. The seclusion provided her with her desired security and solitude, a welcome escape from the hustle and bustle of Tuto sprawled out below.

The only downside was the distance from civilization. However, with her Nervo Pod, she had found delight in the mundane task of everyday driving. She could leisurely scroll through her phone, get lost in a book, or, on a beautiful day like today, savor the luxury of her moon roof, allowing a refreshing breeze to caress her skin as the warm sun kissed her face.

Charlotte marveled at the vast blue sky, dotted with fluffy white clouds, and the green trees that swirled into each other. She raised her arms, reaching, as if trying to touch the sky. Then, a sudden realization washed over her. In a way, she was already touching the sky; from the perspective of the people in Tuto below, she was living in it.

Ever since Charlotte and Jacob had decided to start trying for a child, she found herself frequently drawn to Storks, a charming baby store located, like Hoos, on Tuto's high street—Nox Street. She reveled in browsing the shelves, running her fingers over the soft fabrics of the clothes and stuffed animals.

Sure, she could have easily browsed online like most people, or even requested help from Iris, but she loved the experience of shopping in person; the human interaction, the opportunity to ask questions and receive recommendations from knowledgeable staff, rather than relying on an algorithm. Each visit promised the discovery of something new and wonderful for her future baby.

Charlotte, a no-go zone has been detected along our route to Storks, Iris alerted.

"Iris, turn off the Ambient View Display."

The soothing nature projections vanished, replaced by the stark reality outside. Through the windows she watched as other Nervo Pods and vehicles turned around, seeking alternate destinations. She groaned at the sight.

"Feels like they just keep sprouting up everywhere," Charlotte said, her morning conversation with Jacob still fresh in her mind.

I suggest returning home and shopping online, Iris said.

Charlotte considered her Aux for a moment. She understood the benefits of avoiding no-go zones, often opting for alternate routes. But after years of relying on this system, she had started to notice the negative impact it had on local businesses in those zones. The most significant being the loss of in-person shopping. For some, it meant the potential loss of their business entirely. When possible, Charlotte made a conscious effort to support these establishments. She much preferred backing hard-working individuals over faceless corporations profiting from these no-go zones.

I've never let a no-go zone stop me before, Charlotte thought. "No, Iris. Please proceed with caution."

As you wish, Charlotte.

As her Nervo Pod moved forward, while others turned away, Charlotte couldn't help but reflect on society's deep reliance on technology and social scores. She knew she'd likely take a minor hit to her score for continuing onward. For a brief moment, she felt like a rebel, an outlier, daring to venture into the no-go zones against the tide—a feeling she hadn't experienced in years.

She peered out the window, surveying the city she had grown to love, and noticed its unsettling transformation. She had expected the absence of people but was surprised by how her beloved Tuto had been tainted. Trash littered the streets, gathering in heaps at the edges. Homeless people cooked meals over barrel fires, their clothes tattered. Graffiti marked the alleyways and buildings, among them the infamous Last Patriots symbol—an eagle breaking free from chains.

Charlotte frowned. She had known Tuto was worsening, but she hadn't realized just how much. *How have I let myself become so disconnected?*

Then suddenly, her attention was drawn to a holographic billboard. At its pinnacle, the emblem of the council loomed; a menacing owl, rendered in an eerie shade of crimson, its eyes glowing, as if watching and judging the passersby. Bold letters flashed across the screen, delivering forceful warnings and consequences of the fates awaiting those who dared to defy the council. Accompanying the text were stark images—remote islands cloaked in darkness, their inhabitants hunched in hopelessness, condemned to exile.

Charlotte, we are approaching Storks.

Charlotte tore her gaze from the billboard, shifting her focus to the road ahead. As she entered Nox Street, Hoos came into view, a line of customers stretching out its door. The sight sparked an uneasy thought: how many among them harbored ill intentions for their newly purchased guns? And how many would ultimately face exile, just as the billboard had warned? Her frown deepened, a pang of worry for Jacob tightening in her chest. *I hope he's holding up okay.*

Her Nervo Pod eased to a stop at the edge of Nox Street, humming softly as it powered down. The holographic safety belts dissolved, and the pod's double glass doors whispered open. Stepping out, Charlotte felt the crisp air tingling on her skin as she started toward the store. Through the expansive windows, a holographic display showcased many baby essentials: cribs, sleek Nervo Strollers, and delightful nursery decor. Excitement fluttered in her chest.

When she entered Storks, the scent of lavender and the sound of soft lullabies greeted her. As she started toward the front counter, her attention was snagged on a man approaching from the opposite direction. Dressed in a sharp suit, with wavy ash-blond hair, she recognized him immediately—Richard Woodwin. A flicker of anger flared within her as they passed. Summoning her composure, she plastered on a false, sarcastic smile, which Richard met with a quiet nod and smug smirk before exiting the store.

Her hands had itched to confront him, but she knew it was best to resist that urge, as hard as it was to do. The last thing she wanted was to escalate matters after Jacob's revelations this morning. Instead, she chuckled softly to herself, struck by the irony of the universe weaving Richard into what was already an eventful day.

"*Charlotte.*"

The sound of her name drew her focus back to the front counter. As she approached, her tense shoulders eased at the sight of Roger, his calming presence washing over her like a balm, the anger simmering beneath the surface dissolving.

"Roger, it's so wonderful to see you."

"Likewise."

"I hope you don't mind me asking, but what was Richard doing here?"

Roger frowned. "Since Storks has found itself in a no-go zone, he's been stopping by every few days, trying to buy Storks."

"Ugh, he's been doing the same to Jake. I swear, people like him really piss me off. They could actually use their money to help fix Tuto, but no, they'd rather keep hoarding their wealth, and in the process, cause even more harm."

"I know. And as much as I agree, Lyle and I are seriously considering his offer. Storks just hasn't been the most profitable business for us. Our yoga studio has consistently outperformed it."

"I'm very sorry to hear that."

"Lyle keeps saying it might be wise to accept Richard's offer, before the building's value drops even further," Roger said, his head dipping slowly. "But enough about that. How are you and Jacob doing?"

"Oh, just great. You know, it's kinda crazy. I thought being married for ten years might make things go on autopilot, but I haven't let us get there just yet."

Roger touched his lips with his praying hands, a small smile gracing his face. "That makes me so happy."

"What about you and Lyle?"

"Just as great. Lyle's at the studio now, teaching a session. You know, we'd really love to see you there sometime."

"I know, I know."

"No pressure, of course. Just when you feel compelled. In these dark times, when things seem to be getting worse despite all the council's promises, yoga can bring peace. It helps you connect your mind, body, and spirit."

"It does sound serene," Charlotte said, her hand instinctively resting on her stomach for the first time. She looked down, realizing her gesture might have revealed her news to Roger. He wasn't the person she'd envisioned telling first, but life had its twists. "Maybe I'll stop by soon."

Roger's eyes lit up. "*Oh my.* Are you serious?"

Charlotte nodded, a warm smile spreading, cheeks tinged with blush. "I didn't mean to let it slip, but how could I hide it? I haven't even told Jake yet."

"I'm so happy for you two. Girl, pranayama is going to work wonders for you. Your first session is definitely on me."

"Well, how can I say no to that?"

"You can't. It's how we lure you in."

"Naturally," Charlotte said, rolling her eyes.

"So, does this mean you're here to take a look at *your* crib?"

Of all the cribs at Storks, one had consistently captured Charlotte's attention. Roger knew exactly which one it was.

"It does," Charlotte said.

"Well then, let's go take a fresh look at it, shall we?"

Charlotte followed Roger toward the crib, her gaze drifting around the store she had grown to adore. The walls were adorned with whimsical, hand-painted murals of storks delivering bundles of joy to families. A not so carefully placed stork toy caught her eye, part of a scavenger hunt designed to entertain children while their parents shopped. Storks had a special way of allowing Charlotte to momentarily forget the uncertainty looming over Tuto, offering her a brief escape.

"Here we are," Roger said, dramatically stretching his open arms toward Charlotte's crib.

Charlotte's breath caught for a moment as she neared the crib. Though it was fairly simple, crafted from polished birch, with its chevron-patterned headboard adding a subtle touch, she adored it instantly. It was everything she'd envisioned for the nursery they had prepared.

"What is it about this crib, by the way?" Roger asked. "It's one of my oldest models, and while I'd love to finally sell it, I can't help but think a Nervo Crib would be better. They link with the baby's Aux, keeping the temperature safe, and even include a natural bounce feature."

"It's the simplicity. While that sounds nice and all, I feel like those features take away some of the precious moments of being a mom. When my baby cries,

I want to rock and comfort them myself. Not let them rely on their Aux. It'll bring me fulfillment and joy."

"Spoken like a first-time mother."

Charlotte smiled. "You got me there," she said. "Well, Roger, I'm happy to finally say … I'll take it."

"Yay. I'm so happy for you and Jacob."

"I'm planning to surprise him tonight."

"He is going to freak out."

"Oh, definitely."

"Okay, go ahead and relax here while I get this all rung up. Do you want Lyle to deliver it to you?"

"That would be amazing. And if it's not too much trouble, I need it to be brought upstairs. Is that okay?"

"No trouble at all. Lyle can assemble it for you too, if you like?"

"Oh, no, that's okay. I appreciate the offer, but I know Jake will want to assemble it."

Roger smiled. "Of course."

As Roger scurried toward the counter, Charlotte gazed at her new crib. She imagined all the pieces sprawled out on the floor of the nursery, Jacob hunched over, working to assemble it. She could almost hear the occasional grunt or groan that came with his early forties, paired with his usual determined focus.

In her mind's eye, she pictured herself and Jacob collaborating, moving the completed crib around the room in search of the perfect spot. Perhaps near the door for quick access, and away from the windows to prevent any baby adventures with the drapes. She could almost feel the warmth of their future memories forming, centered around this simple yet significant piece of furniture.

A gentle buzz from her purse pulled Charlotte back to the present moment. *Charlotte, your mother is returning your call*, Iris informed.

Charlotte eagerly reached into her purse and grabbed her buzzing phone. "Iris, answer." Instantly, her phone projected a beaming holograph displaying her mother's face.

"So, what's the big news?"

"Mom, it finally happened," Charlotte said, the words tumbling out in a rush. "I'm pregnant. You're going to be a grandmother."

Her mother's mouth dropped. "*No way! Steve, Steve, get in here. Quickly.*"

"What is it, Nancy? What's going on?" Charlotte's father said in the background.

"Oh, honey, your father is going to cry," Nancy said, her fingers reaching toward her watery eyes. "Wait, *I'm* crying."

"Why are you crying?" Steve asked, joining the scene as he settled next to Nancy.

"Dad, I'm pregnant."

A moment of shock washed over Steve's face. Then, like melting ice, a smile formed, and tears welled in his eyes. Charlotte watched as her parents became overwhelmed with joy, their emotions tangible through the holograph. She felt a warm wave of happiness, knowing she'd just brightened their day.

Perhaps even their entire lives.

Later that night, Charlotte stood on her back deck, gazing at the carefully crafted scene she had prepared. She'd poured her heart and soul into creating the perfect atmosphere, one she and Jacob would cherish forever. String lights were hung, casting a warm, inviting glow over the night. An outdoor fire crackled in the fireplace, filling the air with the scent of pine, reminiscent of her favorite holiday: Christmas.

She turned her gaze toward the round daybed, surrounded by a sea of plush pillows. At the edge rested Jacob's favorite bottle of whiskey, accompanied by an artfully arranged charcuterie board. Beyond the bed, against the wooden wall of her home, hung a large projector screen, waiting for their choice of movie.

At the heart of it all, their new crib sat, wrapped in vibrant green paper, an elegant touch orchestrated by Roger and Lyle. The soft rustle of trees, the chirping of crickets, and the distant flow of the brook filled the air. Charlotte took a deep breath, letting the familiar scents and sounds wash over her.

Everything is just right.

Suddenly, a movement in the corner of her eye yanked her attention away, her gaze snapping toward one of the nearby trees. There, hidden in the darkness, were glowing eyes. Her heart skipped a beat as she recognized an owl perched on a branch. She froze. Her initial reaction was fear, but as she looked closer, awe began to replace it. The owl's feathered form seemed almost otherworldly, its vigilant gaze sending a shiver down her spine. It was thrilling. And a small part of her wished she had her camera.

Then the owl hooted.

Charlotte jolted, her sense of awe shattering. Her heart raced as she watched the owl suddenly take flight and land on the balustrade in front of her, its razor-sharp talons flexing, as if preparing to strike. The owl stood tall, measuring about fifteen to twenty inches in height, its feathered tufts resembling horns.

Startled, Charlotte found herself unsure of what to do next. *Stay calm, Charlotte*, she told herself, trying to convince herself the owl was more scared of her than she was of it. Being this close to the owl was more intimidating than she'd ever imagined. She felt mesmerized and frightened all at once, unable to shake the feeling there was something important about the encounter, something she couldn't fully understand.

The owl hooted again.

Charlotte flinched, barely suppressing a squeal. Quickly glancing toward her bedroom doors, she calculated in her head the distance she'd need to cover. They were only a few steps away, yet in this moment, they felt impossibly far.

Then the owl expanded its wings, its talons gripping the railing as it leaned forward. *It's going to strike*, Charlotte feared. With a startled gasp, she bolted inside, the owl's wings flapping like thunder in her ears. She stumbled as she crossed the threshold, falling to her knees, and quickly slammed the patio doors shut behind her.

Charlotte, are you okay? Iris asked. *Your heart rate spiked abnormally.*

Charlotte took a deep, steadying breath. "Yes, Iris, I'm safe."

Would you like me to call Jacob or alert the authorities?

"No, I'll be all right. Just need some time to gather my thoughts."

As the adrenaline coursing through her veins faded, Charlotte's chest heaved with deep, shaky breaths. Her body trembled, still reacting to the close encounter. After a brief moment of rest, she rose to her feet and fell onto her bed.

Then, out of nowhere, a laugh bubbled up from within her, a release of the fear that had gripped her. It was strange and unexpected, but she couldn't suppress it. The laugh grew, spiraling into uncontrollable giggles, as if she were a songbird caught in the midst of panic, unable to stop her own song.

After a short while, her laughter subsided, and her breathing gradually returned to normal. Despite the danger she faced, she couldn't wait to share the story with Jacob. Much like this morning with the bat, she imagined them laughing together.

But first, she had a surprise to unveil.

Charlotte had decided to pick Jacob up from work tonight, knowing it would be a great start to her plan. She grinned, picturing the shock on his face when she walked into Hoos. Energized by the thought, she sprang from the bed and headed toward her closet, eager to choose the perfect outfit for the evening ahead.

CHAPTER FIVE

DAY ONE OF EXILE

JACOB'S FIRST NIGHT of exile had been unsettling.

As the night deepened, the feeble glow of the fire cast eerie shadows that danced and writhed in the sand. The crackling flames struggled to pierce the thick, suffocating blackness that enveloped Jacob and his fellow exiles. The gunshots they'd heard earlier left them unnerved, as if the very air whispered of impending terror.

He had considered leaving multiple times, but the uncertainty of Eremos felt like quicksand, anchoring him firmly in place, as if the weight of his indecision sank him deeper with each passing minute. Even if he did leave, there was no guarantee he'd find a safer place than where he was now, surrounded by others.

Neither he nor the others had spoken a word about what led them to be sentenced to exile. Their unspoken secrets festered beneath the surface, buried like hidden land mines, threatening to unravel their fragile alliance. Amid the fickleness, survival had become their sole focus, and the dwindling fire offered them a glimmer of hope.

"It's time we faced the bitter reality," Wyatt said, his aged hands shaking as he reached for a charred log from the fire, leaving a darker void in its absence. "We need to find more wood for the fire. Hey kiddo, show me where you found the firewood."

Morgan's eyes darted nervously between the senior and Jacob. His fingers tapped against his jeans as he mustered the courage to speak. "Um, I—I think I should stay here," he stammered.

Wyatt, already standing up, froze and arched an eyebrow. "We're going to need that wood to keep the fire burning, boy."

"I think Morgan is fine here," Jacob said, sensing Morgan's fear of Wyatt. "He's already done his part. I'll help you instead."

Don't do anything stupid, Wyatt, Jacob thought as he stood. He didn't want to use his Talon, be he would if forced.

"I ain't gonna *bite,* for *God's sake,*" Wyatt said, his pride crumbling under the weight of unspoken accusations. "It makes sense for the kid to show me where he found the firewood. Y'all are acting like I'm some kind of child preda—"

An arrow pierced Wyatt's neck, catching his words in his throat.

Jacob recoiled in horror, his eyes bulging as figures emerged from the darkness. Panic gripped him, his heart pounding against his chest. He thrust his arm out in front of Morgan and Alex, a futile shield against the threat closing in around them. There were so many of them, the fire's glow illuminating their tattered garments and tree bark masks.

A thump snapped Jacob back to Wyatt, who'd fallen to his knees, crimson streaks squirting from his neck, staining the sand. With a sickening thud, the senior's body crumpled forward, his lifeless form coming to a rest near the dwindling fire.

"*No way, I actually got him!*" a man shouted, waving a makeshift bow in the air. He stood tall, his spiked hair peeking out above his mask.

"*An excellent shot, my dear,*" another voice said amid a chorus of snickers. The voice was a man's that slithered out slowly. The savage's eyes widened behind his mask as he looked down at Wyatt. "Maw's, let's give Twig a round of applause."

Cheers erupted from the horde. Jacob's hand twitched toward his Talon, torn on whether he should draw the weapon. He bit the insides of his cheeks, fully aware the decision carried deadly consequences.

This beauty holds twenty bullets. Wes's words entered his mind.

It was too dark to count them all, but Jacob knew there were over twenty. He wouldn't be able to kill them all, but he might be able to invoke fear in them, giving them time to escape. But there was also a chance one of them grabbed Morgan or Alex, forcing Jacob to have to choose to save one of them in exchange for the gun. Even worse, what if these savages got their hands on the Talon? Reluctantly, Jacob suppressed his instincts and let his hand fall limp at his side.

I need to play this smart.

The Maws, as they called themselves, inched closer, their circle tightening, cutting off any escape. Firelight glinted in their eyes, holding Jacob frozen in place. Fear coiled around him, suffocating, like a noose drawing tighter with every breath.

"I'm a man of my word, Twig," the savage said. Then slowly he pulled off his mask, revealing a wolfish grin. His cold, slit-like eyes locked onto Jacob, gleaming with sadistic hunger. "You can have an extra serving tonight."

Jacob's gaze stayed sharp, masking the fear clawing at his insides. There was a sinister delight radiating from the savage, feeding off their vulnerability like a predator would, savoring its prey. Escaping his grip would take more than brute force; Jacob knew that. It would demand every shred of his wit, resilience, and determination.

"Thank you, sir," Twig said.

Sir? The savage—clearly their leader—sauntered toward the fire, his movements unnervingly calm. Jacob couldn't look away, his gaze locked on the man.

The savage stretched his arms wide. "No applause for Twig?" he asked, staring at the three of them.

Jacob glanced at Alex and Morgan, their faces mirroring his own fear. The realization hit him—they were looking to him for help. *If only they knew …* He swallowed hard, his previous life's failures resurfacing in his mind. He banished them. Now wasn't the time for doubt.

"We aren't threats to you," he said.

The wild man ignored him, his gaze now fixed on Wyatt's lifeless body. Asserting his dominance, he stepped on Wyatt's head, bent down, and yanked the arrow from the senior's neck. Morgan pressed himself against Jacob's back, hiding from the spectacle as the savage grinned and casually tossed the arrow into the air.

"Fatality," he said, catching the arrow with a flourish.

Then he pointed the arrow at Twig. The tall, wiry man scurried forward to retrieve it, then returned to his spot like an obedient dog. The leader knelt down beside Wyatt's head, pulling a stone blade from his pocket. He grabbed the senior's hair and yanked back, exposing his long neck. He hovered the knife in front of Wyatt's throat, his eyes piercing Jacob's, a grin curling his lips.

Then he sliced from ear to ear.

A torrent of crimson gushed from Wyatt's neck as the savage let out a cruel laugh, his grip on the senior's hair unrelenting. "I'm Daemion," he said. "These are my Maws. And unlike your friend here, we do bite."

The horde rushed forward. Jacob flung his hands into the air in a desperate plea for mercy, his trembling fingers betraying the weight of the Talon hidden at his waist. Rough hands seized him, nails digging into his flesh. He forced himself to stay calm, clinging to the knowledge that rational thinking was his only ally.

The same, however, couldn't be said for Alex. She snarled, throwing punches and kicks at anyone who laid hands on her. Her blows landed with force, cracking masks, but eventually, the sheer number of Maws overwhelmed her, and she was subdued.

"Don't you *fucking touch me!*" she roared.

Jacob's leg wrenched, pulling his attention away from Alex. Morgan held on as two Maws yanked him by the legs. Jacob tried bending down, desperate to help the kid, but the Maws' grip kept him pinned in place.

"*No!*" Morgan screamed.

"You don't have to do this," Jacob said.

His plea hung in the air, unanswered for agonizing seconds. Daemion's cold stare shifted toward Jacob, the flickering flames of the fire dancing in his pupils. Finally, he released his grip on Wyatt's hair, the blood flowing from his neck slowing to a trickle. Jacob held Daemion's stare, a silent exchange passing between predator and prey.

"What do you want from us?" Alex asked.

"You'll learn soon enough, my dear." Daemion stood and crept toward them, pointing his bloody blade at Jacob and Alex. "Pity. You two will be easy. But you . . ." His gaze shifted to Morgan. "You're just a *kid*."

Morgan cowered amid the merciless grip of the Maws. Jacob's protective instincts surged. "Leave him alone."

Daemion released an exaggerated, heavy sigh, his eyes narrowing toward Jacob. "You know, I'm really starting to dislike you."

"What do you want with us?"

"Oh, my dear, have patience. Anticipation is an integral part of the torment."

"You know, you remind me of someone," Alex said, her head and chest pointed upward amid the Maws' grip.

Daemion's eyes widened. "And who might that be?"

"My husband."

Daemion's mouth dropped open before he chuckled darkly. He prowled toward Alex, his long tongue snaking out like a serpent as he licked his hands repeatedly. Then he ran his wet fingers through his tangled hair, as if trying to cleanse himself for her.

"So, you're telling me I have a chance, ya?"

Alex smirked. "Not exactly." Then she spat in his face, causing Daemion to jerk back. "I *killed* my husband."

Daemion slowly leaned forward, unfazed by the saliva trailing down his cheek. A twisted smile spread across his face as he wiped it away with his palm. Then he brought his hand to his mouth and licked Alex's repulsive offering.

"Yum. You taste exquisite, my dear."

"Fuck you!"

Daemion burst into uncontrollable laughter, his movements erratic, limbs flailing, sending sand flying into the air. It was as if he were possessed. Jacob winced, his stomach churning.

Then, as if a switch had been turned off, Daemion abruptly halted his theatrics and pressed a single finger to Alex's forehead, wiggling it in a warning gesture before pulling it away, treating her as if she were a child.

"You're quite the feisty one, aren't ya?" he said, his tongue flicking out briefly. "Oh, the fun we'll have together." He raised his wrist in front of him and mimicked tapping an imaginary watch, his eyes growing wide. "Oh, dear, would you look at that? Time certainly flies when you're having fun. But we best be moving. Maw's, let's move out."

Jacob was thrust forward, his heart racing. Trapped in the relentless grip of the Maws, he was shoved into formation behind Alex and Morgan. The Maws crowded around them, closing in like a suffocating wave. Jacob caught a fleeting glimpse of Wyatt's body being roughly lifted onto a makeshift stretcher, crafted from jackets. *Former victims?*

Then his feet started moving forward, the Maws prodding him toward the dense, unknown jungle. It felt as though he were stepping into the mouth of a terrible beast. There was no other choice but to obey.

For now.

Eremos's terrain had proven unforgiving.

Jacob stumbled over gnarled roots protruding from the ground, threatening to trip him with every step. They crossed a rocky stream, the cold water seeping into his boots and soaking his socks. To make matters worse, he was forced to ascend steep inclines, his muscles burning as he climbed higher and higher.

As if that weren't enough, he was surrounded by a horde of feral individuals, obstructing his view.

With every struggle, a shove, or a verbal lash from the Maws reminded him of his unwelcome status. These savages moved through the darkness with eerie ease, navigating the terrain as though it were second nature. After all, Eremos was their home; Jacob, Alex, and Morgan were nothing more than intruders.

After what felt like an hour or so of trudging, a weary Jacob finally arrived at a small, makeshift camp nestled at the base of a towering rock face. A fence, constructed from tree limbs haphazardly tied together, encircled the camp. *Not much of a fence*, he thought. When it came to it, getting out wouldn't be too hard.

The Maws approached the entrance, where two guards stood with long spears crafted from tree branches. As Jacob passed, they flashed eager smiles, revealing rows of rotten and missing teeth. Inside, he caught sight of hastily constructed huts made from intertwined tree branches scattered about, their roofs thatched. Some stood barely upright, leaning as if they might collapse at any moment.

At the center of the camp, a large teepee fire crackled, its large flames casting a dim light on the figures gathered around it. Men, women, children—mucky faces wearier than Jacob's own. One man was missing an arm. They all glared at him as he passed, his nose wrinkling at the foul stench of unwashed bodies. He wondered if they had once been captives, like him, who'd gradually evolved into products of their harsh environment.

Jacob refused that fate for himself.

"We're home, my dearies."

The Maws continued to shove them along as they followed their master, their jerky, unpredictable movements keeping him off balance. Their snarls crawled under his skin, as if wild animals surrounded him. *Fitting*, he thought, *for an island inhabited by culled criminals.*

"I'm scared, Jacob," Morgan whispered from in front of him.

"Me too, kid. But we have to be strong. One step at a time, okay?"

"*Quiet!*" Twig yelled.

Jacob placed a hand on Morgan's shoulder, hoping to offer him some comfort. The night had terrorized his thoughts. He could only imagine the thoughts racing through the boy's young mind.

"We need to stay quiet and do as they say," Jacob whispered. "Just keep your head down. I'll find a way out of this."

Even if it kills me.

The Maws halted abruptly, causing Jacob to collide into Morgan. His shaky gaze darted through the horde, landing on a large cave carved into the base of the rock face. Inside, torchlight flickered along the jagged walls, illuminating a winding path inside. The flames cast sinister shadows that seemed to mimic chopping motions.

"Prep him," Daemion ordered.

Jacob's breath hitched. He whipped his head over his shoulder, catching a short-lived glimpse of Maws carrying Wyatt toward the cave's gaping mouth. Panic grew in his chest as his mind spiraled, fearing the stretcher would next bear *his* broken form.

"Push 'em in," Daemion commanded.

Hands shoved Jacob forward with a sudden, urgent force. Up ahead, the Maws parted, revealing a massive pit. The earth trembled beneath his unsteady feet as he was driven closer and closer to the edge. Jacob couldn't risk finding out what lay at the bottom of that pit. He turned and hurled himself at the back of the horde. His fists struck tree bark masks, the brittle splintering as one Maw crumpled to his knees. But before Jacob could gain ground, another savage rushed forward to block his escape.

He grunted as he struggled to reposition himself, the relentless Maws continuing their push, Jacob's feet scraping uselessly against the ground. His brief resistance ignited a spark as he caught Alex and Morgan throwing punches and kicks of their own. It was a valiant effort, but hopeless. The sheer number of Maws was just too overwhelming.

The ground grew more unstable, dirt shifting and sliding beneath Jacob's boots. He was edging closer to the pit, powerless to stop it. There simply was no means of escape.

Except . . .

This has to be it, Jacob thought. *There's no other way.*

Jacob reached for the grip of his Talon, but before he could draw it, he tripped over a rock, his feet slipping out from under him, sending him tumbling into the pit. The air rushed past his ears as he fell, the ground rushing up to meet him. He braced for impact, knowing it would hurt. The earth slammed into him, pain searing through every bone in his body. Then, as painful as it was, he rolled his body, trying to avoid the crashing bodies of Alex and Morgan.

Two thuds announced their arrival as they hit the ground, followed by groans of pain. Jacob winced as he slowly pushed himself up, the jagged rocks biting into his palms. With the Talon still resting at the back of his waist, he lifted his gaze toward the pit's edge, where countless tree bark masks loomed above, Daemion's face at the center, a vicious grin curling at the corners of his lips.

"Welcome to exile," he said.

Then he turned on his heel and vanished, the Maws trailing behind him. They were alone now. A soft whimper drew Jacob's attention from the hole above to Morgan, who was gradually pushing himself up.

"This is all my fault," he whimpered. "We're all dead."

"Kid, don't think like that. I'm going to get us out of here."

"Wait," Alex said, rising to her feet. "What do you mean, 'this is all your fault'?"

Morgan froze, his body trembling as tears streamed down his dirty face. He bowed his head, unable to meet their gazes.

"I—I didn't start the fire," he stammered.

Jacob's head dropped into his chest. *No fucking way*, he thought, turning away from the kid as he rubbed the back of his neck.

"I'm sorry," Morgan sniffled.

"You're *sorry?*" Alex barked. "You mean to tell me that Wyatt is dead because of *you?* That we're trapped in this pit because *you* fell for their trap?"

Morgan flinched with every *"you"*, his shoulder slumping as the verbal lashings landed.

"Alex, please," Jacob said, trying to diffuse the situation.

Alex threw her hands up in exasperation and began pacing in a small circle. "I can't fucking believe this," she muttered under her breath.

The situation was spiraling out of control. Jacob felt his own frustration mounting as the gravity of their predicament sank in. Trapped in a pit, with no escape in sight, their blind trust in each other had failed.

"I'm going to figure this out," Jacob said.

Alex laughed. "And just how do you plan to do that? Can't you see? We're trapped at the bottom of a pit by a group of psychopaths. The kids right. We're dead, and it's *his fault.*"

Morgan shrank into himself, turning away and starting toward the opposite wall of the pit. Jacob lowered his head at the sight, a heavy sigh escaping his lips.

"I don't know yet," he said. "But what I do know is I'm not dying here. This is *not* what I came here for."

"What does *that* even mean?"

"Uh ... guys," Morgan interjected.

Jacob turned toward the kid, finding him staring at the ground. Morgan sniffled, brushing his nose with his arm.

"There's like, a man here," he said.

Jacob rushed forward, Alex close behind. When he reached Morgan, he saw a man's body curled up in a fetal position. Strands of disheveled hair veiled his face.

"Do you think he's alive?" Morgan asked.

Jacob kneeled and placed two fingers on the man's neck. "He has a pulse. Just seems to be knocked out."

"What do you think happened to him?"

"Not hard to guess, kid," Jacob said, standing up.

He ran his hand through his hair, his thoughts heavy. Their situation, already dire, had just worsened. He could barely trust Morgan or Alex, and now there was another unknown to deal with. Stepping away, he paced the perimeter of the pit, trying to come up with an escape plan. He just hoped that when the man woke up, he'd be able to help them.

"They beat the shit out of him," Alex said. "That's what happened. And they're going to do the same to us."

"Will you *stop?*" Jacob yelled, whirling around and pointing his finger at Alex.

Both Alex and Morgan froze, their eyes widening at Jacob.

"Just cut it out," he continued, bowing his head, feeling shameful for his outburst. "We're all scared. No need to make it worse, okay?"

Alex nodded, whether out of willingness or fear of him, Jacob couldn't tell. Exhausted, he stumbled toward the back of the pit and slumped against the cold, rough wall. He leaned his back against the damp clay, the coolness soothing the throb in his temples. A deep, gnawing ache spread through his body. His first night of exile, indeed, had been unsettling. And it was far from over.

He let his eyes drift shut, desperately hoping for a moment of respite. He knew sleep wouldn't come, but maybe the darkness could offer an escape from his grim reality. After a while, he saw *her*. He wasn't sure how, but the memories ebbed and flowed, vivid and clear. He saw her smile. Heard her laughter. And surprisingly, felt her warmth.

God, I miss you, Char.

Then suddenly, for the first time in over a year, the darkness was no longer a place of fear, but of comfort. Deep down, he hoped that one day he would be reunited with her.

Home, in the end.

CHAPTER SIX

ONE YEAR BEFORE EXILE

RICHARD HAD UNFORTUNATELY proven right.

In the wake of yesterday's tragic school shooting, Hoos was a hive of activity. People poured into the store, driven by a desperate need to secure protection. Among them were Frank and Dolores, returning to purchase the pistol Jacob had recommended, Dolores's social score teetering on the brink of approval.

"Thanks for choosing Hoos," Jacob said, offering a practiced smile as he handed another firearm to what he hoped would be his last customer of the day.

Normally, he took pride in arming the citizenry. But yesterday's interaction with Richard still weighed on his conscience, like a shadow he couldn't escape. He'd liked to think it hadn't affected him, but even Charlotte had noticed a change when he returned home last night.

Those conflicting thoughts continued to linger, even today. And they were even worse. Throughout the day, as he had assisted the steady stream of customers, he couldn't escape the thought that he *was*, as Richard had implied, part of the problem. And now, as he watched the customer exit Hoos, a nagging worry gnawed at him: *What harm could this one cause?*

You're stronger than you think, Charlotte had told him this morning.

Jacob frowned. As Charlotte had said, he was, after all, just the middleman. The council determined who could purchase a gun. Not him. Yet, as destructive as guns could be, there was no denying their power to prevent harm, too. Those drunk men who had come in last week undoubtedly were full of bad intentions. It was men like them Jacob was offering protection from.

He'd leaned on that sense of purpose to carry him through the day.

With closing time approaching, he began his usual routine. He armed himself with glass cleaner and a cloth and started tackling the display cases to erase the fingerprints and smudges left by the day's shoppers. When he was a child, he embraced the responsibility of tidying up Hoos after a busy day. He took pride in it. His father had instilled that in him. And now, as he cleaned, those cherished memories of his father surfaced. He remembered how his father would stand nearby, sharing stories of the world before Derro, a world that Jacob could only imagine.

Everything in Hoos has a story, Jake. It's our job to let them shine.

Jacob's hand paused as his fingers encountered a grainy texture beneath the cloth. Lifting it, he uncovered the same stubborn grime embedded in one of the glass cases, a mark that had defied his efforts for as long as he could remember. As a boy, it had been a challenge that consumed his youthful determination. But as he grew, the grime persisted, forcing him to live with its presence.

Today, however, felt different.

With all the whirlwind of conflicting emotions he'd been enduring, he longed for an escape. He sprayed the grime with cleaner, feeling a surge of determination, a flicker of the drive he had known as a child, when every imperfection demanded his focus. Pressing the cloth firmly against the grime, he began rubbing with heavy strokes, as though he were sanding rough wood. He pressed his knee against the case for support, its humming merging with his wandering thoughts. The world around him faded.

And unfortunately for Jacob, the escape failed.

He found himself adrift in the corridors of his mind, and no matter how hard he tried to banish it from his thoughts, the haunting news of yesterday's school shooting persisted. Lives had been torn apart; parents robbed of the simple joy of tucking their child into bed, a routine now cruelly and irreparably broken. And the survivors who would be forced to return to hallways that were now scarred into memories of terror they couldn't escape.

That fright shot through Jacob, as if a toxic substance were surging through his veins, poisoning every fiber of his being. How could he carry on with his routine while others endured such unimaginable suffering?

Suddenly, the sound of a jangling bell struck his ears, yanking him out of his mind.

He looked up to find Charlotte stepping inside. His face softened as he realized she'd gotten all dressed up. She wore a black top that was tucked into her jeans, and a tan overcoat that nearly grazed the floor. The sight took him by surprise. He stood speechless, shocked not just by the unexpected visit, but by how stunning she was.

"Char—" Jacob faltered, a smile spreading across his face. "What are you doing here?"

"I wanted to surprise you," she said, walking up to the counter.

When she neared, she leaned over the display case and kissed him. In that fleeting moment, the dark cloud of negativity weighing on his thoughts evaporated.

"Well …" Jacob said, opening his eyes as Charlotte pulled away. "Mission accomplished."

Charlotte chuckled, her lips curving into a playful smirk. Jacob's eyes widened as he took in the sight of her once again.

"And *wow*. You look … amazing."

"Thanks. I've planned the rest of our evening and wanted to ride home with you."

Jacob's heart pulsed as he recalled their planned movie night. "That sounds perfect," he said, letting out a soft sigh. "Today was—"

Charlotte silenced him with a gentle touch of her finger to his lips. "Your shift is officially over, Mr. Hughes. It's now time I took you home."

"You don't have to tell me twice. Let me just grab my things, lock up the back, and then we're out of here."

"Well, hurry," Charlotte said as she moved around the counter. "I'll wrap up."

"All right then," Jacob said, sensing the urgency as he passed Charlotte. He stepped out from behind the counter and headed toward the back of Hoos. "And don't worry about the counters. I'll only be a minute."

Jacob glanced over his shoulder, catching sight of Charlotte putting away the cleaner and cloths anyway. He smiled, admiring how supportive she always was. And undeniably beautiful. His thoughts lingered on her outfit as he entered the back room; the way every garment hugged her form filled him with anticipation for the evening ahead. With urgency, he gathered all his things, locked the back door, secured the inventory room, and then switched off the lights.

The jangling bell sliced through the air.

"Don't you fucking move!"

Jacob flinched, his body instinctively shrinking into the shadows of the back room as two figures stormed through the front door. Dressed in black hoodies and white owl masks, they leveled their arms toward Charlotte.

Guns gripped in their hands.

"Give us all your guns!"

Charlotte screamed, her cry jolting Jacob's body into motion. He dropped his things and immediately reached for his pistol at his waist and then rushed forward. Emerging from the backroom, he aimed his gun at the intruders. His heart sank as he saw Charlotte standing behind the counter, arms raised.

"Jacob!" she shrieked.

In response, one of the intruders leveled his gun at Jacob. "Hey now," the man said calmly, his cold eyes widening from behind the mask. "Let's not do anything stupid."

The man was tall, his athletic frame stretching the fabric of his sweater, outlining his taut arms. Jacob knew he would need to keep his distance.

"Same could be said to you," Jacob replied. "So, I suggest you drop your guns and leave before someone gets hurt."

Jacob's gaze flicked to the second intruder, who had started to lower his weapon.

"Keep your gun pointed at *her*," the other man barked, catching the second intruder dropping his aim.

The second intruder flinched, his aim snapping back to Charlotte. A sizable duffel bag swayed against his legs as his thin form jittered, his feet twitching, as though he were fighting against his instincts. His long, dark hair spilling out of his hood jerked with his head as he shifted his gaze between Jacob and Charlotte.

Jacob's arm shook, his aim shifting erratically between each intruder.

"That's not how we're going to play this," the burly man said, directing his attention back to Jacob. "You listen to me. Drop your gun and slide it over to me."

Jacob froze. His next move was crucial. Sweat beaded on his forehead as he tightened his grip on his pistol. He swallowed hard, desperately searching for a way out of this.

Then his heart sank. *Sid!*

His Aux should have been aware of the danger by now. Sid was programmed to detect threats, and when prompted, alert the Cullers. Yet Sid remained silent. Was Charlotte experiencing the same with Iris? Jacob hovered his finger over the trigger, his mind grappling with Sid's improbable inaction. The Cullers wouldn't arrive in time, if at all. That chilling thought gripped Jacob, forcing a consideration he'd never thought of before—he may have to take a life tonight. His instincts screamed to act, but his conscience countered with the consequences of such a decision.

Firing his gun could set off an unpredictable chain of events. Would his bullet find its mark? Would it kill the intruder, or just wound him? Would the second intruder retaliate, aiming at Jacob—or *worse*, Charlotte? The trigger was a mindful of uncertainty. As loud as his instincts yelled for him to shoot, compliance seemed to be the safest option.

At least for now.

"You can have the guns," he said. "They're all yours. But I'm keeping mine so I can ensure our safety."

"*No*, I'm in charge here. Not you. We're taking your guns. And we're starting with the one in your hands. Trust me, you don't want to find out what happens if you don't obey."

Jacob's resolve wavered. Handing over his gun meant surrendering his only means of protection. It stripped him of all control, leaving him defenseless. How else was he going to protect Charlotte? He cast a quick glance toward her, seeing her arms still raised, her eyes wide, alerted to the danger aimed at her. Flicking his gaze to the second intruder, Jacob noticed something in the man's eyes. Fear? It was strong. Just as strong as what Charlotte and Jacob were experiencing.

Then the second intruder spoke. "Let's just—"

"*Shut up!*" the first intruder snapped. "What did I tell you to do? Keep your gun pointed at *her*. I'll handle the rest."

The second man's feet continued to fidget, as though he were considering fleeing. Instead, he tightened his grip on his pistol and gave what felt like a reluctant nod.

"Now, where were we? Ah, yes … you were about to hand me your gun."

Jacob's pulse quickened, his hands betraying him with a slight tremor. He shifted his focus back to Charlotte. Their eyes met, hers brimming with tears. He tightened his fingers around the pistol's grip. "Please—"

"The hard way, then. If you don't lower your gun in three seconds, he kills her. One—"

"*Okay, I'm lowering it!*" Jacob shouted, raising one arm into the air and carefully lowering the other, setting his gun on the floor.

"Very good. Thanks for making it easy. Now, slide it over to me."

Reluctantly, Jacob slid the pistol across the floor.

The intruder, keeping his pistol trained on Jacob, bent down and grabbed the gun. "I'm proud of you. That's one gun. Now, head on over to these cases and hand me the rest. Then we're out of here."

Jacob quickly obeyed, his legs feeling heavy as he plodded toward the display cases. Stepping behind them, he came face to face with Charlotte. Her eyes flicked downward in a subtle motion, directing his attention. Following her cue, Jacob glanced down and glimpsed Charlotte's hand slipping into her purse.

Realization struck. She was gripping the pepper spray he had given her. Keeping his composure, he gave a slight shake of his head, silently urging her not to act impulsively.

"Let's hurry it up."

The first intruder's growing agitation was palpable. The second intruder, however, continued his unease, his eyes darting rapidly as he slammed the duffel bag onto the counter. Both men kept their guns trained—one on Jacob, the other on Charlotte.

Eager to see them gone, Jacob worked fast to unlock the glass cases and disengage the gun's holographic locks one by one. The humming from the cases grew louder, almost mocking the tension in Hoos. Time seemed to stretch, but finally, he had every firearm packed into the duffel bag. The leader snatched it from him and zipped it shut.

"Good job," he said. "Now, don't forget to call the Cullers when we leave, or else we'll be seeing you again soon."

"Please," Jacob said, releasing a heavy sigh. "Just go."

But his plea fell on deaf ears. Instead, the intruder's eyes locked onto something behind Jacob as he slowly started unzipping the bag.

"Well, would you look at that? You holding out on me? One last gun and we'll be on our way."

Jacob's heart plummeted, and his stomach churned as he realized what the man had seen. His heirloom—the pistol he'd crafted with his father as a boy. His fingers tightened into fists.

"Not that one," he said firmly, shaking his head. "You got what you came for. Now leave."

The intruder cracked his neck as he pulled back the hammer of his pistol, the sharp click sending a jolt through Jacob's body. Charlotte flinched, grabbing his arm in a tight grip.

"This isn't the time to play tough guy."

"I won't let you take it."

The intruder raised his arm, and Jacob tensed, his eyes snapping shut as the man's fist came down violently on the case. The deafening crack made Jacob flinch as Charlotte let out a startled squeal. His eyes shot open at the impact, locking onto the webbed cracks spread across the glass. The store plunged into suffocating silence.

"He made it with his father," Charlotte said, her words tumbling out. "It's all he has left of him."

The intruder tilted his head, considering Charlotte's words. Jacob's chest tightened as he silently hoped the man would back down. He wasn't sure where this newfound resolve had come from, but it anchored him in place.

Then the second intruder broke the silence. "We did the *job*, man, *and* we got what you came for. Let's just go."

The leader snarled, his patience snapping as he jerked his aim toward the second intruder. "How many times do I have to tell you to shut the fu—"

Charlotte sprang into action, leaning over the counter and spraying her pepper spray into the first intruder's eyes. A pained scream ripped through the air as the man dropped his gun, fingers digging into the holes of his owl mask. He stumbled backward, collapsing to his knees, and began blindly clawing at the floor in a desperate search for his weapon.

Jacob stood stock-still, his attention shifting to the second intruder. The man's aim darted wildly between him and Charlotte. Jacob took a slow step back, Charlotte close behind.

Then a gunshot tore through the air.

Jacob's body flinched, bones tightening as he instinctively ducked for cover. Then a *second* gunshot rang out. Panic surged through his veins as he searched for Charlotte. He found her still standing, frozen in place, eyes growing wide, her mouth falling open with a silent scream of agony.

The sight struck Jacob's soul.

Charlotte trembled, her hands pressed against her stomach, blood seeping through the gaps between her fingers. She staggered back, her crimson-stained hand clutching the glass case for support, but as her strength faltered, she crumpled to the floor.

"*Charlotte,*" Jacob cried out.

Heart pounding, he scrambled toward her. When he reached her, he pulled her fragile form into his arms, holding her for dear life. Her eyes, once full of life, were fading, distant and unfocused.

"No, no, no," Jacob whispered, his voice barely audible.

"*Mason, I shot her!*" the second intruder shouted, panic rising in his voice. "Oh, God. What have I done? Look what *you* made me do!"

Jacob lifted his heavy head, gazing through the empty display cases. Mason—the first intruder—stood motionless, his bloodshot, slit-like eyes glaring at the second intruder, his lost gun now found, clenched tightly in his hand. Jacob registered the incident instantly. Mason must have found his pistol and fired it blindly, the bullet missing its mark. That meant the bullet that struck Charlotte came from the second intruder—who, startled by the first gunshot, had fired wildly in his panic.

"What did you just say?" Mason growled.

The second intruder froze, his panic stalling abruptly. The weight of his words settled in. He had just said Mason's name aloud.

"I'm sorry," he stammered. "Mason, I didn't mean to—"

"Shut up!" Mason roared, jabbing his pistol at the other man. You just messed up. And now I have to clean up your mess."

"Sid, alert the Cullers," Jacob hissed, praying they might arrive in time to save her.

Sid didn't respond.

Where are you? Jacob frowned, his tears streaming down his face. He flicked his gaze toward Mason, who was slowly advancing toward him. His world was crumbling. His end was nearing. And there was nothing he could do to stop it. He squeezed Charlotte tighter, slamming his eyes shut, trying to shield himself from what was coming next.

He hoped it would be fast. That way, he could be reunited with her.

"Let's just go," the second intruder urged. "Someone would've heard those shots. The Cullers will be here any minute."

"This will only take a second."

"Please. You don't have to do this. We can just go. *Stop!*"

The world around Jacob seemed to shrink into deafening silence, broken only by the hollow echo of Mason's approaching footsteps. Each thump pulsed in his chest, sending a cold tremor through his bones as he clung toward the woman he loved.

Then the blast of a gunshot reverberated in his ears.

Jacob flinched, eyes snapping open, then bulging at the sight before him. Beyond the shattered glass, slumped against the case, was Mason, blood pouring from his head, staining his owl mask.

Jacob's gaze jerked to the second intruder, who stood motionless, his gun still aimed at Mason, smoke curling from the barrel. Their eyes locked. Jacob saw it—the raw remorse, stark and unmistakable—behind the second intruder's mask.

"I'm sorry," the intruder said. "It wasn't supposed to happen like this."

Jacob saw the sincerity in his tear-filled eyes and heard it in the cracks of his voice. He knew the man meant it. He'd just killed his partner. And in doing so, he saved Jacob's life.

But he'd also torn it apart.

The intruder moved toward the counter, reaching for the duffel bag. Once he had it gripped, he slowly walked backward toward the exit, as if waiting for Jacob to say something. But Jacob was too numb. He couldn't speak, couldn't move. Instead, he watched as the man reached the door, turned, and fled, the soft jingle of the bell ringing in his wake.

Jacob returned his gaze to Charlotte, his heart tightening in a way that felt unbearable. Every piece of him seemed to shatter, scattering into fragments he could never put back together. Tears poured down his face, an unstoppable flood that no amount of willpower could hold back.

"Charlotte," he whispered, a desperate plea for any sign of life.

His eyes drifted shut, unable to bear the sight of her lifeless form. She felt like an empty shell, a hollow casing that could never be filled again. She was gone. He gripped her hands, squeezing tight, the pain of it surging through him.

Then a scream tore from his throat. A raw, primal cry.

Out of breath, the scream subsided. The ringing in his ears faded, replaced by the distant wail of sirens. Exhausted and broken, he laid his head against her chest, his breaths coming in ragged gasps. The Cullers were coming, but deep down, Jacob knew their arrival would be in vain.

With a shuddering breath, he forced his tear-filled eyes to open. The world before him blurred, seen through a haze. Through that veil of sorrow, his gaze landed on the speck of grime ingrained in the glass case—the same one that had tormented him earlier.

But now, its presence felt different. Heaver. Intensified.

And streaked with Charlotte's blood.

CHAPTER SEVEN

DAY TWO OF EXILE

SLEEP ELUDED JACOB.

Trapped in a pit but a feral group of people who called themselves the Maws, rest was impossible. His body rejected the thought of it. Safety was more paramount, and the only way to guarantee it was through unwavering vigilance. So, he remained alert.

The morning sun cast a dim light over the pit, allowing Jacob to observe the weary faces of the other exiles, each one as frightened as he was. Alex rested her head against the wall opposite him, her expression cold whenever their eyes met. Jacob knew he was on her radar, and so far, he had done little to earn her trust. If he was being honest with himself, he didn't know how to. Or maybe, just maybe, he feared her as much as she feared him. His outburst toward her last night certainly hadn't helped. But as the hours dragged on, it became clearer to him that, to survive this, he would need to find a way to mend that rift.

Morgan, on the other hand, had seen something in him that Alex had not. He wasn't entirely sure what, exactly, but whatever it was, it had been enough. The poor kid, after settling close to Jacob, had finally whimpered himself to sleep. It was hard to believe he deserved this. But then again, the kid had been exiled. Jacob could only imagine what for. Pasts were tough, and who was he to judge?

Meanwhile, the mystery man remained unconscious. Jacob's stomach sank as he stared at the man's still form. Throughout the night, he had glanced his way, searching for any sign of life but finding none. *What happened to you?* Jacob wondered. *And when will it happen to me?*

The obvious answer was that he, too, had fallen victim to the Maws' trap. They had proven they had a system in place for capturing exiles, leading Jacob to question their true intentions. Did they see exiles as threats? Bargaining chips? He knew it was only a matter of time before they found out.

He shook his head, the memory of the cave flashing vividly in his mind. *Those shadows ...* the ones he'd seen as Wyatt's lifeless body was carried inside still haunted him. He closed his eyes, steadying his breath and forcing his thoughts to quiet. He needed to find a way out of this pit before the Maws' intentions became clear. Or *worse,* before he faced the horrors waiting inside that cave.

Though as much as he wanted out of here, a troubling thought gnawed at the back of his mind: even if he managed to escape, Eremos harbored other dangers. Other groups just as vicious as the Maws. Other death traps. Michael. The constant struggle for food, water, and shelter. Escape didn't promise freedom. Only another day fighting to survive on Eremos, which, so far, felt like being trapped in a never-waking nightmare.

Suddenly, Jacob's eyes narrowed, darting to the unconscious man. He couldn't be certain, but he swore he had seen movement, a subtle shift. Had the man finally woken? Or had he been awake all along, lying silently, trying to gather information on his new pit mates? It's what Jacob would have done. Not that there was much to overhear. Since learning about Morgan's lie, no one had spoken. Instead, they had slumped against the pit's walls, succumbing to defeat.

Jacob understood why Morgan had lied about making the fire. He was just a kid, too young to fully grasp the potential consequences. Sticking with adults felt safer than facing the dangers of Eremos alone. Jacob couldn't blame him. It was the same reason he had approached the fire. He hung his head, regret pressing down on him as he considered the path not taken. Maybe if he had stayed away, he wouldn't be here now, trapped in the ground.

It felt almost as though he were already dead; buried alive, suffocating under the weight of the inevitable. He scoffed softly at himself. As grim as it was, the thought of death felt oddly comforting, definitely more appealing than enduring another minute on Eremos. At least in death, however uncertain, there was a small hope he'd be reunited with Charlotte.

The thought of her made him lift his heavy head. The morning sky stretched above him, a brilliant blue dotted with clouds. Perhaps Charlotte was up there now, living among them.

From the bottom of the pit, Jacob felt both closer to her and farther away than he had in the past year. Closer, because with death looming, he clung to the fragile hope of reuniting with her up there. But deep down, he knew that hope was a lie, a comforting story he told himself to avoid the truth. And the truth was, his actions, the choices that had led him here, were more likely to condemn him to a hellish place far below the ground. A place where he would be cast even further from her, rather than soaring by her side in the clouds.

The eyes of the Lord are upon the righteous. And His ears are open unto their cry. Michael's words crept into his mind unbidden, offering hope. He shook his head, disgusted with himself. How desperate had he become to find comfort in the words of a madman?

Jacob liked to think he was a righteous person. But after what he had done—and what Eremos would inevitably *force* him to do—he struggled to see himself that way. He wasn't religious, not after all the loss he had endured. How could an all-knowing God allow such unimaginable suffering? Whatever governed the universe, it rewarded survival far more reliably than virtue.

That, sadly, was life. Whether beyond this pit, on Eremos or Derro, it wasn't really living at all. It was survival, teetering on the edge of a pit, one tragedy away from falling in. And righteousness, he'd learned, didn't keep you alive. He knew that kind of life all too well.

"What did you mean last night?"

Jacob jolted, the unexpected voice snapping him out of his thoughts. He turned to find Alex staring at him.

"I'm not sure what you mean," he said.

"You said, 'This is not what I came here for.' What *exactly* did you come here for?"

"I was just frustrated."

"The way you said it, though. It sounded like you came here on purpose."

Jacob scoffed. "That's ridiculous."

"Is it?"

"Why would I want to purposely come here?"

"I don't know, you tell me."

"I'm done with this conversation."

"So, you're just *not* going to answer me?"

"Why does it matter?"

"Because I don't trust you. You arrived much later than the rest of us. It's suspicious. And don't even think about saying it's because you're a bad swimmer or that we need to blindly trust each other. It's bullshit, and look at where it got us."

"Why are you fixated on me instead of trying to find a way out of here?"

"Because I need to know you're not a threat. Getting out of here will not be easy. I need to know if I can count on you to help me. I don't know you. For all I know, you could be just as bad, if not worse, than those bastards up there."

"I'm nothing like them," Jacob said through clenched teeth.

"How am I supposed to know that? Last I checked, you were exiled. Just like them."

Alex had a point. In the eyes of the council, Jacob was no different from the Maws. A criminal. But then again, so was she. And Morgan. The difference was, the Maws … they were a different breed of criminal. Figures of evil. Remnants of the tales Jacob's father had told him about the Anarchy Era. He wondered if the Maws had always been evil, or if Eremos, like the US did so long ago, turned them into the monsters they were now?

What will Eremos turn me into?

"I was exiled," Jacob said. "But I refuse to become anything like them."

"I know what you mean."

Jacob could see in her eyes that she meant it as sincerely as he did. Perhaps their paths weren't so different after all. Both were products of the Derro Council's rule. Both exiled, just for different reasons. And it was those reasons, unfortunately, that lingered just beneath the surface, keeping them from fully trusting one another.

It didn't help that, despite his efforts, Jacob had unwillingly made himself a target. In trying to conceal the Talon at the back of his waist, he had been forced to lie. Alex had seen through that. And yet, amid it all, she wanted to work with him to escape. Mending a fractured trust while trapped in a pit was a daunting task. But it was the only option they had.

Jacob stood and walked over to Alex, making sure their conversation would stay a whisper. Her gaze never left him until he settled beside her. Before speaking, he glanced toward Morgan and the other man. Both seemed to still be sleeping, or at least he hoped they were. He didn't want to frighten the kid more than he already was, and he knew nothing of the other man. He would need to be careful with his words.

"I arrived at the beach late because there was an altercation on the Screech," he confessed. "With Michael, the man with the burnt face."

Alex leaned closer. "What happened?"

"Before he jumped, he challenged Wes. Just faced him down, as if he wanted him to shoot him. I was convinced he would. Absolutely certain. But surprisingly, he didn't. Instead, he fired a shot outside the Screech. My guess, to inject some fear into Michael and prompt him to start running.

"But it didn't work. It was like Michael knew Wes would bluff. Or maybe he was willing to bet his life on it because the moment Wes fired, Michael struck him in the neck. After that, pure chaos. Wes dropped his gun. Michael grabbed it. And before the other Culler could even reach for his gun, Michael shot him in the head."

"Holy shit," Alex gasped, blinking repeatedly as she processed what Jacob had told her. Then her eyes slowly grew wide. "That's why you asked if we'd seen him when you sat down at the fire. You were making sure he wasn't around."

Jacob nodded.

"Fuck, he must've been the one who fired those shots last night."

"I thought the same thing."

"Do you think the Maws had tried taking him too?"

Jacob's brows furrowed. He hadn't considered that, but it made sense. Alex was sharp. Why else would Michael fire his gun? To continue his slaughter, perhaps. Yet, the more Jacob thought about it, the more he realized Michael's mission seemed about something more than just killing anyone he encountered.

"If they did, I'd say they weren't successful," Jacob said.

His stomach churned as regret stirred within him once again. Maybe if he hadn't been so focused on the Maws getting their hands on the Talon, and had instead, like Michael, chosen to use it, they wouldn't all be trapped in this pit. It was hard not to think that way. But with Alex and Morgan looking to him to protect them in that moment, and especially after what had happened the last time he was responsible for protecting someone, choosing to keep it hidden just felt right. He didn't want their blood on his hands.

"So, there's a man up there with a gun that has sixteen rounds left on an island with no guns," Alex whispered, musing. "He may just be the most dangerous person on Eremos."

As far as we know, Jacob feared. Eremos had already proven itself dangerous, even without a gun. The presence of the Talon in the hands of both Michael and Jacob only intensified that threat. Yet Jacob also knew the pistol would make them more than just targets. It would make them irresistible.

And that's where you come in. Richard's words this time crept into his head. *You'll be the one providing them with a false sense of security. An illusion that they can protect themselves when, in reality … you'll only be adding fuel to the fire. And that's where the real power lies.*

The real power, Jacob pondered. Richard was right in the sense that, in times of fear, people flocked to Hoos, seeking guns for protection. Sure, they created a false sense of security, but wasn't that, in a way, still *hope?* And for some, hope was often the only thing that kept them going. To survive. *Perhaps there's a way I can wield that power here on Eremos.*

"Make no mistake, Michael is dangerous," Jacob said. "And psychotic. But the Maws are our immediate threat. We have to find a way out of this pit."

"And how the hell do we do that?"

"There is one thing …"

Jacob wiped his sweaty palms on his jeans, heart pounding as he prepared to do something he dreaded. He fought against his instincts, his mind screaming at him as his fingers closed around the Talon. *This better not backfire.* There was just no other way.

Lifting a single finger to his lips, he urged Alex to remain quiet. "I'm not going to hurt you," he whispered.

Then he revealed the Talon. Alex's head jerked back, her body stiffening in alarm. She was afraid. But then her posture relaxed, and a wave of relief seemed to flood through her. In just a matter of seconds, its presence had given Alex hope.

"How?" she asked.

"Took it from the other Culler before jumping."

"Why didn't you tell us before? Hell, why didn't you *use* it?"

"I've seen firsthand what people are capable of when they want a gun. If I had told anyone, they'd have taken me out at the first chance. And using it against the Maws wouldn't have guaranteed anything but bloodshed. They could have held one of you hostage. And *worse,* forced me to exchange one of you for the gun. There was no way I was going to allow them to get their hands on this."

"But then why tell me?"

"Because like you said, escaping won't be easy. You needed to know you could trust me. This is my way of showing you that you can. That I'm not a threat. Just don't let me regret it."

"Well, you're definitely still a threat," Alex said, a small smile forming. "A threat to the Maws."

Jacob smiled briefly, the grin faltering as the weight of responsibility for the gun settled heavily on him. The damage it could cause in *his* hands felt all too real.

"We have to be careful with how we use this," he said.

"I'll follow your lead. Better in your hands than mine."

I don't know about that …

Alex took a deep breath, her eyes closing as she tilted her head against the pit wall. Though he was glad to have given her some hope, Jacob couldn't shake the gnawing unease. As much as he wanted to trust her, a part of him still resisted. *Will this feeling ever go away?*

Even more disturbing was the prospect of having to kill again. It made him feel sick. His exile had already pushed him to the point of taking lives. And he hated being driven to that brink once more.

He scanned the pit, his eyes darting over every crevice as he searched for a way out. But each possibility crumbled before him. The Talon felt useless without a way out of the pit first.

"If only we could find a way out of this pit," he muttered.

Standing, he tucked the Talon into the back of his jeans and began pacing. His hand scraped against the walls, pushing, probing for any rock or ledge that could aid in climbing. But the Maws had done their work well. The walls were scraped clean.

"Do you think it's possible to lift one of us out of here?" Alex asked.

"Whatever you're about to plan, it's not going to work," a soft voice interjected.

Jacob froze mid-step. The unconscious man was awake. *How much had he heard?*

Slowly, he turned, finding the man propping himself upright, his movements sluggish. The sunlight filtering into the pit illuminated him as he leaned against the wall. Dark strands of hair clung to his face. Jacob's eyes narrowed, his body tensing with renewed alertness.

No, it can't be.

The man moved with labored effort, brushing his hair back like a curtain being drawn. *Those injuries …* Bloodshot eyes. A swollen, bruised nose. Cuts crusted with dried blood.

Is that …

"Any idea you think of, I promise, has already been tried before," the man said. "And failed. The Maws are always watching. Lurking. Waiting to pounce on anyone who tries to escape. So, you might as well give up now."

Jacob's shocked gaze snapped away as Morgan, now awake, scurried to his side, clutching at him for protection. With the kid tucked safely behind him, Jacob turned back to the man, his heart hammering.

The man tilted his head as he leaned forward, his gaze locked onto Jacob's. "You?"

Jacob's hand twitched, readying itself to reach for the Talon.

It's him.

CHAPTER EIGHT

ONE YEAR BEFORE EXILE

THE WORLD AROUND Jacob blurred into a chaotic haze, as if reality itself refused to take shape.

"Mr. Hughes?" a muffled voice broke through the fog, soft and distant, like it was fighting to reach him.

He sat perched on a cold curb outside of Hoos, the surrounding air pulsing with flickers of red lights. His body was stiff, his mind trapped in a cocoon of numbness. He didn't try to leave it. The numbness was safe. Here, in this suspended state, there was no pain, no loss, nothing at all. And for now, that was enough.

"Mr. Hughes, can you hear me?"

This time he could tell the voice was that of a woman. Her words were clear, yet his body resisted responding. Forming a response felt impossible, as though he'd forgotten how to speak. His vacant, foggy gaze shifted down Nox Street, coming to rest on a crowd spilling out of Liberties. They stared at him, worry shadowing their faces. A holographic perimeter surrounded Hoos, preventing them from getting a closer look, but they could still see him—a victim of tragedy.

"He's unresponsive," the woman said.

"Out of my way," another voice snapped, this time a man's.

The commanding voice pulled him away from the onlookers. A muscular figure kneeled before him. Black, form-fitting armor clung to his massive frame, reflecting the glow of flashing red lights. Jacob recognized the man as a Culler, most likely a commander.

"Wakey, wakey," the Culler said, his breath misting the air with the overwhelming stench of tobacco.

Gritty palms tapped Jacob's face, trying to rouse him from his immobilizing trance. His vision cleared, his gaze landing on the badge adorning the Culler's shoulder plate: a white owl. He slammed his eyes shut, the sight unleashing a haunting image of the intruder from tonight, their owl masks piercing his heart like talons.

He opened his eyes, desperate to escape those memories. His senses slowly returned, sharpening with each passing moment. Tobacco. The distant hum of conversation, matching with the hum of the holographic perimeter. The cold curb. Flashing red lights. All of it assaulted him, finally breaking through his numbness.

And now tears, their warm trails streaming down his face. He hated it here. In reality. Where he was forced to face the hard truth. And worse, accept it.

She's gone. And it's all my fault.

"Mr. Hughes, I'm Commander Wes," the Culler said. "I need you to focus, all right? I'm going to do everything in my power to find the bastard responsible, but I need your help. Can you tell me anything about them?"

Jacob bowed his head as he wiped away the tears. Sniffling, he adjusted himself, struggling to find the right words, but they remained elusive.

"Did they have any distinct features? Skin color? Tattoos? Scars? Hair?"

The questions sliced through the dwindling fog still clouding his mind, pulling him back to that haunting moment. He saw the long-haired man, his shaky aim bouncing between him and Charlotte. Then a gunshot echoed, followed by another, their cracks jolting his body and yanking him back to the present.

"Long hair," he said, the words finally breaking free.

"Good," Commander Wes said. "They had long hair. Could you determine whether they were male or female?"

"Male."

"Was the man tall? Short?"

"Average."

"Did he have any tattoos? Identifying marks?"

"None that I saw."

"What about his skin color?"

"Couldn't tell."

"Well, all right," Commander Wes said, releasing a heavy breath.

Jacob knew the Culler wanted more from him. Something to go off of. A lead. And he wished he could give him one.

"Anything else you can think of to help us identify him?"

Jacob raised his head, meeting the Commander's gaze. The Culler's burly form pressed against his uniform, outlining taut muscles. Jacob saw the badge again—the white owl, stark against the black armor.

"They wore owl masks," he said.

"Owl masks, you say?" Wes asked as he stood.

Jacob nodded.

"Any chance you might be remembering them wrong?"

Jacob glared at the Commander. "I know what an owl looks like."

"An owl mask *was* found at the scene, Commander," the second Culler said.

Jacob glanced at her, noting that she appeared rather young, perhaps new to the force. Her age didn't diminish her intimidating presence, though. Sure, the Culler uniform contributed to her hardness, but so did her buzzed head, athletic frame, and long nose. Oddly, the only soft feature Jacob could discern was the scattering of freckles on her cheeks and nose.

"Well, all right," Commander Wes said, though there was a hint of reluctance in his tone. "Alpha, initiate an APB. We're hunting for a male of average height and build, with long hair. Likely on foot, and judging by his dead buddy, may be wearing a dark hoodie. Have the Cullers that capture him report directly to me and only me."

Jacob's father had once explained to him the protocol enforced by the council: all government employees were required to link their Aux to the council's single Aux, known as Alpha. This temporarily severed their personal Aux connection, ensuring the council could supervise their work and prevent conflicts between personal and professional duties.

"Rest assured, Mr. Hughes," the commander said. "We will find him. And when we do, I swear, the bastard will be exiled and put on the first Screech out of here."

Jacob frowned. "And if you don't?"

Wes chuckled as he tilted his head back, arrogantly amused by Jacob's worry. "That's not an option for me. I *always* find my man."

Jacob clung to those words, yet part of him felt that for Commander Wes, hunting criminals was more than just a pursuit of justice. It felt more like a game, a thrill in the chase that he seemed to relish.

"Make sure he gets home safely."

"Yes, Commander."

Commander Wes turned and started toward the crowd of onlookers. "And if he remembers anything else, you let me know right away," he called over his shoulder.

Raindrops began to fall, tapping softly on Jacob's head in a slow, steady rhythm. The second Culler kneeled in front of him, mirroring Wes's earlier posture, raindrops sliding down her armor.

"Do you need a ride home?" she asked.

Home? Jacob's heart plummeted. *"I've planned the rest of our evening and wanted to ride home with you."* Charlotte's words shot into his mind like arrows, each one a piercing reminder of the plans she had made—the plans waiting for him at home, now never to be fulfilled.

Tonight's tragedy returned in an onslaught of images: the man with the shaky aim, the echoing gunshots, Charlotte's lifeless eyes. A lump formed in Jacob's throat as tears poured down his face, tracing his cheeks and mixing with the rain. The plans they had, the future they were robbed of … everything crashed down on him in that moment of heart-wrenching realization.

She's gone. And it's all my fault.

"Mr. Hughes?"

"I'll have my Aux drive me home," he finally said, sniffling.

Then another realization struck him. Sid's improbable inaction. Why hadn't the Aux alerted the Cullers as it was programmed to do? Why hadn't it responded? Would Sid even respond now?

"All right, then. Sometime tomorrow, a Seeker will contact you to provide any updates and go over the case with you again. Just in case any other details come back. The Seeker will be your contact from here on out. Understand?"

Jacob nodded, though his thoughts were racing. "There's actually one more thing. During the robbery … my Aux … it didn't respond. It didn't sense the danger I was encountering."

The Culler stood, her head tilting slightly. "That's impossible. The council's Control Hubs prevent that."

Jacob shot to his feet. "I'm telling you the truth."

"You're saying that during the robbery, you asked your Aux to alert us, and it didn't?"

"Yes, that's exactly what I'm saying. It was like my Aux was gone."

The Culler's eyes narrowed, as though she too were struggling with the impossibility. "Very well. I'll relay this to the Commander." Placing one hand on his shoulder, she offered him a purse with the other. "Here are your wife's belongings. You get yourself home, all right?"

Avoiding the sight of Charlotte's purse, Jacob nodded, though a lingering doubt gnawed at him. He still felt as though the Culler didn't believe him. He watched her leave, his gaze eventually drifting to the onlookers beyond the holographic barrier. He bowed his head, avoiding their stares.

"Sid, I need a ride home."

On my way, Jacob, Sid said. The response was immediate, as though the Aux had never left.

"Sid, why didn't you answer before?"

There was a brief silence, a pause that tightened Jacob's bones as he waited for his Aux to respond.

I am not sure I know what you are referring to, Sid finally said. *I am always here, Jacob.*

Jacob frowned. *But you weren't.* It didn't make sense. For as long as he knew, Sid had always been there; a constant, reliable presence, ready when needed. Yet not tonight.

Jacob, I have arrived.

A soft whine drew his attention to his Nervo Pod approaching the holographic perimeter. He headed toward it, his gaze once again catching the watchful stares of the bystanders. As he neared the humming barrier, his ears picked up the voice of Commander Wes. It was coming from inside a Nervo Pod, this one shaped like a capsule, rather than the cube-like design of Jacob's. The council's owl emblem was emblazoned on it, the creature's red eyes glaring at him.

"I'm telling you, it has to be *them*," Commander Wes yelled.

Jacob's steps faltered as he reached the pod and peered inside. In front of Wes was a holographic projection of a man shaking his head. Wes jerked his head toward Jacob, catching him snooping.

"Move along," he barked. "Alpha, close pod door."

Jacob felt himself growing distant, his head spinning as he started toward his own Nervo Pod. He longed for that numbness again. Settling inside, he leaned his head back, trying to wrap his mind around the implications of what he'd just seen. Who did Wes think the intruders were?

Destination home, Sid said.

Hearing the word *home* caused Jacob's eyes to drift shut. His Nervo Pod accelerated, its whine growing louder as it picked up speed. The sound stirred inside his stomach and made his bones tremble. But it wasn't just the pod's whine that filled him with trepidation; it was the looming plans waiting for him.

Even though he was headed home, Jacob knew, deep down, his home would never truly be home again. Not really, anyway. Instead, like Hoos, his home would become a graveyard.

A haunting, constant reminder of what he had lost.

CHAPTER NINE

DAY TWO OF EXILE

'WHAT THE FUCK?' Alex blurted out. "You guys *know* each other?"

Jacob bit the insides of his cheeks, recognition dawning on him like the morning rays of sunshine beaming down into the pit. The battered face before him conjured the memory of their last encounter; a raid of punches echoing in the recesses of his mind. The visceral anger he had felt that day … it surged through him now, threatening to explode just as violently as it had back then.

It was a Last Patriot. It was Ammon.

"Hardly," Jacob said through clenched teeth.

"It's *really you?*" Ammon said, his hands frantically touching his body and face. "Am I … alive?"

"How long have you been down here?" Jacob asked, ignoring Ammon's questions. The man had clearly been through it.

Ammon rose, his movements labored as he used his hand to steady himself against the wall of the pit. Then he stared at Jacob, his dull eyes stunned.

"How long have I been down here?" he repeated, scratching his head. "I don't know. Five days? Maybe?" Ammon shook his head, eyes narrowing. "I … don't understand. How can you be … here? Why'd they exile *you?*"

Jacob glanced at Alex, who took a few steps backward. "It's alright," he tried assuring her.

"Wait," Ammon said, pulling Jacob's gaze back to him. The Last Patriot's eyes widened, distant, as if he were scared. "You're not … here to—"

"No," Jacob interjected before Ammon could finish. He couldn't afford for Alex or Morgan to be afraid of him. Especially now, considering Jacob had told Alex he had a gun. The Talon rested at the back of his waist, his hand twitching, ready to act should Ammon retaliate. "Finding you here is just a coincidence. One I want out of."

"All right, I need to know what the *hell* is going on here," Alex said, her voice demanding answers. "How do you know each other?"

"I barely know him," Jacob said. "And I don't care to."

"Well, he seems to know you."

Jacob rubbed the back of his head, sensing that his fragile alliance with Alex was cracking, He didn't have time for this. The Maws could return any minute. He needed to pull as much information from Ammon as possible before that happened.

"Alex, I know you need answers. But they're not the answers we need now. What matters *now* is finding a way out of this pit." Jacob pointed at Ammon. "And he knows things we don't."

Alex's eyes narrowed toward him and Ammon. She knew he was right, but he could tell she was still suspicious. Morgan stepped up from behind him, pulling his attention. The kid fidgeted with his fingers. The fear he must be enduring—fear of Ammon, fear of the Maws. Fear of death. If Eremos felt like living in a never-waking nightmare for Jacob, he could only imagine the tolls Morgan must be experiencing.

"We'll find a way out of here," Jacob told Morgan. He turned toward Alex and nodded, subtly suggesting cooperation to show the kid they could work together. "Aren't we, Alex?"

She hesitated, but after a brief contemplation, finally nodded.

"Well, good luck," Ammon said, scoffing. "These people are animals. Monsters, rather. It's only a matter of time before we end up like the others. So, just give up now. There's no hope."

"Others?" Jacob asked.

"Yeah, *others*. I'm not their first, if that's what you're thinking."

"What happened to them?"

Ammon shook his head and closed his eyes, as though the answer to Jacob's question was unbearable to think about. "Did you not just hear what I said?"

Jacob glared at the Last Patriot. "I heard you, but I still want to know. You may have given up, but I haven't. I refuse to die in this pit."

"And why should I help you? After what you did to me?"

"Oh, don't act like you didn't deserve it. You played a role in what happened, and you had the chance to share what you knew."

"And I told them everything I knew. Shit was bigger than me, and you know that. I was a pawn—"

"Ugh, I'm so damn tired of people saying they're pawns," Jacob interrupted. "Like they're being controlled by some unforeseen force. As if they have no control over their own choices."

"Hey, *fuck you!*" Ammon yelled. "You don't know my life. The struggle I've been through. What I've been *forced* to do in order to survive. And after what you did to me, you're not allowed to act like you don't know what I'm talking about. Or did you *choose* to do that?"

Jacob gazed downward, Ammon's words hitting him hard. "I wasn't in the best state of mind then. You had said something ... something that triggered an anger I'd been holding in for the longest year of my life. And unfortunately, you were the recipient of me finally releasing it."

"That why they exile you?"

"No."

"So, you ... found *him?* The man I told you guys about."

Jacob nodded, his eyes darkening. "You could say that," he said calmly.

Ammon's eyes widened, realization striking him. He knew what Jacob had done to get exiled. Not exactly, anyway. But after what Jacob had done to him, it wasn't hard to piece together.

"So, now that you two are done playing catch up, can we talk about how we're going to find a way out of this hellhole?" Alex asked.

Ammon snapped out of thoughts, head bowing slightly as he registered Alex's questions. "What do you want to know?"

"Start from the beginning," Jacob said. "How were you captured?"

Ammon leaned against the wall of the pit, gazing upward, as if he'd been down this road before. With other captives. He mentioned that there were others. Jacob would need to circle back to that and find out what happened to them.

"I was captured on my first night. After I arrived on shore, I went inland. It was getting dark, so I started looking for some form of shelter. Just something I could hide in until daylight. I'd only been walking for like ten minutes before three of them surrounded me. One had a bow."

"Twig, right?" Alex said. "There was a really skinny guy with spiky hair and a bow who killed another exile before capturing us."

Ammon nodded. "That won't be the last time you see him."

"What happened after that?" Jacob asked.

"I made a run for it. Dodged as many arrows as I could before the terrain eventually got me. Tripped over a stump or something. That was all they needed to catch me." He rubbed his hand through his hair. "You can piece together the rest."

"You were captured alone?" Jacob asked. "Earlier you said there were others."

"There *were*. When they threw me down here, there were two people already here."

"What happened to them?" Morgan muttered.

Ammon squinted, finally taking in the kid, frowning as if he couldn't bear the thought of what happened to the others happening to Morgan. "I don't know. Every night or so they come, drop a rope, and then force one of us out."

"Is that why you're all messed up?" Alex asked.

"Sort of," Ammon answered, his eyes flickering toward Jacob. "Two nights ago, there was just me and one other guy left. When they came, Daemion offered us a little *fun*, as he called it. Said he'd give us a chance to earn our freedom." He scoffed. "Fucker called it a pit party. Made us fight each other. Last man standing would be let free."

"So, you like, lost then?" Morgan asked.

Ammon shook his head. "Nah, kid, I won," he said, eyebrows raising slightly. "Wouldn't call it a win myself, though."

"Then what?" Jacob asked.

"Well, like I said, once freedom was on the table, the guy didn't hesitate. Just charged right after me. And those bastards just stood up there, roaring like they'd placed bets or something. I fought back. I mean, what else was I supposed to do? Luckily, it didn't take long. The man was weak. Who knows how long he'd been down here." Ammon glanced at Jacob. "I was *forced* to kill him. Almost as if I was *a*—"

"I get it," Jacob said, raising his hand in a gesture of calm surrender.

"Quick?" Alex asked, scoffing. "I'd say by the looks of you, the other man put up a decent fight."

"Oh, *these?*" Ammon said, pointing at his face. "Wasn't him who gave me these."

"Who did then?"

Ammon nodded toward Jacob. "Ask him," he said tersely.

Jacob sighed, his patience wearing thin. "We don't have time for this. Let's stay focused. If you won, then why are you still down here?"

"Because Daemion tricked us. After they pulled the other guy out, Daemion never dropped the rope. He just stood there with a sly grin spreading wider and wider. Fucker relished it."

Jacob lowered his head, feeling defeated. They were up against *another* madman. In just one night, Eremos had proven itself a relic of the Anarchy Era. He ran a hand through his hair and took a deep breath. Escaping this pit now seemed less of a possibility than ever. It would take a miracle. Fortunately, he had the Talon. But it wasn't the potential destruction the gun could cause that gave him hope; it was the power of attraction it wielded. *And that's where the real power lies.*

"What makes you so confident we can escape this pit?" Ammon asked.

"Because we have something they don't," Jacob said. "Something your *old* friends desired back in Derro."

Ammon tilted his head, eyes narrowing. With the troubled history Jacob had with Ammon, he dreaded the idea of having to work with him. He couldn't fully trust him. But he could say the same for Alex and Morgan. Actually, in a way, he knew Ammon more than he knew them. And as much as he hated admitting it, he needed him.

This better not backfire. Jacob drew the Talon and brandished it for everyone to see. "We have this."

Ammon took a step back. "How the hell—"

"Long story," Jacob said. "But this gives us an advantage. One we need to make sure we take advantage of."

"And just how do you plan to do that?" Ammon asked.

"The gun loses its power down here," Jacob said. "Sure, I can get a few shots off, but they'll just let me fire them until I'm empty. Or, just never come back until we've starved to death."

"So, what are you thinking?"

"You said they come back every night or so and force one of us out, right?"

"Yeah."

"Well then," Jacob drawled, pulling the slide back, the satisfying *click* fueling him once again. "When they do, we need to make sure it's me they pull out of here."

CHAPTER TEN

ONE YEAR BEFORE EXILE

WE ARE HOME, Sid alerted.

Jacob lifted his heavy head, the weight of his guilt pressing down on him as he stepped out of his Nervo Pod and made his way inside. His thoughts still spiraled, those final moments relentless. *I need them to stop!*

Inside felt quiet, save for the thumping of his footsteps and the agonizing flashbacks. Charlotte screaming his name. The blast of two gunshots. Her eyes. The images continued their assault as he wandered aimlessly. Eventually he found himself upstairs, where he began peeling off his wet clothes, still feeling disconnected from himself, unsure of what to do or how to move forward, but removing his clothing somehow felt right.

Jacob's muscles tensed up, his gaze catching blood as he peeled off his shirt, reminding him of Charlotte's stomach. He squeezed his eyes shut, shaking his head, trying to banish the haunting image. But it lingered. His new reality hit him again, deeply, a disturbing realization his entire life had been shattered.

She's gone. And It's all my fault.

Finally opening his eyes, his gaze caught his reflection in the mirror hanging over Charlotte's dresser. Hollow eyes stared back at him. The blood ... streaks of it stained his skin and caked his hands, his bones trembling at the sight. He rushed to the bathroom, desperation driving his actions. The blood was just too much.

"Sid, turn on shower!" he gasped.

Sid didn't respond but obliged the request.

Chest heaving, he desperately tore off the rest of his clothes. Tears welled in his eyes as he opened the glass door and stepped inside. The water scalded his skin as it cascaded over his shoulders, but he barely noticed. His hands were jittery as they frantically worked through the motions, scrubbing his arms, his chest, his face. Each stroke brought a swirl of red down the drain, a fleeting reminder of what he had just endured.

And of what he had lost.

He watched Charlotte's blood disappear, the rest of her life slipping away from him once again. Gone forever. *And it's all my fault.*

Leaning forward, Jacob pressed his forehead against the cool tiles and closed his eyes. The water pounded against his back, a relentless torrent that, unfortunately, couldn't wash the memories away as easily as it did the blood. He'd held her, tried to keep her with him, but it hadn't been enough.

Just like his actions.

Jacob stared down at his hands, Charlotte's blood now faded to pink from the scrubbing. The red stains smeared, diluted, but they clung stubbornly. He told Sid to turn the water hotter, wincing as it stung, yet he kept scrubbing until his hands felt raw. New.

A sob caught in his throat, and he let it out, weeping. He wanted to stand here forever, underwater, until he was clean of his failures. Until he could convince himself this was all just a nightmare he might wake up from. But eventually the pressure waned, the hot water growing cold. Reluctantly, he straightened, letting the water beat his face one last time. Then he told Sid to turn the shower off, silence following. Almost deafening.

Stepping out of the shower, he grabbed a towel and started roughly drying himself. When he was done, he wrapped the towel around his waist and took a deep breath. He didn't leave. Just stood there, the air thickening around him. He was unsure what to do next. He knew he couldn't stay here forever. But maybe, just for a moment longer, he could pretend the water had washed away more than just the blood.

When he finally mustered the courage to step out of his bathroom, he regretted it instantly, his gaze falling on the patio doors across his bedroom. Soft lights shone in, beckoning him outside.

We should do something out here. His words from this morning echoed in his head. He succumbed to the pull, taking hesitant steps closer.

I've planned the rest of our evening and wanted to ride home with you. Charlotte's words this time.

He approached the patio doors, his gaze glimpsing through the glass at what she'd set up for them. A movie screen hung in front of their round daybed. A crafted charcuterie board and a bottle of whiskey waited for him. And there, in the center, was a large, green-wrapped box. He stepped closer, head tilting to examine further. Desperate to see what awaited him, he reached for the door handle.

Then froze.

A shiver of fear crept inside him. He knew the contents of that box threatened to deepen his pain, his guilt, his loss. Opening it would only add more weight to his already burdened heart. The sight alone was doing just that. It hurt. He wanted to numb that ache.

And sadly, he knew exactly how.

Jacob's eyes wandered back to the bottle of whiskey. He needed it, but he couldn't bring himself to go outside. So, instead, he hurriedly retreated from his bedroom and rushed downstairs, eyes brimming, his mind fixated on the only thing he knew could dull the pain.

He reached the bar, grabbed the first bottle within reach, yanked off the cork, and poured the warm liquid down his throat. It burned—a temporary punishment he welcomed, knowing numbness would eventually follow. As long as he kept drinking.

And he planned to do just that.

He carried the bottle upstairs, taking swigs as he wandered back into his bedroom, and then collapsed onto his bed, the towel slackening from his waist as his dull eyes stared up at the ceiling.

With every thought, every ache, every memory, he drank.

Eventually, the ceiling swirled, the ache slowly diminished, and the memories came slower. Every sip ushered him into that state of numbness until his eyes finally closed, his body succumbing to sleep.

Or death.

Jacob didn't care.

The next morning, Jacob reluctantly awoke.

Morning, Jacob, Sid greeted.

He didn't answer his Aux. His head pounded too hard for him to respond. He squinted, the daylight streaming through the windows assaulting him. He rubbed his hands over his face, turning away from the light. Charlotte's side of the bed met him—now empty. The harsh reality of her absence cut through him again, like a knife.

I can't believe she's gone.

He reached for her pillow, his fingers gripping the cold fabric as if clinging to the last traces of her warmth. Squeezing it tight against his chest, he inhaled deeply, hoping to capture one more fleeting moment of her scent.

I should've shot them when I had the chance, he thought, a heavy wish churning in his stomach, yearning for a different outcome. *I should've just handed over the gun. I should've stepped more in front of her.*

The guilt felt insurmountable, pressing him deeper into his bed, preventing him from getting up. Though he knew he should. The Seeker would be reaching out to him today, and he didn't want to miss the call.

A ringing jolted Jacob from his thoughts. His phone was ringing. *Why didn't Sid alert me?*

He shot out of bed, his muscles protesting with each jerky movement as he rushed to grab his jeans from the floor. Hoping it was the Seeker, he fumbled for his phone, but as soon as he retrieved it, he slowly collapsed onto the edge of the bed, realizing it wasn't his phone ringing after all.

The hair on his arms stood up as his eyes flicked toward the ringing sound, landing on Charlotte's purse sitting on her dresser. *That's why*, he realized.

He stood and, with hesitant steps, made his way toward her purse, his heart racing at the thought of who might be calling her. Reaching it, he pulled out her phone just as the ringing stopped, replaced by a notification. The holographic display revealed that Nancy had called. The name struck him like a blow, forcing his eyes shut as a wave of pain washed over him.

No, no, no, he panicked.

A *ping* jolted his eyes open, another notification, this time showing Nancy had texted her. The message projected: "So, how'd it go last night?"

Jacob's mind recalled the image of the green-wrapped box sitting on their back deck. His stomach sank. She had planned more than just a simple movie night. He gazed toward the patio doors, his eyes landing on the box. Curiosity tugged at him, urging him to step outside and open it.

Another ping jerked his eyes back to her phone, alerting him to a new text from Nancy that read, "Was he surprised?"

Despite the overwhelming urge to step outside and open the box, Jacob returned to the edge of his bed instead. He sat there, grappling with the daunting task ahead. His hands trembled as he fought for composure, the insurmountable weight of grief pressing down on him once more. Taking a deep breath, he summoned what little strength he had left, steeling himself to deliver the fateful news to Nancy. Finally, he tapped the notification and started the call.

"Hey you," Nancy answered.

"Nancy," Jacob murmured.

"Jake, dear, is that you?"

"Yes."

"Oh, Jake, you must be so—"

"Nancy, something happened last night."

A somber hush followed.

"What do you mean? Is everything all right?"

Jacob hesitated, the words catching in his throat. He didn't know where to begin, how to convey the magnitude of the tragedy that had shattered their family.

"I … I don't know how to say this. Last night … Hoos was robbed. And Char …"

"Oh, dear God. Is she okay?"

Jacob's head dropped into his chest, tears falling down his face. "Nancy, she was killed," he cried.

"No, no, no," Nancy repeated, the words escaping like a desperate plea.

"Nancy, what's going on?" Steve asked, his voice distant.

"Oh, Steve, it's Charlotte," she spilled.

"What happened?"

Jacob's body tensed for the words he knew would follow. The raw agony in Nancy's cries cut into his heart.

"She's *gone*, Steve," she cried.

"*What do you mean she's gone?*"

Nancy's sobs continued as a shuffling emitted through the phone, as if it had switched hands.

"*Jake, what happened?*"

"I'm sorry, Steve. It's true. I wish it wasn't, but … she died."

"Oh, no," Steve said, his voice cracking but steady. "Jake, I have to call you back, okay? I need to take care of Nancy. We'll … we'll come out there right away."

"Okay," was all Jacob could say.

Separated by miles, but united in grief, Jacob and his in-laws clung to the fragments of their shattered lives. As the call ended, a violent quiet swallowed the room, save for the haunting echoes of Nancy's sobs lingering in Jacob's mind.

Abruptly, another sharp ringing pierced through, jolting Jacob.

Jacob, an unrecognized number is calling you, Sid alerted. *Would you like me to identify it for you?*

"Just answer it and enable the speaker."

Understood, Jacob.

"Hello."

"Mr. Hughes, this is Ezra Pierce. I'm the Seeker assigned to your case. Can we arrange a meeting?"

"Have there been any updates?"

"Not at this time. We're still searching for the man who got away. In the meantime, I need to meet with you, discuss again what happened, and hopefully learn about anything new that might help us find him. Can I swing by now?"

A heavy sigh escaped Jacob's lips. "Okay."

"Great, I'm on my way."

CHAPTER ELEVEN

DAY TWO OF EXILE

JACOB HAD A PLAN.

A risky but cunning plan.

The odds definitely leaned toward failure, but he was ready to risk it all. His plan was no doubt a high-stakes gamble, one he couldn't afford to back down from. He had to go all in.

The Maws had proven to be a ruthless bunch, their savagery fueled by the sadistic leadership of Daemion—a man as brutal as he was unhinged. Yet, like everyone else on Eremos, Daemion fought desperately to survive. And, little did he know, *that* was his weakness.

"Why'd you take it all apart?"

Jacob lifted his gaze to find Morgan settling across from him. The kid drew his knees to his chest, resting his chin atop them, his attention locked on the disassembled Talon lying on the ground. Like Jacob, sweat beaded on Morgan's forehead. The scorching sun had battered them all day, but now, as it finally dipped, a small wave of relief washed over them.

Relief, however, didn't mean rest. Jacob stayed focused on his plan. Pockets of shadows crept across the pit, offering just enough cover to keep him hidden from prying eyes. There was no telling how much time remained before the

Maws returned. Jacob worked with urgency, his hands moving with practiced precision.

"Just wanted to see what I was working with," he said, reassembling the pistol piece by piece.

"You seem to know what you're doing."

"With the gun? Sure. With what comes after I leave this pit … not so much."

"So, you don't think you'll be able to get us out of here?"

Jacob watched as Morgan fidgeted with a strand of curly hair that dangled over his eyes, his gaze fixed on the Talon—their only hope.

"It'll be tough," Jacob admitted. "But I'm going to fight like hell to make sure we do."

"You won't, like, leave us here?"

Jacob paused, his gaze dropping back to the gun. All day he'd sensed that Alex and Ammon doubted his intentions, assuming he'd volunteered to be pulled up just to escape alone. It was a plausible fear. But not one he'd expected Morgan to share. Hearing the kid voice it hit harder than he'd anticipated. It felt real.

The last time someone had relied on him, he had failed. That failure clung to him, relentless and unforgiving, a constant reminder of a bitter truth he had come to accept.

He was no hero.

But sometimes, survival demanded something different. Someone different. And Eremos had forced that out of him.

"I won't leave you behind, kid," Jacob finally said.

Morgan released a heavy breath, a faint smile tugging at his lips.

"You ever fire one of these?" Jacob asked, hoping to divert Morgan's fear.

The kid simply nodded as he watched Jacob reassemble the Talon.

"I built one with my father once," Jacob said. "They're not toys, that's for sure. My father made sure I knew that. He taught me everything I know about firearms."

"You guys *made* an actual gun?"

"We sure did," Jacob said, his voice trailing off as he smiled. "It's one of my fondest memories with my father."

"Have you ever … like … killed anyone before?"

Jacob froze, his hands stilled over the Talon. The question lingered, sharp and unsettling. A heavy silence hung between them, thick as the air in the pit.

Then the quiet shattered as footsteps crunched above them, drawing close.

"Get behind me," Jacob ordered.

Morgan scrambled to comply, Alex and Ammon, too. Desperation bleeding into his motions, Jacob's hands remained steady as he loaded the bullets into the magazine, slammed it into the grip, and pulled back the slide to chamber a round.

The plan was ready.

Jacob stood, drawing a deep breath, silently praying for a miracle. He nodded to Alex as she approached. "No matter what happens," he said, tucking the Talon at the back of his waist, "I'm the one they pull up."

"You better come back for us," she said.

"You three be ready to climb up at a moment's notice," Jacob said, ignoring Alex's comment, his focus unbroken.

"Good luck," Ammon said, nodding slightly.

Jacob narrowed his eyes at the Last Patriot. For a fleeting moment, it felt as though Ammon was setting aside their troubled history. Jacob returned the nod—a silent truce, however temporary—then returned his attention to the edge of the pit.

The crunching footsteps grew louder, closer.

And then Daemion's face emerged.

"Well, hello, my dearies," he drawled. "Are we getting restless down there?"

Jacob bit the insides of his cheeks. Not just from fear, but also to hold his tongue. He refused to give Daemion the satisfaction of a reaction.

"Ah, Ammon, my dear. You're not looking any better. Have you told our newcomers about our little pit parties?"

Jacob's gaze flicked toward Ammon. The Last Patriot's fists were clenched tight, his nostrils flaring as he stared daggers up at Daemion.

"Ew, don't look so tough now," Daemion sneered. "It's not a good look on you. And let's be honest … it wasn't much of a fair fight, was it? But oh, it was fun to watch."

Morgan inched closer to Jacob, drawing Daemion's attention like a predator sensing weakness.

"Impressive, kid. Exiled at such a young age, and yet you cower. Curious. We'll need to toughen you up." Daemion grinned as he curled a finger, beckoning Morgan to come closer. "How about you join me up here? Let me show you around Eremos. Oh, the fun we could have. The plans I have in store."

"Leave him out of this," Jacob said, wrapping his arm around Morgan.

Daemion frowned. "Ugh, you again. Acting all brave and tough. You know, I think I'll save you for last. Watch you break as I pull everyone else out but you. Leave you nothing but a hollow shell."

Jacob's jaw tightened. "Or you can just take me now."

Daemion erupted into a fit of laughter, a chilling, unhinged cackle that promised only pain. "A volunteer? Well, that doesn't sound fun. I'd much rather have the boy. He looks the tastiest."

Jacob's heart skipped a beat as a flood of images sliced through his mind. Wyatt's lifeless body carried into that cave. Daemion's cruel order to prep him. The flickering, chopping shadows he'd seen dance across the cave walls.

The Maws were cannibals. And Jacob had just volunteered himself on a platter.

"You can't have him," Alex said.

"Oh, I most certainly can. And I will. You're in *my* world now. I make the rules." Daemion tilted his head, mockingly tapping his temple. "I thought you'd know that by now. Unfortunate. Well then, a quick reminder. Twig, do it."

Twig pulled back the string of his bow and aimed it at Jacob. "Come on out, kid," the Maw taunted.

Jacob stood in front of Morgan, trying to stay focused on the plan. A plan that now felt even more impossible, twisting his stomach into knots.

"Oh, don't be scared," Twig said, the arrow drawn taut. "It'll be quick. Or maybe not. Maybe I'll make it hurt just a little. I do like to play with my food."

"I'm doing you a favor, little boy," Daemion said. "Your demise on Eremos is inevitable. Best to get it over with now. Twig, shoot them."

"*Wait*," Jacob screamed.

Daemion let out an exasperated sigh. "Damn it, what now?"

"I have information you'll want to know."

"And what's that, my dear?"

Jacob hesitated. This was the first gamble in his plan. He hoped Alex's intuition had been right. Morgan's life was on the line, and this moment would determine whether Jacob had failed him.

"The identity of the man who shot your precious Maws last night," Jacob said.

Twig's eyes widened, darting toward his leader, his aim wavering. "How's he know that?"

"He's bluffing," Daemion said. "That happened away from where we captured you. You only heard the shots and are just biding time—"

"I can get you that gun," Jacob cut in. "It's a Talon, a standard-issue firearm for Cullers with twenty rounds. And after taking into consideration the three bullets that killed your Maws, I'd say there's maybe seventeen left."

Daemion's eyes narrowed. "How do you know that?"

"I'll tell you, but you have to take me instead of the kid."

Daemion paused, his long fingernails scratching at his neck as he considered the offer. Jacob saw it not just in Daemion and Twig's reactions, but in their eyes—Alex's intuition had been right. The people Michael killed last night had been Maws.

"Aren't you curious how a gun got on Eremos?" Jacob pressed, not giving Daemion much time to ponder. He needed the maniac focused on the Talon, not on Morgan.

"What are you doing?" Ammon whispered, concerned to watch Jacob offer up the Talon.

"Improvising."

"Fine, drop the rope," Daemion commanded. "I want to know what he knows. But if I find out you're lying, and this is all just a hoax to save the boy, I'll come back for him. And you'll get to watch as we tear the flesh from his bones."

Jacob didn't hesitate. He rushed toward the wall and grabbed the rope as it dropped. Gripping it tightly, he planted his feet against the cave's wall and climbed. His heart thumped in his chest, each upward tug of the rope digging painfully into his palms. When he finally reached the top, the claws of Maws grabbed him, hoisting him upright. They didn't let go.

Jacob's eyes grew wide with alertness as Daemion sauntered toward him. Those eyes …

"You think you're clever," Daemion said. "Trying to be a hero. Well, let me tell you something. In Eremos, there are no heroes. Only survivors."

Then Daemion fist struck Jacob in the gut, knocking the breath from his lungs. He doubled over, gasping. Hot breath slapped his face as Daemion leaned in close.

"And you, my dear, will not survive this."

Jacob fought for breath, his fight surging within him. He lifted his head, meeting Daemion's stony stare, then snarled.

Daemon's grin widened as he stood tall. Before Jacob could react, his head snapped to the side from a brutal blow to the face. He collapsed to the ground, the sounds of approaching footsteps closing in.

A flurry of kicks rained down on his battered body, coming from every direction. Jacob tried shielding himself, but the Maws were relentless. The world spun into a haze, the edges of his vision darkening. Daemion's cruel laughter faded into a distant echo as the darkness took him.

CHAPTER TWELVE

ONE YEAR BEFORE EXILE

RESTLESS, JACOB OCCUPIED the confines of his living room, fingers drumming anxiously on the armrest of the sofa. The Seeker's brief call had left him grappling with last night's tragedy. The moments replayed in his mind, a continuous loop that made his chest ache and his eyes burn, the skin around them raw from too many tears. He just couldn't stop crying.

The urge to pour a glass of whiskey tugged at him, tempting and persistent. It had dulled the pain last night, but he knew he couldn't afford to lose focus. Not with the Seeker on his way.

Ezra, he mused, the name lingering in his thoughts. Uncommon, yet oddly familiar. He considered the possibility that he'd sold a firearm to someone by that name before, but the connection felt off, like a puzzle piece forced into the wrong slot.

A sudden knock cut through his thoughts, halting his tapping fingers. *Jacob, there is a Seeker at your front door,* Sid informed. *Would you like me to let him in?*

"I've got it," he said, rising from the couch.

He started toward the front door, the thought crossing his mind that he might recognize the man behind it. But upon opening, he met the gaze of a tall, dark-skinned person with sharp features and a no-nonsense expression. The man didn't look familiar at all.

"Jacob Hughes?"

Jacob nodded. "Yes. Ezra, right?"

"That's correct. May I come in?"

"Yes, of course," Jacob said, stepping aside. "Please, come in."

He watched as the Seeker stepped inside, his presence immediately unsettling. He'd never had a Seeker—or even a Culler, for that matter—in his home before. It felt invasive. Ezra's sharp eyes scanned everything, taking in each detail.

He led Ezra to the living room and resumed his spot on the sofa, gesturing for the Seeker to take the chair across from him. Ezra sat, his gaze continuing to rove around the room. He seemed to catalog everything—the framed pictures on the walls, the furniture carefully placed throughout. Beyond the floor-to-ceiling windows, Ezra observed the rain, the steady rhythm of drops drumming against the glass, raising Jacob's anxiety.

"This is quite the home you have here," Ezra said.

"Thanks."

"It's unique. Never seen anything quite like it."

"I'd think working for the council, you'd have seen your fair share of homes. I doubt mine's the most unique."

"That's true, but still, none quite like this. And the photographs … beautiful."

Jacob frowned. "Thanks, but I'm guessing you didn't come all this way just to compliment my home."

"Right, my apologies."

Jacob leaned forward, grabbed the decanter of whiskey from his coffee table, and poured himself a drink. He downed the shot in one gulp. "I don't need your apology. Just need you to find the man who killed my wife."

"And I assure you that is my top priority."

Jacob returned the decanter to the table, taking a moment to lean back into the sofa. He realized how much he was acting like his father, drinking to help grieve. It was all he knew. It had taken strength for his father to stop after Jacob's mother passed. Unfortunately, though, that had always proven short-lived.

Maybe the same will be said for me, he mused.

"I inherited the home from my father," he said. "He had it built as a tribute to my mother. She passed when I was a child. I don't remember her all that well, but my father described her as someone deeply connected to nature."

"I can see the dedication. It's remarkable."

"Thanks."

"So, as I said before, I'm dedicated to finding your wife's killer, and uncovering why all this happened. I've spoken with the assigned Commander, I believe you two have met. He informed me the Cullers searched throughout the night but, unfortunately, were unable to locate the man."

Jacob frowned, Commander Wes's words echoing in his head. *I always find my man.*

"What about the other guy? Mason. They would've known each other."

"We identified him—Mason Rowley. A Tuto native. Was in and out of foster care as a kid, no steady record of employment, and based on what we've uncovered so far, he has minor ties with the Last Patriots. I'm sure you've heard of them."

Last Patriots? That must've been who Commander Wes was referring to last night when he said, "I'm telling you, it has to be them."

"I've heard of them. Seen their symbol spray-painted all over Tuto. So, was Mason part of their rebellion?"

"We're not sure. The Last Patriots mark their allegiance with a simple star tattoo on the wrist. Mason didn't have one. But his online activity and Aux report suggests he was interested in joining."

"So, what … you're saying this rebellion needed guns, and Mason robbed Hoos as some kind of initiation?"

"That's *a* theory. But we're still investigating. There have been other, smaller firearm store robberies over the past few months. This is the first we've seen a potential link to the rebellion. What we don't know yet is how deep Mason was involved. Whether he acted on their behalf or on his own. There's still a lot of uncertainty."

"Is there *anything* you know for certain?"

"Not as much as we'd like, I'm afraid. These men somehow managed to jam the council's AI systems temporarily during the robbery, allowing them to rob Hoos blind."

Jacob's brow furrowed as realization hit. *That must've been why Sid didn't respond.*

"I told one of the Cullers that last night. My Aux … it didn't work during the robbery. It couldn't alert you guys or even register the danger I was in. I thought the council's Control Hubs were supposed to prevent this kind of thing. How is that even possible?"

"It's not supposed to be. This is the first time we've encountered a situation like this."

"So, what, we're like, headed into another Anarchy Era? Criminals just get to commit any crime they want, acting like ghosts?"

"We're trying to get ahead of it. The council is taking this threat seriously. And fortunately, we may have a lead. Our coroner found a subdermal chip implanted in Mason's hand. We believe it acted as a jammer and are working to trace the chip back to its source."

Jacob was at a loss for words. *Jammer?* It didn't make sense. And, unfortunately, only meant the man who killed Charlotte was no closer to being found.

"I'd like you to walk me through what happened again," Ezra said, activating a holographic tablet. "Since the jammer disabled both your security systems and the council's cameras, we only have your account to go on. I know it's difficult, but I'll need you to be as detailed as possible. Any minor detail could help us. Alpha, start recording."

Jacob took a sip of his whiskey, bracing himself to relive last night's events. They had replayed in his mind countless times since he had returned home but recounting them for Ezra somehow felt worse. More painful. Real. But he knew that if there was any chance of finding her killer, it was necessary.

"I was closing up Hoos for the evening when Charlotte walked in. I was surprised to see her. We'd had plans for the night, and she wanted to ride home with me. So, I went to the back to grab my things and make sure everything was locked up. And that's when they came in."

Jacob took a steady breath, his eyes closing briefly as the memories assaulted him.

"They wore owl masks," he continued. "If there *is* a chance these men were Last Patriots, then maybe they wore them as a way to defy the council?"

"It's possible. What happened after that?"

"After they barged in, I drew my gun and rushed out of the back. Pointed it straight at them. Charlotte was behind the counter. They'd already had their guns pointed at her, but as soon as they saw me, Mason—the leader—turned his aim on me. Told me to lower my gun so no one would get hurt."

"How did you handle that?"

I should've shot them.

"I thought about shooting them. But I feared it would turn into a shootout, or *worse*, Charlotte getting shot. That's when I noticed my Aux wasn't working. So, fearing the Cullers wouldn't show up, I told them they could take the guns, but that I was keeping mine. I had to make sure we were safe.

"But then Mason threatened Charlotte's life. Told me if I didn't hand over my gun, that he'd have his partner shoot her. Gave me until the count of three. I didn't know what else to do. So, I handed it over. After that, he ordered me to open the cases and hand over the rest."

Ezra nodded, eyes narrowing on his tablet. "You said Mason was the leader. What made you feel that way?"

"It was just obvious. Whenever the other guy tried speaking, Mason would cut him off. I got the feeling the other intruder was afraid of Mason or inexperienced in such situations."

"Anything else he did to make you think that?"

"He was just erratic and unpredictable. I could sense his discomfort."

Ezra's hand moved with urgency as he jotted notes. "Tell me what happened after you got to the cases."

"When I stepped behind them, Charlotte made a subtle gesture to her purse. She was holding her pepper spray. I gave her a subtle head shake, urging her not to do anything hasty. Then I handed over all the guns. They were about to leave, but Mason noticed an older pistol on display. An heirloom from my father. We'd made it when I was a kid. I told Mason he couldn't have it. Charlotte told them it was from my father, and for a moment, I thought they'd leave ..."

Jacob lowered his head, hiding the tears he couldn't hold back. *I should've just given them the gun.*

"Then what?" Ezra asked softly.

"The second intruder spoke up, urging Mason to leave," Jacob said, sniffling. "That's when Mason snapped. Turned his aim on him."

"Wait, Mason aimed his gun at the other intruder?"

"Yeah."

Ezra's eyes widened. "What happened after that?"

"That's when Charlotte pepper-sprayed Mason. It happened so fast. It shocked me. After that ... chaos. Mason dropped his gun and fell to the floor, blindly searching for it. I thought the other guy would shoot us right away, but he panicked. Kept switching his aim between me and her. Before I had time to even think about what to do, a gunshot went off."

Jacob wiped his eyes on the sleeve of his shirt. *I should've stepped more in front of her.*

"Then right after that, almost instantly, another gunshot fired. I fell to the floor, and that's when I noticed her. She'd been shot ... then she fell to the floor. I scrambled over to her. Just held her while the intruders argued with each other."

She's gone. And it's all my fault.

"Why were they arguing?"

"The second guy had said Mason's name aloud. He was shocked that he'd shot Charlotte. Yelled, 'Mason, I shot her. Look what you made me do.'"

"Is that why he shot Mason?"

"Not exactly," Jacob answered, his mind grappling with what happened next. "Mason told him he needed to clean up his mess, *meaning* kill me. The second guy pleaded for him not to, but Mason wouldn't listen. I could hear him making his way over to me. And that's when I heard the shot."

"The second intruder *saved* your life?"

"He *destroyed* my life."

Ezra lowered his head, nodding as he returned his gaze back to his tablet. "My apologies."

"Just please find him."

"I will. And when I do, ensure he is exiled."

"In times like this, exile doesn't seem like enough justice."

Ezra nodded, understanding the unspoken words in Jacob's response. "Is there anything else you can remember? Something they *did*? Something they *said*?"

Now, don't forget to call the Cullers when we leave, or else we'll be seeing you again soon. Mason's words surfaced in Jacob's mind.

"There was one thing. After I'd handed over all the guns, and it appeared they were about to leave, Mason said something that felt off to me then, but perhaps makes more sense now."

"What did he say?"

"He told me not to forget to call the Cullers, or that they'd be seeing me again."

"Insinuating that once they were gone, you could finally call because your Aux would no longer be jammed," Ezra theorized.

"I guess," Jacob said, his mind focused on Mason's words as he watched the rain pelting the windows.

"Anything else?"

We did the job, *man, and* we got what you came for. The second intruder's word this time. "Yes, the other guy said something too. When he tried urging Mason to go. Right before Mason turned his gun on him."

"What did he say?"

Jacob tilted his head, his mind grappling with the meaning of the words. "He said that they'd done the job *and* gotten what *he'd* come for."

"*And?* Did it sound like he was insinuating that there was another job other than the guns?"

"Maybe. I could be remembering it wrong too."

Ezra nodded, his stylus rapidly moving across the holographic screen. "Well, Mr. Hughes, you've been very helpful, and I appreciate all you've shared with me. I should get going and share all this with Commander Wes. Alpha, stop recording."

Ezra packed his things together and stood, Jacob following suit.

"Thank you," he said, extending a hand toward the Seeker.

"Don't thank me yet," Ezra said, shaking Jacob's hand. "You can thank me when we find him."

Jacob watched as Ezra started toward the front door, but just as the Seeker reached the edge of the hallway, he paused, hesitating, as though a thought had rooted him in place.

"I actually have one more question," he said, turning back. "When he shot her ... just to confirm, was it accidental?"

Jacob bit the insides of his cheeks, his mind still entangled in the events of last night. *It wasn't supposed to happen like this,* the intruder had said. In every replay, it seemed the shot had been fired by accident. But his actions leading up to it were anything but accidental. He had chosen to rob Hoos. Accident or not, he deserved exile.

"Does it matter?" Jacob finally said.

Ezra studied him for a moment, then gave a small nod, his expression softening. "I'll be in touch," he said before turning and leaving.

Once the Seeker departed, a wave of exhaustion swept over Jacob. He turned toward the windows, watching raindrops streak across the glass. Beyond the dark clouds, a sliver of light pierced through, faint yet persistent. Clenching his fists, he fought against the anger boiling inside him. Her killer was still out there. But like the light breaking through the gloom, he held onto a fragile hope that somehow the Cullers would find him.

CHAPTER THIRTEEN

DAY THREE OF EXILE

JACOB'S EYES FLICKERED open, a heavy fog clinging to his mind as the world gradually bled into focus. He winced, the sharp scent of iron cutting through his haze. Lifting his head, he tried inspecting his surroundings, only to be abruptly halted by a searing pain in his ribs.

Then it all came rushing back—each memory slicing its way into his muddled mind: a blow to his face, the thud of boots, and the chorus of sadistic laughter. The Maws had attacked him.

The Talon! he internally screamed, his eyes snapping open. Darkness greeted him, broken only by a dim, flickering light that barely illuminated his surroundings. He tried stepping toward the glow, but his efforts were immediately thwarted. That's when he felt them; the chains, rusted and heavy. He looked down, his heart racing, nearly exploding in his chest at the sight of him. He was naked, his arms and legs bound, spread-eagled, and fastened to a cold stone wall. It was as though he'd been prepared for slaughter.

Entering a state of panic, Jacob threw himself forward as far as his restraints allowed, wrestling against the chains. Dirt and pebbles tumbled onto his back and shoulders as he pulled and twisted, doing his best to ignore the sharp sting of metal biting into his flesh. But he was weak, and the pain became unbearable. Chest heaving, bones aching, he forced himself to stop, to breathe, to assess. There had to be something within reach he could use to help him escape.

Then his eyes adjusted to the dim light, and his stomach dropped. He was in a cave.

Deep gouges scarred the stone walls, as though something—or *someone*—had clawed at them. Cracks like veins snaked across the oppressive ceiling in every direction. Littering the floor were small pebbles, rocks, and what looked like bones, feeding the dread-filled thought that the mountain above was pressing down on him.

No, no, no, Jacob gasped, panic rising within him again. He felt as though he were in the mouth of a beast, waiting to be devoured. His body quivered at the thought. Was Daemion going to cut him up and serve him to the Maws? He squeezed his eyes shut, forcing the terrifying image from his mind. He needed to remain focused and alert. This was just a setback in his plan. Though weak and in pain, there was still a sliver of hope it could work, however improbable.

"You're awake," a low, menacing voice commanded.

The hair on Jacob's arms prickled as his gaze snapped forward. Slowly a figure emerged from the darkness, stepping into the flickering light—Daemion. Jacob's eyes widened as the cannibal sauntered closer, arms clasped behind his back.

"I must say, you're tougher than I thought," Daemion said, grinning. "But I wouldn't be too proud of that."

"What are you … going to do to me?" Jacob asked, each word a struggle.

"Allow me to show you."

Daemion stopped just inches from Jacob's face. Jacob recoiled, trying to pull back, but the stone wall kept him in place. Daemion smirked, his foul breath misting in Jacob's face, causing his nose to scrunch. Then Daemion started to sniff him.

Jacob froze, a shudder creeping through his bones as the cannibal's nose trailed down his neck and across his chest. The shock hit him to his core, the chains anchoring him in place—unable to move, unable to fight, forcing him to endure the violation. There was nothing he could do. Daemion had stripped him of his humanity, reducing him to nothing more than a slab of meat.

"Everyone has their own unique smell," Daemion said, savoring a deep breath as he finally stepped back. "And yours, my dear … is unlike anything I've ever encountered. Reminiscent of pine. Like *Christmas*. Oh, I can't wait to see what else is unique about you."

Anger bubbled within Jacob, prompting him to slam his head forward, aiming for Daemion's face, but the cannibal jerked his head back, as if he'd anticipated the attack.

"No sirree, I don't think so," Daemion said, wagging his finger. "You're in my world now. You volunteered, remember?"

Jacob snarled, the anger simmering now boiling over, causing him to let out a primal scream that tore from his throat as he yanked on the chains. Dirt and debris spiraled into chaotic clouds around him. Daemion stood back, amazed and amused, relishing the struggle of his prey. Spent and gasping for air, Jacob's scream finally faded, and he collapsed forward, nearly hanging from the chains, his head dropping into his heaving chest.

"That was only the preview, dearie. Now for the show."

Daemion lunged forward, seizing Jacob's neck with a brutal grip, and then sank his teeth deep into his shoulder. Pain burst through Jacob like fire, and he screamed in raw agony, thrashing violently against the unyielding chains. Daemion finally pulled back, releasing his bite. Blood dripped from his lips as his eyes fluttered shut, savoring the taste.

"Delicious," he hissed, wiping his mouth with the back of his hand. The motion revealed an X-shaped scar on his wrist. It was jagged, as though someone had carved it into his flesh.

Jacob let his broken, frail body go limp, his chest rising and falling in sharp, ragged breaths. His gaze, however, remained fixed on the brute before him. Warm blood trailed down his chest, each pulse of the bite sending fresh waves of hurt. It was insufferable, and far worse than he could have imagined when he offered himself up.

"Well, well, well, what do we have here?" Daemion said, his fingernail tracing a fresh scar just below Jacob's collarbone. "Looks like someone's been playing with guns. How'd you get it?"

Jacob trembled under the touch. "A friend," he whimpered, struggling to speak the words amid the pain. But if he kept talking, then maybe, just maybe, he could catch his breath. "A friend … who saved my life."

"Saved your life, you say? You must've been in quite the pinch. Tell me, is your friend here on Eremos? Because from the looks of it … you need saving again, dearie."

Jacob frowned. He knew his plan would have taken a miracle. After all, he was no hero. But now it felt less like a plan and more like a sacrifice. One that would offer him up as a feast for the Maws. It was only a matter of time. Part of him almost welcomed it, the relentless torture gnawing at his mind.

"You know, I almost respect your feeble attempt to save the boy," Daemion said, stepping back as he ran his hand through his greasy, frazzled hair. "But if you hadn't been so convincing, I wouldn't have gotten my hands on *this*."

Jacob braced himself for what he already knew was coming. He waited as Daemion reached behind his back and slowly withdrew the Talon. Flames flickered, casting shadows that danced across its chrome finish. The death it promised … and yet, he felt a spark of hope.

This is it …

"Just how in the world did you get your hands on this? It's been *nagging* at me. Eremos doesn't have guns. Derro's council would never allow that. So, tell me, how did it get here?"

Jacob scoffed softly, smiling afterward. "Like I'd ever … tell you."

Daemion growled as he lunged forward, leveling the Talon at Jacob. Slamming his eyes shut, Jacob tensed, bracing for the gunshot, but instead felt the barrel press against his forehead. He opened his eyes to find Daemion inches from his face.

"You know what I think? I think you're a Culler. You and that other guy, the one who killed my Maws. You two are working together, aren't you?"

Even in the face of death, Jacob couldn't help but laugh, though it was short-lived, his ribs stabbing with pain, making him grimace. "You think … that gun makes you … stronger?"

"Ironic words coming from the man I just took it from," Daemion said, pressing the barrel harder into Jacob's forehead. "So why is a Culler on Eremos?"

"I'm definitely not … a Culler."

Daemion paused, weighing Jacob's words, then growled as he pulled the Talon away. "That would make sense," he muttered, scratching his head with the barrel of the Talon. "You did fall for our campfire bait. Not something I'd expect from a Culler. But if you're not a Culler, then how did you get this gun?"

"Does it matter? You … have it now. It's all yours. Who cares … how it got here? Just …" Jacob faltered, his strength waning. "Just pull the trigger. Get this over with."

"You'd like that, wouldn't you? I bet you're just *dying* to meet your demise. Well, don't worry, dearie. It's coming. But … it doesn't have to. I could let you live. Just tell me how you got the gun and if there's more to be found."

Jacob spat on the ground. "Go to hell," he said, scoffing. "I'm not telling you shit."

Daemion frowned. "Odd … I offer you a chance to live, but—"

"You'll just kill me the second I tell you," Jacob cut in. "This is how I survive."

Daemion leaned in close, pressing his forehead against Jacob's. The pressure caused Jacob's head to rise slowly, his nose and lips brushing against Daemion's own, an unsettling, almost intimate contact.

"You're a survivor, huh? Willing to do whatever it takes to stay alive? Then you'd better take my offer. Survival isn't a game, dearie. It's about making tough *choices*."

"Like choosing to eat people?" Jacob shot back.

Daemion bared his teeth. "You just don't get it, do you? Sometimes, the only way to survive is to take drastic measures. And that's what I've been forced to do here. Eating people isn't about choice. It's about *necessity*."

He stepped back, spinning in a circle, the Talon swinging in his hand. "I mean, look around, dearie. We've been dumped on Eremos, an island with scarce resources, but *oddly*, a plentiful supply of people. And when you're faced with starvation … well, you do what you have to do in order to survive."

Jacob's lip curled. "I would never."

"Then you're not much of a survivor," Daemon said, scoffing as he sat on a rock. "You must think you're so superior because you've never eaten human flesh. Cannibalism isn't always what you think it is, ya know? For some, it's a ritual. Not just about satisfying hunger, but about honoring the deceased. It's why we ate the heart, brain, and liver of the Maws your friend killed. To preserve their souls."

Jacob winced, trying to swallow the vomit rising in his throat, the haunting image of Maws feasting on organs flooding his mind. "Then … why take us?"

"Ah, you want to know where *you* come into all of this. Well, other than the *obvious*, I have other motives. You see, when a tribe defeats their enemy, they take them and eat them as a form of domination. It's a way of saying we're *stronger* than you, and we can *consume* you."

"But … we're not your enemy."

"Well, you most certainly aren't my ally, either. Yet that could change. You've got some fight in you. The makings of a survivor. I like that. And clearly you know something I don't." He waved the Talon casually in the air. "Let me share something with you. Maybe then we'll see if you're not my enemy. You see, years ago, during the early days of Eremos, a settlement was born. People realized very quickly they were in a realm of survival, where only savagery prevailed."

His eyes drifted shut, savoring the thought. "Ah, how it must've been like the Anarchy Era all over again," he said, releasing a deep, longing sigh. "So, a select few forged a fragile alliance and birthed Ostria. It began small, like any idea, but eventually evolved into a large settlement. One built around Eremos's most abundant water supply …"

A fleeting realization flashed through Jacob's mind. The memory of his leap from the Screech. The sight of a tall tower and a large pool of water surrounded by towering cliffs. *Was that Ostria?*

"Ostria possesses just about everything one could need to survive," Daemion continued. "While we, on the barren outskirts, are forced to struggle. To *survive*."

"What's this got to do with me?"

"*Because I want it destroyed!* And I'm raising an army to make it happen. There's a plan already in motion to breach their walls. I will bring Ostria to its knees. And you, my dear, could play a part in it. You could survive. Just tell me what I need to know."

"I refuse to be part of your madness," Jacob said, shaking his head as his breath steadied, strength returning. "You're a psychopath, and I won't help you attack innocent people who've escaped the likes of *you.*"

"Innocent? None of us are *innocent.* Not *me.* Not *you.* Not *them.* We were *exiled,* remember? Criminals condemned to Eremos. And they have no right to act as if they're a better class of criminal."

"I'd rather die than join your twisted cult. So, you might as well kill me now, because I'm taking the location of those guns to my grave."

Daemion leaped to his feet, teeth bared. Jacob's outburst had stirred something in him—anger, raw, and immediate. Good. That's exactly what Jacob wanted.

"Well, I guess that answers that," Daemion gritted, fingers tightening around the Talon's grip. "You're choosing to be my enemy then. You realize what that means, don't you?"

Jacob forced a smile, a wide, false grin, one he hoped would stir the anger simmering in Daemion. "You made me your enemy the moment you took me," he said, scoffing. "You can go to hell. I'll meet you there."

Daemion pointed the Talon directly at Jacob.

Jacob's grin grew. *This is it*, he told himself, staring death square in the face. *I'm a dead man. Unless …*

"And as my enemy, dearie. You're on the menu."

An explosion tore through the air.

Jacob's eyes bulged just in time to see the Talon's barrel rupture, tearing Daemon's hand from his wrist and throwing him off his feet. He recoiled from the blast, debris slamming into him. Daemion screamed, a raw, guttural cry ripping from his throat as he fought his way to his feet, disoriented and shocked by the sudden turn of events. Jacob shared that shock, watching Daemion stagger out of the cave, adrenaline fueling his movements, his mangled arm spurting blood.

Then the cave began to shake.

Jacob stumbled, struggling to keep his footing as rocks dislodged from the ceiling.

The cave was collapsing.

Though his plan had worked, he now prayed for the miracle. Planting his feet, he pulled with all his strength against the chains, desperately hoping they'd let loose amid the rattling and shaking of the cave walls. Sweat flew from his face, his bones shaking with the effort, but he didn't relent. He kept pulling, yanking, fighting against the pain, the edges of his vision darkening.

Then suddenly, the stone wall gave way, and the chains ripped free, sending him crashing to the ground. He was free.

And he didn't hesitate. Blocking out all the pain, he seized his clothes and boots and scrambled to his feet. His legs carried him in a desperate sprint toward the cave's exit. Behind him, rock crumbled and fell, nearly grazing his back and heels, pushing him beyond his limits. Just as the ceiling gave way, he leaped, narrowly avoiding the falling stone.

His feet hit the ground hard, the momentum sending him into a roll against the dirt, his knees, shoulders, and head colliding with the ground until he tumbled to a stop. He groaned as he struggled to his knees, his gaze lifting, catching sight of the mouth of the cave caving in, as though the mountain itself had choked on rock, sealing the Maws' lair.

Gut-wrenching screams pierced the air.

Jacob shot to his feet, whipping his head around, his eyes wide at the scene before him. It was as if he'd stepped into the depths of hell. Flames engulfed the Maws' camp, casting a hellish orange glow against the darkness. The inferno devoured everything in its path; shelters, trees, and anything else in reach as a frantic stampede of Maws fled in panic, desperate to escape the destruction.

The mighty man's flame shall kindle, an unquenchable inferno. Michael's eerie words seared into Jacob's mind. *I, the instrument bear witness. The scorched path is not chaos, but divine intent. A flame that devours, yet purifies.*

"What the—"

"*Help!*" a voice screamed, snapping Jacob's attention toward the direction of the pit.

The others! He fumbled with his clothes and boots, yanking them on despite the ache in his strained muscles, and then bolted toward the pit. Sparks of fire rained around him like the dying tears of the trees while flames roared upward, licking hungrily like a beast unleashed, swallowing the forest in its fury. He grimaced, his body growing weak, the all-consuming ache threatening to send him tumbling to the ground. But he persevered, focused on reaching the pit. To save them. *Please don't be late.*

He finally reached the pit, boots skidding to a halt. He peered down, bracing for the worst, but to his immense relief, he saw his fellow exiles huddled together, safe and unharmed. They looked up at him, mouths agape.

"We thought you were dead," Alex said.

"What's going on up there?" Morgan asked.

Jacob ignored them and stepped back, his eyes scanning for the rope. He spotted it tangled at the base of a tree and ran toward it. He urgently grabbed the end and rushed back to the pit, dropping the rope down.

"Hurry!" he urged.

Jacob saw Ammon grab the rope just before a massive weight slammed into him, throwing him off his feet. The impact hit him like a freight train, sending him crashing onto his back with a painful thud. Legs tightened around his waist as someone collapsed on top of him, hands shooting to his neck, squeezing tightly. His eyes flew open to find Twig's crazed face glaring down at him.

"What the hell did you do?" Twig grunted.

Screams rang in Jacob's ears as he fought for air, his fingers clawing at Twig's hands, desperate to break free. His vision blurred, the edges of his thoughts fraying as he struggled to stay conscious. But he was too weak. Twig's grip tightened, his fingers digging deeper into Jacob's flesh, choking the life out of him.

He felt rooted to the ground, as if he were sinking into its soil, death pulling him downward. He closed his eyes, resigned to his fate, and waited for the inevitable darkness to swallow him whole. The distant echoes of screams faded as he slipped further away.

And then he saw her—Charlotte.

She was sitting on a peaceful beach. *Their* beach. She fixed her gaze on the endless expanse of the ocean, the soft breeze gently dancing in her hair. Turning, she glanced over her shoulder and smiled. His heart fluttered. Her face … so beautiful.

"Come on, *you*," she called, waving him toward her.

Drawn by the pull of her presence, he started toward her. He could feel the warmth of the sun on his skin and the soft sand between his toes. It felt … almost … real.

And then it was all gone.

His eyes snapped open, catching a blur of motion, followed by a dull thud as his lungs struggled to draw air. Twig's grip on his neck loosened, and Jacob watched as the Maws's blurred form crumpled beside him. He coughed and sputtered, fighting for breath as his vision slowly cleared, revealing a hazy figure standing over him, clutching a rock.

It was Ammon.

"Come on, let's get out of here," he said, pulling Jacob to his feet.

Jacob's limbs shook, his muscles threatening to give way as he struggled to stand. He lifted his gaze and quickly spotted Alex and Morgan behind Ammon. They stared back at him, worry in their eyes, then darted their gazes toward the whimpering trees and frantic cries piercing the air. A fresh surge of determination flooded through Jacob as oxygen filled his lungs. They had to keep moving, pressing forward until they'd escaped the Maws and whatever nightmare Michael had cast.

"How?" Alex asked.

"No time … to explain," Jacob wheezed. "We have to go. Come on."

Jacob started toward the edge of the camp, the others close behind. Ammon passed him, leading the way, while Alex and Morgan stayed close, ensuring he didn't get left behind. Jacob struggled to keep pace, his battered body protesting every step—shortness of breath, stabbing ribs, pulsing shoulder. But he didn't stop. He kept moving amid the pain, determined to escape.

"Move faster," Ammon said, casting quick glances over his shoulder.

Jacob gritted his teeth, picking up speed, his focus on the makeshift fence ahead, and the darkness beyond. Flames curled around him like fiery claws, searing heat prickling his skin as he wove between burning trees and crumbling shelters.

Then Morgan tripped, his body collapsing on the dirt. Jacob skidded to a stop, nearly tripping over the kid. He reached down, grabbed Morgan by his shirt and pulled him up.

"I've got you," he said, glancing back to make sure no one was in pursuit. "You're okay, kid. Come on, we have to keep—"

Jacob slowly stood, his eyes catching something in the distance. Amid the flames and smoke, a figure paced through the camp, its cloudless form moving with ease, making its way toward them.

"Run," Jacob said, pushing Morgan forward.

The kid burst into a sprint, Jacob right behind him. He didn't look back, yet his mind raced. Ammon and Alex had stopped at the edge of the fence, waiting for them to catch up. Once Jacob finally reached them, his eyes caught their gazes, widening in shock at the scene behind him.

He yanked his head around, his eyes locking on the inferno consuming the Maws' camp. Then he saw it. The figure from before, emerging from the gaps in the flames. He tensed as recognition hit him like a blow, his fears coming to reality.

Michael loomed ahead, his burned face twisting into a vile grin—the Talon gripped tightly in his hand. The madman's words forced themselves to the forefront of Jacob's mind. *What you're staring at is a reminder of where they once were.*

"Is that—"

"Michael," Jacob said, stealing the name from Morgan's tongue as he stepped backward, nearly stumbling into Alex and Ammon. *"Run!"*

With a surge of desperation, Jacob sprinted into the darkness—deeper into Eremos, and deeper into this nightmare that refused to end.

CHAPTER FOURTEEN

TEN MONTHS BEFORE EXILE

JACOB TRIED TO disappear into the sea of faces, but his stood out like a lighthouse, impossible to miss.

The courtyard buzzed with muted chatter, the soft clinking of glasses, and the scent of pine. Lanterns strung between the trees, casting a warm glow over the gathering, but Jacob felt cold. Despite the carefully crafted facade of composure, a part of him felt irreparably fractured, like a cracked mirror held together by will alone. He moved among the guests, his movements stiff, his mind a thousand miles away.

Every step he took, every conversation he engaged in, carried memories of Charlotte, their bittersweet tendrils weaving through his thoughts. Each person present held a fragment of her life, a piece of her essence that he both longed for and feared to confront. They were the keepers of her stories, the witnesses to her journey, and now, they had gathered to celebrate her life.

A life that was tragically cut short.

A pang tugged at his heart as he caught sight of Steve and Nancy. Their slack facial expressions revealed their own battle with grief, but despite their overwhelming pain, they moved among the attendees, offering solace and support to those seeking comfort.

He frowned, raising his tumbler of whiskey to his lips, and sipped. Watching the strength of Charlotte's parents filled him with admiration, but more strongly, with guilt. Amid their own grief, unlike him, they embraced the other mourners, their touch conveying empathy, even as tears welled in their eyes.

Why can't I be as strong as them? he thought. *Look at them, carrying their grief with such grace while I hide and wallow in my own guilt. How did I become so weak? Or had I always been this weak?*

You're stronger than you think. Charlotte's words this time entered his mind, offering comfort. Jacob's lips trembled, the thought of her bringing tears to his eyes. Even though she was gone, her words lived on.

A gentle touch on his arm jolted him out of his turmoil. He sniffled, wiping his eyes as he quickly turned to find two unfamiliar faces, their puffy red eyes mirroring his own ache.

"Hey, Jacob," one of them said. "I'm Roger, and this is my husband, Lyle. We used to own Storks. It's just further down Nox Street from Hoos."

Storks? Jacob recalled the name of the store. Ezra, the Seeker assigned to his case, had mentioned that Charlotte had visited Storks earlier that fateful day. Now the forsaken, green-wrapped box loomed above them on the deck, untouched. Even from where he stood, he could feel its pull—a magnetic curiosity drawing him to uncover its contents. He had little doubt that whatever lay inside had come from Storks.

If only he had the courage to open it.

"*Used* to own?" Jacob asked.

"We unfortunately had to sell it," Lyle said, frowning. "We just weren't getting the same traffic since the no-go zone went up. Plus, Woodwin Realty made us an offer we couldn't refuse."

Jacob took another sip of whiskey at the mention of Woodwin Realty—Richard's real estate company. *You'll only be adding fuel to the fire.* His words continued to haunt Jacob's mind.

And unfortunately, he'd been right.

The guns in Hoos were the reason Charlotte died, and he couldn't shake the thought that the gun responsible for her death was one he had put into Derro. He'd struggled to set foot in Hoos since.

"You might not be familiar with us, but we knew Charlotte," Roger said. "We wanted to offer our deepest sympathies for your loss."

"Thank you."

"We can only imagine what you must be going through," Lyle added.

Roger frowned. "In the short, cherished moments I had the privilege of spending with her, she'd left a memorable mark. I will always treasure the warm affection she brought every time she came into Storks."

The weight of their words settled on Jacob's shoulders like a comforting blanket. He had always known the impact Charlotte had on his life, but now he realized just how profound that impact was on everyone around her.

"She loved your store," he said. "And thank you for your kind words. They mean a lot. I'm honored to meet you both. Thank you for coming."

With a gentle nod, he stepped away, emptying his tumbler of whiskey down his throat as he started toward the doors of his home. He'd grown weary of maintaining his composure, trying to be strong for those around him, and now yearned for respite, where he could allow his emotions to surface without restraint. Entering his home, he made his way to the bar where he refilled his glass. After taking a drink, his eyes locked onto the door of Charlotte's photo room, left slightly ajar.

Wondering who had trespassed into her room, he hurried over and entered but found nobody inside. Rows of framed photographs adorning the walls pulled him further in, each one capturing a *moment frozen in time*, as Charlotte would say. Some depicted the beauty left in Derro—pictures of oceans, nature, and wildlife—while others showed a time before the council's dominance; billboards covered in graffiti, statues and landmarks destroyed.

Venturing further in, Jacob's eyes landed on a small, solitary photo pinned to the wall above her desk. He walked over and, after placing his glass down, carefully unpinned it, a soft smile forming on his lips. The photo captured the back of Charlotte's form, a silhouette framed against the endless expanse of the ocean at their cherished beach. A picture he had taken.

Come on, you, she had said that day after he took the photo.

"She had quite the eye, didn't she?"

Jacob jolted out of his reverie, swiftly folding the small photo and tucking it into the fold of his suit jacket. He sniffled, wiped his eyes, then turned toward the familiar voice, finding comfort in the sight of Steve standing at the threshold.

"Yes, she did," he replied.

"She caught sight of you," Steve added, stepping deeper into her room.

Jacob smiled, his heart briefly filling with joy, an emotion he'd forgotten he could feel. "She did, didn't she?"

Steve nodded as he approached. "How are you holding up?"

"I'm trying."

"Me too, Jake," Steve said, placing a weathered hand on Jacob's shoulder. "Grief is tough. It has its own course, its own ebb and flow. There's going to be moments when the pain feels unbearable. And it can change who you are."

Jacob bowed his head, Steve's words absorbing into him like a salve to his wounded soul.

"But there will also be moments of relief," Steve continued. "Tiny flickers of light that'll remind you of all the love you two shared. And she *really* loved you. Search for the tiny flickers, Jake."

Jacob frowned, feeling tears welling in his eyes. In the depths of his grief, he'd lost sight of the intricacies of healing. And as much as he wanted to heal, his path felt obscured by his guilt. He couldn't escape it. Searching for those tiny flickers of light felt impossible when the world around him was complete darkness, where her killer remained hidden. Jacob bit the insides of his cheeks, his heart burning for justice, burying his path of healing in ash.

"I can imagine how lonely you must feel," Steve said. "Especially with the loss of your father and the absence of your mother. But I want you to know that you're not alone. You will always have Nancy and me."

Steve pulled Jacob into his arms. Jacob folded into the hug, embracing a comfort he hadn't experienced in a long time. A longing fulfilled after being absent from his life for far too long. A comfort and strength only a father could offer, and Steve stepped into the role with open arms. Charlotte had spoken of Steve's fortitude, and now, amid their shared grief, Jacob could finally comprehend the truth in her words.

"She's gone," Jacob cried. "And it's all my fault."

"Son …" Steve's voice cracked.

"I should've shot them. I should've given them the gun. I should've stepped more in front of her."

"It's not your fault."

"But it *is.*"

"You can't blame yourself."

"Steve, are you in here?"

Jacob gently pulled away, hastily swiping the tears from his face. Sniffling, he turned toward the door as a slender figure entered. It was Nancy, her red, swollen eyes squinting as she cautiously stepped inside. Her gaze settled on Charlotte's pictures, her fingers tracing each one as she passed. His heart sank, the memory of her cries that morning still echoing in his head.

"Oh, Jake," Nancy said, her weathered eyes noticing him.

Jacob started toward her and hugged her gentle form. "Hey, Nancy."

"Have there been any updates from the Seeker?"

Jacob frowned, shaking his head. "I spoke with Ezra just before the funeral, and they still haven't found him. I'm sorry."

"They will," Nancy said, patting Jacob on the chest.

How? Jacob thought, marveling at Nancy's inner strength. He wished he could be as strong as her. *But I'm weak.*

"Jake … there's something I must tell you," Nancy said, her hand shaking as she lowered it from his chest. "And it won't be easy to hear."

"Dear, I'm not so sure now is the best time—"

"We've waited long enough, Steve. He deserves to know."

Jacob's heart raced. "Deserve to know what?"

"It's about Charlotte," Nancy said, frowning as a tear fell down her cheek. "Jake, dear … she was pregnant."

Breath escaped from Jacob's lungs, a crushing blow as if a heavy force had slammed into his stomach. He staggered, the walls of the room seeming to close in as his vision blurred. *She was …* Flashes of that night tore through his mind—her lifeless body, blood pooling from her stomach. He squeezed his eyes shut, tears spilling as he tried in vain to banish the images.

"Son, are you all right?" Steve asked.

"Pregnant?"

"She called us earlier that day and shared the news," Nancy said, gripping Jacob's arms tightly as she wept. "I'm so sorry, Jake."

I've planned the rest of our evening and wanted to ride home with you. Charlotte's words from that night. Jacob's heart ached as he imagined the evening she had planned for them—shared dreams of parenthood that had finally seemed within reach, now obliterated. *I was finally going to be a father.*

His hands tightened into fists, a fire of anger igniting within him. Her killer was still out there, unpunished for the lives he had destroyed. Healing seemed inconceivable until they found him. Jacob's jaw clenched, his fists shaking as Steve and Nancy clung to him, their cries cutting through him, fueling an ember of justice into a relentless thirst for revenge.

I won't let him get away with this, Jacob vowed to himself. *He'll pay for what he did to you and our unborn child.*

CHAPTER FIFTEEN

DAY THREE OF EXILE

EVEN AS THE SUN rose, Jacob couldn't shake the feeling that he was still trapped in a nightmare.

His aching, bruised muscles remained locked in tension, ready to propel him into a sprint at the slightest hint of danger, which, unfortunately, seemed to hide in every crevice on Eremos. Hours had slipped by since his daring escape from the Maws, but his mind still reeled from the chaos. A miracle had been his only hope of surviving, and strangely enough, one had come.

Michael had set the Maws' camp ablaze, offering them a chance to flee. Jacob and the others had run through the night, distancing themselves from the inferno as much as they could. But it wasn't just the flames they sought to escape. Danger seemed to loom everywhere.

Eremos, stripped of its feral inhabitants, might have been breathtaking. Its lush landscape sprawled before him, a visual feast of vibrant green. Tropical plants flourished, their leaves a riot of shapes and textures, while vines coiled and hung from colossal trees like nature's curtains. The thick foliage offered cover, a slight relief from the relentless sun that beat down on them, but it did little to ease Jacob's frayed nerves or the rapid, jerky rhythm of his gaze, ever vigilant for signs of pursuit.

Surprisingly, Jacob found himself not counting Michael among the threats pursuing them. Dangerous, yes—Michael had proven that—but the madman seemed driven by some inscrutable, divine purpose he couldn't begin to understand. After all, Michael hadn't fired at him or the others when he'd had the chance last night, unlike his actions toward the Culler on the Screech or the Maws the night before. Jacob couldn't fathom why. He'd mulled over Michael's words throughout the night, replaying their encounter aboard the Screech. They felt foreign to him. Cryptic.

What you're staring at is a reminder of where they once were. Michael had declared about his burned face.

Who's they? Jacob pondered.

Almost instantly, Michael's response came to him. *They are the evildoers. The wicked ones.*

Jacob wrestled with the implications. If Michael's burned face served as a reminder of where "they once were," did he consider the Maws as evildoers? Wicked ones? And if so, what did that imply for Eremos, an island inhabited by those exiled for their crimes?

The mighty man's flame shall kindle, an unquenchable inferno. I, the instrument, bear witness.

Words that hinted at an impending conflagration. Michael, it seemed, saw himself as the executioner of this inferno. His actions last night had confirmed that. The image of the madman's burned visage, framed against the Maws' blazing settlement, still flickered in Jacob's mind.

The scorched path is not chaos, but divine intent. A flame that devours, yet purifies.

Jacob furrowed his brow, sweat trickling down the bridge of his nose as he mulled over the enigmatic words, aligning them in his mind like pieces of a puzzle. *Divine intent? Devours, yet purifies?* Was the divine purpose meant to cleanse Eremos of its wickedness?

"You guys hear that?" Ammon called from up ahead.

Jacob's legs came to a stop, his focus ripping away from his thoughts as he focused on his surroundings, his ears growing alert.

"It sounds like water," Ammon said as he sprinted ahead.

Alex and Morgan pursued.

"Come on," the kid said, glancing over his shoulder, urging Jacob.

He picked up his pace, gaining speed, his heart racing as he trailed a path that twisted and turned beneath his feet. Jagged branches clawed at his exposed skin, leaving thin red lines in their wakes. His tongue, dry and swollen, begged for the cool touch of water, his hope heightening as he dodged foliage that slapped at him from the others ahead.

Eventually the foliage gradually yielded, and his feet skidded to a halt at the sight of a small stream. Its undulations glimmered in the sunlight, a shimmering oasis promising relief. He rushed to the stream's edge and fell to his knees. As he cupped his hands in the cool water, its touch instantly soothed his dirty hands; then he scooped water toward his mouth and drank. The cool liquid rushed down his throat, a refreshing cascade that cooled his parched insides. Closing his eyes, he gave a shaky laugh as he embraced the sweet relief of finally quenching his thirst.

"Thank God," Alex said, pressing her wet palms into her eyes. "I don't know how much longer I could've gone."

"Let's stay here forever," Morgan said, sighing, a slow smile widening.

"We should rest here for a bit," Ammon said, his hands reaching back into the stream for a refill. "We can regain our strength and plan our next move."

Jacob's eyebrows pinched as he ran his wet hands through his hair. *We? Our move?* It was surprising to hear Ammon speak as if they were allies. Despite their successful escape, he'd assumed their paths would eventually diverge.

Especially after what he had done to Ammon.

Yet, Ammon's demeanor and words hinted at a different inclination, suggesting more than a transient partnership. The weight of recent events pressed on Jacob's shoulders, and he bit down on the insides of his cheeks, grappling with a dilemma. Could he trust the Last Patriot, who, in a crucial moment, saved his life from the menace of Twig? Trust, after all, was fragile here on Eremos. The notion lingered like a shadow at the edges of his mind.

"We should stay alert, though," Ammon said, taking off his shirt and tossing it into the water. After soaking it, he rolled it up and wrung it out, then focused his gaze on Jacob. "You still got the gun, right?"

Jacob absentmindedly shook his head, still in contemplation. "No."

"No?" Ammon repeated, his eyes narrowing. "What happened to it?"

"How'd you escape then?" Morgan asked.

"What the hell?" Alex snapped, her glare cutting into Jacob. The frustration in her voice made it clear—losing their best weapon for survival was a blow she wasn't ready to accept.

Jacob, however, didn't see it that way. Not anymore.

"Daemion was unpredictable," he said. "You guys saw how crazy he was. And based on what you told us, Ammon, he didn't follow through with anything he said. That pit was a game for him. So, I crafted a plan."

Alex clenched her jaw. "What kind of plan involves giving up our most important tool for survival?"

"One that allowed us to escape," Jacob said.

A heavy silence settled over them, broken only by the gentle murmur of the stream. Alex frowned. It was clear she regretted complaining about the loss of the Talon, especially after Jacob had led them to safety. He didn't take it personally. He understood how much comfort weapons brought people—how here, on Eremos, that sense of security was magnified. But for him, the Talon hadn't been a source of safety. If anything, it had made him a target, a weight that only fed his anxiety.

"I didn't know what I was offering myself up to," he said, breaking the silence. "All I knew was that I had to catch Daemion and the Maws off guard. So, while we were in the pit, I disassembled as much of the gun as I could and lodged a tiny rock into the barrel. Then I used the gunpowder from a couple of bullets and mixed it with clay from the pit to create a blockage for the bullet to hit."

Ammon's head flinched back. "You did *what?*"

"I rigged it to explode. I figured Daemion would feel powerful with the gun in his hands, so I baited him into pulling the trigger. The moment he did, the gun blew up."

"So, *that's* what we heard," Alex said. "Dude, that's insanity."

"It's badass!" Morgan said, smiling.

Jacob rubbed the back of his head, a faint smile tugging at his lips. "Honestly, it's sheer luck I made it out of there alive. Daemion had me chained up in their cave. When the explosion went off, it caused the whole thing to collapse. I just kept tugging at the chains until, miraculously, they broke loose. I barely got out before the whole place came down."

"How did you even come up with something like that?" Ammon asked, his eyebrows practically touching his hairline.

"Read it in a book once."

"A *book?*" Alex spat.

"Well, the idea came from the book. But the execution? That was all me. The gun used hollow-point rounds. They expand on impact. I figured that by lodging a rock into the barrel, the expanding round would trigger an eruption."

"Damn," Alex muttered. "You had a man killed by his own hand. You're some kind of crazy."

Jacob winced, a frown pulling at his brow. "Well, I'm not actually so sure Daemion's dead. The explosion blew his hand off, but when the cave collapsed, he'd recovered enough to flee. I didn't see him when I made it out. There's a chance he bled out, but we can't be certain."

"I damn well hope he bled out," Alex said. "Otherwise, we've got two madmen to worry about. And one of them has a gun."

"Yeah, about that," Ammon said. "Can someone catch me up to speed on what the hell happened last night? This Michael guy … did he burn down the Maws' camp?"

"Looks that way," Jacob said.

"How'd he have a gun?" Morgan asked.

"Yeah, kid has a point," Ammon said. "You had a gun, and now he has one. How?"

Jacob shared an understanding glance with Alex. Other than the *why* Michael had potentially burned down the Maws' camp, they both knew the answers to these questions. Of course, Jacob had his theories, but he wasn't ready to share that information yet. They sounded far-fetched in his mind, and he could only imagine how implausible they seemed spoken out loud.

"He got the gun because he attacked Wes on the Screech," Alex said.

"He attacked Wes?" Ammon asked.

Morgan stiffened, drawing Jacob's attention. The poor kid had been through hell, his eyes sharp and unblinking, drilling into anyone who spoke.

"Maybe not in front of the kid," Jacob muttered.

"Why the hell not?" Alex said. "After what he saw, he deserves to know."

"I want to know," Morgan said, nodding at Jacob.

Morgan's eagerness gave him pause, and after a brief silence, Jacob raised his hands in a conceding gesture. "All right, if you insist, kid."

"So, what happened after Michael attacked Wes?" Ammon asked.

"Easier if I just start from the beginning," Jacob said, taking a deep breath. "I was sitting next to Michael on the Screech. We had an unsettling exchange. He was rambling about his burnt face, saying he'd been *'spared'*. And the way he talked—it was like he believed he had some higher purpose. It was a lot to process, especially since I'd just come to. I was foggy, dizzy, and honestly trying to figure out what the hell was going on. But it was obvious he wasn't afraid of Eremos.

"Then everyone started to jump, and eventually it was just me and him left. He went first, and that's when he attacked Wes. Wes had his gun pointed at him to get him to run, but he just stood there, leaning his head into the barrel like he was daring Wes to shoot.

"And then Wes did. Just not at Michael. He fired outside the Screech, aiming past Michael, probably thinking he could scare him into running. But Michael saw it coming, and the second Wes pulled that trigger, Michael struck him in the neck.

"After that, it was chaos. Wes dropped his gun. The second Culler stepped in and tried to shoot Michael, but he was too slow. Michael had already grabbed

Wes's gun and shot him. Then he jumped out. I followed shortly after with the other Culler's gun."

"Whoa," Morgan said, exhaling a deep breath, as if he'd been holding it the entire time.

"That's wild," Ammon muttered, blinking as he tried to process what Jacob had just told them. "*Madman* is right. But torching the Maws' camp? What is he, some kind of pyromaniac?"

"Oh, no doubt," Alex said. "The dude's face says it all."

"He's definitely deranged," Jacob said. "And one thing I know for certain, thanks to you, Alex, is that the Maws tried snatching him, just like they did to us. And when they did, he fought back. Shot them. After that, well, it's just theories."

"That's not all we're certain of," Ammon said, stepping closer to Jacob. "We also know that *you* fought back. Without you, man, none of us would be standing here right now. So, let me be the first to say …" Ammon's voice trailed off as he smiled and placed a hand on Jacob's shoulder. "Thank—"

Jacob flinched, his breath hitching as pain shot through him. His shoulder dipped, the sharp sting of Daemion's bite from the night before flaring up.

"Sorry!" Ammon blurted, yanking his hand back. His expression shifted from gratitude to concern. "What happened?"

"It's … alright," Jacob said through clenched teeth, wincing. "You didn't know."

Slowly, he pulled his collar down past his shoulder and inspected the wound. His breath caught as his eyes widened. The bite mark was raw and jagged, an oval of torn flesh with half-moon punctures oozing blood. The inflamed skin throbbed in rhythm with his pulse, each beat radiating a sharp sting outward.

Alex gasped. "Oh my God, did he *fucking bite you?*"

"Yeah," Jacob muttered, groaning as he eased his collar back into place.

"Wicked," Morgan said.

Ammon frowned. "That doesn't look good, man."

Jacob straightened, rolling his shoulders despite the discomfort. He inhaled deeply, trying to swallow his worry. "Yeah, I know," he said, raising his brows. "I think I'll just head further downstream, take a dip, and see if I can clean it up."

"Can I come?" Morgan asked.

Jacob shook his head gently. "Probably best you stay here, kid. I won't be long. Just need a moment."

Morgan sighed. "Okay."

Jacob shifted his gaze to Ammon and Alex, giving each a quick nod. "I'll be back in a few."

They nodded in return, their understanding clear, but their concern more so. Both exchanged a glance with each other, their eyes heavy with unspoken worry, silently grappling with everything Jacob had endured.

He walked a short distance away, making sure to remain within earshot should anything happen. Had it not been for the inferno, he knew more than likely this stream served as another death trap for the Maws, or any other exile here. Still, best to be alert.

After finding a small pool where the current slowed, he shed his clothes, leaving only his boxers, then eased himself into the water. The cool embrace of the stream washed over him, each ripple feeling like a thousand tiny fingers kneading his aching muscles and searing skin. The bite on his shoulder pulsed harder, a painful throb that radiated through him, but he gritted his teeth and endured it, hoping the water would stave off any lurking infection.

He transitioned onto his back, letting the water cradle him as he floated, gazing up at the canopy above. Sunlight filtered through the dense leaves, painting a dappled pattern of light and shadow across his chest. He closed his eyes, surrendering to the pull of his thoughts.

The vision from last night flooded his mind, where, on the brink of death, he had somehow seen Charlotte. He didn't entirely know how, but he was sure it had happened. Then again, after everything he'd endured, maybe it was just his mind playing tricks on him.

Yet the moment had felt real, as if Charlotte had been there to comfort him as he faced death. She had always been his source of comfort.

You're stronger than you think, she'd say.

And last night, I had been. He clung to her words, knowing strength would be vital in navigating what lay ahead in his new life on Eremos—a life he wasn't sure held any promise.

Suddenly, his eyes flew open. He gradually sat up, memories from the cave flashing through his mind to something Daemion had said. The words came in fragments: *A select few forged a fragile alliance and birthed Ostria—a large settlement built around Eremos's most abundant water supply—possesses just about everything one could need to survive.*

Perhaps Ostria could be his promising future? A place where he could survive and start anew.

His thoughts shifted to his jump from the Screech as he recalled seeing a wide clearing atop a high mountain, encircled by towering cliffs with waterfalls plunging into a pool below. And there, standing tall, a tower.

If only he could find Ostria. It felt like a longshot, but it was all he had to lean on. And from what little he'd seen of Eremos, Ostria seemed to offer the best chance he had of survival.

I want it destroyed! Daemion's words continued. *And I'm raising an army to make it happen. There's already a plan in motion.*

If Daemion was still alive, he posed a serious threat to Ostria. They needed to be warned about his planned attack, an assault he insisted was already underway. Understanding Michael's divine mission was equally crucial. From what Jacob had gathered, the madman's intentions seemed clear: to engulf all of Eremos in flames. The inferno he'd ignited, combined with the heat of the land, would surely spread to Ostria. They'd need to prepare.

Informing the others was just as important, though Jacob wasn't sure how to begin without sounding like a lunatic himself. But given their recent conversation, perhaps they might as least entertain his theories. His gaze drifted toward them ahead. They looked weary and their eyes darted anxiously. He frowned, realizing that even after finding water, the stream couldn't wash away the fear still gripping them.

We? Our move? Ammon's words reentered his mind. Jacob knew he couldn't find Ostria on his own.

Perhaps Ostria could be our next move.

CHAPTER SIXTEEN

TEN MONTHS BEFORE EXILE

BEYOND THE GLASS French doors of Jacob's home, traversing the expansive courtyard and following a winding trail, nestled within a small clearing embraced by towering trees, rested the graves of Ava Hughes, Henry Hughes, and now, Charlotte Hughes.

The wind whispered through the leaves, a melancholy symphony that accompanied Jacob in his silent grief. It felt as though he was gazing into his past lives.

And a life that never was.

Jacob wept as he kneeled before her grave, head bowed. Staring at the stone too long hurt, as if a vise tightened around his heart with every passing moment.

"I can't believe we'd finally done it. We were going to be parents."

After a few years of marriage, the two of them had tirelessly tried for a child but unfortunately failed. There were, of course, advanced treatment options to boost their chances; however, they both concluded that those routes didn't align with their preferences for a natural conception. They had accepted that if unsuccessful, it simply wasn't meant to be. So, they had agreed to stop actively trying and instead embraced the uncertainty of waiting for the right moment to come. Even if that moment never arrived.

Sadly, for them, that moment had arrived. But it had been torn away faster than it took to happen.

"You would've made an incredible mother, Char."

A couple of months had passed since that tragic night, and the Cullers still hadn't found her killer. Ezra insisted he was investigating diligently, yet he had brought no new information. Jacob still didn't understand how the intruders had jammed the council's Aux systems, or whether Mason, the deceased intruder with alleged ties to the Last Patriots, had acted alone or on behalf of the rebellion.

We did the job, *man, and we got what you came for.* The killer's words still echoed in Jacob's mind, the *"and"* lingering like an unsolved riddle. Mason had made it very clear he wanted the guns. But then, what was the *"job"*?

He had considered whether low social scores prevented the intruders from obtaining guns legally. If they were tied to the Last Patriots, others in the group might face the same restrictions. But they did have two that night. Perhaps obtained through those smaller robberies Ezra had mentioned? Was their mission to arm the rebellion? If so, then what had Mason *"come"* for? He'd only demanded the guns.

Jacob bit the insides of his cheeks, frustration mounting. Something was missing, and each replay of that tragic night brought no answers. Only pain. The Cullers had proven no more helpful, their efforts falling short of their promises. *I always find my man,* Wes had assured him. But assurances felt hollow as the Cullers' efforts proved futile.

The thirst for justice and the weight of helplessness was overwhelming. Each night, as Jacob drowned himself in whiskey, the urge to take matters into his own hands grew stronger. Yet deep down, he knew such a pursuit would change him—turn him into someone, or something, he wasn't. Besides, even if he could summon the courage, he wouldn't know where to start.

Jacob, the Seeker from before is at your front door, Sid alerted.

Jacob stiffened, the unexpected announcement catching him off guard. *Why is Ezra here?* He hadn't been expecting him. Maybe he had an update? *Finally.*

He hoped that was the case, though the thought that Ezra might bring bad news made his palms sweat.

"Sid, request to connect to his Aux and lead him out here."

If Ezra came bearing bad news, having him come out here would serve as a reminder of what's at stake.

Very well, Jacob. I will do so now.

After a brief wait, Jacob's gaze caught Ezra making his way down the trail, his long trench coat swaying with every step. The moment Ezra's eyes fell on the tombstones his expression turned crestfallen.

"I'm still amazed by your home," Ezra said as he approached.

"Thanks. I wish I could feel the same, but with her gone, it just doesn't feel much like home anymore. My home is where she is."

Ezra frowned. "I understand."

"So, do you finally have an update?"

"Unfortunately, I don't. We've actually hit a hiccup in the case, I'm afraid. Wes, the commander of the Culler team assigned to your case, was removed from the investigation. I'm catching his replacement up—"

"*Removed?* I don't understand. Why? And what does this mean for my case?"

"Wes was demoted. But I assure you, finding her killer is still my top priority."

"Is this why you haven't found him? Because of your commander's lack of work ethic?"

"I know how frustrating this must be, but I assure you, as much as I don't care for the guy, he was good at what he did. He, like me, shared a common goal. To help restore law and order. However, he had trouble leaving justice up to the council. Often took matters into his own hands, and that's something the council won't stand for."

"So, what, he killed people?"

"He was determined to stop the Last Patriots, and it often led to drastic measures. The council had given him a second chance, but this last occurrence was the final one."

"This is completely uncalled for. You said you were going to do everything in your power to find him."

"And I assure you, I am. You're not the only one I've had to deliver bad news to. Crime is on the rise, and we're struggling to keep up. I just got a missing child case in Otus, and last week a man burned down his entire apartment building, killing almost everyone inside. He claimed it was his divine—"

"I don't care about anyone else. I only care about finding *him*."

"Like I said, we are doing everything—"

"Are you? Because it almost seems like having Mason dead at the scene is enough for you. Closed case." Jacob shook his head as he scoffed. "Are you just waiting for the other intruder to commit another crime? Can't find him, so you're just what, hoping he falls into your lap?"

Ezra bowed his head, taking the punches as they came. Jacob sighed as he rubbed the back of his neck, suddenly aware of the harshness in his words. He could only imagine the pressure Ezra faced as a Seeker, drowning in the chaos of Derro's rising crime, but truthfully, it was hard for Jacob to care. He deserved answers. Justice.

"I could have just called you, Mr. Hughes," Ezra said. "But I wanted to tell you in person. You deserved that."

"I appreciate that. And I'm sorry for my outburst. You didn't deserve that. It's just been so hard going on these past couple of months with no new information."

"I get it. It's not much, but I did learn that Mason frequented the bar Liberties. Like Hoos, it's also on Nox Street. Bank statements showed Mason had stopped in there many times before robbing Hoos. I went to see if I could review any security footage, but unfortunately, it was jammed each time he visited. The owner, a man named Bel, only found out once we reviewed the footage."

If that's the truth, no one's Aux would've worked, Jacob thought, remembering how Sid hadn't responded that night. "No customers complained about their Aux not working?"

"I had the same question. Asked Bel and his employees. All said they'd never experienced their Aux not working, nor had they received any complaints. Told me people came there to drink their problems away, one of those being their Aux."

That makes no sense. Not one *person complained.* "Maybe some of the employees are Last Patriots?" Jacob theorized.

"It's a possibility. I did a background check on each of them, and for the most part, they're clean. Social scores weren't the greatest and most hadn't had any trouble with the law."

"Of course," Jacob said, sighing as he closed his eyes. "At this rate, it feels like we'll never find him."

"Cases like this can take time."

"Yeah, except time moves slow when you don't have anyone to spend it with," Jacob said, turning his gaze toward Charlotte's headstone. Silence settled between them, broken only by the soft rustle of the wind.

"So, how long were you two married?" Ezra said, breaking the stillness.

"Little over ten years."

"Wow. You guys meet here in Tuto?"

"Yes. *Luckily.*"

"Luckily?"

"She'd been on a trip when we met. Was just passing through Tuto when I scrambled into her on Nox Street, right outside Hoos. She'd had her camera in her hand and was capturing some pictures. Said she'd been traveling all around Derro."

Ezra let out a soft scoff. "Luckily is right."

"She was on her way back home to Strix and was only staying for the night. I still don't know what came over me that day. She was just so beautiful. So, I asked if I could tag along. Show her around Tuto. I'd grown up here, so I knew some great spots for her. And surprisingly, she said yes. We spent the rest of the day just driving around. Wound up here to end the night. She fell in love with this house. Took more photos here, I felt, than she'd taken all that day."

"That's quite the meet-cute."

A slow, fond smile spread across Jacob's face. "The next morning, she had to leave," he continued. "I didn't want her to go. And apparently neither did she. So, she stayed another night. Then another. Wound up staying for a few weeks before she finally went home. But by then we were both madly in love. When the time finally came for her to go home, I asked if I could tag along again. I hadn't gotten out of Tuto in a long time, and it sounded fun, searching for some good out of all the bad in Derro."

"Photographs have a way of doing that, don't they? I personally have an appreciation for them, even though it's considered a dying art. They have a way of allowing you to live in a past moment, and I enjoy finding meaning or purpose in each one."

"Charlotte did always say she was freezing moments in time, often ones that could never be repeated."

"Exactly. I've actually got this one photograph in my home that I purchased years back. I look at it almost every day."

"What's it depict?"

"It's a picture of an old billboard here in Tuto from before the Collapse, covered in graffiti and just weathered by time. But it stood in the enormous shadow of a new Derro surveillance tower. Made me think about the clash between the past and present. And even with how dark Derro may seem, a darker time existed before it. The picture was called—"

"Echoes of Eras," Jacob softly interjected, his eyes closing as a tear slipped down his cheek.

"Well, yeah. But how'd you know that?"

"Because Charlotte took that photo. I was with her."

Ezra's head flinched back, his eyes rapidly blinking. "So, Charlotte is *Char*?"

"Char is a nickname I'd always called her. She wound up using it as her signature for all her photos."

"Oh my God!" Ezra said, still stunned. "That's …"

Jacob laughed softly, the weight of surprise cutting through his earlier frustration. He was just as stunned, and surprisingly, he had forgotten that as much as Charlotte's words still lived in him, so did her photography. There were of course many others, like Ezra, who had come across her work.

"I thought your name sounded familiar," Jacob said, connecting the dots. "That was one of the first photographs she'd sold after moving here with me. She must've told me your name when you bought it."

Ezra shook his head. "I don't even know what to say."

"Just use it as motivation. Find her killer."

"I will."

"I know you will."

Jacob had no doubts about Ezra's motivation to find Charlotte's killer. But he also knew he could no longer rely solely on him or the Cullers. They had their hands full with more cases than just his. It was time he stepped in and started a search of his own. And thanks to Ezra, he knew just where to start.

He needed to visit Liberties.

CHAPTER SEVENTEEN

DAY THREE OF EXILE

AFTER TREKKING DOWN the stream throughout the day, ensuring they distanced themselves further from the inferno, Jacob and the others set up camp for the evening. The sun embarked on its gradual descent, casting the stream in a warm glow as he and Morgan settled by its side, watching Ammon trying to kindle a fire. Insects buzzed and chirped, forming a relentless symphony as Ammon raced against the sun to ignite a flame before nightfall.

"Come on, spark, you little shit," Ammon grunted, his hands rapidly spinning a stick against a dry piece of bark. "Excuse the cursing, kid."

Morgan rolled his eyes. "Shit, I don't care."

The three of them chuckled, and Jacob couldn't help but smile. It felt nice to laugh and see Morgan come to life a little more. However, his smile quickly faltered. He, for the moment, felt safe, but here on Eremos, safety felt forever fleeting. If he were honest with himself, he dreaded the approaching night. He'd caught his left leg bouncing with nervous energy more times than he could count, his mind swarming with memories of the last time he'd sat around a fire. At least now, the fire would actually be made by one of them.

Ostria continued to linger in his thoughts. He had yet to disclose the settlement to the others, primarily because he wasn't certain of its location on

Eremos. It could take days to find, and even if they did, he feared the possibility of not being let in. Daemion's mention of a plan to invade Ostria's walls had revealed safeguards against exiles. The prospect was hopeful amid the constant fear gripping him, but the longer he pondered, the more Ostria felt out of reach; like chasing an elusive dream.

"You got it," Morgan said, drawing Jacob's attention back to Ammon. "That's it."

Ammon's hands moved with increasing speed as he spun the stick, his motions a blur of controlled chaos, beads of sweat dotting his forehead. Jacob leaned forward, eyes widening with anticipation as wisps of smoke curled upward, carrying the faint scent of smoldering wood. Then, a spark leaped from the rotating stick, igniting a tiny ember that clung to the dry tinder beneath. Jacob's breath caught as the ember blossomed into a fragile flame.

"Don't lose it this time," Morgan said.

Ammon carefully blew on the ember, coaxing the flame to grow. Then he swiftly fed the fire with larger sticks and branches, the flames surging with an insatiable appetite. The warmth was instantaneous, wrapping around Jacob like a comforting blanket, calming his nerves. Yet, like his smile from before, the calm was short-lived as the sight of the fire reminded him of the looming threat of the inferno.

"Impressive," he said.

"Thanks," Ammon said, glancing up at Jacob as he continued to feed the fire.

"Where did you learn to do that?"

"Kinda taught myself. Back in Derro, I wasn't as fortunate as most. Spent some time homeless, living under bridges and such. You learn a few things in order to survive. Eremos kinda reminds me of those nights."

Jacob wore a somber smile. The past year had been the toughest of his life, yet Ammon's words reminded him of his fortune in Derro. He had the privilege of generational wealth, which allowed him to maintain an excellent social score. Others, however, were forced to survive under harsh circumstances, often driving them to commit acts that further lowered their social scores.

"*Holy shit*, we have fire," Alex gasped as she approached, her hands wringing out her wet hair. "One of you guys *actually* made it, right?"

Ammon offered a courtesy laugh. "Yes, I did."

"Good," Alex said, settling in their tight circle around the fire, her eyes lingering on Ammon longer than usual.

"Good rinse?" he asked.

Alex expelled a relaxing breath. "Definitely."

As the two of them continued to chat, Jacob shifted his attention to Morgan, checking on him after Alex's unabashed honesty. The kid's head hung low. Jacob frowned at the sight. All it had taken was one fear-provoking question to shatter the relief Morgan had just felt. Earlier, Morgan had again expressed to Jacob how bad he felt about not being honest about starting the fire. He wanted to apologize to Alex too but was both nervous and afraid. Alex could be intimidating, but Jacob had encouraged Morgan to be brave. He just needed a little push.

He leaned toward the kid and softly elbowed him, drawing his attention. He smiled and nodded toward Alex, silently urging Morgan to follow through with his apology. Morgan drew a deep breath, then nodded.

"Uh, hey Alex. I really need to, like, say I'm sorry for not telling you about the fire. I totally lied when you first arrived, and, um, that lie just kept growing. I didn't know what to do, and well, I just didn't want to be alone."

Alex's face softened. "It's all right, kid. I shouldn't have assumed you'd made it. My own fault, really. But we all managed to escape, and that's all that matters now."

Ammon scoffed. "Hell, I'm glad you lied. If you hadn't, I'd still be stuck in that pit. Or worse, dead."

That remark brought Morgan's head back up, a faint smile forming. Jacob, like the others, couldn't help but return the gesture, a newfound sense of camaraderie settling among them. It was an interesting turn of events—how one wrong inaction could yield both unfortunate *and* fortunate outcomes. But then again, that was the nature of decision-making: choosing a path with the highest chance of success. Or, in Morgan's case, survival. And that was something they all could relate to.

"And now, thanks to *you*, we've got fire," Jacob said, nodding toward Ammon.

"Yeah, now if only we had some food to cook on it," Ammon quipped.

"We could give bugs a shot," Morgan said, smirking. "You know, extra protein and all."

"Hard pass," Alex said, curling her lip. "Unless we have to."

"I think I saw some fish in the stream earlier," Ammon said. "I could try making some kind of net or trap to catch one."

Jacob's eyebrows rose. "You could do that?"

"Key word there was *try*."

"I might be able to help with the net," Alex said. "When I was a kid, my mom taught me how to tie all kinds of knots. If we find enough thin vines, I'm sure I could tie something up."

"That would definitely be useful," Ammon said, nodding as he added more branches to the fire.

Jacob's stomach growled. He hadn't eaten since being exiled, and that "last meal" Wes had given him had long worn off. All this talk of fish had his mind drifting toward his favorite foods in Derro.

"I don't know about you guys, but I could really go for a big, juicy burger right about now," he said.

"Dude, yes," Morgan said, pointing a finger at Jacob. "Or, even better, some pizza."

Alex rolled her eyes. "Guys, we're stranded on Eremos, and you're talking about food we'll *never* have again?"

"It's been *forever* since I've had a slice of pepperoni pizza," Ammon said.

"See, even Ammon gets it," Jacob said.

"Sounds so good," Morgan said, licking his lips. "I *love* pizza. Especially with pineapple. Nothing better."

"*Whoa*, hold the Aux," Ammon said. "Pineapple does *not* belong on pizza."

"It sure as hell does," Morgan fired back.

"I'm gonna have to side with the kid on this one," Jacob chimed in. "Nothing better than a little sweet and spicy."

Ammon bowed his shaking head. "Wow. Alex, help me out here."

Alex frowned, but then a small smirk began to form. "You guys are ridiculous. We're in a survival situation, and you're arguing about pizza toppings."

"A man can dream, can't he?" Jacob said, shrugging with a wide grin, then wincing as the movement aggravated his bite.

Morgan scoffed. "Who said it has to be a dream? I say we go boar hunting. Get all survival and shit. Make our own damn pepperoni."

"All right now, calm down there," Ammon said, laughing.

Alex rolled her eyes again, prompting Jacob to chuckle at the sight. She had easily become their voice of reason, but even she couldn't resist their silly conversation.

"*Ah*," Morgan said, a heavy breath escaping him as he looked at the starry sky. "I miss pizza *so* much."

"Same, kid," Ammon said. "But I think what I miss the most are my books. They were my comfort. Took me to other worlds and made me feel like I could get through anything."

Jacob smiled softly. Knowing what he knew about the Last Patriot's past, learning of his fondness for reading was unexpected. He imagined Ammon during those homeless nights under a bridge, finding comfort in a book. He didn't peg Ammon as the reading type, but then again, did reading really have a type?

"I wish I had my morning coffee," Alex said warmly, then frowned. "It sure would make waking up here a hell of a lot less dreadful."

"I wish I could still have Alice," Morgan said.

"*Who's* Alice?" Alex asked, smirking. "A girlfriend?"

"No, she's my Aux. She helped me get through everything. Would be nice if she was here to help me get through exile."

Jacob frowned. He knew all too well how different it felt without his Aux. Sid had always been there for him through the lows of life. Growing up with a father who was a widower and wasn't always as present as he should have been. Growing up without a mother. His father's death. And then Charlotte's. His frown deepened. Sid had been there during the good times too, but it was the bad times when Jacob needed his Aux the most, even if he didn't realize it at the time.

"Do you think our Auxes can still hear us?" Morgan asked. "Sometimes I catch myself thinking things, and I can't tell if it's just me or Alice."

I am always here. Jacob recalled Sid's words from the night Charlotte died. Of course, it wasn't really Sid speaking to him this time. Just Jacob's memory of Sid. But, as Morgan suggested, was there really a difference? Sid had always been the voice in Jacob's head. Perhaps even now, Sid was listening, just wasn't capable of giving a reply.

"I'd like to think that, even if we can't hear our Auxes, they can still hear us," Jacob said. "Maybe they're trying to help us in whatever way they can."

Then a sudden thought came to him, his mind recalling that vision of Charlotte on the beach. *Was that how I'd seen her last night? Had Sid taken me to her, like he had before?*

"I think you're right," Morgan said, pulling Jacob from his thoughts. The kid smiled, clearly pleased with Jacob's answer.

Alex scoffed. "Spoken like two people with great social scores," she said, shaking her head. "My Aux just repeatedly denied me things, constantly reminding me of my failures."

"Yeah, same," Ammon said. "Though my Aux did teach me a lot about surviving. Like how to make a fire. Which was just useful."

"Speaking of surviving, any ideas for what we should do in the morning?"

"You mean besides trying to stay alive?" Ammon quipped.

Alex frowned, her eyes narrowing toward him. "Ha, ha, very funny."

Ostria, Jacob thought. As elusive as it felt, trying to find the settlement gave them all a common purpose. A reason to keep going. And hopefully, a shot at a second chance.

"I might have an idea," Jacob said. "When Daemion had me chained in the cave, he mentioned something interesting. Said there was a place here on

Eremos, surrounded by a huge freshwater source. Apparently, people created it in the early days to escape all the anarchy. Daemion claimed it has everything needed to survive. Called it Ostria."

"Ostria?" Ammon repeated, raising an eyebrow.

"It's like a settlement?" Alex asked.

"That's what Daemion called it."

"Do you know where it is?" Morgan asked, eyes widening.

"Not for certain. But when I jumped out of the Screech, I saw a large clearing at the top of a mountain surrounded by cliffs with waterfalls falling into a pool of water. There was also a tall tower. Could be there."

"Why'd Daemion tell you about it?" Ammon asked.

"After he learned I had a gun, he thought there was more to be found. Said he had a plan that was already in motion to invade Ostria's walls."

"*Walls?*" Alex spat. "Do you think they'll even let us in?"

Ammon scoffed. "Probably not. Why else would Daemion want to invade it?"

"He told me he wanted to destroy it," Jacob said.

"And there was a plan already in motion?" Alex asked.

Jacob nodded. "Hopefully not anymore. Hopefully he's dead."

"Yeah, but not *every single one* of the Maws is," Alex said. "I'm sure plenty were able to escape the fire."

"I know it sounds like a longshot, but what other options do we have?" Jacob asked.

"Sounds like a death sentence to me," Alex said.

"We are *literally* serving out our death sentence," Jacob said. "My thought is, if we can find Ostria, we can tell them about Daemion's plan and Michael's possession of the gun. Both are threats to Ostria. Perhaps that will give us enough leverage to negotiate our way in."

"That could work," Ammon said, shrugging. "Count me in. It's only a matter of time before we're faced with danger again. Might as well try to find Ostria while we're at it."

"Yeah, me too," Morgan said, trying to sound confident.

The three of them turned toward Alex, who remained skeptical, her lips pursed in thought. After a moment of silence, she nodded, but with a tight expression Jacob interpreted as her not being fully committed.

"All right, I guess you can count me in too," she finally said.

Ammon grinned. "Glad you said yes. I would've felt bad leaving you all alone out here."

"Oh, shut up," Alex said, trying to fight a smile. "I'm going to bed."

"That's a good idea," Jacob said. "We can rest up and start searching for Ostria in the morning. You guys get some rest. I can take the first watch."

"Nah, let me take the first watch," Ammon said. "Least I can do."

Least you can do? Jacob thought. The offer seemed genuine, but a nagging doubt lingered. Had their escape been enough for Ammon to forgive what Jacob had done to him?

Jacob had saved his life, after all. But then again, Ammon had saved his, too.

Still, he couldn't shake the suspicion that Ammon might have plans of his own, acting kindly in the hope of escaping during the night to find Ostria alone. Jacob had entertained a similar thought himself, the allure of self-reliance tempting him.

Yet a newfound sense of responsibility anchored him to Morgan and Alex. After everything they had endured, he couldn't bring himself to leave them behind. If Ammon did flee in the night, it would put more weight on Jacob's shoulders to lead them to Ostria. But he'd understand, given their rough history.

However, Jacob would be lying to himself if he hoped that wouldn't happen. The Last Patriot had already proven himself useful.

"Thanks," Jacob finally replied. "Just wake me when you get tired."

"Deal," Ammon said.

The ground shifted as Morgan and Alex settled into their makeshift beds. Jacob followed suit and reclined on the soil of Eremos, his body yearning for sleep. But his mind wrestled against it. Like Ostria, sleep seemed elusive. It was hard to rest, let alone sleep, when dangers lurked nearby.

Was this how Ammon felt on those homeless nights? Jacob thought.

The earth shifted again, drawing his attention to Morgan, who had inched closer to him. Jacob smiled. Turning his gaze upward, he found comfort in the stars piercing through the canopy of foliage—a reassuring sight, reminding him that, like the stars, he wasn't alone tonight. He had people to rely on, and they, in turn, relied on him.

He just hoped it would stay that way.

As his eyes drifted shut, the sounds of Eremos serenaded him: the soft rustle of foliage in the wind, chirping insects, and the occasional hoot of an owl. Those gentle sounds lulled him to sleep until finally he succumbed to slumber.

Jacob's eyes snapped open.

He was greeted by an inky sky, yet shadows flickered on the greenery above, cast by the campfire. The steady current of the stream, combined with the crackling of kindling, offered a tempting lull back to sleep.

Then a rustle of leaves beside him jerked his gaze toward the foliage. His pulse quickened as he registered Morgan was no longer at his side. He quickly searched his surroundings, his heart pounding fiercely as the realization struck him.

They're all gone.

He catapulted upright, propelled by a surge of raw instinct and an urgent need to catch up with them, but he struggled to stand. In the flickering light, his frantic gaze landed down below him, only to be met with a nightmare that froze him in sheer horror.

His legs were severed, leaving nothing but stumps at the bottom of his knees that oozed with blood. He panicked, an agonizing scream clawing at his throat, only to emerge as mere rasping breaths.

He yanked his head up, eyes bulging so wide they threatened to pop from their sockets. Another rustle of greenery and Daemion emerged from the dense vegetation, his eyes piercing with feral hunger. In one hand, he clutched a charred leg, and in the other, nothing but a sleeve—no hand in sight.

"You thought you could escape me?" he said, snarling as he lifted the leg to his mouth. "Did you forget what I told you? We are *stronger* than you. And we will *consume* you."

Jacob flinched as Daemion sank his teeth into the scorched flesh. He squeezed his eyes shut at the sight, the repulsive sounds of tearing sinew slithering in his insides. He threw himself on his stomach, digging his elbows into the earth, trying desperately to crawl away from the abomination.

Then abruptly, he came to a halt. The rising terror paralyzed him as his head collided with a series of mucky feet. Heart pounding, he slowly looked up, his eyes gaping at the tree-bark masks glaring down on him.

"Oh, you won't be getting away this time," Daemion sneered. "No, no, I made sure of that. You have to pay for what you did. And oh, it will be painful."

The Maws lunged for him, their fingernails digging into his skin as they flipped him onto his back like they would a slab of meat and then raised him back up into a sitting position. A blaze of pain jabbed at his bite, a cruel reminder of what was coming. His gaze locked on Daemion, who sauntered toward the fire.

"I have to say, your little plan was impressive," Daemion said. "I never saw it coming. Too bad it was all foiled by your new friend."

Jacob's gaze shifted toward a shuffling of foliage behind Daemion. He watched in horror as Morgan and Alex appeared, their bodies being yanked toward the fire by Maws. Ammon strolled in behind them, his chin dipped into his slumped posture, his eyes avoiding Jacob's.

"He's a smart one," Daemion said. "Knows what it takes to *survive* on Eremos. Unlike you, dearie."

Jacob's mouth fell open. *Ammon betrayed us.*

"*Bring the boy to me,*" Daemion demanded.

Jacob screamed internally, his shoulders jerking forward in a helpless attempt to intervene as Maws dragged Morgan toward Daemion. The kid fought against the grip, but he was no match for the Maws. Jacob tried to yell desperate pleas for Daemion to stop, but no sound escaped his mouth, as if the horror had choked him.

"Your legs were merely an appetizer," Daemion said. "But your friends? Oh, dearie, they're our *feast.*"

Suddenly, Jacob's gaze snapped toward Alex, catching a swift slice. Her knees gave out, body going limp as blood poured from her neck. Ammon looked away, his face ashen at the sight. Jacob couldn't turn away if he wanted to. He was frozen in shock as he watched the Maws holding her up by her hair, preventing her lifeless, twitching form from collapsing.

Daemion smiled at the sight, his tongue flicking out of his mouth. "Funny," he murmured, "how the body just *knows* to give in, like gravity's final judgment. It's as if the earth itself can't wait to claim them."

Then he shifted his attention to a flailing Morgan as a Maw approached. Jacob fought against the clenches holding him down, but then went still, his mouth falling open at the sight of Daemion tossing the kid on top of the fire. Morgan screamed as he tried to escape the devouring flames, but it was too late. Maws placed heavy rocks on top of him, rooting him in place.

"Ah, I love a good sear," Daemion sneered, his eyes glaring into Jacob. "Now watch as I *consume.*"

"*No!*" Jacob finally screamed.

He shot awake, gasping for air, his hands scrambling at his chest, as if trying to escape the lingering horror. His eyes darted around quickly, registering the truth: *It was only a nightmare.* His shoulders slumped in relief, and his frantic breath slowly settled, the iron grip of fear loosening as reality returned.

His legs were intact. Morgan and Alex slept soundly beside him. And Ammon sat by the fire, wide-eyed, silently observing him.

"You all right?" he asked.

Jacob nodded, though his body still trembled. He gradually pushed himself to his feet and made his way toward the stream, his dry mouth craving water. After a few long drinks, his nerves began to settle, but his eyes still darted to the dark vegetation where, in his nightmare, Morgan and Alex had been dragged out of. He turned his gaze back to the fire, locking eyes with Ammon. *How long was he watching me sleep?*

He made his way back toward the campfire, his mind still reeling from the nightmare. In it, Ammon had betrayed them—Jacob's fear of not being able to trust him had come true. Or was it revenge for what Jacob had done to him? Either way, Ammon was still here. And Jacob knew that, in order to move forward with any sense of peace, he needed to make amends.

"You sure you're okay?" Ammon asked.

"I'll be fine," he said, settling near the fire. "Just a nightmare. Nothing I haven't been used to over the last year. Only this time, no whiskey to drown it away."

"I know how that is. Here, have some of this." Ammon handed Jacob a flat rock with chopped up fish. "It's no 'juicy burger,' but it'll help."

Jacob's eyes widened, and he didn't hesitate. He grabbed the rock and started devouring the fish. "How'd you catch this?" he mumbled.

"Got lucky. Took me a while, though. Just stood in the stream with my hands dipped in, hoping to feel for any subtle movement."

"You caught this with your *bare* hands?"

"Pretty wild, right? I just felt this quick, slippery flicker and closed my hands around it. No hesitation." Ammon smiled. "Probably my most exciting moment on Eremos."

"What, escaping the Maws wasn't exciting enough?"

"Definitely not. That's another nightmare I'm trying very hard to forget."

Jacob nodded, understanding that, although he had just woken from a nightmare, he felt as if he were still living one. Ammon, too, had been trapped in his own nightmare on Eremos far longer than Jacob. And it could worsen at any moment. Daemion could reveal himself alive, Michael was still out there plotting his next arson, and for all they knew, someone could be watching them right now.

"I'd lost all hope in that pit," Ammon said, his eyes growing distant as he stared into the fire. "And then you came along. The last person I'd *ever* expect to see. I thought I was hallucinating. Of all their islands …"

Jacob paused, chewing thoughtfully on a piece of fish. He glanced over at Ammon, the campfire casting shadows on the Last Patriot's battered face. Memories of that day resurfaced in his mind, reminding him of what he had done, and unfortunately, of what he had become.

"Life is strange …" he finally replied.

"The strangest."

"Hey, listen, about what happened—"

Ammon raised a hand, a silent barricade against Jacob's impending apology. "Don't apologize. I deserved what you did to me. Just like I deserved exile. I've done a lot of bad shit in my life."

Jacob wiped at his mouth, a bit caught off guard by Ammon's unexpected words. Even after what he had done to him, Ammon refused his apology, as if he deemed his battered face and his exile as the due price for his transgressions. Jacob understood all too well.

"We've all done bad shit," he said. "Me included. I've done things I never thought I was capable of."

Ammon nodded, his gaze lingering on the flickering flames. "So, that's really why you were exiled? You found him?"

Jacob hesitated, his mind threatening to conjure moments from that night. He knew Ammon could piece together what he had done. And now, like Ammon, exile was his punishment.

"Yeah, thanks to you."

"I was only using you to save my ass from exile."

"Can't say I blame you, though. Especially after everything we've been through."

"Derro wasn't much better," Ammon said, his fingers tracing the star tattoo on his wrist. "At least for me. Trying to survive every day. Being denied life's necessities because of my social score. The system's fucked. The lower your score drops, the harder it is to climb back up. That's what got me exiled. I never wanted to be a criminal. And I hated doing what I *felt* I *had* to do just to survive."

People can hate so much that they'll rip the world apart. Those *last* words crept into Jacob's mind. "Is that why you became a Last Patriot?"

Ammon nodded. "It was the only way to fight back. It's wild, feeling like you're doing some good in the world, only to realize it's also wrong. You know, fighting for change, a better way of life. For some, that'd be called heroic." He frowned. "But I'm no hero. And none of that justified what I did to you. For that, I'm sorry."

Jacob nodded, accepting Ammon's apology, though he didn't think it was necessary. Unlike Jacob, who had assaulted him, Ammon was merely an opportunist, trying to save himself from exile. And had Ammon not, Jacob might never have found Charlotte's killer.

"So, you and me? We good?" he asked.

"Yeah, man, we're good."

"Here, you can have the rest," Jacob said, handing him back the rock of fish.

Ammon grabbed the rock, scooped up the rest of the fish, and tossed it into his mouth. "Needs salt," he mumbled.

Jacob chuckled. "You should sleep. I'll take watch. It'll be daylight soon, and you're going to need your energy for tomorrow's trek."

"That's right … *Ostria*," Ammon said dramatically as he reclined onto his back. "You think we'll find it?"

"I hope so."

Ammon closed his eyes and yawned. "So, what was the book called?"

"Book?"

"The one you used to blow Daemion's hand off."

Jacob's eyes grew distant. "It was called *Crimson Hands*."

Ammon scoffed, a laugh bubbling up. "No way," he said, barely holding it back.

"I'm serious," Jacob replied, his own laugh creeping into his voice.

"Oh, the irony," Ammon muttered, grinning as his words slowed, sleep pulling at him. "That's … that's good."

Jacob smiled, but as the minutes stretched on, his grin slowly faded. The fire crackled softly, its warmth a comfort. Eventually, he stood, needing to relieve himself. He wandered a short distance from the camp, finding a shadowy spot near the edge of the greenery.

His thoughts churned with the weight of tomorrow—what path to take, what dangers might lie ahead. Death traps, ambushes, worse. Yet, amid the uncertainty, there was an odd comfort in knowing he wasn't alone.

Suddenly, a gritty hand clamped over his mouth.

"Scream and I'll fucking snap your neck."

CHAPTER EIGHTEEN

SEVEN MONTHS BEFORE EXILE

THE FORLORN CORNER of Liberties had become Jacob's new sanctuary. It was the spot where, for countless nights over the past month, he had slumped in a booth, just as he did tonight. From this booth, he had the best view of the entrance, and his eyes scanned every person who walked in and out, searching for *him.*

He nursed a tumbler of whiskey, his third or fourth, he wasn't sure. At first, his nights at the bar were driven by a relentless focus, a promise of familiarity, a visceral recognition that would hit him like a sucker punch to the gut. But as the evenings passed without a trace, the man he sought began to feel more and more like a ghost, and his determination gradually gave way to drinking.

I've become my father. A desperate widower with a drinking problem. The only difference was that he had Jacob to keep him going. *I have no one else to live for.*

The front door of Liberties swung open, its rusty hinges screeching in protest. Jacob watched as a man entered, but he immediately knew it wasn't him. The hair wasn't long enough, and the color was wrong. He frowned, wrestling with the possibility that those distinct features might have been nothing more than a disguise. The man wore an owl mask. What's to say he didn't wear a wig, too?

I'll never find him. This is just a waste of time.

Time seemed to have lost all meaning since her death. That night felt like an eternity ago, the agony of endless nights and sunless days stretching into a blurred blend of memory and pain. Each sip of whiskey served as a bitter companion in his distorted timeline, attempting to fill the void left by unanswered questions and no justice.

He took another sip of whiskey and closed his eyes, trying to will away the memories threatening to resurface. He heard the gunshots. Saw her dead body on the floor. Then her hands, blood pouring between her fingers, holding onto a life they had worked so hard to create. He sniffled and wiped his nose with his sleeve, catching a faint scent of gun oil. He scowled, the smell another reminder of his shortcomings. What had once filled him with reverence now only filled him with sorrow.

I should've shot them. I should've just given them the gun. I should've stepped more in front of her.

The deafening chorus of regrets intensified as his mind replayed those haunting last moments, the pivotal instances where his actions fell short, where his failure to act decisively had cost him. If only he had acted on one of them. Things would have ended differently. Charlotte could still be alive. *We could be planning for the birth of our child.*

The green box still settled on their deck, its presence threatening to desecrate their once-shared sanctuary. He hadn't stepped out there since that morning with her, and he couldn't bear the idea of trying. The pain he was already enduring was difficult enough. Opening the box would only increase the pain. With a trembling hand, he emptied his glass in one reckless motion, seeking solace in its numbing embrace.

"Sid, refill," he uttered, placing his tumbler onto the holographic panel embedded in the table.

The automatic liquor dispenser attached to his booth whirred to life, pouring a calculated portion of whiskey into his glass. He frowned. Night after night, he had hoped Sid wouldn't respond, just as the Aux hadn't that night. He imagined the severance happening instantaneously, perhaps triggered by someone entering Liberties with the same chip Mason had.

Then he'd have a lead.

But sadly, every night passed without a single indication of losing connection to Sid. At least this whiskey dulled the sting of disappointment.

Your refill is complete, Sid said. *You have one more left.*

Great, Jacob sighed, his frown deepening. *Nothing better than being cut off by AI.*

"To hell with them council's social scores," a familiar voice hollered. "I reckon I want a damn drink from that top shelf."

Turning his head toward the voice, Jacob recognized Frank, a longtime Hoos customer, arguing with his Aux. His ginger beard hung low enough to brush the table as he heaved his round form out of the booth.

"That damn council thinks they're playin' God, tryin' to dictate what I *can* and *can't* have," Frank grumbled, his head down as he started toward the exit. Making his way, he lifted his head, his footsteps halting and his eyebrows furrowing as he locked eyes with Jacob. "*Jacob,* is that you?"

Do I look that bad? Since Charlotte's death, he'd avoided mirrors at all costs. It was difficult for him not to acknowledge the growing scruffiness, with all the itching, but he never realized his appearance had become almost unrecognizable. Then again, he didn't care. Unrecognizable was precisely what he aimed for.

"Hey, Frank."

"Goodness, I almost didn't recognize ya," Frank said, settling into Jacob's booth, taking the seat across from him. "How ya holding up?"

"I'm hanging in there," he said, tracing the rim of his tumbler.

"I reckon you've probably heard this more times than you can count, but the missus and me, we're mighty sorry for your loss."

Jacob heard the entrance door open and lifted his head to see who had entered, but Frank's round form blocked his view. He peeked his head out, attempting to catch a glimpse, only to discover it was just someone leaving.

"Thanks, Frank."

"Charlotte … she was like a beacon of light 'round here."

Jacob took a sip of whiskey, frowning at the mere mention of her name, realizing he was no closer to achieving justice for her. Especially with Frank obstructing his view.

"You know what? You should come over for dinner one of these nights. Dolores makes a mean chicken and dumplin's. My *favorite*. And she always cooks up more than we can handle. We'd be downright thrilled to have you join us."

"Thanks, but I don't want to be a burden."

"Aw, c'mon now, Jacob. It's the least we could do for ya."

Jacob? Not bud? I guess he did know my name. Or he does now. Just took the death of my wife.

"I don't know when I'll be ready for an evening like that, but when I am, I'll let you know."

"Well, all righty then, I get it. You just holler at me when you're ready."

Frank started to hoist himself out of the booth, but paused, his gaze shifting back to Jacob as if there was something else on his mind. "Jacob, I reckon it ain't my place to say, but have you … talked to anyone?"

Jacob's nostrils flared. "Why does everyone keep saying I need to talk to someone?"

"We're just worried 'bout ya, is all. I ain't never seen you like this. Talking to someone can help."

"I don't deserve help."

"Well, sure you do."

"She's gone, and it's all my fault."

"Now, wait just a minute. It ain't your fault. You can't control what others do. And you sure as heck ain't responsible for the awful things *they choose* to do."

"Not responsible? I've sold guns to thousands of people, Frank. What's to say the gun that killed her isn't one *I* sold? That *I* put out in Derro?"

"Not everyone you sell a gun to is a no-good scoundrel. I'd reckon most are law-abiding citizens. Hell, you sold one to me and Dolores. Thanks to you, we can protect ourselves."

I wished it felt that way.

"That's what you do, son. You help folks. You offer protection."

You'll only be adding fuel to the fire. Richard's words haunted his mind.

"You're not understanding me," Jacob said, gritting his teeth. "I've been *putting* guns into Derro. Increasing the likelihood of them ending up in the hands of ruthless people who use them to hurt others. And now she's dead. Because of *me.*"

"You didn't pull that trigger. That ain't on you. Guns don't be killin' people. People be killin' people."

Jacob slammed his fists onto the table, the tumbler rattling and crashing, its remaining whiskey spilling. "*They were there for the guns, Frank!*" he roared. Then he snatched his glass and hastily placed it onto the holographic panel. "Sid, refill."

Frank had gone completely still, his dull, weathered eyes gazing toward Jacob as the liquor dispenser poured Jacob's final refill.

Your refill is complete, Jacob, Sid said. *You have no refills left.*

Jacob took a sip of his freshly poured whiskey as he observed Frank heaving himself out of the booth. Just as the senior was about to walk away, he hesitated, a final thought dawning.

"Jacob … I can't rightly fathom what you're goin' through," he said, his mouth opening slightly as he collected his thoughts. "But you ain't gotta be alone in this. Offer still stands whenever you're ready."

Jacob bit the insides of his cheeks as he watched Frank leave. While a large part of him still fumed in anger, a smaller part felt regretful. He knew Frank was only trying to help, but he wasn't ready to receive any. Instead, he drank. And with each sip, his mind grew hazier, and he struggled to keep his unsteady eyes focused on the entrance of Liberties until he finished his last drink.

Unable to drown in his pain any longer, he unsteadily stood and dragged his feet out of Liberties. "Sid, pay my tab."

Your tab has been settled.

He stumbled out of Liberties, greeted by a darkened Nox Street. The cool wind brushed against his skin as he sighed. Another night was ending with him no closer to finding her killer. The task proved daunting, and he had hoped for at least a lead by now.

His glassy eyes drifted toward Hoos. He still hadn't set foot inside since that night, and he couldn't fathom ever doing so again. The purpose his father had instilled in him as a boy—selling guns for protection—had lost its meaning.

Suddenly, his gaze caught something flying and landing on the eaves of Hoos. Its wide, circular eyes gleamed at him. "What the …" he slurred. *Is that an* owl?

The owl hooted. Jacob stood mesmerized by its presence. The creature had chosen to land on Hoos and stare at him, as if delivering a message sent solely for him. It was as though he were stuck in a trance by the owl's hypnotic gaze, unable to look away, until the owl hooted again, snapping him out of it. Then it took flight and disappeared into the darkness.

Feeling at a loss for words and more intoxicated than he'd care to admit, he started down Nox Street, hoping to walk it off. He hung his head low, his staggered steps guiding him aimlessly. Pockets of light and shadow fought for his gaze as he walked beneath the streetlights, his steps carrying him in and out of their reach. Growing dizzier, he glanced up, his eyes catching a dark figure emerging from a side alley ahead, moving toward him.

Nox Street is still in a no-go zone, he remembered.

He slowed his unsteady pace, his heart quickening as he fought against his drunkenness to become more alert. The figure approached, hands in jacket pockets, the streetlights casting a blurred silhouette of a thin, hooded man. Jacob tensed, readying to defend himself, but the man simply passed. Jacob halted, his stare fixed on the man's retreating back.

You're just being paranoid, he told himself.

Turning on his heel, he resumed walking but was abruptly stopped as his face collided with someone's chest.

"Bit late for a stroll, don't you think?" a man's voice slurred.

Jacob staggered backward, his gaze fixed on a burly, hooded figure before him, eyes like slits tearing into him. Hurried footsteps thudded behind him. Jacob whipped his head around, spotting the original man sprinting toward him.

This was a trap. "Sid alert the Cullers!"

I've alerted the Cullers and provided them with access to your precise location.

Jacob didn't hesitate. Turning swiftly, he threw a fist into the burly attacker's jaw. Then he sprinted toward the side alleyway next to him but was immediately tackled at the waist. The other assailant forced him backward relentlessly. Jacob slammed his fists onto the man's back, but the attacker persisted, driving him into the wall, his head colliding with brick.

Dazed and blurry, he tried blocking out the pain, but more followed as the attacker struck him in the face. The blow caused his body to fold, threatening to send him to the pavement, but the attacker gripped him in place.

"You're gonna regret you did that."

A clicking noise caused his pounding heart to skip a thump, his blurred vision preventing him from seeing what the attacker held. But he didn't need to see it to know what it was. *He's got a knife!*

"Let's see how strong you are now."

"*Halt,*" a voice declared.

"*Shit,* a Culler! Let's go."

Jacob crumpled onto the ground as the assailant released his grip, footsteps speeding away from him. The cool cement soothed his throbbing face as his lungs fought to catch his breath. A pair of black boots entered his view.

"Are you crazy or something?" a woman's voice asked.

"Huh?" Jacob slurred.

"That explains it. You're *drunk.* You're sure as hell lucky I was patrolling this no-go zone."

"I was just …." Jacob faltered, struggling to find the right words. He didn't have an excuse. He'd been careless.

"Yeah, yeah," the Culler said, nudging Jacob's body with her boot. "Get up."

He gradually rose to his feet, groaning with the effort. Then two hands grabbed him and pulled him up more quickly than he expected. Through his blurred vision, he spotted an armored Culler with a buzzed head, a long nose, and—

"Freckles," he muttered, recognizing the Culler from that night.

"Yeah, nice try," she said, scoffing. "Get home before you kill yourself."

Jacob's wandering gaze landed on the Culler's shoulder plate. There it was again—the owl. The sight reminded him of the owl he had just seen on the roof of Hoos. And then of that night.

"*Hey*, are you hearing me?"

Jacob shook his head, trying to snap out of it. "I'll have my Aux drive me home."

"Good."

"Sid, I need a ride home."

On my way.

"What's the fucking point of no-go zones if no one listens to them?" the Culler muttered to herself.

As Jacob waited for Sid to approach with his Nervo Pod, he glanced back at the store the attackers had just thrown him into. A large holographic sign flickered to life, displaying the words, "Sold by Woodwin Realty." The hologram shifted, now showing Richard's smug face smiling back at him. Jacob's lip curled as he read the additional message: "No-go zone got your business in the red? Turn crisis into capital. Richard Woodwin. Reshaping no-go zones for a promising future."

The store was Storks. From what Jacob could see, the entire store was empty. Richard had done nothing with it yet. *Probably waiting till he owns all of Nox Street,* he mused. *Maybe I should just sell, after all.* Except Jacob wasn't in the red. He was well in the black. And that's what terrified him the most. *I profit off everyone's fear.*

Jacob, I'm approaching your location.

The distant whine of his Nervo Pod rang in his ears, growing louder as it approached. When it stopped, the sleek doors whispered open, and he stepped inside, his body slumping into the plush seat.

"Do me a favor, and stop entering no-go zones," the Culler said. "We've got better shit to do than this."

Hard to do when your business is in one, he thought, frowning. *And when you're trying to find the man who murdered your wife.*

The Nervo Pod's doors closed on the Culler, ending their conversation. Holographic seat belts wrapped around him, securing him in place. He touched his cheek and winced, catching the sight of blood on his fingers as he pulled them away. The Nervo Pod hummed to life, its battery whining as it drove forward.

Destination home, Sid said.

"No, not home," Jacob pleaded. "Anywhere but there, Sid. Just … take me to Charlotte. Please."

Sid paused, indicating a moment of contemplation regarding Jacob's request. *Very well, Jacob,* his Aux finally said.

Jacob grabbed the bottle of whiskey resting in the seat beside him and removed the cap. Leaning his head back, he closed his eyes and savored the fiery liquid. His plan was simple: drink until oblivion, whether through sleep or death. He still didn't care. All that mattered was that when he woke up, he would be with her.

CHAPTER NINETEEN

DAY FOUR OF EXILE

I'M A DEAD MAN.

Jacob's legs flailed frantically, seeking purchase as someone yanked him by the head and shoulders, dragging him deeper into the dense foliage. A gritty palm clamped over his mouth, stifling any cry for help, its grip like a vise.

Looking upward, he strained to identify his attacker, but darkness shrouded them. His heart and mind raced, fear pulsating through his veins. Was it Daemion? Michael? Or was he about to face a new threat? Desperation clawed at him, hoping Ammon had heard the struggle, but the memory of closed eyes suggested a slumbering obliviousness.

His body jerked to a halt, the dragging finally ceasing. Gasping for air, he heaved as the bulky figure loomed over him, patting his waist and pockets.

"Where the hell is it?"

It? Suddenly, the figure effortlessly flipped Jacob's body onto its side, then frantically patted Jacob's back.

"*Fuck.* Where's the gun, dammit?"

Gun? Who the hell just grabbed—

The man grappled on top of him, knees pressing into his ribs, forcing a muffled cry to escape his lips. He closed his eyes in agony, the gritty palm muffling his scream. A nose brushed against his, causing him to snap his eyes open, then widen at the face hovering over him.

It can't be.

But it was.

There was no mistaking the stench of tobacco, or the armor marked with a white owl on the shoulder plate. *It's Wes!*

"I'm going to remove my hand so we can talk, and I swear, if you scream, I'll snap your neck," Wes threatened. "Nod if you understand."

He nodded, trying to gulp down his scream as Wes's hand tightened around his mouth. Then the Culler lifted his hand away.

"Now, where's the damn gun you took?"

"I destroyed it."

"*You what?*"

A dark blur suddenly threw Wes off Jacob, sending the Culler to the ground. Jacob scrambled to his feet, wincing amid the pain stabbing his shoulder and ribs. Fighting for breath, he squinted at a shadowy figure grappling with the Culler, limbs entangled until the figure struck Wes in the face.

"Are you okay?"

Startled, Jacob jerked his head over his shoulder, only to be filled with relief as he found Alex and Morgan behind him. But if they're here, then ... *Ammon's fighting Wes.*

Whipping his attention back to the scuffle, he could see Ammon still on top of Wes, raining down strikes, attempting to find impact through the Culler's bulky arms. Jacob rushed toward them and pulled Ammon off. The Last Patriot continued to flail his arms and legs, resisting Jacob's effort to separate them.

"What the *hell* are you doing?" Ammon grunted.

"It's *Wes.*"

Ammon's eyes jerked toward Wes, then back to Jacob. "Wes?"

"Wait, Wes, as in Wes, the Culler who dumped us here?" Alex interjected.

"I'm just as shocked as you."

"What the fuck is he doing *here?*" Alex asked.

"He was looking for the gun," Jacob said, his breath steadying.

Wes gradually rose, his hand grabbing at his jaw, wincing at the touch. "I gotta give it to ya. You can throw a punch."

"Why are you looking for the gun?" Alex asked as she glared at Wes. "We don't have it anymore."

"Calm down, princess. I'm aware of that now. Jacob here apparently destroyed it. What kind of idiot destroys a gun? Why even take it then?"

"An idiot who wanted to escape from a group of cannibals," Jacob fired back.

"Did it ever occur to you to *shoot* the gun? Seeing as you were once an owner of a gun store, I'd think you'd know how to use one."

"My time of killing is done," Jacob replied firmly.

"Is that why you're here?" Ammon asked. "The council wants you to find the guns you let get taken?"

"No," Wes said, frowning. "I'm here because I was exiled."

"*Exiled?*" Alex spat. "Exiled, like all of us, exiled?"

Wes exhaled sharply. "I'm afraid so."

There's no way, Jacob thought. He had never heard of a Culler being exiled before.

"All because of that crispy little shit."

Michael, he realized. "The council exiled you for what happened with Michael?"

"Unfortunately," Wes said through gritted teeth. "Those fuckers. After everything I did for Derro."

Jacob knew the council wasn't pleased with Wes. They had demoted him from Charlotte's case after taking matters of justice into his own hands too many times, trying to break members of the Last Patriots. The incident on the Screech must have been the final straw. *But why exile him?* Michael was the one who killed the other Culler. Not Wes.

"I don't understand," he said. "You didn't kill Allen. Michael did. So, why'd they exile you?"

Wes scoffed. "The council didn't see it that way. They said my *carelessness* is the reason he died."

"They're not wrong," Alex said. "Serves you right."

"Shut that foul mouth of yours, you little—"

"Little what?" Alex cut off, rushing over to Wes. "Finish it. I fucking dare you."

Wes smirked, holding back a laugh. "Bitch."

Alex struck Wes in the face.

Wes staggered back, clutching his face, but Alex didn't stop. She lunged forward, fists flying, seeking more impact.

"Oh shit," Ammon said, head jerking back in shock.

He rushed over, hooked his arms around Alex, and yanked her back. Alex thrashed, arms flailing, fighting against his grip, but Ammon held on.

"No, let me at him," Alex demanded.

Wes grinned, wiping a trickle of blood from his lip.

"You really know how to make friends, Wes," Jacob said.

"Friends were never my strong suit," Wes said, massaging his jaw as he glared at Ammon. "Careful with her. She hits harder than you."

Morgan inched closer to Jacob, catching Wes's glare. The kid shrunk amid the gaze, his body growing still.

"Well, would you look at that," Wes said. "This is quite the bunch. You've got a former gun store owner who doesn't use guns. A Last Patriot. A woman. And a kid. Crazy what Eremos brings together. I mean, I'm not surprised to see you three together, but I sure as hell am surprised to see *you*." He narrowed his eyes at Ammon. "You weren't with their group. And after what *he* did to your face?"

"That's in the past," Ammon said.

"Clearly," Wes said, chuckling to himself as he surveyed them all. "It's interesting. I know exactly what all of you *did* to get exiled. Oh, how I could break your little alliance so fast."

"What we did no longer matters," Jacob said.

"Oh, but it will."

"We don't have what you're looking for," Morgan said, trying to sound confident. "So, just leave."

"Yeah, you see, kid, I don't want to. If you haven't noticed, I'm a Culler. Thousands of criminals are here because of me. That's why I grabbed you. I'm a dead man walking. I needed that gun. And considering I still don't have it. I think we could work together."

Alex scoffed. "You're kidding, right? You're insane if you think we're going to help you."

"It's not just me that needs helping," Wes said, snarling.

"What's that supposed to mean?" Jacob asked.

"It means you're just as soon as dead as me. Let me break it down for your weary minds. You were captured on your first night here. You destroyed your biggest defense advantage to escape only to be captured by the likes of me shortly afterwards. I'd say things haven't worked out so great for ya."

"We'll be fine," Ammon said.

"Oh, and then there's Prince Charring. Boy, do you guys need to worry about him."

Jacob furrowed a brow, lost in thought. If Wes knew why they were all exiled, he would know why Michael was too, perhaps even have insight into the madman's cryptic words. "What do you know about Michael?"

"You mean other than the fact that he's *insane*? I know he believes he's some kind of tool to be used to deliver God's judgment or some shit."

I, the instrument, bear witness.

"God's judgment?" Ammon said.

"Fucker burned down his entire apartment building, claiming he was purging Derro of its wicked and evilness. Said the righteous would be spared. Guy's a nut job. And now he's *here*."

I exist here solely because I was … spared.

Jacob's mind swirled, recalling Michael's words as the puzzle finally came together. *Evildoers. Wicked ones. I, the instrument. A flame that devours, yet purifies.* Michael burned down his apartment building in an act of purification and the deliverance of God's judgment. He did the same to the Maws' camp. *My suspicions were right.*

"You're gonna make me state the obvious?" Wes asked mockingly.

"He's gonna try and burn down all of Eremos," Jacob answered.

"Ding, ding, ding, there go the church bells," Wes said. "Eremos is inhabited by the wicked and evil of Derro. It's gonna be like Sodom and Gomorrah out here. Fucking biblical."

"What's Sodom and Gomorrah?" Morgan asked.

"Something from the Bible, kid," Ammon said.

Morgan furrowed a brow. "What's the Bible?"

"So, what, you want us to help you find him?" Jacob asked.

"Fuck that," Alex spat. "How can one man burn down an entire island?"

"We all saw what he did to the Maws' camp," Ammon said. "Given the heat and the absence of any means to contain it, that fire is likely still raging."

"Plus, he's got a gun," Jacob said. "With bullets. Which means gunpowder. Which means highly flammable. And combustible."

Alex rolled her eyes, frowning. "I get it. I'm still not working with the Culler."

"Even if I can show you where Ostria is?"

"You know about Ostria?" Morgan asked, voice rising with promise.

"Sure do, kid. And my guess is they don't let any of you in. But I can change that. I can help you get in. I'll vouch for some made-up crime that isn't as bad as what you really did."

"How do you know about Ostria?" Jacob asked.

"I saw it every time I flew over Eremos."

So that was it, Jacob thought, remembering the clearing he saw when he jumped from the Screech.

"Plus, it was on the council's radar for some time," Wes continued. "What? You think the council isn't watching their islands? They've got cameras all around here. Surveillance doesn't stop in Derro. They've gotta make sure no one tries to build a boat or some shit and try escaping. Not that they'd get very far."

"*Was* on the council's radar?" Ammon asked.

"The council wasn't sure what they were building. When it became obvious they were only building a settlement, they became less worried."

"How do you know they won't let us in?" Morgan asked.

"Because, kid, they've worked hard to build what they have. It's their home. You think they're gonna risk destroying it by just letting anyone in?"

Alex folded her arms across her chest. "We have a plan."

"Well, whatever it is, I doubt it'll work."

Wes was right. Jacob knew there was no guarantee they would be granted refuge in Ostria. Having a Culler with them who could relay the danger Ostria faced brought them credibility. But then again, Wes was a Culler. Ostria might want nothing to do with him.

"Whether our plan works or not, I don't trust you," Jacob said. "And my gut tells me you need us more than we need you. Seeing as you're a Culler and all. Hell, I bet they don't even let *you* in."

Wes scowled. "You don't want to make an enemy out of me."

"Just shut up already," Alex said. "We're not helping you out, okay? So, stop the begging and get."

"Fine," Wes grumbled as he turned on his heel and started toward the foliage. "But just wait. I can't wait to see the looks on all your faces when I find that other gun. Then we'll see who's really begging."

"Good luck finding it," Alex jabbed.

"I found you, didn't I?" Wes fired back. "I always find my man."

Not always, Jacob thought, watching Wes disappear into the greenery.

"Well, that was unexpected," Ammon said.

"Definitely," Jacob said.

His gaze lingered on the spot where Wes had vanished, the realization settling in. Wes's presence on Eremos was all the confirmation he needed. Destroying the Talon had been the right choice. Had he not, Wes would have gotten his hands on the weapon, leaving them all dead, just like he had done with the Last Patriots.

"You good?" Ammon asked.

"As good as I can be. Thanks for saving my life … again."

"Eh, don't mention it."

"So, now what?" Alex asked.

Jacob inhaled sharply, wincing against the sharp bite of pain. The journey ahead would be perilous; that much was certain. More dangers lay in wait, both from new enemies and old ones. Food and water were already scarce on Eremos, and leaving the stream behind felt like a gamble. Yet the looming threat of the inferno felt even more urgent. There was no question. They had to leave.

"Ammon, you think you can catch another fish?" he asked.

"You *caught a fish?*" Morgan said.

Ammon smiled. "I'm happy to *try.*"

"Well then, let's catch some breakfast fast, eat up, and then find our way to Ostria."

CHAPTER TWENTY

SEVEN MONTHS BEFORE EXILE

JACOB AWOKE TO the roaring of waves.

A low groan escaped his lips as he tried to pry open his eyes, only to be assaulted by the harsh sunlight. He squinted and raised his hand to shield his face from the piercing rays. His head throbbed with a relentless pulse, and his mouth was dry, as if he had spent the night chewing on cotton. Both sensations served as reminders of yet another failed attempt to find Charlotte's killer—and, unfortunately, of the close call that had almost claimed his life.

Digging his hands into the grainy sand, he gradually sat up, the ocean spinning in a dizzying haze. A deep breath steadied him, and as he scanned his surroundings, the beach unfolded before him; vast and empty, with the sand stretching as far as the eye could see. To his right, a towering rock sea stack jutted out of the shoreline like a giant's finger pointing toward the horizon.

This is our beach, he realized. *Take me to her.* His words from last night resurfaced, and a natural smile tugged at his lips as he grasped what Sid had done for him.

"Sid, thank you."

You're welcome, Jacob.

In front of him, waves persistently raced toward the shore, churning up white foam as they crashed against the sand and ended near his feet. *So close*, he mused, a sentiment he wished he could echo about finding her killer. Instead, he felt adrift at sea, unable to navigate his way home. *I need to find him.*

He closed his eyes, defeat settling heavily on his shoulders. A soft wind passed by, bringing with it the scent of salty air, stirring memories of their road trips to this beach. He smiled, recalling how lucky they had been to find it. Jacob, following Charlotte's advice to embrace the unknown, had asked Sid to take them to any beach. Sid had brought them here.

From then on, it had become a tradition. Summer after summer, Sid or Iris would bring them back. The combined joy and laughter from their travel games flashed before him, their favorite being Truth or Lie. Despite Charlotte's statements always seeming far-fetched, he was consistently surprised to discover they were true.

One memorable anecdote stood out, when she shared, *"I once was arrested and spent the night in a jail cell."* Jacob hadn't believed it for a second and immediately called, *"Lie!"*

To his astonishment, it was true.

She went on to explain that Cullers had found her trespassing in a forbidden zone. She had been trying to capture a sunrise with her camera. They had only kept her overnight for a background and Aux check, ensuring she had no ulterior motives beyond the photograph.

A small laugh escaped Jacob's lips at the recollection. "You were always on the hunt for things to capture," he said, as if she were sitting right next to him.

She hardly left home without her camera, as if she saw each trip through fresh eyes. She even let Jacob take a photo from time to time, a thought that reminded him of the one he had found in her room. He reached into his pocket to retrieve it and carefully unfolded the picture. There she was, seated in the sand, the photo capturing the back of her form as she gazed toward the ocean, completely in her element.

Tears brimmed in Jacob's eyes as he lifted the picture directly in front of him. Then it hit him. He was now sitting nearly close to where she had been that day. He smiled, a warm sensation flooding through him, a calming presence he could feel, as if she were right there with him.

Come on, you, she had said to him after taking the photo.

He wept, the tears flowing freely down his cheeks, leaving salty trails in their wake. The memory of that day came rushing back to him. As wonderful as it had been, he couldn't escape the shadow of the not-so-great part. Restless and agitated, he'd wanted to go home sooner than she had. She'd pleaded with him to stay longer, to watch the sunset and savor the moment. But he'd insisted on leaving. Reflecting on it now, he became overwhelmed with regret. He wished he had listened and stayed. To watch that sunset. To seize every precious moment with her.

But she's gone. And it's all my fault.

He clenched his fists in the sand, an unresolved anger building within him. *But there will also be movements of relief.* Steve's voice interrupted his thoughts. Slowly, he released his grip on the sand, watching it flow through his fingers as his body gradually relaxed. *Little tiny flickers of light that'll remind you of all the love you two shared. And she really loved you. Search for the tiny flickers, Jake.*

With a heavy heart, he allowed himself to experience the flicker of light Sid had gifted him. His Aux had brought him here, knowing this was their spot, a beacon in the darkness that had clouded his everyday life since her death. Embracing this moment of relief, he resolved not to leave the beach. Not just yet. He needed to be here. Needed to feel close to her.

Suddenly, his phone rang, causing him to tense.

Jacob, an unrecognized number is calling you, Sid informed. *Shall I identify it for you?*

Groaning, he fished his phone out of his pocket and eyed the unfamiliar number with suspicion. He frowned, the ringing acting as a powerful pull away from the relief of his pain. For a moment, he hesitated, considering ignoring the call. But as the ringing persisted, he felt compelled to answer. *Maybe it's Ezra.*

"Sid, answer call."

Certainly.

The holographic display flickered to life, but just as the call was on the brink of connecting, the battery died, its hologram dissipating. *Your phone has died,* Sid alerted. *Might I suggest returning to your Nervo Pod to charge it?*

Jacob scowled, frustration mounting. But then, gradually, a small smile tugged at the corners of his mouth. Perhaps it was a sign, another reminder that he should live in the moment. Just as Charlotte would. *Come on, you.* Her words echoed in his head.

He stayed on their beach until the sun collapsed, watching as the sky turned a brilliant shade of orange and pink. He owed it to her. But most importantly, he owed it to himself. Though as peaceful and relaxed as he felt, he dreaded what came after the sunset. Darkness. Another day was ending without an update on her case or a lead to follow.

When the sun completed its long descent, he stood and made his way back to his Nervo Pod. Settling in, he subconsciously placed his phone on the holographic charger, leaving it floating.

Where to? Sid asked.

"Liberties."

Very well.

Jacob reclined his head back, his mind still lingering on the sunset he had just witnessed. It would be a couple of hours before he arrived at Liberties, where he planned to spend another night until last call, watching the entrance vigilantly. So, he closed his eyes and welcomed the idea of drifting off to sleep.

Then a chime emitted from his phone, snapping his eyes back open. He frowned, suppressing the urge to sit up and grab it.

"Sid, is the notification anything of importance?"

You have a voicemail, Sid said. *From the number that called you earlier. Would you like me to play the voicemail?*

Jacob released a sigh. "Sure. Play it through the Nervo Pod."

"Hi, this message is for Jacob Hughes," a woman's voice resonated from the Nervo Pod's speakers. "I represent Woodwin Realty, and I understand your business, Hoos, is still stuck in a no-go zone, with no sign of the council lifting the restrictions. If your business is facing challenges, know that Woodwin Realty specializes in turning adversity into opportunity. We've saved numerous owners from financial burdens amidst the challenges of no-go zones, and we're confident we can do the same for you. Time is of the essence, so let's discuss how we can reshape your future. Act now—"

"Sid, stop."

And that's where you come in. Richard's words continued to haunt his mind. *You'll be the one providing them with a false sense of security. An illusion that they can protect themselves when in reality ... you'll only be adding fuel to the fire.*

As much as he loathed the man, his mind wandered to the actual idea of selling Hoos. Richard had proven right, and working there didn't feel the same anymore. Not after what happened to Charlotte. *And* his father. There was no legacy left for him to uphold. Selling Hoos could help him finally move on, shedding a burden he no longer wished to hold.

The only burden he wanted was the weight of finding her killer. And when he did, ensure he could never hurt anyone again.

CHAPTER TWENTY-ONE

DAY FOUR OF EXILE

JACOB PUSHED THROUGH the dense vegetation of Eremos, the thick greenery brushing against his sweaty skin. His clothes clung uncomfortably, like a second layer, and beads of sweat inched down his forehead, stinging his eyes. He trailed behind the others, desperate to discover any signs of Ostria.

Since last night's encounter with Wes, who had confirmed his suspicions about Michael, the scorching heat felt like a suffocating reminder of what was pursuing them. The madman had set his divine purpose to burn Eremos in motion, and it felt like only a matter of time before they faced its flames again.

Jacob ran a hand through his wet hair and drew a steadying breath, trying to will away the fears in his mind. Yet, for every fear he pushed away, another one took its place.

We're in trouble if Wes gets his hands on that Talon.

Strangely, the prospect of Wes finding Michael filled him with both fear and hope. Hope, because discovering the madman would put an end to any further outbreaks. Yet fear, because it would mean Wes possessing the Talon. A firearm in a Culler's hands posed a threat in its own right, and if anyone on Eremos could stop Michael, it was Wes.

Or perhaps Daemion, assuming he was still alive. That would be a clash of insanity against insanity. It was plausible that Daemion might actively pursue Michel too, seeking the only person he knew had a gun after losing the one Jacob had destroyed—a weapon he desperately wanted for his planned attack. Jacob knew better than anyone how desperation, anger, and fear could twist a person's soul, driving them to do whatever it took to hold a gun in their hands.

We are stronger *than you. And we will* consume *you.* Daemion's words still haunted Jacob's mind, just as last night's nightmare had. In it, Daemion had pursued them, seeking revenge for Jacob's actions in the cave. That fear had kept Jacob constantly looking over his shoulder. However, the longer he pondered, the more he realized that pursuit offered little beyond revenge. Daemion most certainly desired the Talon more.

As hopeful as that thought made Jacob, he couldn't shake the feeling that the convergence of these individuals' paths was all but inevitable.

"I don't think I've ever seen leaves this big before," Morgan said, pulling Jacob from his thoughts. "They're bigger than my *head.*"

Jacob smiled. Seeing Morgan enjoy the little things brought him temporary relief from the terror that had been stirring in his mind. There was no doubt the events Jacob had endured on Eremos had left him forever scarred. He could only imagine the profound toll the horrors had taken on Morgan's tender psyche. So, seeing him in good spirits felt like a weight being lifted from his shoulders.

"You know, kid, come to think of it, I don't think I've ever seen leaves this big before either," he said, letting his fingers graze the leaves as he passed.

"So cool, right?"

"Definite—"

Jacob's words escaped him as his knees buckled, sending him crumpling to the dirt. His vision blurred, then darkened as his face collided with the earth. His head recoiled, panic surging through his veins, prompting him to rise, but his body failed him.

"Guys!" Morgan yelled, alerting the others up ahead.

"What happened?" Alex asked.

"He just fell," Morgan said, the words rushing out.

Jacob's ears caught the muffled rustle of twigs crunching as the others approached. He tried to rise again, his arms trembling with the effort, the abrupt collapse leaving him disoriented.

"Hey, not so fast," Ammon said, grabbing Jacob by his armpits and helping him to his feet. "Nice and slow. That's it."

"You okay?" Morgan asked.

With Ammon's help, Jacob straightened, his feet finding purchase on the ground. He drew in a breath but struggled to find air, as though he was suffocating under a pillow with only the tiniest opening for breath.

"I'm good," he lied. "Just tripped."

"It's the heat," Alex said. "We've been walking all day. We should rest."

"Good idea," Ammon said. "We've probably already burned off that fish from this morning. We need to regain our strength."

"We can't afford … to waste any sunlight," Jacob urged between breaths as he shook his head. "We need to find shelter before nightfall. We have to keep moving. I'll be okay."

Alex frowned. "You don't look okay."

"She's right," Ammon said, pinching the skin at his throat.

"How's your bite?" Alex asked.

Jacob closed his eyes, a sense of dread mounting at the mention of his wound. He had pushed through all day, suppressing the festering bite, but now his mind seemed too weary to block out the pain any longer. And apparently, so did his body. Opening his eyes, he carefully pulled his shirt's collar over his shoulder and checked on the lesion.

"It's good," he lied again.

Alex winced. "It's looking infected."

"That's *gnarly*," Morgan drawled.

"It's swelling big time, man," Ammon said, biting his lips. "And there's pus forming."

"Do you feel cold?" Alex asked.

Jacob sighed. "No. Like I said, I just tripped. The heat got the best of me."

"If you start to feel cold, it means you have a fever, and the infection is getting worse," Alex said.

Jacob released his collar, covering the wound again, and started to walk. "All the more reason to keep moving," he muttered bitterly.

Reluctantly acknowledging the truth, he knew the others were right. His bite was worsening. It didn't help that his shirt had clung to it all day in the heat and his sweat. Despite the oppressive heat, he had yet to experience chills, a fleeting relief. *Would probably be a nice break from this damn heat, though.*

But dwelling on the bite was a luxury they didn't have. There was no practical way to treat it in their current surroundings. Unless Eremos offered natural remedies that could help. And even if it did, he wouldn't know where to look. Wiping the sweat from his forehead, he readied himself to press on. *I need to find Ostria fast.*

With determined steps, he led the way, pushing through the thick greenery once more. After struggling through the dense vegetation for some time, they finally came face to face with a steep mountain that promised shelter. Nestled in the rocky terrain was a large overhang with a weathered formation of coarse gray rock that stretched out like a protective arm extending from the cliff side.

"We should make camp here," Jacob said. "The overhang should keep us hidden for the night. Tomorrow we'll find a way up this mountain. So, relax while you can."

"Find a way, like … hike up the mountain?" Morgan groaned, slowly sinking to the ground, relieved to have finally stopped walking.

"Afraid so," Jacob replied, bending down to sit. He slumped against the mountain, working to catch his breath. "I don't like the idea any more than you do. But we need to reach higher ground if we're going to find Ostria. Or at least a sign of it."

"This should do," Ammon said, nodding as he scanned the area. "I'll go gather some firewood before nightfall."

"Thanks," Jacob said.

"I'll help," Alex said.

Ammon smiled. "All right, let's go."

As Ammon and Alex searched for firewood, Jacob and Morgan found a moment of respite under the overhang. Morgan remained on his back, while Jacob leaned against the rock face, observing the stone structure above them. Irregular patterns and crevices etched its weathered surface, reminding him of the Maws' cavern. *Better not collapse.*

"Do you think they'll find us here?" Morgan asked.

He glanced at the kid, who was nervously tapping his shoes together. He felt the same unease about the approaching night. There were no guarantees of safety here. Still, he knew he had to project confidence. He didn't want to lie to Morgan, but he wanted to reassure him, to make him feel as safe as possible.

"The overhang should keep us hidden," he said. "Just gonna be another night, like last night."

"But Wes snatched you last night."

He frowned, realizing very quickly he wasn't great at this. "Yeah, you're right. He did. But he's not worried about us anymore."

"Yeah, he's after that Michael guy," Morgan said, shaking his head with a grimace. "Ugh, he's one freaky-looking dude. Do you think Wes will find him?"

"I don't know. But something tells me he will."

"'Cause if he doesn't, then Michael's gonna burn down all of Eremos?"

"It's possible," Jacob said, his fingers drumming nervously against the ground. "The fire he started at the Maws' camp will definitely have spread in this heat. But we've got a good head start on it."

"Fire doesn't stop while we're sleeping."

Jacob's fingers tapped faster. "You're right again, kid."

"I learned in school that wildfires can spread at an average speed of, like, fifteen miles per hour. That's faster than most people can run."

Jacob's jaw tightened. "That doesn't sound promising."

"Do you think Daemion is still alive?"

"All right, kid, I get it," Jacob said, slapping his hand against the rock face, the sharp sound cutting through the air.

Morgan froze, his fidgeting feet suddenly still. "I'm sorry," he mumbled. "I've been told I ramble a lot and don't have a filter. It happens when I get nervous. And scared."

Jacob leaned his head back against the rock face with a soft thud. *Dammit, Jacob, he's just scared.* "You don't need to apologize," he said, his voice softer now. "We've been through a lot. If anything, I should be the one apologizing. I shouldn't have snapped. I guess … I'm just as scared as you are."

A tense silence lingered. Though Morgan unconsciously frayed Jacob's nerves, the kid had changed. Gone was the timid child he had first met, cowering behind his knees. Now, he was someone still hesitant, but beginning to open up, quietly shedding his reclusive nature bit by bit. Jacob felt a growing fondness for the kid, accompanied by an instinct to protect him. Yet the harsh truth gnawed at him: keeping Morgan safe on Eremos was a near-impossible task.

"I would've never guessed that," Jacob said, breaking the silence.

"What's that?"

"That people tell you that you ramble."

"Well, that's because I wasn't comfortable around you guys yet. But that's changing. I *am* scared. But I feel safe with you."

"I'm glad, kid."

"You never answered my question, though."

"What question?"

"About killing anyone. Have you ever killed someone before?"

Jacob frowned, recalling Morgan asking him the question in the pit. Right before Daemion came. *He may feel safe around me, but he still doesn't know me.* "I've done what I've had to do," he finally answered.

"That's such an *easy* answer."

"Well … it's a *hard* question."

"It's actually an *easy* question."

"If it's so *easy*, then you answer it."

Morgan went still. Jacob's fingers started tapping the ground again as he realized he'd just put the kid on the spot. But in fairness, so had Morgan. And Jacob didn't know Morgan any more than Morgan knew him. His gaze narrowed, curiosity tugging at his brain. *Why were you exiled, kid?*

"Fair enough," Morgan finally said. "I guess it's the answer that's hard."

A sudden snap of twigs and the distant sound of footsteps jerked Jacob's attention. Morgan scrambled to his feet, eyes widening. A flood of relief followed shortly after as Jacob saw Ammon and Alex emerging from the foliage, their arms laden with branches, laughter resonating between them.

"Hope we didn't scare ya," Ammon said, entering the overhang.

"Only a little," Morgan said.

"Well, next time we'll try harder," Alex said, smirking.

Ammon dropped the firewood onto the ground and started emptying his pockets, pulling out an assortment of leaves, grass, and sticks, and began rubbing them together. "We'll have a fire soon."

"Why are you rubbing them together?" Morgan asked.

"It's the tinder for the fire. It helps it catch quicker. At least, that's what Nell told me. My Aux." Ammon handed some to Morgan. "Here, give it a try."

"All right." With a furrowed brow, Morgan started rubbing the tinder together.

"Super easy, right? Now, want to help me make the fire?"

Morgan's eyes lit up. "Sure!"

"Cool, let's do it."

With Ammon's help, Morgan quickly kindled the fire. Flickering flames sprang to life, their warm glow spreading across the overhang. The crackle of kindling filled the air as the fire steadily grew, casting dancing shadows in its light.

"Holy shit, I can't believe I actually did it."

"Nice work," Ammon said, smiling.

Soon they were all sitting in a circle around the fire, a natural camaraderie taking root among them. The moment reminded him of his fireside times he'd shared with Charlotte on their beach. He longed to relive those memories with her, a yearning that cut deeper than the punctures in his shoulder.

Yet, as he reflected on the past year—spent mostly in solitude, hunting Charlotte's killer, and grappling with the events that led to his exile—he never imagined finding solace or connection again, let alone here.

I have nothing else to live for. His plea from *that* night resurfaced in his mind. Back then, he couldn't see it behind all his guilt, pain, anger, and hate. But now he could, and with the realization, a sense of hope.

"You guys up for a game or something?" Morgan asked.

"What, like a campfire game?" Alex asked.

Morgan shrugged. "Yeah, sure, a campfire game."

"Any favorites in mind?" Ammon asked.

"Nah, not really. I do know my way around a bunch of video games, though."

"I've got one," Jacob said. "Ever played Truth or Lie?"

"Nope, never heard of it," Morgan said, shaking his head.

"It's fun. Each one of us takes a turn sharing something about ourselves, and the rest of us have to guess if it's the truth or a lie." He paused, a bittersweet smile forming. "My wife and I used to play it before she ..."

His voice trailed off, a lump forming in his throat as the weight of Charlotte's death settled heavily on his shoulders. It took him by surprise; how easily the words had begun to flow out for him to these strangers, as if the act of sharing his loss brought a strange comfort. He rubbed his palm as tears brimmed in his eyes.

"I'm game," Ammon said, breaking the momentary stillness.

He glanced at Ammon, detecting an unspoken understanding in his eyes. After all, Ammon was the only one on Eremos, besides Wes now, who knew about Charlotte's death. It felt, in a way, as if Ammon were extending a hand to him in this emotional moment.

"Could be fun, I guess," Alex said.

"Cool, let's do it."

Jacob quickly wiped his eyes, trying to regain his composure. He could feel a flush creeping across his cheeks as he swallowed the lump in his throat. *Damn, I could use a drink*, he thought, feeling embarrassed.

"I'll go first," Ammon said. He rubbed his hands together in deep thought. "Okay, here's one. I can play the piano."

Jacob smiled as he exchanged intrigued glances with Alex and Morgan, eager to unravel the truth behind Ammon's claim. He could envision Ammon as someone who might have played the guitar with his outward rough appearance, but the piano? He couldn't see it.

"Nah, I'm calling lie," Alex said, narrowing her eyes toward Ammon.

Ammon, taking in the skepticism, playfully keyed an air piano, eliciting a chuckle out of Morgan. Alex frowned jokingly.

"I think it's true," Morgan said, watching Ammon's epic air piano performance. "I mean, like, look at him go."

"You know what that means?" Ammon asked, a lively tone in his voice as he cast a glance at Jacob. "Tiebreaker falls on you, man."

Jacob's smile widened. He was having fun, something he had forgotten he was capable of experiencing. "I'm gonna have to side with Alex on this one. I say lie."

Ammon grinned mischievously. "Crescendo, please," he said, jamming down on his imaginary piano. "It's … *true*."

"*Yes*," Morgan said, throwing his fist in the air in a grand gesture. "I knew it."

"No shot," Alex said, giving Ammon a good-natured push. "You're lying."

"It's true, I swear. My grandfather taught me when I was a kid."

"Yeah, I still can't see it," Jacob said.

"Oh, come on," Ammon sighed. "Kid, you go next."

"Okay, let me think," Morgan said, taking a moment to gather his thoughts.

"Careful now," Ammon said. "The audience is tough out there."

"Okay, I've got one," Morgan said, his eyes growing wide. "I know sign language."

"That's true," Ammon immediately said.

"Oh, definitely," Alex fired right after.

"I feel like that's true, too, kid," Jacob said.

"*Really?*" Morgan moaned. "How is it that obvious?" He signed a word that Jacob interpreted as a curse by the look on his face.

"Told you it was a tough crowd," Ammon said.

"Yeah, yeah," Morgan replied, rolling his eyes.

As the game progressed, and the sun dipped, the air seemed to lighten. With each round, the burdens of their circumstances and pasts momentarily lifted, and Jacob's perception began to shift. They were no longer just fellow exiles to him, but people with unique stories and experiences. Bonds were forming—fragile yet meaningful—offering strength and a sliver of hope. Maybe, just maybe, they could face the challenges ahead.

Together.

CHAPTER TWENTY-TWO

SEVEN MONTHS BEFORE EXILE

YOU HAVE ARRIVED at your destination, Sid announced. *Please exercise caution, Jacob. You're in a no-go zone.*

"Yeah, yeah," he said, rising from his seat.

Peering through the window of his Nervo Pod, he spotted a holographic sign beaming the word "Liberties" in bold, glowing letters. He stepped out, the cold air biting at his skin as a soft wind brushed against his face. *Winter's coming.*

He turned his head, scanning a dimly lit Nox Street, with streetlights casting an eerie glow on the empty sidewalks. He frowned, memories of last night's near-death incident flashing in his mind. A knot twisted in his stomach when his gaze fell on Storks. Those men had a method, a sinister system of trapping their prey. He could almost feel their presence now, lurking in the shadows, silently waiting for their next unsuspecting victim to step into the light.

How many others like me fell into their trap? How many died? And who will be their next victim?

Jacob would need to be more cautious moving forward. Hunting Charlotte's killer was bound to be dangerous, filled with life-threatening moments he couldn't afford to face recklessly. Fortunately, he already knew what he needed to ensure his safety.

He glanced over his shoulder toward Hoos. He hadn't dared to step inside since that night; until now. Like his customers, he needed something. That something was a gun.

Biting the insides of his cheek, he carried his dragging footsteps toward Hoos. At the entrance, he hesitated, his hand resting on the door handle. He closed his eyes, knowing that stepping inside would be like entering a nightmare—a nightmare he dreaded reliving. *Just be in and out.*

Drawing a deep breath, he steadied himself and then unlocked the door and entered. The jingling bell announced his entry, triggering memories of when the intruders had barged in. Opening his eyes, he tried banishing the memory, only to be greeted by a reality that was no better. He saw the cracked display case, the image of Mason's lifeless eyes flashing in his mind. He looked away and hastily started toward the front counter and stepped behind it.

With his head down, he pressed on toward the purpose that brought him here. And there it was—the blue pistol in its glass case. The one he had built with his father. The same one Mason had coveted and Jacob had refused to give him.

The very decision that had cost Charlotte her life.

Reaching the display shelf, he removed the gun from its case and gripped it tightly. His fingers traced the smooth metal, pausing on tiny spots of rust. The firearm had changed over the years, slowly decaying, just like Jacob himself. It seemed to dare him to use it in a way he had never considered before.

I will find you, he vowed, his fingers turning white as he squeezed the grip. *I don't care if it kills me.*

Placing the gun onto the counter, he reached for the boxes of ammunition from the wooden crates above. Opening one, he spilled the bullets onto the glass in a metallic cascade. Then he grabbed the gun, ejected the magazine, and started loading the bullets one by one. Once fully loaded, he pulled the slide back, chambering a round, the sharp *click* fueling his thirst for revenge.

As he lifted his head, his eyes caught sight of a dark stain on the counter. Charlotte's blood. It was now ingrained into the speck of grime, an indelible mark of that horrific night. Her grimaced face flashed before him, followed by the clutching of her stomach. He watched her fall, her bloodied hand sliding down the glass as she collapsed. A harsh reminder of his failure to protect her.

Unable to bear the sight any longer, he shuffled toward the exit. His hand reached for the door, but his steps faltered. He pivoted on his heel, his gaze sweeping over Hoos one last time. The voicemail from Woodwin Realty lingered in his thoughts. Hoos wasn't just a business; it was his life, his purpose, his father's legacy. Selling it felt inherently wrong, a betrayal of everything he stood for.

Yet, as he gazed at the shattered remnants of that tragic night, he realized Hoos had become tainted. To persist in the wake of Charlotte's and his father's fates would be a greater betrayal than selling it. He knew this yet wasn't sure he was ready to accept it. For now, he turned and stepped out of Hoos, the bell's jingle announcing his departure.

"*Get away from me!*" a woman cried.

Jacob whipped his gaze down Nox Street, his eyes widening at the sight of two hooded figures attacking a woman. The same spot he had been ambushed the night before.

Without thinking, he burst into a sprint, his breath misting in the cool air, the pistol gripped tightly in his hand. He wasn't sure what compelled him, but he knew one thing: *Something has to be done.*

Ahead, the larger of the two figures shoved the woman deeper into the side alleyway, their forms disappearing into the shadows. Jacob's heart pounded as he pushed his legs harder, his determination drowning out the biting chill of the night.

Reaching the edge of the alley, he raised his gun and leveled it at the thugs. Lights along the brick walls illuminated the space in intervals, casting deep pockets of darkness where the glow ended. And there, sprawled on the ground, was a woman. The larger thug loomed over her, while the thinner one kneeled near her head, tightly restraining her hands.

"*Get off her!*" Jacob demanded.

The attackers snapped their gazes toward Jacob. "Shit," one of them grunted.

"I said, get the hell off her. *Now.* Let's go."

Slowly, both men stood, their hands raised in surrender as they stepped away from the woman. She scrambled to her feet, her disheveled red hair framing a face streaked with makeup and tears. Her clothes were torn from the struggle, and her wide, terrified eyes now glimmered with relief.

"Thank you," she stammered.

"Go," Jacob urged, motioning his head toward the alley's exit. "Hurry."

She nodded quickly and bolted past him, her footsteps fading into the distance. Jacob didn't move as he kept his gun trained on the two thugs.

"You guys are sick," he said. "Attacking innocent people. You're the reason the world's a mess."

"Hey, it's the guy from last night," the lean one said, snorting. His hoodie hung low on his wiry frame, and an involuntary jitter ran through his body, one Jacob couldn't solely attribute to the cold.

"I know," the other one calmly replied. His burly frame confirmed he was the one Jacob had punched. "Come back to kill us?"

Jacob tightened his grip on the gun, alternating its aim between the two of them. *What am I doing?* He'd only wanted to ensure the woman didn't get hurt. But she was gone now. He could leave. He *should* leave. But … *What if they know something?*

"Maybe," he finally said. "Unless … either of you can tell me anything you might know about the Hoos robbery."

"Hoos? You talking about the robbery that killed that girl?"

"We had nothing to do with that."

The wiry man's eyes darted nervously. "He's right. We *swear.*"

"Wait. You're him. The owner. Her husband. Jacob, right?"

Jacob froze, his heart racing. *Shit, they know who I am.* The situation was slipping out of his control. His legs tensed, urging him to run, be he didn't. He needed a lead, something to keep him going.

"I'm trying to find her killer," he said.

"Well, we don't know shit," the burly thug said. "And even if we did, we wouldn't risk telling you. Now hurry off, because we all know you aren't gonna shoot us. Doing so would just trigger all our Auxes and alert the Cullers."

"They're probably already on the way," Jacob said, trying to sound confident.

"Doubt it," the other one said, chuckling darkly. "Your Aux. It's programmed to sense danger. Increased pulse and heart rate, right? Don't you think it would've picked up on your actions, considering you ran over her with a gun in hand? Yet … it's *silent*."

"Now, if you *shoot*, then your Aux is programmed to signal the Cullers. And I'm betting you don't want them catching you shooting us."

Jacob hadn't realized it, but the men were right. Sid hadn't reacted to his racing pulse or his elevated heartbeat as he sprinted over. But Sid *had* responded last night. *Did these guys have jammers now? Were they Last Patriots?* It was too dark to check for any star tattoos.

"Auxes are always listening, yet when committing a crime, they're ever so silent. Want to guess why?"

"You've got a jammer," Jacob said.

"Jammer? That shit don't work. Everyone knows the council's Control Hubs prevent that."

"It's 'cause the council *wants* us committing crimes. More crimes means more no-go zones. That way, they control what we all think. Keeps us scared and needing them."

"Yeah, no-go zones aren't just for protecting. They're all about control."

"Bullshit," Jacob said. "My Aux alerted the Cullers last night when you attacked me."

"That's 'cause you were the victim. Now, you're not. Now you're on the brink of committing a crime. Your Aux knows that. It could alert the Cullers right now, but it doesn't. It waits until the victim alerts it. Then the Cullers respond based on their social score."

You're lucky I was patrolling this area. The Culler's words from last night crept into Jacob's mind. *Shit, were they* actually *right?*

"Go ahead," the lean thug said. "Try it. Speak to your Aux."

Jacob bit his lip, fingers fidgeting around the pistol. *No, these guys are just trying to confuse me. The council wouldn't allow that.*

"It won't matter," he said. "I doubt the Cullers will be here as fast as they were last night. I bet your social scores aren't high enough for them to make you a priority. It's why you use a knife. The council won't grant you a gun."

"Fuck you," the burly thug barked, scowling. "We're trying to *survive* out here. We do what we *have* to do. It's all a means of ensuring us another day. Not everyone has it as good as you."

"That doesn't justify your actions."

"Says the man who's pointing a gun at us?"

"I was stopping you from hurting that woman."

"And you *did*. Yet you're still here."

"We were never going to hurt her—"

"That's because I'm trying to find the man who *murdered* my wife."

"Well, you're not going to find him here, man," the lean thug said, scoffing. "We had nothing to do with that. You said it yourself. We're using knives. If either of us were the man who killed your wife, we'd probably be using the guns we robbed from you."

Shit, he's got a point. But then again, they could've just sold them to the Last Patriots.

"You know, you ought to be more careful moving forward," the burly thug said, smirking. "You wouldn't want to risk getting exiled. Not gonna find your man while stranded on an island."

The other thug laughed. "Yeah, unless the dude *was* exiled."

"True. People be getting exiled every day. You could be looking for a dead man."

Jacob shook his head, dismissing the thought of her killer being exiled. His plan to gather information about that night was failing. These men seemed oblivious. But he was desperate. He needed something. Anything.

"What if I pay you?" he asked. "You said you're trying to survive, right? You tell me what you know about that night, and I'll pay you both."

Both men exchanged glances, silently weighing his offer. The dim light stressed their wrinkled foreheads, uncertain of how to move forward, as if caught between the prospect of immediate gain and the risks of betrayal.

"How much we talking here?" the larger one asked, breaking the silence.

"Depends on the importance of your information."

"Yeah, I don't know. That shit's above us. And we're not gonna ruin our primary source of income for some petty cash."

Petty cash? "What the hell does that mean?"

"It means there's bigger shit at play here. Derro isn't the only one profiting off crime. We're just pawns."

"So, what, Hoos getting robbed had something to do with the Last Patriots?"

"Last Patriots? You think *they're* responsible?"

"I don't know. One of her killers had ties with them. Mason. Mason Rowley. You guys know him?"

"Never heard of him."

"Yeah, me neither. We aren't the only criminals in Tuto, dude."

"Listen, man, I'll be straight with you, 'cause I can tell you're grasping at straws here," the burly thug said. "The Last Patriots are a *movement*. They see themselves as the last defenders of a faded era. Trying to bring back a government that truly represents the people, whatever the hell that means. That sound like someone who wants to rob a gun store and take an innocent life?"

"They're a rebellion," Jacob said. "And for a rebellion to be effective, they'll need to be armed. That's why they were after the guns. They're made up of people who can't get them. Like you."

"Maybe, but I doubt it, dude. This Mason guy. He have a star tattoo on his wrist?"

"No, but—"

"Well, there you go. The star tattoo's supposed to be the mark of a Last Patriot. Stars for the old states of America, only now they stand for the people." The wiry thug held out his wrist, revealing bare skin. "See? No star here. And if this Mason guy didn't have one either, he was definitely no Last Patriot. They don't just let anyone in."

"He's right. I've also heard rumors that they've crept themselves into key positions within the Derro government. Trying to dismantle the council's control from within. Not rob a gun store."

"There's always a use for a pawn," Jacob said. "That's what you called yourself earlier, isn't it?"

The burly thug scowled. "We're not the pawns you're looking for."

As much as Jacob didn't want to believe them, he couldn't deny their logic. What if Mason wasn't working with the Last Patriots? And if that were true, then what were his plans for the guns? And what was the other job her killer had mentioned that night? The unanswered questions swirled in his mind.

Even worse, there was a chance, just as these men joked, that her killer had been exiled. He could have been involved in another crime, arrested, and then put on a one-way Screech to one of the many council's islands. The more Jacob uncovered, the further her killer seemed beyond his reach. Yet he refused to accept that as a possibility.

"There, we gave you some shit. So how about that pay?"

Jacob, feeling defeated, lowered his aim, turned, and walked out of the alley. Disappointment weighed him down as he realized once again, he was still no closer to finding *him*. *This must be how Ezra feels. And he has multiple investigations to pursue.*

"Hey, you said you'd pay us!"

"You said it wasn't worth it," Jacob fired back as he turned down Nox Street. "Besides, if it's such a profitable venture, why not just commit another crime?"

He started toward Liberties. After what he had just gone through, he needed a drink. The encounter had left a bitter taste in his mouth, one he looked forward to washing down. And despite the unsettling turn of events, or perhaps because of it, he remained resolute. *I will find him. Even if it means getting exiled.*

Stepping into Liberties, its door screeching his arrival, he hurried over to his corner and slid into the booth where he planned to continue watching every patron enter.

"Sid, the usual."

Right away, Jacob.

Jacob frowned. *Still here, I guess.* He licked his lips, eager to drink so he could forget about what had just happened. Yet, as the night went on, those two men lingered in his thoughts. It was people like them he and his father had sought to protect others from by selling guns. The notion brought a sobering realization over him as he contemplated the path ahead—a path that would almost certainly end with him pulling the trigger.

Without his gun, he might have been more inclined to leave the pursuit of justice to Ezra and the Cullers. But unfortunately, he had a gun, just like the countless others who had purchased one from him. Each firearm held the power to shape fates, for better or worse. Including his own. *And that's where the real power lies …*

As the weight of this understanding settled, clarity emerged. He was ready. Despite the sentimental burden of ending his father's legacy, he knew it was time to move on. Selling guns would never feel the same again.

People do *kill people. And I refuse to enable them.*

CHAPTER TWENTY-THREE
DAY FIVE OF EXILE

AFTER ANOTHER RESTLESS night spent on the unforgiving ground, the next day's journey began with Jacob's muscles screaming. In his prime, he could have handled this trek effortlessly. Hiking had always been a common escape for Charlotte, venturing with her camera, searching for beauty in a dark world, and Jacob had always been able to keep up.

Now, not so much. After a long year of immersing himself in little but the solace of whiskey, neglecting exercise, and now enduring scarce food, water, and a painful bite, his body felt on the verge of collapse.

He winced. The mountain's steep slope had proven unrelenting. Every step he climbed was a struggle, often requiring him to dig his hands into the earth and crawl his way up. Beads of sweat rolled down his face, stinging his eyes, and parching his tongue as he battled through another scorching day on Eremos.

Fortunately, he had felt no chills, but with every ache of his bones and pulse from his bite, he feared the impending fever. It didn't help that he was also fighting an empty stomach and dehydration. The fish remnants from yesterday morning had faded away, and since leaving the stream, they had yet to encounter another fresh water source.

I have to keep moving. Digging his hands deeper into the earth, he pressed forward, fueled by the determination to reach Ostria. After a while, his steps faltered, and his nose wrinkled at a pungent scent. He stood upright, gazing across Eremos's expanse, where he saw a dark cloud of smoke billowing into the air. The inferno was encroaching.

"Uh, guys, do you smell that?" Morgan asked from up ahead.

"It's the fire," Jacob said. "We have to keep moving and get up this mountain."

"It's definitely spreading," Alex said, shielding her eyes from the sun as she gazed at the inferno in the distance.

"It's still pretty far," Jacob said. "But it won't be for long."

"He's right," Morgan said. "I learned that smoke can travel hundreds of miles from an active fire."

"We'd better hurry then," Ammon said.

Drawing a deep breath, Jacob pressed on. As he climbed, the scent slowly intensified, its acrid odor stinging his eyes and nose. The surrounding air grew hazy, making it even more of a struggle to breathe, and eventually, tiny flakes of ash drifted by like dark confetti. From up here, he could hear the distant snapping and occasional roars of the fire echoing in the distance, heightening his urgency.

As he crawled, he hugged the mountain, following the safest route upward. When possible, he clutched tree roots protruding from the side of the mountain, using them to pull himself up. When the slope steepened, it forced him to rely more on his fellow exiles for help. Ammon, leading the way, would reach downward to pull them up when needed, and Jacob, positioned at the bottom, offered gentle pushes to propel them forward as they all stumbled and slid.

Finally, after what felt like an eternity in hell, the rugged terrain beneath them leveled. Gasping for breath, he emerged onto a plateau filled with thick vegetation and towering trees. His face softened at the instant relief he felt seeing the flat expanse, yet his aching muscles continued their protest. From this high, the distant roar of the inferno was quieter now, the scent of the wildfire still lingering, though much less intensely, filling him with the hopeful thought the threat was diminishing. However, the sight down below, where ash settled on the ground like a somber blanket, covering the terrain with a layer of darkened flakes, only diminished that hope.

With a heaving chest, he gathered with the others, taking stock of their surroundings. A burned-orange sun hid behind a smoky sky, casting an eerie hue over the landscape. It hung just above the horizon in the west, indicating it was late afternoon. They'd hiked almost all day.

"We made it," Ammon said, still catching his breath.

"We'll need to keep moving, though," Jacob said, wiping sweat from his forehead. "It'll be dark soon, and it's hard to tell how fast that fire is spreading. Hopefully the mountain will slow it down, but our biggest priority should be finding shelter and water."

"Hate to say it, but unlike humans, fires actually travel uphill much faster than downhill," Morgan said.

Alex frowned. "Thanks for that, kid."

"Any idea where we go from here?" Ammon asked.

Jacob scanned the horizon, squinting through the haze. "Hard to tell from here, but if we keep moving ahead of the fire, the air might clear a bit, and we should be able to get our bearings." He pointed toward a ridge in the distance. "Let's head that way. Ostria was surrounded by cliffs. It could be over that ridge."

Alex groaned. "Fuck me, that seems far."

"If it seems far, it's most likely farther," Morgan said. "Our eyes actually—"

"Okay, we get it," Alex said.

"Jacob's right," Ammon said. "Let's head towards the ridge until we find proper shelter."

A series of groans followed as they resumed their journey. Jacob swept his arms through the tall grasses, pushing aside the invasive greenery, his skin itching with every movement. After a while, his steps grew increasingly labored. He noticed the others exchanging concerned glances, their eyes lingering on the pallor of his face, which betrayed the pain he was trying to conceal.

"Let's stop for the night," Ammon said. "It's getting harder to see with night so close, and we've yet to find proper shelter. The tall grass should keep us hidden and offer a nice break from sleeping on the ground."

"Not here," Jacob said. "It's too open."

"There's no guarantee we'll find anything better," Alex said.

"Plus, you're really not looking so great," Morgan said. "Worse, actually."

"It's the infection," Alex said. "How's your temp? Are you cold?"

"I'm fine. And I refuse to be the reason we risk our safety by not finding a better shelter or water. So, can we please keep moving?"

He saw a collective shaking of heads as he pressed forward. He knew the others likely thought he was being bitter, but stopping wasn't an option. If he slept, he feared he might not wake up. His condition was worsening, his vision growing hazier by the minute. Still, he could make out the distant ridge silhouetted against the darkening orange sky, where the setting sun burned like a red orb.

"Hold it right there!"

Jacob jolted, his limbs tensing at the sight of figures emerging from the tall grass around them. He frowned, biting his cheeks. *Not again.*

Through his blurred vision, he could see men and women clad in weather-worn clothing and balaclava masks fashioned from shirts. Each of them bore makeshift weapons, such as sharp sticks or clubs. He tried to speak but was too weak.

"Whoa, there," Ammon called out, his hands raised. "We mean no harm."

"What are you doing in Last Patriot territory?" one of them asked.

Last Patriot? Jacob repeated in his head, wondering if he'd heard the man correctly.

"We were just passing through," Alex quickly replied. "Trying to find Ostria."

The group erupted in a chorus of laughter. "Ostria?" someone sneered. "Trying to find safety, are ya? Well, good luck. The council doesn't just let anyone in."

Council? The word echoed faintly in his mind, distant and hollow. His vision grew blurrier, his body swaying as he struggled to stay upright. The edges of his consciousnesses darkened, threatening to close in.

"Wait, did you say Last Patriot?" Ammon asked.

"Yeah, you deaf or something?"

"No, it's just that … *I'm* a Last Patriot."

"Show me your mark."

Jacob glanced at Ammon, his balance slipping from under him, and pieced together what looked like Ammon sticking his wrist out toward the figures—*the Last Patriots?* He tried speaking again, but before any words could escape his lips, his strength finally gave way, and he crumpled to the ground, unconscious.

And then he saw her—Charlotte.

She was sitting on a peaceful beach. *Their* beach. She fixed her gaze on the endless expanse of the ocean, the soft breeze gently dancing in her hair. Turning, she glanced over her shoulder and smiled. His heart fluttered. Her face … so beautiful.

"Come on, *you*," she called, waving him toward her.

Drawn by the pull of her presence, he started toward her. He could feel the warmth of the sun on his skin and the soft sand between his toes. It felt … almost … real. *Is it really her?*

With cautious steps, he approached her, his heart thundering in his chest. As he drew closer, her form became clearer, her presence almost tangible. A smile broke across his face, tears of joy welling in his eyes as he reached out a trembling hand to touch her. But the moment his fingers brushed against her shoulder, she vanished, and Jacob's eyes snapped open.

CHAPTER TWENTY-FOUR

SEVEN MONTHS BEFORE EXILE

THE SUN POURED through the floor-to-ceiling windows, rousing Jacob from his slumber. With a groan, he shifted in bed, feeling the familiar ache in his muscles and the dryness in his mouth that had become his constant companions since Charlotte's death.

He dragged himself upright and sat at the bed's edge. Rubbing his eyes with the heels of his palms, he tried to relieve his throbbing headache. Drawing a deep breath, his mind wandered to last night, where he had held those thugs at gunpoint, searching for answers, only to come home with nothing. Another day loomed ahead, filled with the same relentless search.

Good morning, Jacob.

"Hey Sid," he murmured, stretching his arms.

Steve and Nancy attempted to reach you earlier this morning. Would you like to call them back?

He sighed, letting his arms fall back to his side. His gaze landed on his nightstand, where the remnants of last night's whiskey pulled at him. Reaching for the glass, he grabbed it and drained what remained in one large gulp, savoring the burn.

"Not right now, Sid."

May I suggest a reminder for this evening? Sid persisted gently. *They have been reaching out since the funeral, and they may provide you with some comfort.*

"It's just too hard. Can you just handle the call for me?"

I can initiate a Clone Call on your behalf. Are you giving consent for this?

"Yes. Just let them know I'm managing and that there have been no updates on Charlotte's case. You can fill in the rest as needed."

Understood, Jacob. Starting Clone Call now.

As Sid called Steve and Nancy, Jacob stood and headed toward the bathroom to take a shower. Just as he stepped inside, a sharp knock at the front door froze him in place. *Who could that be?*

Then his stomach plummeted as an icy shiver crawled down his spine. *You're him. The owner. Her husband. Jacob, right?* The thug's words crept into his mind. Those men had figured out who he was. *Did they find where I live?*

Starting toward the front door, he bit the insides of his cheeks, hoping he was just being paranoid. *It's probably just Ezra.*

Upon reaching the door, he peered through the peephole, relieved to find it was, in fact, Ezra. Only this time, he wasn't alone. A woman Jacob didn't recognize stood next to him. He swung the door open, desperately hoping they were here with an update.

"Jacob, good afternoon," Ezra greeted. "This is Commander Brody. She's replaced Wes. Can we come in?"

Jacob, momentarily taken aback, regarded the commander. Strands of silver streaked her black hair, which was pulled tightly into a bun. Her face bore the perpetual hardness of someone accustomed to scowling, and her piercing eyes locked onto him, unrelenting, as though she was scrutinizing his every move.

"Yes," he finally said, stepping aside.

He led the Seeker and Culler to the living room, his mind swirling. Upon entering, he extended his arms toward two chairs, in which Ezra and Commander Brody sat. Jacob followed suit, sitting on the couch in front of them.

"Late night?" Commander Brody asked, noticing Jacob still in his pajamas.

"Um, yeah," he said, his guard suddenly going up. "Please tell me you have an update."

"Jacob, this isn't going to be an easy conversation," Ezra said gently. "Unfortunately, we're not here regarding your case."

"What do you mean?"

"We're—"

"We're here to discuss what happened last night," Commander Brody cut in.

Last night? Shit, they know. "Are you referring to me saving that woman?"

"Yes," Ezra said, nodding. "Can you tell us what happened?"

Jacob blinked rapidly, stuck in a state of confusion. "I don't understand. Am I in trouble here?"

"No, we—"

"We simply need your account of events," Commander Brody interjected.

"I *saved* that woman. What else is there you need to know?"

"We know you saved her," Ezra said, leaning forward. "She came into the station this morning and explained everything. Your actions were heroic."

I'm no hero.

"But that's not why we are here," Commander Brody said. "We're here because of what happened after that. Those men you saved that woman from. They were found dead under a bridge a few hours ago."

"Dead?" Jacob repeated, head jerking back.

"An ironic turn of events, considering we have footage of you holding them at gunpoint."

"Well, I certainly had nothing to do with it, if that's what you're implying."

"We're not saying you did," Ezra said, raising a calming hand. "But as you know, we're required to investigate every lead. And you may have been the last person to see them alive."

Ezra grabbed his stylus and activated his holographic tablet, his movements deliberate and measured, just as they had been during that morning, when he had interviewed Jacob. But now, the air felt heavier—different—and Jacob couldn't shake the feeling that this wasn't a simple conversation anymore. It was an interrogation.

"If you could please tell us more about your encounter, it may help us identify who killed them," Ezra continued. "Then we'll be on our way. Alpha start recording."

Jacob regarded Ezra, sensing the truth in his words. He could tell Ezra didn't want to be here anymore than Jacob wanted them here. Ezra had an obligation to find Charlotte's killer, but as he'd said, they were required to investigate every lead.

This lead, however, felt driven more by Commander Brody. The Culler's sharp eyes locked onto Jacob, studying him with unnerving intensity. It was as if she were dissecting his every move and every word with the precision of a human lie detector.

"We have footage of you exiting your Nervo Pod and then entering your gun store before the altercation," she said. "Why don't you start from there?"

Shit, the gun.

His palms started to sweat. The footage they had would have shown him leaving Hoos with the gun. Ezra and the commander both knew this. It didn't prove he was responsible for their deaths. But it was suspicious. And it hinted at him needing the gun for something. He slowly rubbed his palms down his thighs, drying them as he reclined into the couch.

"I was headed to Liberties after spending the day at the beach. Charlotte and I … we have a beach we frequent, and I wanted to feel closer to her. I've been considering the idea of selling Hoos. After what happened, I haven't been able to find a reason, other than continuing with my father's legacy, to step back inside. Going to the beach was my way of clearing my head."

Commander Brody grunted. "I'm sorry for your loss. I know it must be difficult. But rest assured, we're still working on your case." She leaned back, crossing one leg over the other. "It seems that since her death, you've been frequenting Liberties almost every night. Care to explain why?"

Jacob glanced at Ezra, knowing there was no secret between them about why he'd been going to Liberties every night. It all traced back to the update Ezra had given him a few months ago. *Shit, grabbing that gun now only makes me look more suspicious.*

"To drink," he said. "To be around other people. Helps me deal with my pain. Blocks out all the negative voices in my head."

"Is that also why you got that gun from Hoos?"

Jacob's eyes bulged, surprised by Commander Brody's bluntness. "What the fuck is that supposed to mean?"

"It's a valid concern, don't you think? After what happened with your—"

"What the commander means to ask," Ezra cut in calmly, "is why you grabbed the gun?"

Jacob clenched his fingers in his palms. *Fucking Cullers are all the same, I swear.*

"Like I said before, I've been considering selling Hoos, and after thinking about it all day at the beach, I decided to move forward with it. I'd planned to call Woodwin Realty and start the process. I grabbed the gun only because it's an heirloom. My father and I built it when I was a kid. It's all I wanted from Hoos before I sold it."

"I see," Commander Brody said, her eyes growing distant. "If I recall, this is the same gun Mason wanted, yes? Not much of an heirloom anymore, I'd say. Not after what happened to your wife … and your father."

"*That's enough,*" Jacob barked, shooting to his feet. "This good Seeker/bad Culler tactic is pissing me off. I didn't kill those thugs. Now, unless I'm under arrest, I'm asking you to leave."

"I'm afraid that's not possible," Commander Brody said. "We have more questions to ask. Would you like to do that here or at the station?"

Jacob scowled, rage simmering inside of him. He glanced toward Ezra, who had a painful look on his face, as if he shared Jacob's negative feelings.

"Jacob," he said softly, "you're not under arrest. Just let us ask our questions, and then we'll be on our way."

Jacob jabbed a finger at Ezra and bared his teeth. "You should be hunting for her killer," he gritted. "Not interrogating me for the deaths of thugs." He slowly sat back on the couch, knowing he had no other choice. "They deserved what they got for what they did to *me* and that woman. And every other person they've attacked."

Ezra furrowed a brow. "What did they do to you?"

"They attacked me, too. The night before. I had drank too much at Liberties and decided to walk it off. That's when they attacked me. They were going to stab me, but luckily a Culler showed up. So, they ran.

"And don't even think about asking if that's why I held them at gunpoint," he said, shifting his attention to Commander Brody. "Me entering Hoos to grab my gun, and those men attacking that woman, were merely coincidence. I just didn't want what happened to my wife to happen to her."

"So, why continue to hold them at gunpoint?" she probed. "The woman had left. But you stayed."

Jacob glanced at Ezra, their eyes meeting briefly. Ezra wasn't a fool. He knew without a doubt why Jacob had been going to Liberties every night. Commander Brody, knowing about his case, probably just as well connected the dots. But they needed to hear it from him.

"I asked them if they knew anything about why Hoos was robbed. It's been months, and you've given me no updates. Figured they might know something that I could tell you guys to help. But they didn't. I went to Liberties afterwards, as I'm sure you saw."

"We do have footage of you leaving and entering Liberties, as well as you leaving later that night," Ezra said, pausing from his notes. "You sure you learned nothing new?"

"Or maybe he did," Commander Brody said, smirking. "Maybe he found out that one of them was who we'd been looking for. The man who shot his wife. So, he let them go and went into Liberties. That way, he could have an alibi for their deaths."

"I didn't kill them. And they're not *him*. My wife's killer is still out there."

"You understand taking justice into your own hands is punishable by means of exile, don't you?" Commander Brody continued. "The council places great emphasis on delivering justice. It's why they demoted Wes to exile duty. So, I'd tread lightly if I were you. Otherwise, you may be seeing him soon."

Jacob scrunched his nose. "Are we done here?"

"Yes, we're done," she said, standing up. "We'll let you get back to your day, with selling Hoos and all. It's a shame it's come to that."

Ezra stood as well, offering Jacob a nod. "I'll let you know if we find any updates on Char's case. If you think of anything else that happened that night, please let me know."

Char? Jacob met Ezra's gaze, sensing a deliberate choice in the name. He read between the lines, interpreting it as Ezra's way of emphasizing Charlotte's importance to him. But there was also a hidden understanding, as if Ezra knew Jacob would continue his pursuit and silently wanted to offer his support.

"I will," Jacob said.

"Why the name Hoos?" Commander Brody asked, standing at the threshold of the living room, her gaze scanning the pictures Charlotte had taken. "Just seems like an odd name for a gun store."

He frowned, remembering his father's reasoning. "It's a homophone of our last name. *Hughes* and *Hoos*. My father had a unique sense of humor. And he thought it would bring favor from the council."

"Interesting," the commander said, nodding thoughtfully, her eyes lingering on a picture. "And a shame. Family business having to end." She tore her gaze away from the picture and turned to Jacob. "One less thing for you to worry about, though. And I'm sure Woodwin Realty will get you a substantial amount for it, even with it being in a no-go zone."

"Best of luck with that," Ezra said. "I know it'll be hard to let go."

"Thanks."

"I'll be in touch."

Jacob watched them both depart, feeling troubled. *Who killed those thugs last night?* The commander wanted it to be him, but Ezra knew he hadn't, and that brought him some inner peace. Yet it wasn't so much the question of *who* killed them that troubled him. It was the *why.*

Jacob, I've completed your Clone Call request, Sid informed.

"Thanks, Sid," he replied absentmindedly. Then he frowned, realizing that, amid his exchange with Ezra and Commander Brody, another conversation had taken place: his Clone Call with Steve and Nancy. "How'd it go?"

They miss you and are worried about you, Sid answered. *But like you, they are managing.*

Jacob's frown deepened. *We all seem to be.*

CHAPTER TWENTY-FIVE

DAY SIX OF EXILE

JACOB'S EYES SNAPPED open, his vision revealing an unfamiliar setting. It wasn't the beach with Charlotte that he had been dreaming of, but somewhere different. *Was that even a dream? A vision? Sid, somehow?* He still wasn't sure. But one thing he knew for certain: it had felt almost … real.

Groaning, he surveyed the room. A burned-orange sunlight filtered through the narrow gaps in the walls, casting a soft, eerie glow over the interior. He found himself in a makeshift hut constructed from bamboo, far more sophisticated than anything he had seen at the Maws' camp.

How long have I been out?

Then it all came rushing back. They had been ambushed. *What are you doing in Last Patriot territory?* Words he'd heard before passing out. *Am I in their camp?*

Carefully rising from the coarse cot, he winced as a sharp pain shot through his shoulder upon straightening. He quickly put his hand to his bite and was surprised to see the wound wrapped in what looked like clothing scraps. The makeshift bandage, though rough and frayed at the edges, filled him with relief. With cautious fingers, he started to peel away the cloth, but before he could inspect it further, the door to the hut swung open.

"Well, *don't touch it*," a feeble woman's voice said. Her lip curled in disapproval as she entered the room. "You'll damage my dressing."

My dressing? "You did this?"

"Yes," the woman said, wiping her sweaty face with the sleeve of her tattered shirt as she picked up a large bowl at the table across from him. She carried it over and placed it on the ground before sitting next to Jacob. Inside the bowl, he glimpsed water. Lots of it. His eyes bulged at the sight.

"Consider yourself lucky," she said, dipping a smaller bowl into the larger bowl of water. "I was beginning to doubt my treatment." She offered the bowl to him. "Drink. It's clean."

He cautiously accepted the bowl, giving it a quick sniff before downing the water. With each swallow, the primal urge to quench his thirst overwhelmed him until he drained the bowl, leaving his lungs gasping for air.

"You stopped the infection?" he asked between breaths.

"Hard to know for certain," she said, dipping another clothing scrap into the water. Then she wrung it out, droplets of water cascading on the ground. "But you waking is a good sign. Your friends mentioned the bite happened a few nights ago. Is that right?"

"I'm not sure," he said, handing her back the empty bowl. She grabbed it and filled it with more water. "I guess that depends on how long I was unconscious."

"Since last night," she said, returning the bowl of water to him. "You've been out all night and most of today. Sun will set soon."

"Then yes, a few nights sound about right." Jacob took another drink of water. "My friends, are they okay?"

The woman smiled. "They're fine but also worried about you. The young one …." Her voice trailed off, as if she were trying to remember his name.

"Morgan."

"Yes, Morgan, that's it. Sweet kid. Reminds me of my son when he was that age." Her smile widened. "He kept checking in on you."

Jacob smiled at the thought as he took another drink of water. "Where is he?"

"Settling in with your friends. You'll see them soon."

"And your son?" Jacob asked, wondering if she had him on Eremos. "Is he … here?"

The woman jerked her weathered eyes toward him, the question catching her off guard. After a brief silence, she frowned. "Not here. Unfortunately."

"I'm sorry," Jacob said, fearing he had just opened a wound.

"Let's look at your bite," she said, brushing off his apology. "I'm hopeful we caught it before it became too infected."

With gentle hands, she unwrapped the dressing, and to Jacob's relief, the sight was far better than he expected. His skin, once inflamed, now appeared clean around the newly stitched punctures, and the redness and swelling had noticeably subsided.

"It definitely looks better," the woman said as she dabbed at the wound with a wet clothing scrap.

Jacob winced at her touch. "It does. Thank you."

"You're welcome. Name's Jaci by the way."

"Jacob," he introduced. "So, Jaci … would you mind telling me exactly where I am?"

"You're in the Last Patriots settlement."

"I thought that's what I heard before I passed out. I just can't seem to escape those guys."

"Yeah, kind of ironic, isn't it? The Derro Council exiled all of them to Eremos, trying to quell their rebellion in Derro, and now they live here. Almost as if getting exiled was part of their plan."

Them? Their rebellion? Their plan? Jacob's eyes narrowed at Jaci. She seemed to speak as if she wasn't a Last Patriot. *But why?* And was she right? Was getting exiled part of their plan? Or was it simply a fallback for those who were captured? That made the most sense, considering what they did to Derro's Control Hubs.

"It didn't happen all at once, but over time, they were able to create this settlement. It's not much, but it's a foundation on which a new nation could be built. Or at least, that's what Myla promises."

"Who's Myla?" Jacob asked, the name pulling him from his thoughts.

"She's the one in charge around here. The president, as she likes to be called." Jaci rolled her eyes. "You know, 'cause the Last Patriots stick to the old values of the US."

"You continue to speak as if you're not one of them."

Jaci paused from nursing his bite. "Well, that's because I'm *technically* not," she said, standing up and making her way to the table across from them. As she did, Jacob watched with interest.

"Then why are you here?" he asked.

Jaci frowned as she turned from the table and returned next to him, another bowl in her hand. "I'm here because I was exiled," she said. "But not for being a Last Patriot. I've just been fortunate enough to earn my place here. Help is hard to find on Eremos, as are safe havens. But you're well aware of that."

Jacob nodded solemnly. His exile had felt like the hardest struggle of his life. But, then again, so had the last year in Derro. Enduring the loss of Charlotte. Hunting down her killer.

The pursuit that had led him here.

"Then again," Jacob said, "as my father would always tell me, 'You are the company you keep.' So, in a way, I am a Last Patriot. Guilty by association. Guess that's what exile demanded of me."

"I know that feeling," Jacob said. "The urge to change who you are, just to survive another day."

Jaci scoffed. "And you just got here," she said, smirking.

"Fair enough."

"I know your exile hasn't been the easiest, though. Your friends have told us quite the story. They paint you as a hero."

"I'm no hero. More of a teamwork effort. Just survival instincts kicking in."

"That's the thing about survival," Jaci mused, stirring a concoction that resembled honey. "Everyone strives to live, yet the outcome is inevitable. I mean, who the hell wants to live just to die?"

Sadly, Jacob understood. After a grueling year spent hunting Charlotte's murderer, he had faced his own reckoning, ultimately choosing death over exile. But his attempt had failed, and exile became his fate. Though, in the eyes of Derro, he was already dead, as exile and death were the same. Survival, he realized, indeed led to some *form* of demise, whether it be the finality of actual death or the sentence of exile.

"True," he said. "Or perhaps survival merely leads to exile? Seems just as inevitable."

"Indeed, survival does seem to be the recurring theme, doesn't it?"

"My father would say that division would be the recurring theme."

"He wasn't mistaken. Division is a constant presence. But I'd argue that survival precedes it. Division is merely a consequence."

"And what would you say is the consequence of division?"

"Well, I'd think that one would be obvious to you. History has shown us that there can only be one consequence of division."

"And that is?"

"Anarchy."

Jacob nodded, thoughts swirling as he considered Jaci's insight. It struck him how many criminals he had encountered, both in Derro and Eremos, who justified their actions as necessary for survival, unwittingly fueling further division. The catalyst for the Anarchy Era, as Jacob's father had preached.

But Jacob knew his own actions weren't solely driven by survival. Vengeance fueled them. For what *he* did to her. He wondered if the same applied for others. Certainly, not every crime committed was justified by survival or vengeance. Daemion and Michael had proven that. So perhaps Anarchy was just as inevitable? Before being exiled, Derro had seemed on track of entering another Anarchy Era, while Eremos appeared to be in one of its own.

"History has a knack for repeating itself, doesn't it?" he mused.

"Indeed. Makes you wonder if true peace is ever attainable."

"Yeah, it does …" he said, voice trailing off as his thoughts drifted.

Jacob could never recall living in a state of peace. In Derro, life was an unending battle, a constant struggle for some. For Jacob, however, not so much. He recognized his own comfort and privilege, knowing full well that most had it worse than he did. Yet everyone seemed to navigate their own challenges, much like the people here on Eremos did. It made sense for Eremos to lack peace. It was, after all, an island of exile for Derro's miscreants. But then again, not every criminal was a bad person. The thought made him think about Ostria.

"I'm going to apply this to your wound now," Jaci said, breaking the silence. "No need to worry. It's just honey. It'll aid in healing your bite and hopefully repair some of that tissue damage."

Honey, of all things? "Okay," he said, grateful for the treatment.

As Jaci carefully applied the warm honey to his skin, his mind wandered back to Ostria. Daemion had spoken of it as the ultimate haven on Eremos. So much so that he had plans to lead an assault to it. Ostria was Jacob and his friends' beacon of peace, a place where they could hopefully live safely. Why then was Jaci content to stay with the Last Patriots? *Is Ostria harder to access than we'd anticipated?*

"Why not seek refuge in Ostria? That's where we were headed before we ran into you guys."

Jaci frowned. "I wish I could, but I already have. But that was a long time ago. I can't go back there now."

"Why not?"

"Because I was exiled."

"So was everyone else on Eremos …"

Jaci shook her head as she placed a clean scrap of cloth over his wound. "No, you're not getting it," she said, extending her other wrist to Jacob, showing him a scarred X carved into it. "I was exiled *from* Ostria."

Jacob's eyes widened. He'd seen that scar before.

"I've seen that before," he said. "Daemion, the cannibal who bit me, had the same one. Why do you have it too?"

"It's a marking," she answered, securing his new dressing. "From Ostria's council. To show I've been exiled."

The council doesn't just let anyone in. More words he had heard before passing out. He shook his head, trying to understand all Jaci was telling him amid his groggy state. *Ostria had a council?*

"I'm sorry. This is just a lot to take in at the moment. You were exiled from Ostria by the council?"

"Yes, we all were. Well, most of us, anyway. There are some who have decided not to seek refuge in Ostria. Mostly Last Patriots." Jaci paused. "And, sadly, there are some who will never have the chance."

"What about Ostria's council? Do they work for Derro?"

Jaci suppressed a laugh. "Definitely not," she said, rolling her eyes. "Although they try acting like they do. But really, they're no different from you or me. Just criminals exiled by Derro."

"And the X is their marking?"

Jaci nodded. "It's their way of making sure they don't let someone they've exiled back in."

Back in? His eyes grew wide as a realization settled in. *That must mean …* "Was Daemion once a citizen of Ostria?"

"Unfortunately, he was. I was there at the same time he was. Like me, he sought refuge. However, he struggled to reintegrate into society, and eventually, his true intentions became clear. He sought refuge as a ploy to rally an army, turning many citizens against the council. He even tried to overthrow them and claim Ostria for himself. Fortunately, he failed. The council exiled him thereafter."

Jacob sat stunned. Daemion was once a citizen of Ostria, but only in hopes of overthrowing the council. And now there was a plan in motion for a second attempt. Only this time, he didn't want to rule it. He wanted to destroy it, leaving nothing but an island reigned by anarchy. Did Jaci and the Last Patriots know this?

He shifted his gaze toward Jaci, who watched him closely. He could tell that she understood the shock and confusion he was experiencing. She had likely witnessed it in others before.

"It's why the council has strict rules for granting refuge now," she continued. "Their decisions are not infallible, but they are driven by the desire to create peace and ensure the survival of their community."

Jacob silently prayed their warning of the planned attack would be enough to grant them refuge.

"Before Daemion bit me, he had mentioned a plan to attack Ostria. Claimed the plan was already in motion."

"He said *that?*" Jaci asked, eyes locking with his.

Jacob nodded. "He seemed confident. Almost cocky."

"Interesting."

"Why so?" Jacob asked, sensing there was more to Jaci's reaction.

"It's just more evidence of what you said. History has a way of repeating itself. Anarchy. Councils. Exile. Daemion's attack. Let's just hope, like your friends said, that he succumbed to his wounds."

"Yeah …" Jacob said, though he wanted to say more. There was something in Jaci's demeanor. A hesitation. He got the sense she was holding something crucial from him.

"Well, I'm finished," Jaci said, rising from the cot. "I'll have some food brought to you. Help yourself to more water. And I'll inform your friends you're awake. They'll be happy to see you."

She started toward the door, her footsteps faltering as she paused at the threshold. "Tell me," she said, glancing over her shoulder. "What was your plan once you reached Ostria?"

"We intended to warn them about Daemion's attack. Help them prepare before it's too late."

Jaci nodded, though her gaze searched his face for something more he couldn't quite discern.

"Also," he said, sensing Jaci's skepticism, "as I'm sure you know, there's a wildfire heading this way. A madman who believes he's purging Eremos of its wickedness started it. We hoped both our warnings would persuade Ostria to grant us refuge."

"We were wondering how the fire started. Your friends told us about him, too. Sadly, the wildfire is spreading rapidly. It's drawing nearer by the minute, and while preparations are underway, I fear we lack the resources to stop it."

Jacob bit the insides of his cheeks, grappling with the magnitude of the inferno. By now, the smoke and flames were no doubt visible to Ostria. Given Eremos's scarce resources, he dreaded that, as Jaci said, they might be powerless to halt its advance.

"And your friend, Ammon," Jaci said, pulling Jacob from his thoughts. "Can he be trusted?"

"What do you mean?"

"He's … one of them. I saw the star on his wrist."

This was the first time Jaci had expressed any fear of the Last Patriots. Jacob wasn't sure how to respond. *Is she trying to see what I think of them?*

"Ammon was a Last Patriot, but he's proven himself trustworthy. We have a history in Derro. Before we were exiled, he helped me find someone I'd been searching for for a long time. And here on Eremos, he's saved my life twice now. I trust him."

"Very well," Jaci said, nodding. "Rest up. Myla will want to speak with you when she returns tomorrow."

With that, she slipped out of the hut, leaving him to grapple with the weight of their conversation. Now alone, a chilling thought crept into his mind. *Did I just unwittingly paint myself as a threat to the Last Patriots?*

CHAPTER TWENTY-SIX

SIX MONTHS BEFORE EXILE

THE ROOM ENVELOPED itself in stillness, disrupted only by the measured ticking of an opulent grandfather clock. Each passing second served as a bitter reminder of what Jacob had lost.

And of what he was about to lose.

Haven't seen one of those in a long time, he thought as he sat at the end of a long table, nervously tapping his fingers against its glossy surface, waiting anxiously.

The last time he had seen a grandfather clock was when he was a kid scouring antique shows with his father, looking for parts for the gun they were making. His father had ingrained in him a soft spot for antiques, and he'd always been fond of the grandfather clock. So much so that he had always asked his father to buy one for Hoos, but because they're not made anymore, they're godly expensive. Without a doubt, this one cost a fortune.

He rose from the chair and approached for a closer inspection. Taking in the impressive stature, towering at what he estimated to be eight feet tall, his eyes widened. Crafted from rich rosewood and adorned with intricate designs and patterns, the clock exuded a timeless elegance. He couldn't resist reaching out and touching its face, his fingers delicately tracing the silver-chased details and hallmark numerals.

This thing's ancient.

His gaze drifted from the clock to the books crammed into the bookcase beside it. Nowadays, most people listen to books, their Auxes serving as narrators. Bookshelves were a rare sight in a world where everyone had an all-knowing AI chip. As his fingers traced the spines, his eyes paused on an aged hardback, sealed in a plastic protector, bearing a title he instantly recognized.

It actually reminds me of a book my father made me read when I was a kid. One of his personal favorites. Crimson Hands. *Ever heard of it?* Richard's words entered his mind from that day he came into Hoos, trying to buy it.

Jacob scowled, recalling how Richard had used the book to draw parallels between its protagonist, Tyrell Macy—who knowingly sent out faulty firearms that caused the deaths of American soldiers during the Anarchy Era—and himself, a man who knowingly sold firearms destined to cause loss of life.

Well, Richard, you're about to seal the deal.

Turning away from the bookcase, his gaze shifted back to the long table in the center of the room. His eyes landed on a control panel embedded on its surface. Curiosity getting the better of him, he leaned in for a closer look. There was a series of buttons, one standing out among the rest. Labeled "Map," it all but begged to be pressed, and he couldn't resist giving it a push.

Instantly, a large holographic map materialized, floating above the table. Jacob, still leaning over, found himself immersed in its projection. He straightened and took a step back to better grasp what he was seeing. Vividly highlighted areas pulsated with data, each containing a series of ominous red pins. His eyes narrowed with recognition; it was a map of Tuto, and the highlighted zones were unmistakably no-go zones.

He zeroed in on Nox Street, his eyes tracing the holographic representation until he found Hoos, untouched by a red pin. Then he shifted his attention to Storks, and as suspected, the foreboding red pin marked it. *What are you planning?*

"Interesting, isn't it?" a fragile voice announced.

Startled, Jacob jerked his head toward the unexpected voice to find a tall and lean elderly man standing at the room's threshold. He boasted a crown of smoky-gray hair that was slicked back, stressing a receding hairline, and a matching goatee. Leaning on a sturdy cane, he entered the room with hesitant steps, his suit not fitting his body as it once had. It didn't take long for Jacob to recognize the distinct features.

This was Richard's father.

"I'm sorry," Jacob said, feeling caught. "I was just—"

Mr. Woodwin dismissed Jacob's explanation with a wave of his hand, his legs dragging his feet toward the other side of the table. "Not necessary, Jacob. We've got nothing to hide."

"Hello, Jacob," a honeyed voice greeted.

Jacob turned to find Richard entering the room, a grin plastered on his face as he made his way next to his father. Clad in a navy blazer over a crisp white dress shirt, paired with denim jeans and a belt showcasing an imposing "W" emblem, he oozed his usual air of smug confidence.

"So, what do you think?" Mr. Woodwin asked, gesturing with his cane toward the map.

"It's … interesting."

"Has a way of opening your eyes, doesn't it?" Richard said, securing his ash-blond hair in a bun.

"What do you mean?" Jacob asked.

"Look at all the no-go zones. They're everywhere. Hell, before we know it, Tuto will be one large no-go zone."

Mr. Woodwin scoffed. "Wouldn't surprise me if we entered into another Anarchy Era. Derro, after all, originates from the land of the great big dogs, and it is a dog-eat-dog world."

"Let's hope it doesn't come to that," Richard said. "The council is exiling criminals every day. They have it under control."

No-go zones aren't just for protecting. They're all about control. Those dead thug's words resurrected into Jacob's mind. "And yet, the no-go zones just keep popping up," he rebutted.

"And when they do, we'll be there to swoop in and save people from their struggling businesses," Richard said. "Just like we did for *you.*"

"You didn't save me. Hoos was doing just fine. I'm selling because of what happened. I just want it over with. And you're lucky enough to be the one profiting from it."

"Our deepest condolences for your loss, Jacob," Mr. Woodwin said, placing a trembling hand over his heart. His gaze shifted to his son, his expression hardening into a scowl.

Frowning, Richard took a seat immediately. "I didn't mean—"

Mr. Woodwin silenced his son with a dismissive wave. "What you went through and your loss," he said, turning his attention back to Jacob, "it's *tragic.* A shame the man hasn't come forward and turned himself in. Some people, I swear, they'd rather watch the entire world burn before they'll take blame."

"I too, am incredibly sorry for your loss," Richard said. "I hope the Cullers find her killer soon, so you can begin to mourn properly."

"Thanks."

"Have they found anything to identify the man?" Richard asked.

Jacob shook his head. "Unfortunately, no."

"Let's hope they do soon," Mr. Woodwin said. He fished into his suit jacket and retrieved a stylus pen. "So, shall we add another pin to the map?"

Jacob nodded and took a seat at the table. His eyes grew distant as a reel of memories tied to Hoos played out in his mind, like a poignant film. Each scene unfolded vividly: the joy of building his first gun with his father, the camaraderie with the customers, and the serendipitous moment he met Charlotte—a moment that forever altered his life.

But as the pleasant memories faded, darker ones began to surface. The heart-wrenching loss of his father, the weight of his inherited legacy, the ever-present shadow of danger accompanying every firearm he sold, and, worst of all, the haunting night he lost Charlotte. His jaw tightened as he struggled against the searing image of her that refused to fade. With a sharp inhale, he shoved the pain aside, steeling himself to confront the reality before him.

"I'd like to get this over with," he finally said.

"Understandable," Mr. Woodwin said, handing Jacob the stylus. "Let's make the sale of Hoos final, shall we?"

Jacob reached for the stylus, and as he grabbed it, the holographic map in front of him vanished. Taking its place was an array of documents neatly laid out in front of them. With a tap on the first one, Richard initiated the signing process, and the paperwork expanded across the table.

The transaction had begun.

As Richard explained each document, Jacob's mind drifted further and further away. The words spoken to him faded into a distant murmur, and his signature, once steady, grew increasingly frantic with each passing slide. Each document felt like it was pulling him deeper into detachment, stripping away a piece of his life—one he still wasn't sure how to navigate afterward.

Yet, to move forward with even a semblance of peace, he knew it must be done.

When the signing finally ended, he rubbed his sweaty palms against his jeans and took a deep breath, as if he had been holding it the entire time. "Is everything in order?" he asked, standing up.

"Yes, you're all set," Richard said, pressing a button that made the holographic documents vanish.

"Congratulations, Jacob," Mr. Woodwin said, extending his arm toward him.

Jacob shook his hand. "Thanks."

Richard stood up and stretched out his hand as well, which Jacob shook. "I'll process the paperwork tonight, and you should have the funds wired into your account first thing in the morning."

Jacob responded with a nod, then turned and started toward the exit. After a few steps, he halted, curiosity getting the best of him. "What's the goal here?" he asked, retracing his steps toward the table. "Why the interest in purchasing businesses within no-go zones?"

"Oh, we're just the middleman," Mr. Woodwin said. "It's the council that's buying these businesses. We've only been contracted by them to facilitate the transactions."

"The *council* is buying them?" Jacob repeated back, voice rising. "The ones who decide when a no-go zone goes up or down?"

"Well …" Mr. Woodwin faltered. "I suppose so."

"And that's not *concerning* to you?" Jacob asked, hands clenched into fists. *The council just stole Hoos from me.*

"It's not uncommon for a government to contract with real estate professionals when acquiring properties or land, Jacob." Richard said. "It's just businesses."

Derro isn't the only one profiting off crime. More words from those thugs entered Jacob's mind.

"Oddly …" Mr. Woodwin said, a fond smile growing, "it reminds me of one of my favorite books. *Crimson Hands.* I had Richard read it when he was a boy. It's an old piece of literature, written shortly after the Anarchy Era, but its themes are timeless if you ask me. You ever heard of it?"

Jacob frowned. "Actually, I have," he said. "It appears your fondness for the book carried down to Richard. He mentioned it the last time he tried to buy Hoos from me, though, not quite with the same enthusiasm as you."

Mr. Woodwin's smile faltered into a scowl, which he directed at Richard. "Well …" he said, shifting his stance with his cane. "I'm sorry to hear that."

"He told me selling guns contributed to Tuto's crime problem. That my actions were no different from Tyrell Macy's with his faulty guns. Only I sell them, and they're later used in crimes. Or *worse*, in a death."

"I was only—"

"That's enough," Mr. Woodwin said, silencing Richard once again. "Jacob, please let me—"

"His words have haunted my mind ever since that day. And as you can see, it worked. He got the sale. And I blame myself for my wife's death." Jacob shifted his gaze toward Richard. "You may not have *saved* me, but with your guys' logic, you may have just saved Tuto. Let's hope now these no-go zones start going down."

He turned away from the Woodwins and started toward the exit, leaving a final thought hanging in the air. "But I doubt it," he said. "The council still needs more businesses to buy, and you have more pins to place."

CHAPTER TWENTY-SEVEN

DAY SIX OF EXILE

LATER THAT DAY, Jacob stood at the threshold of the bamboo hut he had awoken in, greeted by the sprawling view of the Last Patriots settlement unfolding before him. He stared in astonishment. The sky was ablaze with a burned orange hue as the sun, a fiery red orb, dipped below the horizon, casting a hellish glow upon the settlement. It felt surreal, almost apocalyptic. He had never witnessed anything quite like it.

It was as if the very heavens had ignited, consumed by the inferno threatening to engulf all of Eremos.

The air hung heavy and hazy, the acrid smoke mingling with the fading light of the sunset, obscuring his view. As he squinted through the haze, he could make out clusters of bamboo huts scattered across the terrain. People moved among them with urgency.

Along the perimeter, others worked frantically, digging a trench around the settlement and then filling it with sand to serve as a firebreak for the inferno. Great idea; however, not so great execution. They had started too late. Even if they could finish in time, the trench wasn't wide enough. Jaci was right. They were, indeed, powerless to halt the inferno's advance.

As everyone around him displayed a clear sense of purpose, driven by the instinct to protect their home, Jacob couldn't help but admire the semblance of order amid the chaos. Each person seemed to know their role, their actions seamless, as if fighting for survival was normal to them. Which, coming from what he knew of the Last Patriots, was undeniably true.

Yet despite the unity he witnessed in front of him, he couldn't shake his earlier conversation with Jaci. She had spoken as though she wasn't one of them and had even expressed doubt in Ammon, leading Jacob to believe she didn't trust the Last Patriots. But he also considered the idea that it was a test, perhaps meant to get him to speak his true feelings about the group. He drummed his fingers against his jeans. *What am I not seeing here?*

"*Jacob!*"

The call of his name jolted him from his musing, his attention swiftly being drawn to Morgan's approach. As the kid ran toward him, Jacob noticed Alex and Ammon emerging from the smoky haze behind Morgan.

"Hey, kid," Jacob said, offering a small smile.

"You look better," Morgan said.

"I *feel* better. Especially now that I've got some food in me."

Shortly after Jaci had left, another woman arrived with a small portion of fish. He had devoured it in five bites. Alongside it, a small bowl of cantaloupe, which was, to his surprise, extremely refreshing amid the heat.

"Can you believe all of this?" Morgan asked, gesturing around them. "It's wild, right?"

"It's ... something," Jacob said, his eyes wandering over the settlement once more.

"You're *alive*," Alex quipped as she neared.

Jacob scoffed. "For now," he said, a wry smile forming.

"Glad to see you're okay," Ammon said. "You had us worried."

"Me too," Jacob replied.

And your friend, Ammon—can he be trusted? Jaci's words of caution lingered.

"What do you make of all this?" Jacob asked, his gaze probing Ammon's expression.

"I'm not sure," he said, taking a moment to collect his thoughts, his eyes surveying the settlement. "It's unexpected, that's for sure."

"Did the Last Patriots have a plan to start anew here if exiled?"

"If there was a plan, I wasn't aware of it. I joined the Last Patriots barely a year before my exile."

"It makes sense," Alex said. "For them to work together here, as they did in Derro. It's easier when everyone shares a common goal."

"Goals can change, though," Ammon said, his fingers absently tracing his star tattoo. "In Derro, their goal was clear: to destroy the council's Control Hubs. But here, I'm not so sure."

Their goal? Jacob found it odd. Here, on Eremos, were people Ammon could relate to, people who could make him feel at home and part of a community. Yet, even after everything he had done for the Last Patriots' cause, he, like Jaci, spoke as though they were detached from the collective. It left Jacob questioning just how much they truly understood the Last Patriots' intentions.

Then a realization struck him. *It's a foundation on which a new nation could be built—or at least that's what Myla promises.* More of Jaci's words entered his mind. Myla, the self-proclaimed president, had pledged to her people the promise of building a new nation here on Eremos. But to build this new nation, the old one would need to be dismantled.

Ostria, he realized, his stomach sinking. Daemion had said there was a plan already in motion. *Could this be the plan he was referring to?*

"Why do you have that look on your face?" Alex asked.

They're trying to do what they couldn't in Derro, he thought, connecting the dots. He scanned their surroundings, ensuring privacy, before gesturing toward the hut. "We need to talk."

As Jacob made his way inside, he could feel the eyes of the others piercing into him, eager for an explanation.

"Uh, what's happening?" Morgan asked.

"Okay, this might seem wild at first, but just stay with me," Jacob said, his voice lowering. "I think the Last Patriots might be working with the Maws to attack Ostria."

Alex narrowed her eyes. "What makes you think that?"

"Remember when I said Daemion spoke of a plan to attack Ostria? And how it was already in motion? Well, what if the Last Patriots are that plan in motion? Alex, you said yourself, 'it's easier when everyone shares a common goal.'"

"I don't know, man," Ammon said. "Who would want to work with Daemion? The guy's a monster."

Jacob nodded, agreeing with Ammon. Indeed, Daemion's manic nature made him an unlikely ally for such a coordinated assault. "I'm not sure," he admitted. "But what I do know is that the Last Patriots want to establish a new nation here. To do that, they need to dismantle the old one. Just like they tried to do in Derro."

"Now that makes sense," Ammon said. "That Daemion part, though? I'm still not sure."

"How do you know all of this?" Alex asked.

"I sort of pieced it together myself, but Jaci, the woman who treated my bite, she was the one who revealed their goal of wanting to build a new nation here. Their leader, Myla, or 'president,' as she likes to call herself, has promised it."

"Why would she tell you all of this?" Alex pressed. "You're an outsider. Hell, you're not even a Last Patriot. It doesn't make sense."

"Because I wish for the attack to not happen," a fragile voice answered unexpectedly, causing Jacob to whirl around in surprise. It was Jaci, slowly making her way inside. "And I'm not alone. There are others who feel the same way."

"So, I was right?" Jacob asked. "The Last Patriots are working with Daemion?"

"Well, I can't confirm *that* for certain," Jaci said, closing the door, but not before checking for any lurkers outside. She turned to face them, hands clasped behind her. "But their goals seem aligned. When you mentioned Daemion's planned attack on Ostria, I realized this situation was even more dire than I feared. And … I'm hoping you can help."

"What are *we* supposed to do?" Morgan asked, looking dumbfounded.

"What you've already planned to do," Jaci said. "Warn them. Help them prepare. The inferno has sped up the timetable of the attack. Myla believes it will catch them off guard while their attention is diverted. She'll return tomorrow, and word is she'll mobilize her army toward Ostria shortly after. You *do not* want to be here when she returns."

"Why?" Jacob asked.

"Because she'll have you marked," Jaci said, rolling up her sleeve to reveal her X marking. "It's her method of trapping you. She brands the same X as Ostria does to its exiles, ensuring you can never find refuge."

"*Exiles?*" Ammon echoed.

"Ostria, like Derro, uses exile as punishment," Jaci said, offering clarification. "They mark their exiles with an X carved into their wrists."

"And I saw the same one on Daemion's wrist when I was in the cave," Jacob said.

"Wait, hold up," Alex chimed in. "Are you saying Daemion was once a citizen of Ostria?"

"He was," Jaci replied. "Just like me. But that was many years ago. He was exiled for trying to overthrow the council. He wanted to rule Ostria himself."

"I don't understand," Ammon said. "If they exiled you, like they did Daemion, then why don't you, or these others you mentioned, want the attack to happen?"

Jaci frowned, letting her sleeve fall back down. "We all have our reasons. Most people fear the anarchy that will ensue. I share that fear. But I also have *personal* motivations. I have a son. He and his father reside in Ostria. He was born there. Ostria is his home."

"But if the attack succeeds, you'd have the chance to be reunited with them," Alex said. "Wouldn't you want that?"

"There's no guarantee of that. And even if there were, at what cost?" Jaci took a deep breath, fighting back the sadness threatening to surface. "I miss my son dearly. And while Ostria isn't without flaws, they've built something here. A sanctuary, a place for people to call home. There are others, like my son, who were born within its walls. They don't deserve to see their home destroyed. It's my own fault I was exiled, and I live with that every day. But I refuse to let others suffer because of it."

"Why were you exiled?" Morgan asked.

Jaci turned, narrowing her eyes at Morgan, studying him intently. "Why were *you* exiled?" she countered.

Morgan's head bowed slightly. "Fair enough," he muttered.

"This is …" Ammon said, his head shaking in disbelief.

"Overwhelming, I know," Jaci said. "But I can't think of any other way to warn them. I'm barred from returning, but *you* have a chance."

"But we don't even know where Ostria is," Alex said. "We may not even make it in time."

"But I do," Jaci said. "It's a day's journey from here. I will guide you there." She tilted her head. "Well, at least part of the way. Just enough for you to glimpse its walls. Then you're on your own, I'm afraid. I can't risk you being seen with me. May hurt your chances of getting in."

Jacob glanced at his fellow exiles, wondering their thoughts. The plan wasn't drastically different from their previous one: find Ostria, warn them, seek refuge. If anything, it was an improvement. They now had a guide who could lead them there. No more wandering aimlessly. And staying here only increased the risk of being marked.

"If you help us, what happens to you afterwards?" Alex asked. "Won't they suspect you helped us?"

"I'll do what I've always done," Jaci said, turning her gaze to Jacob. "Survive."

Jacob nodded. "Just like we all have," he said. "Personally, I think there's only one answer. We go. Unless anyone has any objections."

"I'm with you," Morgan said.

"I'm in," Ammon said. "I refuse to stay here any longer. My time with the Last Patriots is over."

Alex nodded. "Okay."

"Thank you," Jaci said.

"Likewise," Jacob replied.

"Now gather your things," Jaci said. "The sun has almost set. Once night falls, we depart."

As the inferno painted the night sky in hues of fiery red, Jacob and the others trailed behind Jaci, who guided them through the Last Patriots settlement with haste. They moved swiftly, aiming to blend in and avoid attracting unwanted notice. Though they weren't technically prisoners, the risk of being caught leaving loomed over them, a potential spark for suspicion they could ill afford.

Fortunately, Jaci had lent them extra shirts, which they fashioned into makeshift balaclava masks, covering their heads and faces entirely, with only their eyes exposed for visibility. While their primary goal was to shield themselves from the thickening smoke, they also appreciated the added benefit of concealment that the masks provided.

Jacob's heartbeat quickened as they neared the perimeter, passing workers still focused on the firebreak. They moved past smoothly, following a narrow path toward a lone guard who loomed ahead. Jacob exchanged a glance with Ammon, their eyes conveying an unspoken understanding—they needed to find a way past the guard without arousing suspicion.

The guard raised his hand in warning as they approached, halting their advance with a stern gaze. Clutched in his other hand was a long spear.

"Where are you guys going?" he asked, his voice a low growl.

"We're headed to Eagle Creek," Jaci said. "I need to harvest more remedies for the man we brought in last night."

"No one is supposed to leave," the guard said, eyes narrowing on each of them. "Myla will be returning soon."

"I thought she wasn't due back until tomorrow," Ammon said, trying to blend in.

"Negative. A messenger arrived earlier and informed us she decided to trek through the night. The fire is getting bad out there."

"Oh," Jaci said, her head beginning to bow. "Well, nonetheless, I still need more remedies. We'll be back before she arrives." She stepped forward, but the guard placed a hand in front of her, halting her steps.

"I'm afraid that's not possible," the guard said.

"Come on, man," Ammon pressed. "Desperate times call for desperate measures. Myla will want to speak with that man when he wakes up. You know this. Gotta *earn* your star, am I right?"

The guard paused, his eyes scanning Ammon up and down. "You got that right. You get yours yet?"

"You bet I did," Ammon said, showing his wrist to the guard. "Got exiled because of it. What about you?"

The guard straightened his posture, a proud smile spreading across his face as he displayed his wrist. "Same."

"Hell yeah," Ammon said. "You see, my friends here though, they don't have theirs. And with the planned attack, they're eager to show their support. Anything for the star. You know how it is."

Jacob stood stunned as he watched Ammon banter with the guard as if he were still one of them. Meanwhile, the guard paused, continuing his scrutiny. Jacob bit at the insides of his cheeks, hoping Ammon's ploy had worked.

"Well, all right then," the guard finally said. "You guys go ahead now, but hurry back. That damn fire isn't getting any slower. Best be careful."

"You're the man," Ammon said, placing his hand on the guard's shoulder as he passed.

Jacob and the others fell in step behind him. He shot Ammon a wide-eyed glance, his eyebrows raised in disbelief. They kept their body language neutral, though, striving to appear as casual as possible, but beneath the surface, their insides cheered.

"Hold up," the guard called.

Jacob's steps faltered. He turned slowly, eyes growing alert as the guard approached. He swallowed hard.

"Jaci, aren't these the people we found last night?" he asked.

"I'm not sure what you mean," Jaci quickly replied.

"Something feels off," the guard said, his knuckles whitening as he tightened his grip on the spear. His eyes darted between them, suspicion deepening. "There were two men, a woman, and a kid we brought back. What's *really* going on here?"

Before anyone could answer, Morgan moved like a coiled spring snapping loose and kicked the guard hard between the legs. The guard let out a strangled gasp, doubling over as the spear slipped from his grip. Wasting no time, Morgan closed the gap and swung his fist into the guard's jaw. The force of the blow sent him sprawling to the ground, where he landed with a heavy thud.

"Holy shit," Alex said.

Jacob stood frozen, his mouth slowly dropping, his eyes fixed on the crumpled guard. He shifted his attention to Morgan, who turned toward them, shaking out his hand with a faint grimace before a grin crept onto his face.

"Kid ..." Jacob said as he stood in shock.

"*What?*" Morgan said, shrugging. He patted Ammon's shoulder. "Desperate times, right? Plus, now when Jaci comes back alone, she can say we forced her to show us the way out."

"That's ... actually a good point," Ammon said.

"Yeah, and as much as I appreciate it and all, we really need to leave before we're seen," Jaci expressed urgently. "Now."

CHAPTER TWENTY-EIGHT

FOUR MONTHS BEFORE EXILE

IT WAS SNOWING.

Jacob frowned as he watched the flakes fall gracefully from the floor-to-ceiling window of his bedroom. Normally, he'd smile, especially when Charlotte was around. It was impossible not to smile when she did, and snow always made her smile.

His wandering eyes stopped at the sight of the large green box she had left for him on their back deck. The snow had risen a few inches, reaching halfway up the box. Part of him wanted to save it from the elements, to protect the gift she wanted to surprise him with. But even as he mustered up the courage to step outside, it wasn't enough for him to act.

You're only delaying the inevitable, he told himself.

Deep down, he suspected what hid within the green box, his conclusions mostly stemming from Charlotte's visit with Storks. Which, sadly, was the sole reason he was afraid to open it. For too long, they had desired to add to their family. And they had gotten so close.

I wish I could've seen you that day. I bet I could've seen a new smile from you.

"Sid, can you tell me something?"

How can I help, Jacob?

"How was Charlotte the day she visited Storks?"

Part of being married allowed for Jacob and Charlotte's Auxes to be connected, if they chose to do so, which they did. This allowed Sid to know what Iris knew.

Charlotte had visited Storks often, Jacob, Sid replied. *Each time she felt excited and hopeful. Especially on her last visit.*

When she bought that, Jacob said to himself, his eyes glued on the box.

"Can you tell me what she bought, Sid? On her last visit?"

Yes, I can, Jacob. But I will not. Charlotte intended this gift to be a surprise for you. Iris had made that very clear. It's best if you are the one to open it.

Jacob scoffed. "Fine."

He started toward the patio doors, his heavy feet thumping on the hardwood floor. As he drew nearer, his steps slowly came to a halt, his hand resting on the doorknob. *You can do this.* Just as he turned the knob, a sudden chime from his doorbell stopped him. He frowned. *Of course.*

"Sid, who is it?"

There is a Mr. Woodwin at your door, Sid said.

He scowled. *Richard? What the hell does he want?*

He departed his bedroom, clomped down the stairs, and started toward the front door. Pulling it open, his eyes widened as he was met not by Richard, but by Richard's father. The elder was bundled in a snow jacket, but it was obvious he was wearing an expensive suit underneath. He leaned into his cane, which was planted in the snow, his other hand clasping a black briefcase.

"Jacob, I apologize for showing up at your home unannounced," Mr. Woodwin said.

"Why are you here?" Jacob asked bluntly, giving Mr. Woodwin the cold shoulder.

The elder sighed, his expression crestfallen. "Well, after learning how my son handled trying to purchase Hoos, I wanted to come by and apologize."

"That was over a month ago. Besides, it should be him apologizing, not you."

"Indeed, you are correct. And I have urged him to take responsibility for his actions. However, I am apologizing for my own conduct, not his."

Jacob's eyes narrowed on Mr. Woodwin. He hadn't expected an apology from him and found himself curious about the reason behind it. "I'm listening," he said.

"I must confess, our recent encounter has left a lasting impression on me. I failed to recognize the detrimental impact of my involvement in assisting the council with their no-go zone purchases. Initially, I justified it as a means of saving people from their struggling businesses. Yet, upon deeper reflection, I now understand the potential harm it will eventually inflict. My intentions were misguided and clouded by greed. In retrospect, I found myself drawing parallels to Tyrell Macy from *Crimson Hands*, a book you know by now I hold dear. However, despite admonishing his actions, I inadvertently mirrored his misdeeds."

What is it with this family's fascination with that damn book?

"I cannot discern the council's final intentions in purchasing these businesses," Mr. Woodwin continued. "Nevertheless, I am adamant about severing ties with them. I've already instructed Richard to end our contract with them. I believed it was imperative for you to be informed of this decision."

"It won't matter. They'll only find another real estate company. Their plan has always been the same. Control. Whatever they're planning will only increase that control."

Mr. Woodwin frowned as he nodded. "You're likely correct."

Jacob strangely empathized with Mr. Woodwin, though he was reluctant to admit it. Opting to sell Hoos was, in part, his effort to avoid exacerbating Tuto's crime problem. Yet he also recognized the presence of other gun stores in the city. Regardless of his involvement, people would still find their means of protection. And unfortunately, harm.

But at least it wouldn't weigh on his conscience any longer.

"Will that be all?" Jacob asked.

"Yes, however," Mr. Woodwin said, nodding as he opened his briefcase, "before I take my leave, there is one more matter I wish to discuss with you." With care, he retrieved a book from the briefcase, cradling it in his hands. "This is one of my personal copies, and despite my son's misjudgments, I hope that, like *Crimson Hands* has done for me, it will show that perhaps the sale of Hoos was a blessing in disguise."

"I don't want that book."

"Surely you won't refuse my gift," Mr. Woodwin insisted gently. "Read it or let it sit untouched; it's entirely your choice. However, there may come a moment, and perhaps that moment has already arrived, when you begin to question your purpose. You might even find yourself regretting the sale of Hoos. In such times, this book might provide you with … assurance."

This fucking family, I swear. Gonna be the death of me.

"I'll take your gift," Jacob said, frowning as he grabbed the book. "If that's what you want to call it."

"I understand your hesitation. But sometimes, the greatest gifts come in unexpected forms. Until we meet again."

Jacob nodded in silent acknowledgement as he observed Mr. Woodwin's departure, his thoughts swirling. *The greatest gifts come in unexpected forms …*

His gaze drifted to the book in his hands. Just moments ago, he had wrestled with the courage to open the gift Charlotte had given him. And now, here he stood, holding yet another unexpected offering.

And like Charlotte's gift, he struggled to muster the courage to unveil its contents. *I need a drink.*

His body shivered as he shut the front door. Mr. Woodwin's encounter lingered in his mind as he moved with purpose toward the living room, seeking solace in the familiar ritual of pouring himself a glass of whiskey.

As he lifted the glass to his lips and sipped, his eyes wandered to Charlotte's gift. He had been on the brink of unveiling its contents earlier, but now, with each passing moment and drink, the distance between him and the gift seemed to grow.

Seeking a distraction from his inner turmoil, he resolved to lose himself in some mindless television. "Sid, turn on TV."

A holographic screen materialized over the fireplace mantle instantly, casting a gentle blue glow across the room. His eyes narrowed, locking onto the bold letters displayed on the screen, spelling out "Breaking News."

"Sid, turn it up."

As the volume rose, his eyes grew wide in shock as he beheld the aerial footage unfolding on the screen. Massive plumes of smoke billowed into the sky, their dark tendrils curling downward to meet the snowy ground, where an inferno blazed fiercely. The scene showed the aftermath of a devastating explosion, the remnants of a heavily guarded building engulfed in flames amid a densely forested landscape.

"As reports flood in from all corners of Derro, the aftermath of the explosion at one of the council's vital Control Hubs is evident. A scene of pure chaos and ruin. Citizens are being left stranded and disconnected as countless Auxes remain inoperable, plunging affected regions into disarray.

"The council has confirmed that the notorious rebel group, the Last Patriots, is responsible for this act of terrorism. The extent of the damage and the regions affected are still being assessed, with citizens grappling with the sudden loss of essential services and communication. Amid the turmoil, the council assures the public that their Redundancy Hubs are mobilizing to take over. As the situation continues to unfold, we remain committed to providing updates as they emerge …"

"Sid, are you still there?"

Yes, Jacob, I am always here. How can I be of assistance?

Jacob exhaled a shaky breath, grateful for Sid's swift response and steady presence amid the chaos happening in Derro. The revelation that the Last Patriots had somehow found a Control Hub sent a wave of dread coursing through him. *But how?*

I've also heard rumors that they've crept themselves into key positions within the Derro government. Those departed thug's words revived in Jacob's mind. *Trying to dismantle the council's control from within.*

Maybe that's how, he pondered.

As he grappled with the implications of the attack, Jacob's mind raced with all the potential consequences. Losing Control Hubs would destabilize Derro's infrastructure, plunging the world into turmoil. *We could be faced with another Anarchy Era.*

He sank onto the couch, struggling with the anxiety in his gut. Taking deep, deliberate breaths, he tried to calm his nerves, but the weight of the crisis pressed relentlessly down on him. With his breathing failing to bring relief, he succumbed to more drinking. Leaning back, he rested his head on the couch, his gaze wandering to the ceiling.

"You're here now, Sid," he murmured. "But you might not be for long."

Over the next month, the Last Patriots had successfully destroyed two more Control Hubs, pushing Derro to the brink of mayhem. Rolling blackouts plagued the cities, leaving people in darkness as they waited for more of the council's Redundancy Hubs to take over. Streets once bustling with life now lay deserted, illuminated only by the sporadic flickers of emergency lights.

Derro was starting to feel like one large no-go zone.

Meanwhile, the council had imposed a strict curfew from 9 p.m. to 4 a.m., ostensibly because the council wanted to ensure safety while they deployed Cullers to protect the remaining Control Hubs. However, during Jacob's mindless scrolling on social media, he encountered a prevailing sentiment, leading him to believe the curfew was far more tyrannical.

People were claiming the council had plenty of Cullers at their disposal and only used the curfew to quell any hint of brewing chaos among the populace. It was a tactic to maintain control, a constant reminder of the council's iron grip on power, ensuring that anarchy could not spark.

To ensure they prevented another Anarchy Era.

Was another Anarchy Era what the Last Patriots wanted? Jacob pondered, sipping his morning coffee, which he laced with whiskey for an extra kick. He gazed out his living room window at the white, foggy morning, the cloudy, snowy mist shrouding the woods in an eerie silence. Anxious energy pulsed through him, evident in the bouncing of his left leg and the soreness of his cheeks as he contemplated the Last Patriots' motives.

Then a realization struck him. Those thugs had described the Last Patriots as a movement, one that saw itself as the last defenders of a faded era, trying to bring back a government that truly represents the people. Based on their words alone, Jacob concluded the rebellion aimed to bring back America—the supposed land of the free and home of the brave. *But at what cost?*

Innocent people would die, adding to the already hundreds of casualties among those who worked in the destroyed Control Hubs. Even if the Last Patriots destroyed them all, which seemed highly unlikely, it wouldn't obliterate Derro entirely. It would only dismantle the technology used for control. The council still maintained an army of Cullers, ready to enforce their will.

The notion had Jacob grappling with the Last Patriots' end goal. Were they truly fighting for a better tomorrow? Or were they merely agents of chaos, intent on dismantling the fragile semblance of order that remained?

He recalled the first time his father had told him about the Anarchy Era, and the countless times he had heard him recount it to others in Hoos. *It was pure chaos, Jake. Picture society unraveling at its seams. Criminality running rampant, unchecked, with no effective governance to restore order. The whole world seemed to spiral into a lawless abyss. That was, until the council emerged.*

Maybe that's it, he realized. It wasn't so much anarchy the Last Patriots were aiming for. It was the destruction of Derro. Anarchy was merely a natural side effect. Then, a new group of leaders could emerge once again, saving the populace, just as the Derro Council did all those years ago.

Jacob sighed and took another sip of his coffee. It was a lot to process, and escape felt impossible. The past month had been an uphill battle, wrestling with himself as the persistent gnaw of uncertainty refused to let go.

But the scariest thought of all stemmed from an unnamed guilt—a guilt that threatened to consume him. It was the knowledge that the man who robbed Hoos of its guns, killing Charlotte in the process, might have delivered those firearms to the Last Patriots. In doing so, he had armed the rebellion with the means to destroy the Control Hubs. Ezra had mentioned there had been other, smaller robberies before Hoos. The connections were too coincidental to ignore, and even if Jacob tried, he couldn't.

So, he continued to drink, desperate to escape the insurmountable weight of responsibility bearing down on his conscience. Unintentionally, he had played a part in unleashing chaos and violence upon Derro. *How can I live with myself, knowing the bloodshed and destruction that my inaction had caused? It's all my fault. I should've shot them.*

Placing his empty mug on the coffee table, he reached for the bottle of whiskey to refill it. As he did so, his gaze wandered to the book Mr. Woodwin had gifted him. *Crimson Hands* lay abandoned on the table since that day, its presence a constant tug.

How alike am I to this Tyrell Macy? he wondered, pouring himself another glass of whiskey. With drink in hand, he grabbed the book and settled back into the sofa. Taking a sip, he rested his right foot on his left knee and then placed the drink on the armrest before opening the book. His eyes scanned the yellow-tinged pages, noticing several passages underlined in faded ink.

Are these Mr. Woodwin's markings or Richard's? His brow furrowed in concentration as he leaned in closer and read the passages, trying to absorb their meaning.

I like to stay well-acquainted with my ignorance, he read from the first underlined passage. Initially, it struck him as an expression of openness to learning. Yet he couldn't be certain without grasping the full context.

Wanting to delve deeper, he sought help from Sid, giving him an excuse to check in on his Aux and ensure its continued presence. Since the destruction of the most recent Control Hub, Sid had been operating more slowly than usual. Unlike other people in Derro, who had lost all connections to their Auxes, Jacob had only experienced Sid's reduced responsiveness. Tuto, being the largest and most central city in Derro, had yet to feel the full impact of the recent events compared to other areas.

However, it felt like it was only a matter of time.

"Sid, are you familiar with the book *Crimson Hands*?"

Yes, Crimson Hands is a book written by Desmond Locke, Sid replied after a brief silence. *It was published shortly after the Anarchy Era and deals with themes of guilt, responsibility, and the consequences of decisions.*

Jacob frowned. "Great," he muttered as he reached for his mug of whiskey and took a sip.

Would you like to know more? Sid asked.

Nervously tapping his fingers, Jacob considered Sid's question. The themes of the book alone were more than enough to make him feel guilty about his choices—and his indecision. But as he continued to reread the underlined quote, he realized perhaps it was best to remain open to learning.

"Yes, I would," he finally answered. "In the beginning of the book, there's a quote spoken by a character named Drew Macy. The quote says, 'I like to stay well-acquainted with my ignorance.' Can you explain what that means?"

The response from Sid was delayed once again but eventually arrived. *In the context of* Crimson Hands, *the quote you're referencing suggests Drew Macy is telling his father, Tyrell, that, unlike him, he dreams of improving himself. It's a quote that reflects humility.*

"Thanks, Sid."

Jacob leaned closer, rereading the quote and continuing from there. Drew Macy went on to explain to his father that he had a talent for ignoring things. To which his father responded, "I turn a blind eye when I have to, ignoring what I have to ignore."

Just like I did all that time, Jacob realized. *I thought I was helping Tuto with every gun sold, but I was only risking lives. I single-handedly put more guns into Tuto, all to receive a profit. How could I not have seen it for so long?*

The answer came to him instantly in the form of his father's words. *Son, oiling your gun is a ritual. It's a connection. To those who came before us and a responsibility to those who follow.*

Jacob closed his eyes in reflection. *Of course, I never saw it. I was raised respecting guns.*

Mr. Woodwin had proven correct. *Crimson Hands* had struck a chord of truth within Jacob. Even the first underlined quote had provided him with a sense of assurance. Selling Hoos was the right decision, even if it meant not furthering his father's legacy. As far as Jacob was concerned, after witnessing the terrible tragedies caused by the use of guns, Hoos wasn't much of a legacy anymore.

Intrigued further, he continued to read, the pages engrossing him in thought as he turned each one with renewed interest, forgetting all about his whiskey. After devouring thirty pages, his eyes came to a halt at another underlined passage.

People can hate so much that they'll rip the world apart, he read. The words surprisingly paralleled the current issues plaguing Derro. The world felt as if it was being ripped apart and on the brink of extinction once again.

Jacob mirrored that hate. The council's hidden agenda with their no-go zone purchases left him feeling frustrated. He also harbored self-loathing for Charlotte's death. So much so that he'd spent nearly every waking moment trying to hunt down her killer—another form of hate he embodied. The killer was a product of the council's failure to restore law and order, driving Jacob to take matters into his own hands—a pursuit that had consumed him, leading to his need for revenge.

Sadly, though, that pursuit now seemed futile amid the current state of Derro. With the imposed curfew, Jacob couldn't venture to Liberties past 9 p.m. and Ezra and the Cullers were preoccupied with the Last Patriots. Her killer now seemed far more elusive than ever.

Feeling the guilt surfacing, he grabbed his forgotten whiskey and took a drink. Then he focused his attention on another underlined sentence on the same page as the one he had just read.

Some people, the sicker they become, the longer they survive, he read. He scowled, his hands squeezing the edges of the book. The words drew forth memories of Richard leaving Hoos that day when he wrote a blank check. It was as if Richard had encountered this quote before, or perhaps heard his father speak it. But instead of being inspired toward positive change like his father, Richard had twisted its meaning, justifying his ruthless pursuit of wealth and rationalizing his business decisions.

I have a legacy to uphold, Richard had said that day.

How many legacies have you destroyed in your own pursuit? Hoos. Storks. Those were just the two Jacob was most aware of, but there were undoubtedly more businesses marked by red pins on the map he'd seen at Woodwin Realty. It seemed as if Richard was blatantly ignorant of the damage the council was causing with their no-go zone schemes, merely seeking a profit from it.

"Just like Tyrell Macy," Jacob murmured as he closed the book. *We all have blood on our hands.* Taking another sip of whiskey, he scratched his head, wondering how *Crimson Hands* ended. Did Tyrell ever learn from his actions? Curiosity getting the better of him, he decided to take a shortcut and ask Sid.

"Sid, how does *Crimson Hands* end?"

After a brief silence of waiting, Sid finally responded. *In the end of* Crimson Hands, *Tyrell Macy, overwhelmed by guilt for his role in selling defective firearms during the Anarchy Era, commits suicide. The book concludes with a sense of tragedy and the consequences of past actions.*

"Damn," Jacob muttered, running his hand through his hair. The ending was a bit of a shock. Apparently, Tyrell had finally seen his blatant ignorance and felt remorse for his actions. So profoundly, it had caused him to take his own life.

The thought of choosing a similar path, sadly, whispered to Jacob from the dark corners of his mind. The regretful "what-ifs" threatened to resurface once again. Refusing to let guilt consume him, he took a swig of his whiskey and swallowed those thoughts away. That was a choice he could never come back from, one that would only dishonor Charlotte's memory.

Instead, he rose from the couch and climbed upstairs to his father's study. With trepidation, he slowly opened the door, banishing any fragmented memories of that tragic day. Walking over to the bookcases lined with novels and old photographs, he reached for the empty glass case he'd placed there after selling Hoos. Retrieving the heirloom he'd made with his father from the back of his waistline, he placed the pistol in the glass case and returned it to the shelf.

My relationship with guns has come to an end.

CHAPTER TWENTY-NINE

DAY SEVEN OF EXILE

"OSTRIA ISN'T MUCH further," Jaci called out from up ahead.

"Oh, thank God," Alex gasped.

Jacob breathed a sigh of relief as a flicker of hope ignited in his chest. They had been navigating Eremos's unforgiving terrain throughout the night, with only the ominous glow of the burned orange sky lighting their path. The past couple of hours had been the hardest. They had been forced to scale a steep incline. Exhausted and sore, Jacob's legs screamed with every step, a struggle he'd grown accustomed to during his exile but now amplified by the effects of the inferno.

The air hung heavy, carrying with it the scent of charred timber and smoke. Every labored breath served as a reminder of the relentless blaze consuming Eremos, and despite the balaclava mask he'd fashioned to shield his face, Jacob still felt the sting of smoke in his eyes, the burn on his nose, and the scratchiness in his throat.

As he pressed on, the overwhelming weight of their inability to halt the advancing inferno bore down on him, a grim realization settling in his chest, dwindling the sliver of hope he'd just felt. Their desperate plan to warn Ostria of the attack launched by the Maws and Last Patriots felt increasingly futile against the encroaching inferno. The flames presented a more terrifying threat, one that was far more destructive and uncontrollable, rendering their efforts to alert Ostria almost insignificant in comparison.

We need another miracle. But miracles were acts of God. And according to Michael, the inferno he set was him delivering God's judgment. Michael was merely the instrument. Even praying felt fruitless. *We're dead men walking.*

"Do you think Ostria's council will be like Derro's?" Ammon asked, pulling Jacob from his thoughts as he sidled up next to him.

"Hard to say," Jacob said between puffs as he fought to catch his breath. "We've never seen Derro's council. No one knew who they were."

"True, but we do know how they governed," Ammon grunted, taking another step up. "It just has me thinking, is all. What are we about to walk ourselves into? Another Derro?"

"I don't think it'll be *exactly* like Derro. But I do think it'll be similar. During the Anarchy Era, people looked for leaders to stop all the anarchy. They got a council. It's usually the strongest who ends up in command. The same happened here on Eremos. Only this time, we know *who* those leaders are."

"We do?"

"They're criminals," Jacob said, nodding as he glanced at Ammon. "Just like you and me. It's like Jaci told me. They only *try* to be like Derro's council."

Ammon frowned. "That makes me think they'll be *worse.*"

"Why?"

"Because criminals don't have a reputation for being good people. And if it's the strongest who ends up in command, then here on Eremos, it's the strongest criminals we're about to face."

Jacob's eyebrows drew together as he processed Ammon's insight. "Well, just because we're all criminals doesn't mean we're all inherently bad. Some of us simply made bad choices. In my life, I've learned the world is rarely black and white. There are always shades of gray."

Ammon nodded, his gaze absent as he looked ahead. "It's hard to see any gray with all the bad I've done."

"I know what you mean. We do what we think is right, even when it means doing something bad. But sometimes, the world needs people willing to do bad things."

"I've heard that before. The Last Patriots lived by that code."

"Not just them. Look at what the Derro Council did with their Derro Act. Exiling criminals to stop all the bad from taking hold again. Ostria's council has done the same with people like Daemion. It's an unfortunate way of life. We chose the path with the highest chance of success. Or, in our case, survival."

Ammon nodded, but Jacob could tell he was still grappling with his own demons. After all, he was a Last Patriot. And despite those poor decisions weighing him down, he believed he was doing what was right to bring a better way of life.

Or perhaps Ammo was worried Ostria wouldn't let him in? Jacob shared that fear. Not just for himself, but for his fellow exiles too. The idea of leaving any of them behind unsettled him deeply. They had come this far, and he was determined to make sure they all found refuge.

"Besides, you're nothing like them," he said, pulling Ammon from his absent gaze. "You have something they lack."

"Oh, yeah? And what's that?"

Jacob smiled. "Remorse."

Ammon's face softened.

"*Welcome* to Ostria."

Jacob looked up to find Jaci at the ridge's pinnacle. She glanced down and smiled, as if to hint at what lay beyond. It still surprised him how effortlessly she navigated Eremos's rugged terrain at her age—far better than he ever could.

"Well, here we go," Jacob said.

Ammon took a deep breath. "Time to find out what Ostria is really about."

Jacob fought his way to the top, boots crunching against the rugged ground as he climbed. Each step forward was laborious, a constant fight. When he finally reached the top, chest heaving, lungs protesting, he interlocked his hands at the back of his head, trying to catch his breath. But it wasn't just the large incline that caught his breath. It was the sight of Ostria below, sprawling and wondrous.

As the fiery orb of the rising sun cast its burning light upon the landscape, his gaze swept across the expansive panorama before him. Amid the smoky haze, his gaze landed on a towering marvel—the central tower of Ostria, standing tall and commanding attention. Surrounding the tower, like loyal subjects paying homage to their sovereign, were humble dwellings crafted from sturdy timber, their roofs adorned with rustic thatch. Around the perimeter, imposing stakes stood close together, creating a palisade for protection.

"Whoa," Morgan gasped.

"Well, shit, would you look at that," Alex said. "Hey, kid, truth or lie. I'm staring at Ostria right now."

Morgan smiled. "*Truth.*"

"It's quite the sight, isn't it?" Jaci said.

"It looks … almost unreal," Ammon said. "This must've taken years."

"Indeed," Jaci said. "I was told the stake walls were the council's first priority. The vast clearing stretching before Ostria was once densely forested, inhabited by thousands of trees. By clearing them, they ensured their defense in two ways: first, with the formidable walls you see surrounding Ostria, and second, by creating an open expanse that allows for early detection of approaching threats."

Jacob couldn't stop his eyes from tracing the stake walls. Strangely, they filled him with false hope. Large and towering, they offered safety. But one major weakness stood out that destroyed all the hope kindling inside of him. Fire. *Everything burns.*

"Kind of reminds me of what a prison might've looked like," Ammon said.

Jaci nodded her tilting head as she processed Ammon's words. "Well," she said, "everywhere can be a prison if you allow it."

"Is that water I'm hearing?" Morgan asked.

Jaci chuckled softly. "Yes," she answered. "It's hard to see through all the smoke, but beyond the council tower is a large pool of water that flows through Ostria. The council strategically built around it. What you're hearing are waterfalls feeding it."

"That tower is huge," Alex said.

"Hard to miss, isn't it? That was the point. The council built the tower to stand as a beacon of hope. Especially for new exiles when they jumped from the Screech. It symbolizes unity, strength, and resilience—*our* collective hope for a better future. Inside that tower is where you'll meet with the council. It's there they'll decide whether to grant you refuge."

Our collective hope? After all this time, even after Ostria's council exiled her, Jaci still considered herself one of them. The thought perplexed Jacob at first, but as he reflected, it started to make sense. Ostria was home to Jaci's son and husband. Therefore, it would always be her home.

My home is where she is. Jacob's own words echoing in his head. His home, in the end.

"You guys should get going," Jaci said. "Myla and her Last Patriots will have already set forth here. They'll all be here by sunset. The Maws, most likely too. With or without Daemion."

"So, what, we just approach their walls?" Alex asked.

"Yes. They'll see you before you see them."

"Thank you, Jaci," Ammon said, smiling. "For everything."

"I wish you could come with us," Morgan said.

"Me too, Morgan," Jaci said, smiling through teary eyes.

Jacob started toward her, his shoulders sagging with the weight of his gratitude. Their arrival to Ostria was bittersweet, made possible only through her. She had risked her life and security on Eremos for their sake, and for the sake of Ostria, all to protect her family.

"I'll tell the council everything you've done for us," Jacob said. "I'll do everything I can to make sure you can be reunited with your son and husband."

A heavy sigh escaped Jaci's lips. "That's too much of a burden to hold on to. I can't ask that of you. Just, if you're able, find my son and tell him how much I love him."

Jacob smiled, feeling a knot forming in his throat. *Your mother loved you so much, Jake.* His father's words entered his mind. *She told you all the time.*

"I can do that," he finally replied. "What's his name?"

"His name is Ellis, and his father's name is Abe," she said, smiling. "He'll be a young man by now. I wonder if he'll still have my eyes."

"I'll find them," Jacob said, "and when I do, I'll make sure they know how heroic you are."

Jaci shook her head modestly, her smile widening. "I'm no hero. Just survival instincts kicking in," she said, echoing Jacob's own words from yesterday.

A wistful smile formed on Jacob's face. He had grown up without ever truly knowing his own mother, his memories shrouded in haze like the smoke around them. But if he had been given the chance to grow up with her, he'd have wagered she'd have been like Jaci.

"Now go," Jaci urged. "And it's crucial you keep quiet about how you found Ostria. And the markings. The less you know, the better."

"Got it," Jacob said. "You stay safe out there."

"You too, Jacob," she echoed softly.

With a determined exhale, Jacob turned to the others and gathered them close.

"Time to go?" Morgan asked.

"Yes, but there's something we've gotta do first."

"What's that?" Alex asked.

Jacob gestured with a nod of his head toward Ammon. "Find a way to hide that star tattoo."

Ammon frowned. "Great."

"Let's go," Jacob said.

With resolute strides, Jacob and his companions descended the ridge toward Ostria, their spirits momentarily lifted by the hope, false or not, of a new beginning.

CHAPTER THIRTY

THE FINAL DAYS BEFORE EXILE

THERE IT WAS, glaring down at him.

"*Hoos Responsible for Arming Last Patriots?*"

Jacob lay in his bed, engulfed by the embrace of complete darkness, save for the piercing holographic glow of his phone displaying the title of the article he was afraid to read. The room seemed to hold its breath, creating an eerie stillness within its walls, leaving nothing but the echo of his depressed inner voice.

I already know what it says. It's an article about my failures.

Overwhelmed by compulsion, he surrendered to the urge and clicked on the link to reveal the contents of the article. His eyebrows furrowed as he scrolled to the start and read.

> "*The devastating terror attacks on Derro's Control Hubs that claimed the lives of at least 486 people and disrupted the nation's Aux stability, have etched a grim mark in the annals of Derro's history. The council's vow to exile all Last Patriots and their collaborators underscores the gravity of the situation, with citizens demanding justice and answers for the mysteries surrounding the origins and motives of these perpetrators.*

*"How did the Last Patriots breach the heavily for-
tified Control Hubs? What drove them to orchestrate
such a violent rebellion? And perhaps most importantly,
how did they amass such a formidable arsenal?*

*"As the populace clamors for answers, the council
has initiated a comprehensive investigation, deploying
Cullers and Seekers to interrogate these apprehended
public enemies. Yet, amid the anticipation for revelations within the confines of the council's imposed curfew,
speculation runs rampant.*

*"Among the plethora of theories circulating online,
one particular incident emerges as a potential nexus: the
tragic robbery at Hoos, Tuto's foremost gun store, nearly
a year ago. The brazen event, marked by the loss of one
of Hoos's owners, Charlotte Hughes, remains unsolved.
Could there be a connection between this unresolved
crime and the recent wave of terror?"*

Jacob swiped out of the article, unable to read further. He tossed his phone to
the end of the bed, desperate to distance himself from the painful truth he'd
been avoiding since witnessing the first Control Hub attack a few months ago.

Seeking solace, his gaze landed on the marijuana vape pen on his nightstand.
He sat upright, leaning against the headboard, and reached for it, craving the
familiar relief. Sadly, whiskey just didn't have the same effect anymore. Placing
the pen to his lips, he inhaled deeply, letting the vapor swirl in his lungs as he
tilted his head up. With closed eyes, he exhaled, surrendering to the numbing
embrace.

As his head slowly bowed, his eyes opened and landed on the patio doors. A
powerful pull tugged at his soul, urging him to step outside and finally confront
the haunted space. Even within the walls of his home, Charlotte's absence was
inescapable. The house felt quieter now—no longer the peaceful quiet they

once cherished, but a *violent* silence, a deafening stillness that only amplified his regrets and let his tormented thoughts echo relentlessly in his mind.

He swung his feet out of bed and stood up, his bare feet touching the cold hardwood floor. Another reminder of her absence. Everything felt harder and colder. Even the floorboards seemed to mourn her. He yearned for her presence, her gentle touch and comforting words that had always soothed his troubled spirit in times of uncertainty.

You're stronger than you think. Her words echoed in his head as he started toward the patio doors.

I wasn't that day.

Drawing near, his steps faltered. He gripped the door handle, summoning the courage to step outside. The back deck had been their sanctuary, the place where they'd connected the most. Happy memories of them together filled his mind, and he couldn't bear losing that connection.

But perhaps I can be strong enough today.

With a deep breath, he surrendered to the never-ending pull and finally stepped outside. The biting cold hit him the instant he crossed the threshold, every gust like a barrage of icy needles against his skin. He hugged his arms tightly around his body, the frigid air seeping through his clothes, sending chills deep into his bones.

Slipping on his boots, he started toward the box. Each step through the snow felt heavy, as if the weight of the world bore down on him. The string lights Charlotte had hung still clung to their places, though their once-vibrant glow had faded into a feeble flicker. The projection screen now hung in tatters, its surface marred by patches of mold. And nearby, the handcrafted charcuterie board lay in ruins, its carefully arranged delicacies reduced to scattered remnants, plundered by scavenging wildlife.

As Jacob approached the box, he winced. The outdoor space she'd created now felt desecrated, and opening her gift would only deepen that violation. Yet stronger than his apprehension was the irresistible pull that had tugged at him since that fateful night.

And he could no longer resist that urge.

He started to tear away the hanging pieces of the soggy box and wilted wrapping paper. It wasn't long before he could discern its contents, the realization stunning him with what he'd suspected all along.

It's a crib.

His body stiffened, his legs trembling as if they might give way, threatening to send him to his knees in the snow. An avalanche of sorrow crashed over him without warning, his heart sinking like a stone in water. Warm tears streamed down his face as he finally surrendered to the sorrow he had carried for far too long.

Time passed in a flurry as he remained riveted by the sight. The grief was unbearable as he envisioned the dreams they once shared coming to fruition with this crib. But amid his grief, a flicker of determination ignited within him. Charlotte knew he would have wanted to assemble the crib.

And he planned to do just that. For her.

Driven by a newfound purpose, he tore away the remaining soaked remnants of the box with fervor, his hands trembling. Then, with great care, he lifted the pieces of the crib and carried them inside, placing them in the empty spare bedroom they had prepared.

Once he had placed every piece in the room, he quickly put on warm clothes and grabbed his toolbox, determined to bring purpose to the barren space. He settled on the carpeted floor, transforming it into a makeshift workshop. The crib pieces lay scattered before him as he studied the instructions with immense attention, as if assembling this crib held the key to rebuilding his shattered life.

After understanding each step and familiarizing himself with the hardware, he set to work. He started by laying the headboard and footboard across from each other, their smooth birch emanating a sweet scent. He could almost feel Charlotte's delicate touch, as if a fragment of her life had been intricately carved into the very essence of this crib.

He carried that essence with him throughout the assembly. In the house's stillness, the only sounds were the soft rustling of the instructions and the gentle drumming of the screwdriver against the wooden frame. With each completed step, Jacob felt a sense of purpose growing within him, eclipsing the pain he had consumed for far too long.

When he finally finished, he checked all the screws for tightness before stepping back in awe. As the first rays of dawn filtered into the room, they bathed the crib in a warm, golden light. A breath caught in Jacob's throat as his eyes fixed on the crib Charlotte had chosen.

It's perfect.

"Hey, *you*," Charlotte said as she entered the bedroom, her eyes widening at the sight of the crib. "Oh, my goodness, it's *beautiful*."

Jacob smiled warmly as he watched her move gracefully through the nursery, her face aglow with maternal love; a sight he'd always longed to see. The scene unfolded before him like a vision. He observed the room coming together: Charlotte hanging her cherished photographs on the walls, just as she had throughout their home; organizing the bookshelf with children's stories waiting to be told; and neatly placing tiny baby garments in the dresser drawers, each piece a token of the precious moments to come.

Moments Jacob knew she would capture through her lens.

A soft coo transformed the scene. He watched as the rocking chair creaked gently while Charlotte swayed back and forth, her arms cradling their baby against her chest. The coos filled the air, tender melodies that soothed his ears. He smiled, eyes brimming with tears as Charlotte carefully transferred their little one into the embrace of the crib he had just assembled. The baby's tiny fingers grasped at the air as they drifted into a peaceful slumber.

"I love our baby so much it hurts," Charlotte whispered, smiling as she quietly slipped out of the room.

The scene was beautiful. And then it wasn't.

The fleeting beauty of the vision dissolved into a harsh reality. His smile faltered as the heaviness of his loss crashed over him like a wave. The imagined coos were nothing more than a cruel illusion. He would never hold his child, never soothe their cries, and never experience the joy of parenthood. It felt as though an invisible hand had gripped his chest and squeezed with an unbearable force, wringing out every last trace of joy, leaving only a hollow ache behind.

Suddenly, with the screwdriver still clenched in his trembling hand, a dark temptation crept into his thoughts. The pain, both physical and emotional, had become unbearable. All he wanted was an end to the torment, a reprieve from the crushing mass of his grief.

And sadly, the screwdriver felt like a viable escape. The whiskey had dulled its effect, and getting high only conjured visions he couldn't bear. The thought of hurting himself as penance for failing to protect her and their unborn child took root like a poisonous vine, entangling his mind. Every part of him recoiled from the idea, yet in the suffocating grip of his sorrow, it held a perverse allure—an escape from the overwhelming guilt.

But then, like a beacon cutting through the darkness of his mind, a knock shattered the chains of his despair, jolting him back to the present. Slowly, almost reluctantly, he loosened the grip on the screwdriver, strength draining from his fingers as he strained to determine if the knocking he'd heard was real.

Then a knock came again, insistent and undeniable. Someone was at his front door. Sid's slow responsiveness had increased as he registered his Aux hadn't alerted him. Or perhaps Sid was gone forever? With a steadying breath, he released the screwdriver, letting it clatter into the toolbox with a metallic clink.

Jacob, Ezra is at the front door, Sid finally alerted.

"I guess you're still here after all," he muttered as he exited the room and started toward the stairs. Reaching the bottom, his heart quickened, wondering what news Ezra had. *Did he finally find her killer?*

A gust of frigid air swept into the warmth of the house as he opened the front door, carrying with it the brilliant glow of the morning sun shimmering upon the pristine blanket of snow outside. On the porch stood Ezra, dressed in a sturdy jacket and beanie, his breath hanging in the air.

"What is it?" Jacob's words tumbled forth in a rush.

Ezra met his gaze with a determined expression. "We may have something."

CHAPTER THIRTY-ONE

DAY SEVEN OF EXILE

JACOB CAUTIOUSLY NEARED Ostria, the palisade rising before him. Made of thick tree trunks planted firmly into the earth, the palisade wrapped around the settlement, its intimidating spikes designed to ward off intruders. Indeed, it was a formidable barrier.

For now, he feared.

His gaze lifted beyond the palisade to the central tower of Ostria, a towering structure of timber reinforced with stone. The rounded shape of the tower tapered slightly as it rose, with a spiral staircase winding its way to a platform at the top, bordered by sturdy railings. From this vantage point, the tower loomed as an imposing presence, its silhouette stark against the fiery hues streaking the sky.

Jacob bit the insides of his cheek, his gaze lingering on the tower. Within those walls, Ostria's council would soon decide their fate—a judgment that could shape the rest of their lives on Eremos.

If they even let us in.

Jaci had explained how the tower once stood as a beacon of hope for new exiles, but since Daemion's banishment, Ostria's council had imposed stricter rules for granting refuge. Indeed, Jacob had felt a spark of hope when he first glimpsed Ostria from the Screech. Now, however, that hope waned at the thought of him and his fellow exiles being denied entry.

"Do you really think this will work?" Ammon asked, casting a worried glance at him as they walked through the vast clearing of grass dotted with patches of ash.

"I can't think of a better idea," Jacob said.

"You guys could go on without me."

"That's not an option, Ammon. We're all in this together."

Ammon exhaled deeply. "I just don't want to be the reason you don't get in."

Jacob's gaze fell to Ammon's arms, now smeared in soot to conceal his Last Patriot tattoo. It wasn't a foolproof plan, but amid the ash blanketing Eremos from the inferno, it was their best chance to avoid detection. He, Alex, and Morgan had similarly disguised their arms and faces, aiming to draw any scrutiny away from Ammon.

"It'll work," Jacob said.

"Look!" Morgan whispered urgently, pointing ahead.

At the center of the palisade, massive wooden doors swung open, revealing the gateway into Ostria. Through the haze, a group of figures emerged, their silhouettes blurred but unmistakably Jacob could tell they clutched spears in their hands.

"Well, let's hope you're right," Ammon said, casting a glance at Jacob.

As uncertain as Jacob was, he remained resolute, leading their small band forward, each step bringing them closer to the people of Ostria. Eventually they came into focus, and Jacob could see that, like them, they wore makeshift balaclavas to conceal their faces, leaving only their eyes visible. The heat pressed their clothing against their skin, but unlike the tattered garments he had seen elsewhere on Eremos, their attire was simple yet tidy. It served as a reminder that they were stepping into unfamiliar territory, still unsure of what awaited them beyond those walls.

A petite figure with wizened eyes stepped forward from the group, strands of white hair peeking out from beneath their balaclava, hinting at their age. The others fell into formation, their bodies tense, poised to protect.

"Don't take another step," commanded a woman's voice.

Jacob halted, his eyes studying the woman before them. It was clear she was the group's leader—perhaps even a councilor of Ostria. He hoped so. And he knew from this point forward, every move would need to be intentional and cautious to avoid any missteps that might label them as threats.

"Why do you approach Ostria?" the woman asked.

Alex elbowed Jacob softly. "You're up," she whispered in jest.

Taking a steadying breath, Jacob pulled down his balaclava, signaling the others to do the same. "We mean no harm," he said. "We've come seeking refuge within your walls."

"How long has it been since Derro cast you out?"

"Roughly a week. Though it's hard to say exactly. Our days have blended together. The journey here was challenging."

"From the looks of you, I have no doubts about that," the woman said as she approached, her arms clasped behind her. "Your swift arrival intrigues me, though. Few ever reach Ostria, let alone within a week. And yet, here you stand."

"We had some help along the way," Jacob said, gesturing upward. "Your tower, specifically. I spotted it when I jumped from the Screech, along with the pool of water behind it. Water has been scarce. Your tower has been our beacon of hope."

"Indeed, that is its purpose," the woman said, pulling down her balaclava to reveal a soft, wrinkled face. "Are any of you marked?"

"Marked?" Jacob echoed, feigning ignorance.

"Show me your wrists."

Jacob nodded to the others, gesturing for them to reveal their wrists. His unease grew. He had expected this moment, but now that it had arrived, his confidence wavered. *It's going to work,* he repeated to himself, though the mantra did little to calm his nerves.

"Gerrick, check them," the woman said.

The group gave a wide berth to a burly man who started toward them, obeying the command without hesitation. Each of his steps sent a muted thud against the earth, his broad shoulders swaying as he neared. He reached Jacob first, grasping his wrists with a tight grip. Wiping away the soot, Gerrick's eyes narrowed as he inspected them. Jacob couldn't ignore the man's bloodshot eye, surrounded by a patchwork of purple and blue bruises. Their eyes met briefly, and Gerrick scowled before releasing Jacob's wrists.

Gerrick moved along the line, performing the same curt inspection with Alex and Morgan. He cleared them just as quickly, and rightly so. They weren't marked. When Gerrick reached Ammon, Jacob's heart raced. Anxiety crawled through him as he watched the brute seize Ammon's wrists and wipe away the soot.

Then suddenly, he yanked Ammon's wrist upward for a closer look. It was the one with the Last Patriot tattoo. Jacob's pulse quickened, his eyes darting around, searching for any sign of movement from Ostria's group. His gaze drifted back to Ammon, who stared wide-eyed at Gerrick. Finally, the man released Ammon's wrists.

"No marking, Monique," Gerrick said. "Just ash."

"Very well, thank you, Gerrick."

Jacob breathed a huge sigh of relief. He could have sworn they were just about to get caught.

"Please," Alex said, her voice strained. "We aren't threats to you."

"How can we be so certain?" Monique countered. "Indeed, you don't appear threatening at first glance, but looks can be deceiving. You were *exiled*, after all. Derro saw fit to cast you out for actions deemed grievous enough to warrant such punishment. And now you come here, seeking refuge within our walls."

"But isn't that how *everyone* arrived here?" Ammon asked.

"Yes, however, due to *unfortunate* past circumstances, we must be selective with who we allow into our sanctuary."

"Jacob, tell them about the attack," Morgan said, his words tumbling out.

"An *attack?*" Monique echoed, her eyes widening. "What does the boy mean?"

Jacob frowned. *Ah, come on, kid, not like this.* He sighed. "We've come to warn you that Ostria is under threat," he said. "We hoped you'd grant us refuge in return. The Maws and Last Patriots plan to strike tonight, taking advantage of the chaos caused by the encroaching wildfire."

The group behind Monique exchanged worried glances, murmurs erupting among them. Monique raised her hand, silencing the rising chatter.

"How certain are you of this attack?" she asked.

"It's inevitable," Jacob answered. "During our first night here, the Maws captured us, and their leader, Daemion, disclosed their plans to me."

Monique's eyes narrowed. "Why would he reveal such information to a captive?"

"He wanted something I couldn't give him."

"And what was that?"

Jacob hesitated, knowing he needed to tread carefully from here. "Guns."

"Guns?" Monique repeated, her eyebrows shooting up. "Certainly, there are no firearms on Eremos."

"Unfortunately, that is no longer the case. There is *a* gun here on Eremos. Wielded by a madman who used the gunpowder from the bullets to burn down the Maws' camp. He's the one responsible for the wildfire sweeping across Eremos."

Monique tilted her head as she processed Jacob's words. Indeed, they sounded strange, but they needed to be said. He just hoped Monique believed him. It helped that the effects of the inferno had spread to Ostria.

"How did this madman come by a gun?" she finally asked.

"He took it from a Culler before jumping from the Screech. I saw the whole thing. He struck one Culler in the neck, causing him to drop his gun. Then he used that gun to kill another Culler."

"He's got some twisted belief that burning down Eremos is his God-given mission," Ammon said. "And the fire is God's wrath, purging Eremos of its wickedness."

"And that lunatic is still out there," Alex said. "Just like the Maws and Last Patriots. It's only a matter of time before they all arrive here."

"Indeed, that is concerning," Monique said. "However, I still fail to understand. If this madman already possesses the gun, why would Daemion believe *you* could help him acquire more?"

Jacob drew a breath, weighing his next words. "Well," he said, "that's because I had a gun, too. After the madman jumped from the Screech, I took the other gun from the Culler he had killed before jumping. But I don't have it anymore. I destroyed it to escape from the Maws."

"You *destroyed* the gun to escape?"

"Yes. On the same night of our abduction, the madman used his gun to shoot and kill two Maws. Daemion knew their deaths couldn't have been caused by my gun because he was there during our capture, and the madman's actions occurred elsewhere. So, as far as he knew, there were at least two guns on Eremos. He hoped there were more so he could arm his forces for the attack, and I led him to believe there were. It wasn't easy to do, but I knew it was the only way to get us out of there alive."

"And we are simply expected to believe you destroyed this gun? That seems like an unlikely method to escape."

"You're welcome to check us," Jacob said, spreading his arms. "You'll find we're unarmed."

"We're not here to hurt anyone," Ammon said. "We only want to warn you of the attack and help you prepare for it."

"Well, if this madman was capable of burning down the Maws' camp, as you said, then it suggests their forces have been significantly weakened," Monique countered.

"Even so, the Last Patriots are still a threat," Jacob said. "In Derro, they were on the edge of open conflict with the council and had successfully sabotaged three Control Hubs before they were thwarted. Their failure there only fuels their determination here."

Monique straightened, her eyes contemplative as she studied each of them. After a brief moment, she nodded. "Very well," she said. "Though your tale sounds strange, it carries a weight of truth too heavy to dismiss. The rest of the council must be informed immediately. Gerrick, have them checked."

"Does this mean you'll let us in?" Morgan asked.

"It means I will convene with the rest of the council so you can present all the information you have regarding this supposed attack," Monique said. "If we deem your information credible, accepting your warning will likely secure you refuge. However, I must emphasize that there are no assurances. The decision will rest with the majority vote of the council."

The rest of the council? As Gerrick and a few others approached, patting them down in search of weapons, Monique's words registered fully in his head. Did this mean she was a councilor of Ostria's council?

Suddenly, his shoulders felt lighter, his body less tense. There was a chance he'd just convinced a councilor to let them inside Ostria. He just desperately hoped her influence would be enough to impress upon the rest of the council the urgency of the attack and secure their refuge. While it wasn't a guarantee, it was a step in the right direction—an accomplishment they'd worked for diligently since escaping the Maws. He adjusted his clothing, rumpled from the search, and nodded to Monique.

"We understand," he said.

"Very well, then," Monique said, motioning for them to follow. "If this attack is as imminent as you claim, we cannot afford to waste any time. Come now."

Jacob started toward Ostria, following the group. He exchanged relieved smiles with the others, all happy they had made it this far—just a stone's throw away from potential safety. Though the looming threat of tonight's attack still worried him, the waning hope he had felt earlier began to refuel within him. He clung to it, believing that their warning to the council would be enough.

As he approached the palisade, he fell into step behind Monique and her group, crossing a flat wooden bridge, his gaze drawn to the freshly dug trench below, which, like the palisade, wrapped around Ostria. Water filled its depths, clearly creating an effective firebreak for the inferno and adding another line of defense.

Stepping into Ostria, the wooden doors closed behind him, sealing the palisade. Jacob didn't glance back. His attention was fixed ahead, drawn to the vibrancy of life around him. Ostria thrummed with the energy of a hive. Clusters of people hurried about, hauling buckets of water and distributing them along the palisade and around the dwellings. Some doused the stockade and huts with water, saturating the wood to prevent it from igniting, their faces marked by fatigue, yet resolute.

There was a palpable sense of unity among the people of Ostria, reminiscent of what he had witnessed with the Last Patriots yesterday. Strangely, it contrasted with the perpetual division he had experienced in Derro, making him see that survival didn't always lead to anarchy. It could also foster solidarity.

Though, as heartening as this unity was, he knew the impending attack would soon test it, their determination giving way to a desperate struggle for survival. Jacob had witnessed firsthand the extremes people would go to in the name of survival, and sadly, he knew the cost all too well.

But he was determined to help, already planning strategies to share with the council for their defense. These were people who had embraced their exile, learned from their faults, and started anew. They had built Ostria from nothing, forging a way of life that defied the wickedness surrounding them. Ostria was their home. It was Jaci's home. And Jacob hoped it could be his, at least for now.

"Jacob, come on," Morgan called from up ahead.

Jacob hurried to catch up, traversing a dirt path that stirred clouds of dust with every step. His gaze wandered over the evolving settlement. Homes and buildings made of timber and stone leaned against one another for shared support. They were larger than he had imagined, spacious enough to house multiple families.

Ahead, the path opened into a bustling marketplace. Children ran about, their laughter filling the air. Vendors shouted their wares, and shops stood alongside what appeared to be a health center. Most people barely glanced at him, too preoccupied with conversations or their own tasks. Jacob loved it.

He marveled at the ingenuity of the community: blacksmiths forging iron tools and weapons, potters shaping clay into elegant vessels, and workers in a communal garden racing to harvest crops before the inferno reached them. Each person moved with purpose, something Jacob hadn't felt in far too long. But after everything he had endured, he could feel a flicker of it returning, filling the hollow space inside him. And surprisingly, he welcomed it.

Finally catching up with the others, he exited the marketplace and followed another dirt path shaded by trees. The thunderous cascade of waterfalls grew louder, heralding their approach to a shimmering pool ahead. Aching with thirst, his gaze fixed on the oasis, its glistening surface promising relief.

They emerged into a small clearing, the pool just steps away. Its tranquil waters, cradled by the embrace of lush trees, were a sight he hadn't dared imagine. Circular dining platforms, constructed from timber, dotted the area, with some already occupied. Jacob's eyes met those of a tall man seated with his family. Their demeanor shifted to one of apprehension, and he immediately understood. The wariness etched on their faces wasn't hostility; it was fear—fear of strangers entering their home. He couldn't blame them. If their positions were reversed, he would have felt the same.

"You are to wait here while the council is convened," Monique said, pulling Jacob's attention to her. She turned to Gerrick. "Ensure they are provided with sustenance."

Gerrick nodded. "Understood."

With a nod, Monique turned and started back down the dirt path. Jacob watched her retreat until his attention was drawn back to Gerrick, who was now speaking in hushed tones with his comrades. It appeared he was delegating tasks, perhaps sending a few to fetch the promised food and ensuring the others stayed alert. But to Jacob's surprise, it was Gerrick himself who set off down the dirt path after Monique. He narrowed his eyes, unease prickling at the back of his mind. For someone who seemed like Ostria's muscle, Gerrick's departure felt unexpected. Jacob had assumed he'd stay to keep a close eye on them.

"Food is on its way," a woman's voice announced, interrupting his thoughts.

Jacob turned to see her approaching, a spear gripped firmly in her hand. Her posture was relaxed but watchful. "For now, you can rest and enjoy the pool. You may drink from it, but swimming is strictly forbidden."

Jacob wasted no time. Dropping to his knees at the water's edge, he plunged his hands into the cool pool, scooping up handfuls and pouring them into his mouth. The sensation was a balm to his parched throat and weary soul. Beside him, Morgan, Alex, and Ammon followed suit, eagerly quenching their thirst, their relief palpable in the clearing's stillness.

When his thirst was finally sated, Jacob sank onto the soft earth, his body heavy with exhaustion. He closed his eyes, allowing the tranquility of the surroundings to wash over him. The steady roar of the waterfalls blended with the hum of insects and faint murmurs from the nearby settlement, creating a rare moment of calm.

Since Charlotte's death, silence had often felt like a weapon, amplifying his doubts and regrets. But here, with the hope of refuge, the stillness felt less oppressive, a faint promise of peace. For the first time since his exile, he allowed himself to exhale fully, even if only for a moment.

The thought of the council meeting intruded on his reprieve. Monique's belief in their warning was a crucial step, but convincing the rest of the council was another battle entirely. He would need to present himself not just as a bearer of bad news, but as someone valuable—someone capable of contributing to their survival and future.

He began mentally rehearsing what he would say. He considered mentioning his skills, his willingness to work, and his determination to integrate into their community. Yet a shadow loomed over his resolve: the crime that had led to his exile.

Would they ask? Of course, they would. He dreaded the moment, knowing the truth could shift their perception of him. Still, he resolved to be honest, even if it meant revealing the worst of himself.

But that was a concern for later. For now, the attack loomed larger than any personal reckoning. That had to be his focus so he could ensure the council understood the severity of the threat and prepare to survive it. Everything else could wait.

Jacob's eyes snapped open as someone settled beside him. Morgan sat cross-legged, staring at the waterfalls in the distance, his expression distant. Stifling a groan, Jacob pushed himself upright.

"You get enough to drink?" he asked.

Morgan nodded but didn't respond, his hands fidgeting in his lap. After a moment, he sniffled, lowering his head.

Jacob frowned. "You all right?" he asked, leaning closer.

Morgan turned toward him, his eyes glistening with unshed tears. "They're not going to let me in, are they?"

The question hit Jacob heavily. He hesitated, then placed a hand on Morgan's shoulder. "Hey, try not to think that way," he said gently. "It's normal to feel scared. Hell, I feel it too. But you're a good kid who, like everyone else here, made a mistake. They'll see that."

Morgan sniffled again, quickly swiping at his eyes. "But what if they don't?" he whispered.

Jacob gave his shoulder a reassuring squeeze. "I refuse to let myself think that way. And I won't let you face this alone, okay? We're in this together. You, me, Alex, and Ammon. No one gets left behind."

Morgan frowned, his shoulders slumping. "I wish I was strong enough to think that way."

Jacob chuckled softly. "Kid, you're stronger than you think."

Morgan managed a small, tentative smile, his tears drying. As they sat together, Jacob felt a quiet warmth stir in his chest. Seeing Morgan find comfort in his presence felt … right. Like he was doing something that mattered.

The moment reminded him of that morning with Charlotte, on their back deck, when she comforted him, her steady presence pulling him out of his turmoil. The pain of that loss still lingered, but now, for the first time, he could see how far he'd come.

He couldn't help but wonder if she could see it too, this version of him, stronger, steadier. A part of him liked to think she could.

"Hey, Jacob," Morgan said hesitantly, "there's something I need to tell you."

"Sure, what's up?"

Morgan drew a breath as he fished into his pocket. "I took something from you I want to give back. When we were stuck in the pit, I took these when you were taking the gun apart."

He opened his hand to reveal three bullets. Jacob's eyes grew alert as he extended his hand, letting Morgan spill the bullets into his palm. Glancing quickly around, hoping no one was watching, he stuffed the bullets into his pocket.

"I know it was wrong," Morgan rushed on. "But I was scared. I thought you might not come back. I thought if I took them you'd have to."

Jacob's face softened. "It's okay. I understand."

"I'm sorry."

"No need to apologize," Jacob said, offering a reassuring smile. "No harm done. Plus, they're almost useless without a gun."

"So, you're not mad at me?"

"No, I'm not mad at you," Jacob said, chuckling softly.

Morgan smiled. "Thanks, by the way," he said, meeting Jacob's eyes. "For coming back. And for getting us here. I'd be dead for sure by now if it weren't for you."

Jacob's smile widened. "Don't mention it, kid."

"Hey, guys," Ammon called out. "Food's here."

Jacob glanced over his shoulder, seeing Ammon wave them toward him. He was sitting at a table, with Alex by his side. Gerrick must have returned.

"Let's get some grub," Jacob said, patting Morgan's back.

Morgan sprang up eagerly. Jacob struggled to follow, his aching muscles still in protest. As he approached the table, he saw fresh faces placing platters of fruit and meat in front of them—but no sign of Gerrick. His absence gnawed at Jacob's mind. Monique's departure made sense. She had to gather the council. *But Gerrick? Why hadn't he returned?*

"You good?" Ammon asked, mouth full of food.

Jacob snapped out of his musings and nodded, taking a seat next to Morgan. The smell of fresh fruit and meat assaulted his senses, the hazy air and drifting ash doing little to dampen his appetite. Nothing could ruin this meal for him.

"I am now," he said with a grin, grabbing a piece of fruit. But as he chewed, that flicker of unease refused to fade. It made him consider whether Gerrick had actually seen Ammon's Last Patriot tattoo. If he had, why hadn't he said anything?

You're just being paranoid, he finally told himself.

He just hoped he was right.

CHAPTER THIRTY-TWO

THE FINAL DAYS BEFORE EXILE

OH MY GOD, Jacob screamed in his head.

His heart quickened in his chest as he scrambled to pull on a snug jacket and boots, his mind racing with potential revelations Ezra brought. *Could this be it? Did Ezra finally find him?* Hope surged within him, mingling with a sense of renewed vigor as he hurried to join Ezra outside.

Stepping into the cool morning air, he followed Ezra into a sleek, black Culler Nervo Pod, the haunting owl of the council's owl emblem glaring at him. He stepped inside and settled into the plush seating, his left leg starting its nervous bounce.

"Alpha, take us to the station," Ezra requested.

"Right away, Ezra," Alpha said, the Auxes words emanating from the pod's speakers.

The Nervo Pod began its descent, navigation down Jacob's snakelike hill toward downtown Tuto, its wheels splashing through the wet snow. Jacob leaned forward, eager to learn more about what Ezra had discovered.

"So, did you find him?" he asked.

"Does the name Ammon Curran ring any bells for you?"

"No, not that I can think of, anyway."

"As you might know, we've been busy rounding up Last Patriots since the first Control Hub attack. We apprehended a group last night, and one of them—this Ammon—claims to have valuable information on what happened at Hoos that night. He's willing to talk, but only if it gets him out of exile."

"Then it's true, right? The men who robbed us were connected to the Last Patriots?"

"That's still unclear, but their goals seem aligned. Remember, Mason didn't have a star tattoo. And unfortunately, your case, it's become tangled in a widespread theory going around online. Some people believe that the men who robbed Hoos armed the Last Patriots for their attacks. Ammon could know nothing."

Jacob sighed and leaned back in his seat, grappling with the implications of Ezra's words. He knew the theory had gained traction online. It was possible this Last Patriot might be nothing more than a desperate opportunist, using the whispers of the internet to save himself from exile.

"That's why I'm bringing you in," Ezra continued. "I need you to put eyes on him. See if he shows any signs of being her killer."

"You think he could be Charlotte's killer?"

"It's possible, yeah. He could be deliberately diverting our attention. This is the biggest lead we've got, and I'm not excluding any possibilities."

"Then I have to speak with him."

Ezra frowned. "I'm afraid that's not possible. The council won't allow it. I can promise you'll see him and hear his voice during the interrogation, though."

Jacob let out a deep, resigned sigh. He had expected that answer from Ezra, though he had hoped for a different one. An overwhelming pressure settled heavily on him. He desperately wanted this man to be her killer, but almost a year had passed since that night, and he doubted hearing this man's voice would confirm it. Seeing him wouldn't help either, considering he'd worn a mask.

"I know how challenging all this will be for you," Ezra said. "I haven't mentioned it before, but I've also experienced the pain of losing a loved one. So, when I say I understand how you're feeling, I truly mean it."

"Who was it you lost?"

"My older brother."

"Did you find his killer?"

"Sadly, finding his killer wasn't hard. He took his own life. Just like …" Ezra's voice trailed off.

"I'm sorry to hear that."

"It wasn't much of a shock. My brother battled with mental illness. Towards the end, he had gotten lost in conspiracy theories. Even tried finding ways to join the Last Patriots. He'd always say, 'It's not the land of the *free* anymore.' I guess it had all become too much for him, so he chose his own form of exile."

Own form of exile … Jacob, sadly, understood all too well. Just moments ago, he had considered a similar option. He frowned, realizing that in that moment, with the screwdriver in his hand, logic and reason had seemed hidden from his mind. It was as if the very concept of self-harm lurked in the darkest corners of his mind, waiting for the weakest moment to seize control. He had been so close to choosing his own form of exile.

"Should we find Charlotte's killer today," Ezra said, pulling Jacob from his thoughts, "have you come to terms with the justice of exile?"

Jacob leaned forward. "I'm not sure I understand what you mean."

"It's just … I've been down this road before, many times. For some, exile alone isn't enough justice, something you told me yourself when we first met. If that's the case, there are people I know who can help. They helped me through the loss of my brother, and I believe they can offer you the same guidance and understanding."

Jacob processed the question. He'd been so fixated on Charlotte's killer that he'd failed to entertain what would happen after? Exile would be the punishment; justice served.

But Charlotte would still be gone.

"The only acceptable form of justice would be to have Charlotte back," Jacob finally said. "That can't happen. So, I guess his exile will have to do."

My own form of exile, that is.

"All right," Ezra said, his gaze shifting to the window. "Looks like we're here."

Jacob looked beyond the window, where the sight of Tuto's Culler Station made his eyes widen. The towering structure broadened as it rose, piercing the sky. Neon lights outlined its sleek form, stretching all the way to its roof, which spread out like the wings of an owl, dominating the skyline with an authoritative presence.

Flying overhead were machine orbs—security drones scanning the perimeter for threats. As he observed them circling, his gaze caught sight of a Screech hovering in the air before landing on top of the station. *More Last Patriots?*

The sounds of chanting reached his ears, pulling his attention away from the sky and back to the road. A mob of protesters stood before a holographic barrier, their voices raised in anger as the Nervo Pod approached the security checkpoint.

Among them, like a formidable leader, was a short woman with round spectacles and a pointed nose. Her passionate voice boomed from a megaphone as she led the crowd in chants, their shouts reverberating from the pod's windows.

"Exile is vile! Exile is futile!"

As they reached the checkpoint, a large holographic screen smoothly emerged from the floor, scanning both Jacob's and Ezra's faces. While Jacob was being scanned, his gaze fell on the sorrowful eyes of a man and woman protester holding a sign that read, "Exile isn't for the juvenile!"

Sadly, exile didn't discriminate based on age.

"Seeker Ezra Pierce, cleared for entry," Alpha announced. "Tuto citizen Jacob Hughes, no criminal record, sufficient social score, cleared for entry."

The holographic barrier in front of the pod vanished, and an army of Cullers came rushing through, dispersing the protesters as the pod glided past. Once they cleared the crowd, the pod descended into a dark tunnel, its interior instantly illuminated by soft lights.

"Are we underground?" Jacob asked.

"Indeed. Security is paramount for the council."

It made Jacob wonder how the Last Patriots had managed to take down the Control Hubs. For the longest time, no one knew where they were, yet the rebellion had not only found them but repeatedly breached them. Seeing the formidable security firsthand, Jacob couldn't shake the thought proposed by those dead thugs: Had the Last Patriots *actually* infiltrated key positions within the Derro government? It was the only explanation that made sense.

They ascended a short incline and emerged from the tunnel into a vast garage lined with other Nervo Pods, each marked with the council's owl emblem.

"You ready?" Ezra asked.

Jacob nodded, though he found himself biting the insides of his cheeks, nervous to find out what lay ahead.

"All right," Ezra said.

Once the Nervo Pod came to a stop, they stepped out and walked toward a thick cement door. Jacob's gaze flicked to the camera overhead as it emitted a holographic beam, scanning them both. Moments later, Alpha announced their clearance to enter, and a soft, mechanical hiss accompanied the cement doors parting.

Jacob followed Ezra inside, his gaze sweeping over the station. Holographic displays lined the walls, broadcasting real-time news and images of wanted criminals. The floors gleamed with a polished material, reflecting their footsteps like mirrors, creating a weightless sensation with each step. They came to a stop at an elevator.

"Alpha, take us to the interrogation block," Ezra requested.

After another holographic scan, access was granted, and the elevator doors whispered open. As Jacob stepped inside, he noticed the back of the elevator was entirely glass, offering a view of the outside as they ascended. He could still see the protesters gathered in the distance, their signs waving in the air.

"Exile is futile?" he mused aloud, turning to Ezra. "Were you always a supporter of exile?"

"It's all I've ever known. Not much different from what came before."

"Prison systems?"

"Exactly. Exile has been part of human history since the dawn of time. Before Derro, the US banished criminals to prisons. Now the council exiles them to remote locations. Same concept, different execution, no pun intended. I mean, even Adam and Eve were banished from the Garden of Eden."

Jacob shifted his attention back to the protesters, their forms shrinking into tiny specks as they ascended. "Adam and Eve … the first exiles," he murmured.

When the elevator reached its destination, rising at least twenty stories, the doors sighed open. Jacob's gaze immediately locked onto the unexpected sight before him. Standing at the threshold of the elevator was Wes, the former commander of the Cullers. Beside him stood a younger man Jacob didn't recognize, a scar above his left eyebrow marking his face. Their imposing figures blocked Jacob's view of what appeared to be a standing holographic stretcher behind them. The stretcher resembled a log-shaped capsule that contained a human body with folded arms and closed eyes, as if in a peaceful slumber.

"Well, would you look at that," Wes drawled, a smirk tugging at the corners of his mouth as he eyed Ezra and Jacob.

"Wes," Ezra replied, his tone flat.

"What's *he* doing here?" Wes asked, recognizing who Jacob was.

"We're following up on a lead," Ezra said. "Now, if you could step aside—"

"I was right, wasn't I?" Wes pressed. "Those men who killed his wife. They were Last Patriots."

"You know I can't tell you that," Ezra said.

"Whatever," Wes muttered, scowling. "I know it was *them*. It's how they got armed for their assault on the Control Hubs. I knew it was coming then, but no one would listen."

"Wes, that's enough," Ezra said firmly. "Step aside and get back to your exile duties."

Wes's scowl deepened, but he complied with Ezra's command, silently moving aside and pivoting the stretcher roughly out of their path. As Jacob followed Ezra past Wes and the other Culler, he gave a brief nod of acknowledgement. Wes had voiced his suspicions about the men who killed Charlotte being Last Patriots, but the council hadn't acted on them. Or maybe Wes's brutal methods of extracting information had clouded the council's judgment. Still, Wes had been onto something.

"Ya know, Ezra," Wes said, stepping into the elevator. "Exile duty's not so bad. You oughta try it sometime." He laughed to himself. "The looks on their faces. Gets me every time."

Ezra ignored Wes's last remark and kept walking. Jacob stayed close, but as the elevator doors began to close, he glanced back, catching sight of Wes's smirk. After all this time without justice for Charlotte's death, Jacob found himself strangely relating to Wes's brand of lethal justice.

They eventually arrived at a steel door and stepped inside after another holographic scan. Ezra led Jacob into a small, plain room, furnished with only a few chairs facing a sleek, transparent pane of glass that was seamlessly integrated into the wall. Beyond it was another room, a metal table at its center, flanked by three chairs. On the table lay two half-moon shaped devices, their reflective surfaces glinting under the harsh lighting.

"That's where I'll question him," Ezra said. "You'll watch from in here. Commander Brody is bringing him up now."

Jacob nodded, the tension in his stomach tightening as he sank into one of the chairs. In just a few moments, he hoped to face the man who had destroyed his life. But deep down, there lurked the nagging suspicion that this man was nothing more than an opportunist, using Jacob's case to escape exile. He forced that thought down, knowing he needed to manage his hope carefully.

"You doing all right?" Ezra asked, settling into the chair next to Jacob.

"Just nervous," he said, his eyes staring blankly into the room beyond. "I really hope this ends with us finally finding him."

"You remember what you told me that day when we learned I'd purchase one of Charlotte's photographs?"

"Use it as motivation," Jacob said, the words coming back to him.

Ezra nodded. "Since that day, I've done just that. Every time I leave my house, I stand in front of it. It grounds me. Reminds me of what's at stake. To find her killer. And when I come home, it's a reminder of my failure to do so." He drew a breath. "I know this last year hasn't given us the answers we both wanted, but I assure you, when I question this man, that will be my only goal—answers. No stone will be left unturned."

The sound of the door opening snapped Jacob's attention to the entrance of the room beyond the mirror. An olive-skinned man, clad in a red jumpsuit, with a scruffy beard and shoulder-length hair, walked in, his hands bound by holocuffs. Commander Brody followed closely behind. She ordered the man to sit, and then she released his restraints. After a brief pause, she instructed him to place his hands on the half-moon devices at the center of the table. The man complied, and in an instant, his hands were bound again with holographic restraints.

"I'm going in now," Ezra said. "If you need or remember anything, just knock on the mirror."

Jacob nodded as he watched Ezra rise and start toward the door. His left leg began its involuntary bouncing as his gaze shifted beyond the mirror to the people in the interrogation room. Ezra settled into a chair next to the commander, requested Alpha to start recording, and then silence fell. No one spoke.

"Well, aren't you going to ask me questions?" the Last Patriot finally asked, breaking the silence.

Jacob listened to each word, noting how they were spoken, and tried to find recognition. He felt there was a sense of familiarity, but also feared that it could just be him wanting it to sound like *him*. He knew he couldn't let his eagerness cloud his judgment. The last thing he wanted was to exile the wrong man.

"We were waiting for you," Ezra said, leaning back in his seat. "You're the one who is claiming to have information to share with us."

"Unless you were lying?" Commander Brody said. "Is that it? You just buying as much time as possible before you're exiled to Eremos?"

"*Eremos?*" Ammon shrieked.

"Well, of course," Commander Brody said. "Seems like a fitting exile for all you Last Patriots. Or should I say terrorists?"

"But if I tell you guys what happened that night, I can avoid exile?"

"That all depends on how valuable the information is."

"Tell me, Ammon," Ezra said, leaning forward. "Does it make you feel good to hinder someone's pursuit of justice in exchange for your own freedom?"

"It's not like *that*. I'm trying to help."

Ezra scowled. "Then talk. Tell us what you know, and we'll see just how *helpful* you're trying to be."

"All right," Ammon said, taking a deep breath and nodding, as if convincing himself he was making the right choice by talking. "A little over a year ago, a childhood friend reached out to me with a job for some quick cash. We'd grown up in foster care together and used to take on shady work now and then. You know, just trying to survive another day."

The Last Patriot scoffed as he shook his head in disbelief. "But that's always easier said than done. Once your social score's as low as mine, getting it back up is like trying to climb out of an endless pit. I'd been working on it, trying to leave that life behind, but he'd known I was struggling, living on the streets and such. So, he told me about this guy he'd met who was paying top dollar for easy jobs."

"Easy jobs?" Commander Brody probed.

"As in committing a crime," Ammon said. "He told me the guy didn't care what kind of crime it was, only that it was committed in a certain area. And that the Cullers were called."

Don't forget to call the Cullers. Mason's threat from that night echoed in Jacob's mind.

"Do you know who this guy is?" Commander Brody dug deeper.

"I have no idea, but trust me, if I did, I'd tell you. Dude's been trying to kill me, I swear."

"Why would he want to kill you?" Ezra asked.

"Because I told my friend I wouldn't do the job. The guy is tying up loose ends. Who do you think killed those two thugs a few months back?"

"Are you suggesting that the man who hired your friend *also* killed those two men?"

Ammon shrugged. "I don't know. I doubt *he* killed them. Probably hired someone to do it for him. Just like he tried doing to me."

"Okay, so how does this all correlate with what happened at Hoos?" Ezra asked.

"The job *was* Hoos. Mason told me all we had to do was hold it up, intimidate the employees, steal some stuff, and get out. That's it. No one was supposed to die."

"Mason, as in Mason Rowley? That's your childhood friend?" Commander Brody asked.

"Yes, but I didn't take the job," Ammon blurted. "It was too risky. Nothing about it screamed *easy*. I mean, robbing a gun store? Come on. That sounded like a death sentence to me."

Jacob clenched his teeth, his hands squeezing into fists. *They were friends.*

"And we're just supposed to believe you?" Ezra said.

Ammon scoffed. "That would be easier, but I don't expect you to. I have an alibi for that night. I was at work. I was the chef at Liberties."

Ezra raised an eyebrow. "Liberties, huh? The bar Mason just happened to frequent a series of times before he and *supposedly* not you robbed Hoos?"

"Yeah, he needed someone he could trust to do the job with. He'd come by a lot, trying to get me to do it with him, saying he was having trouble finding someone else. Begged me to change my mind. But I didn't. I swear."

As Ammon had explained himself, Ezra had flipped through a series of case notes on his holographic tablet. "Ah, here it is," he said. "Liberties list of employees. Your name isn't listed on it."

"That's because I don't work there anymore, hence the, 'I *was* the chef at Liberties.' I got fired a week or so after that night. But Bel, the owner, he'll still vouch for me being there. Hell, I'd even be on their security footage."

"Yeah, well, sadly Liberties and any other store near it doesn't have much footage from that night," Ezra said, his eyes still tracing something on the tablet. "Mason had somehow managed to jam the footage and the council's Aux system. Do you know anything about that?"

"Jam? I didn't even know that was possible."

Commander Brody frowned. "And let me guess, if you *did* know anything, you'd definitely tell us."

"I thought the council's Control Hubs prevented that?" Ammon asked.

"You mean the ones you and your pals destroyed?" Ezra said.

"Yeah, exactly. That's why I was sent to destroy them. We're trying to spark change. These Auxes and their social scores dictate everything about our lives. They don't eliminate crime. They create criminals. Make one wrong move, and you're condemned to a life of poverty."

"Spark change?" Commander Brody interjected. "How does robbing a gun store and murdering an innocent woman and her unborn child spark change?"

Ammon squeezed his eyes shut, hands clenching into fists. "From what I know about that night, her death was an accident. Like I've said, when Mason approached me about the job, he said we just had to scare the owners, steal a few things, and make sure the Callers were called. He *never* mentioned killing. Or guns."

"Accident or not, his actions led to her death," Ezra said. "And he was definitely there for the guns. He made that very clear. Can you think of any reason why?"

Ammon shook his head. "If he wanted guns, then the job had changed since he'd asked me to do it with him."

"It wasn't to arm the rebellion?" Commander Brody probed.

"I have no clue. Mason *wasn't* a Last Patriot. But he *wanted* to be."

"Do you think he tried robbing Hoos of its guns so he could bring them to the Last Patriots in exchange for joining them?"

"I don't know. I mean, it's possible. But he died—"

"And yet the rebellion still got their arsenal," Commander Brody interrupted. "You know, I find it ironic. You claim to have wanted to distance yourself from that kind of life, yet here you are—a Last Patriot. Perhaps you did take the job with Mason. And when you ran out of Hoos looking for safety, there was only one group of people who could offer it to you. In exchange for guns."

"No," Ammon said through gritted teeth. "I already told you. I have an alibi. Her death isn't my fault."

"Well, I do see your name here," Ezra said, looking up from his tablet. "Under the list of former employees."

"*See*, I told you. I'm not lying."

"This doesn't prove you're not lying, Ammon," Ezra said. "Just proves you were telling the truth about working at Liberties. Mason could've still changed your mind. You could've still done the job."

Ammon sighed. "I don't know what else to say to convince you guys I didn't take the job. Check the cameras. Once they're back online or whatever, you'll see me on them. Guaranteed."

"Why not?" Commander Brody asked.

Ammon's eyes narrowed. "What do you mean?"

"Why didn't you take the job? You said you'd been struggling, and Mason offered you a chance to earn, as you put it, top dollar."

"I already told you. The job wasn't as easy as he made it sound. I was trying to do the right thing and work on improving my social score."

"But you said yourself that's a task easier said than done," Ezra countered. "Maybe you finally figured that out and took Mason up on his offer?"

Ammon shook his arms violently, frustration pouring out. "You're not looking for me," he snapped. "You're looking for whoever Mason wound up finding to do the job with."

"Except we haven't been able to do that," Ezra said. "You were supposed to help with that, remember?"

"Find the guy who hired Mason, the same one who's been *trying* to kill me, and you can find that woman's killer."

"But you don't know who that is either," Commander Brody said, shaking her head in frustration. "Ammon, if you're looking to avoid exile, you're going to have to do better than this."

Ammon frowned. "All Mason ever told me was that the man who hired him knew that if enough crimes were committed in an area, the council would eventually label it a no-go zone."

"But Hoos was already in a no-go zone the night of the robbery," Ezra said.

"Maybe the guy wanted to make sure it stayed that way," Ammon said, shrugging.

Ezra nodded, appearing to process Ammon's words, as did Jacob. Was someone within the Derro government making sure that the no-go zone declarations remained in effect? After all, the council was buying out businesses within these zones, for reasons Jacob still didn't know.

"Did Mason ever explain why it was so important that these certain areas be declared a no-go zone?" Ezra asked.

"He had his theories, but they were just speculations."

"Elaborate," Commander Brody ordered.

"He thought it was part of some large scheme to buy out struggling businesses within these no-go zones."

"So, Mason figured the person hiring all these criminals aimed to create or maintain a no-go zone in that area? All so he could swoop in and buy these struggling businesses?" Ezra surmised.

Jacob's stomach dropped. *No, it can't be.*

"That's what Mason speculated," Ammon said. "You know, the guy probably works in real estate."

Jacob leaped out of his seat and banged on the window, alerting Ezra to his sudden realization, though he was still struggling with it himself, anger rising within him. *It doesn't make sense*, he thought, knowing it was the council that was buying these struggling businesses. Ezra turned his attention to the window, then stood up and started toward the door. Jacob followed urgently, exited the room, and approached the door to the interrogation room.

"Hey, what's going on?" Ezra asked, sticking his head out of the room.

"He said something," Jacob said, struggling to find the right words as he fought the anger bubbling inside of him. Then his ears caught Ammon's voice beyond the room.

"Who's that?" The Last Patriot asked.

"None of your business," Commander Brody said.

"Was I right? Does the guy work in real estate? I mean, it makes sense if you ask me."

"It's perverse if you ask me," Commander Brody said. "Taking advantage of people like that. Just *sick*."

Ammon scoffed. "Mason used to always say the sicker people get, the longer they survive."

The words hit Jacob like a physical blow. His mind went black, and then, overcome by a surge of fury, all he saw was red. The anger coursing through his veins erupted like lava, unstoppable and scorching.

Without thinking, he charged forward, slamming through the door and sending Ezra sprawling to the floor.

"What the *hell?*" Ammon yelped, shrinking into his seat as Jacob stormed toward him.

Commander Brody shot to her feet, her chair screeching against the floor. "Just what do you—"

But Jacob didn't hear her. Rage had consumed him, a deafening roar in his mind silencing everything else. He barreled past the commander, his focus locked on the Last Patriot. Grabbing a fistful of Ammon's hair, Jacob yanked his head back with brutal force. Ammon barely had time to cry out before the first punch landed. Then another. And another. The sickening thud of flesh meeting flesh echoed in Jacob's muted ears, his knuckles stinging, his vision blurred, though he didn't stop. He couldn't.

A pair of hands gripped his shoulders and yanked him back. He spun, shrugging them off with a violent twist before driving his shoulder into their chest. The force sent the person stumbling into the wall, collapsing in a heap.

Jacob turned back to Ammon, his fury undiminished. Grabbing a fistful of hair, he yanked Ammon's head up again and delivered another crushing blow. Before he could strike again, a heavy weight slammed into him from behind, taking him to the ground.

"What the hell are you doing?" Ezra grunted, his arms locking tightly around Jacob, restraining him.

Jacob thrashed against the hold, his breath ragged, his vision clouded with fury. Then, as if struck by a jolt of clarity, his eyes widened in horror. He froze, his body going limp as the weight of his actions hit him like a hammer.

Commander Brody leaned against the wall, cradling her head, wincing in pain. Jacob's gaze shifted to the Last Patriot, and his stomach dropped. Ammon slumped over the side of the chair, his hands still bound by the holocuffs. Blood oozed from his nose and eyes, pooling on the floor beneath him.

Jacob stared, paralyzed. He'd just beaten someone unconscious, unleashing a pain he'd long reserved for someone else—Charlotte's killer. The realization twisted in his gut, of how he'd just reacted to those words—words someone had spoken to him once before, and words he'd read recently in a book. His thoughts sharpened, a single name rising from the fog: *Richard Woodwin.*

His hands curled into trembling fists, anger reigniting within him, this time controlled and deadly. Those words had confirmed it. Richard had hired those men. *His actions murdered my wife and unborn child. And now, even if it means my exile, I'm going to kill him.*

CHAPTER THIRTY-THREE

DAY SEVEN OF EXILE

THIS IS IT, Jacob thought, steeling himself for his appearance before Ostria's council.

He followed behind the heavy thumps of Gerrick, who had finally returned with news that the council was ready to see them. Alex, Ammon, and Morgan sidled close to him, their gazes fixed on the imposing tower ahead.

Jacob tapped his fingers against his jeans, the rhythm a poor substitute for the words scrambling in his head. He had tried planning what to say, how he'd say it, but the words slipped away the harder he tried to grasp them. Eventually, he decided it was just best to improvise. Choosing to journey all this way to warn the council of the attack had to be forthcoming enough to show they could be trusted.

He turned a corner and walked through a wooden fenced entrance, its giant doors secured open, welcoming them in. Unveiling before him lay a sprawling courtyard, its cobblestone pavement a striking departure from the narrow dirt path they had been traversing. People moved purposefully between dwellings, and children ran through the open space, their laughter a brief respite from the serious visages of the adults. He wondered how many of the children, like Morgan, had been exiled here, or if, like Jaci's son, they'd been born here, sheltered from the world beyond.

Pressing onward, a young girl with braided red hair stopped in her tracks, eyeing Jacob and the others. He waved and offered a smile, which she promptly returned before running off again with her friends. He watched her depart, his smile widening.

Redirecting his attention ahead, his gaze settled on the far end of the courtyard, where the tower loomed, casting its long shadow over the surrounding dwellings like a silent sentinel. He took a deep breath, trying to shake off his doubts and the weight of responsibility resting on his shoulders. Coming to Ostria had been his idea, their potential refuge, its tower their beacon of hope, where the council now waited within its walls. Jacob wrung his hands, silently praying it hadn't all been in vain.

Reaching the base of the tower, they climbed a set of stairs leading to a stoop where two imposing wooden doors awaited. Gerrick pushed them open, the protesting hinges screeching into the dimly lit chamber beyond. Torches flickered along the walls, their flames casting long, dancing shadows on the rough-hewn stone.

Inside, the air was cool, wrapping around Jacob and soothing his heated skin. He proceeded down a short, narrow corridor and emerged into a vast chamber. His gaze immediately fell upon the staircase that wound along the chamber's walls to its dizzying height. The wooden steps seamlessly integrated with the stone structure, creating an unbroken flow from the exterior staircase to the interior.

At the far end of the chamber, a semicircle of people sat around a long, weathered table. Monique occupied the central seat, flanked by two men. On her left, an elderly man with a powder-white beard squinted his aged eyes toward them as they approached. To her right, drawing Jacob's attention, was a much younger man. He hadn't experienced someone so youthful to be appointed a councilor. Though he sported a healthy head of blond, curly hair and his face was clean-shaven, he held a commanding presence.

As Jacob and the others neared, his knot of anxiety tightened in his stomach. Before them stood a long wooden platform, with railings rising from the base, creating a symbolic barrier between the commoners and the councilors—an unmistakable sign of the distance he still had to overcome in his search for refuge.

"You are to approach the council by standing on the platform," Gerrick said. "We will treat any attempt to move beyond it as a threat, punishable by immediate exile."

"Thank you, Gerrick," Monique said with a nod. "But I'm confident there is nothing to worry about. These people have journeyed all this way to warn us of an attack. A gesture of good faith. Wouldn't you agree?"

"Unless, of course, they're here to *initiate* the attack," the young councilor said, leaning forward with piercing eyes.

"Now, Ellis," the old man said, inserting himself gently into the conversation, "let's hear them out before jumping to conclusions."

Ellis? Jacob narrowed his eyes toward the young councilor. Ellis was the name of Jaci's son. *Could it really be?*

"Father, it doesn't make *any* sense," Ellis said, shaking his head. "They came here seeking protection at the very place that is *supposedly* soon to be attacked. No, I'm not buying it."

Father? Jacob's heart skipped a beat, his mind reeling with the implications. If this aged councilor's name was Abe, as Jacob suspected, there was no doubt he was Jaci's husband, and Ellis her son.

"Ellis, as I've already informed you, they're not marked," Monique said.

"*Exactly*," Ellis said. "The very people we'd *least* suspect."

"Do we really look like the bunch to start a war?" Alex said.

Ellis scoffed. "Derro cast you out. Don't feign innocence."

"Enough," Monique said. "We're wasting valuable time."

Ellis started to interject, but his father swiftly intervened. "Ellis, let them share what they know. We will decide from there. For now, hold your tongue."

Ellis scowled, and with a frustrated huff, leaned back in his chair. His gaze, however, remained fixed on Jacob and the others, suspicion burning in his eyes.

"Jacob, I have already shared with Abe and Ellis what you've told me about the planned attack by the Maws and Last Patriots," Monique said. "What we hope to see from you, if possible, is more … *concrete* evidence."

His name is Abe! Jacob's eyebrows shot up. He couldn't believe his ears. Yet here they were—Jaci's husband and son, councilors on Ostria's council. He stood stunned, unsure whether he should say anything to them. His mind screamed to do so, but he didn't want to jeopardize their chances of being granted refuge.

"We could just wait for the attack to happen," Alex muttered under her breath.

Jacob disregarded the remark, trying to narrow his attention to the council's request. He sifted through his thoughts, searching for anything to corroborate their claims, but found nothing. His mind was still reeling from the revelation of Abe and Ellis. And unfortunately, Jaci and Daemion's account of the attack remained his only constant, yet disclosing them as their source—both Ostria exiles—would only invite deeper scrutiny and suspicion, especially from Ellis, sadly. He frowned, wondering why Jaci hadn't disclosed the familial tie. *Did she even know?*

"Jacob," Ammon said, cutting through Jacob's thoughts. He offered a reassuring nod. "Show them the bite."

Of course, Jacob thought, returning the nod to Ammon. Revealing the bite would not only validate their escape from the Maws but also portray them as victims rather than threats.

He cautiously removed his shirt, his achy body stabbing with the movement. Monique's mouth fell open as she leaned forward in her chair, her eyes widening. Abe leaned forward as well, his weathered eyebrows raised in surprise, studying the bruises. Meanwhile, Ellis only tilted his head slightly, his expression inscrutable.

"On our first night of exile, Daemion and the Maws captured us," Jacob said. "They did this to me; beat me unconscious. When I finally woke up, Daemion had me chained up in their cave. And that's when he bit me."

Leaning forward, he carefully peeled off Jaci's dressing, revealing the grotesque signature left by Daemion. Though the bite looked better than it had, the councilors still appeared shocked—all except Ellis, anyway.

Abe cleared his throat. "That must have been quite the ordeal," he said, "and I'm sorry you and your friends had to endure that. Daemion, unfortunately, has been a thorn in our side since we exiled him all those years ago."

"Indeed," Monique said.

Ellis scoffed. "I'm sorry, but I fail to see how this validates the supposed attack."

Jacob bit the insides of his cheek, frustration beginning to simmer. "Daemion told me about his plan to attack Ostria while I was in their cave. This proves—"

"Proves nothing," Ellis interjected. "Sure, it shows that Daemion bit you, but for all we know, he may have recruited you as well. This could very well be a ploy between the two of you to initiate the attack."

"That's not true," Jacob said.

"And we're just supposed to believe you?" Ellis said. "Just like we're supposed to believe there's a gun on Eremos." He chuckled dismissively. "There's never been guns here. And I refuse to believe your improbable story of how a madman could disarm a Culler, allowing him and you to bring guns here."

"But it's *true*," Alex said. "How can you not see the evidence? That madman used the bullets to start the fire that burned down the Maws' camp. And now it's spreading all across Eremos."

"Very well," Ellis said, raising a single eyebrow. "I'll entertain your theory for a moment. Jacob, let us assume everything you've told us is true—that you brought a firearm to Eremos. You expect me to believe that you allowed yourself and your companions to be captured, all while in possession of a gun? Please explain how that makes sense."

"Using the gun wouldn't have guaranteed our safety," Jacob said, his words rushing out. "There were more Maws than bullets. One of them could've grabbed any of us and negotiated their life for the gun. Revealing it, or even firing it, would've only led to bloodshed, or *worse*, the gun falling into Daemion's hands."

"My son raises a valid point, Jacob," Abe said. "I fail to see any concrete evidence of this gun's presence. Monique told us you claimed to have destroyed it during your escape. A rather peculiar decision, wouldn't you agree?"

Ellis scoffed, a faint laugh escaping him. "Most people, when faced with such a weapon, would wield it without a second thought, using it for its *intended* purpose."

"I didn't want to risk anyone's life," Jacob said.

"That's a hard stance to maintain in the face of a supposed attack," Ellis replied.

"Indeed," Abe said. "There is a time for everything, and a season for every activity under the heavens, Jacob."

"That includes a time to kill," Ellis added, raising his chin.

"Well, my time to kill has passed," Jacob said.

"That is," Ellis said, smirking, "until it begins again. After all, seasons do come and go."

Jacob's jaw tightened, his frustration threatening to boil over. He was struggling to break through Ellis's skepticism. Nervously tapping his jeans, his fingers drummed against the bullets in his pocket. *The bullets!* They would serve as tangible, concrete evidence of the Talon's presence in Eremos.

Hope surged within him, softening his expression as he lowered his gaze to Morgan, offering a grateful smile. They owed the bullets to him. Once again, the kid had reminded Jacob that a single decision—even a wrong one in the moment—could lead to a positive outcome. He fished the bullets from his pocket, then cleared his throat and raised his gaze to address the council.

"If you doubt the existence of the gun, perhaps this will change your mind," he said, placing *two* bullets on the balustrade, their tips facing upward. He hesitated, though he wasn't entirely sure why, and kept one bullet hidden in his pocket.

"These," he continued, pointing to the two bullets, "are leftovers from the gun I destroyed to escape the Maws. I sabotaged it by crafting an obstruction in the barrel, rigging it so that when fired, the gun would explode."

He turned his gaze toward Ellis. "Like you, I understand that most people, once they hold a gun, would likely use it without hesitation. In fact, I'd bet my life on it. I knew Daemion would shoot, and when he did, the gun exploded in his hand, causing the cave to collapse. I barely escaped with my life."

Jacob paused, letting the words linger in the air. "Consider what Daemion could've done with the gun during his planned attack. I wanted to ensure it couldn't be used to kill. And by rigging it to explode, I not only rendered it useless for future violence, but I also forced Daemion to confront the consequences of his own violent intentions."

A heavy silence settled over the chamber. Monique exchanged glances with Ellis and Abe, their expressions veiled in contemplation. Jacob did the same, looking at his fellow exiles, their supportive—and surprised—smiles offering silent encouragement.

"Well, I must say," Monique said, breaking the silence, "your actions and commitment to preserving life—even in the face of danger—are commendable. And frankly, surprising. You don't sound like the typical exile we encounter."

"Indeed," Abe said. "It makes me curious what you did for Derro to exile you." He paused, his gaze lingering thoughtfully on Jacob. "But we're not here to pass judgment on your past transgressions. You've already faced the scrutiny of Derro's council, as have many others here in Eremos. That's precisely why we built Ostria. At its core, it offers a second chance."

A smile tugged at Jacob's lips as he felt the tension in the chamber shift. "Thank you."

"Based on the evidence presented, I find Jacob's account credible," Monique said. "We must prepare for the attack."

"Indeed," Abe agreed. "Ellis, mobilize the barracks for defense and assign a team to escort women, children, and those unable to fight to the caves for safety. Another crew should reinforce the traps around the perimeter of the palisade. Our top priority is fortifying our defenses and ensuring the safety of our people."

Ellis scowled. "Just like that?" he said, scoffing. "He shows you some bruises and a couple of bullets, and suddenly, we're supposed to believe he's different from any other exile?"

"Ellis," Abe interjected calmly.

"And now you issue me commands as if I have no say in whether they're granted refuge," Ellis pressed. "Ostria appointed me as a councilor too—"

"That's enough," Abe said sharply, rising abruptly. His voice thundered through the chamber, silencing Ellis and the others. After a brief pause, he composed himself and adjusted his clothing. "Act as a councilor should."

Ellis's scowl deepened, his piercing eyes fixed on Abe.

"Ellis, it's clear Jacob and his companions don't have your support," Monique said. "In light of that, I suggest you mobilize our forces, giving them time to prepare for the attack while Abe and I deliberate on our decision. When you return, you can present your case."

Ellis shot to his feet and kicked his chair with a loud crash that echoed through the stone chamber. *"How are they any different from Mother?"* he shouted. Then he stormed toward the wooden doors, kicking them open with a forceful slam before storming out of the chamber.

Jacob frowned, now understanding Ellis's hard scrutiny more deeply. It wasn't just distrust; Ellis was wrestling with the pain of his mother's exile. The realization cemented for Jacob that Ellis was, indeed, Jaci's son.

It made sense now why Ellis had questioned them the way he had. After all, Jacob and his companions did not differ from Jaci, or any other exile, for that matter. Whatever Jaci had done to earn her exile, it had clearly led her to a point of remorse, prompting her to risk her safety by helping them reach Ostria.

Strangely, her actions revealed some people were capable of growth and redemption, given the chance. Unfortunately, exile denied them that opportunity.

"In the meantime, Gerrick," Monique said, patiently waiting for Gerrick to redirect his attention from the swinging doors left in Ellis's wake. "Please escort Jacob and his companions to the Sanctuary Halls. They are to wait there while we deliberate."

"Thank you," Ammon said.

"You can thank your friend," Monique said, gesturing toward Jacob.

"Come on," Gerrick ordered.

Jacob smiled, nodding toward the councilors before falling in step behind the others. He gingerly pulled on his shirt, mindful of the bruises still throbbing beneath it. As he smoothed the fabric down, his eyes caught Morgan sidling up beside him.

"I thought I gave you *three* bullets," Morgan whispered.

Jacob placed a reassuring hand on Morgan's shoulder and shook his head slightly, signaling him to stay quiet. He leaned closer. "Kept one," he murmured. "Just in case."

"Just a moment," Abe said.

Jacob's steps faltered. He straightened his body and turned to face the aged councilor, heart quickening.

"The other individual, this madman who caused the inferno," Abe continued. "Are you certain he still possesses the other firearm?"

Jacob breathed a soft sigh of relief. "I'd say it's highly likely. We saw him with it at the Maws' camp during our escape."

Abe frowned. "Very well."

As Jacob turned away, a troubling thought stopped him in his tracks. There was a chance that Wes had found Michael, as he said he would. If successful, it was possible Wes now had the Talon.

"However," Jacob said, directing his attention back to the council, "there's also a chance the gun has changed hands."

"How so?" Monique asked, leaning forward.

"The Culler I mentioned, the one the madman disarmed on the Screech. When he returned to Derro, the council exiled him for causing the death of another Culler. Now he's here on Eremos. We ran into him on our way here. He assaulted me, demanding the gun I had taken. When he found out I had destroyed mine, his focus shifted to the madman."

"A Culler here on Eremos?" Abe said, his brow furrowed. "I've never known Derro to exile one of their own."

"Should we be concerned about him?" Monique asked.

You don't want to make an enemy out of me. Wes's words entered Jacob's mind.

"The Culler made his intentions clear," Jacob said. "When he found the madman, he was going to seek refuge here, likely intending to present the madman to you to gain your favor and protection in return."

"How confident are you that this Culler will find him?" Abe asked.

"He prides himself on always finding his man," Jacob said.

Abe nodded gravely, his eyes growing distant. "Understood. Then it's only a matter of time before he brings us both the madman and the other gun."

"And when he does, we'll be ready," Monique said, smiling. "Just as we are prepared for the attack tonight, thanks to all four of you."

"Indeed," Abe said, nodding as he gestured toward the exit with a fragile hand. "You may now follow Gerrick to the Sanctuary Halls."

Jacob returned the nod, his gaze lingering on the two bullets arranged on the balustrade. It struck him how, despite his exile, guns still seemed to weave through his life. They followed him, even now, with the heavy weight of the single bullet still tucked in his pocket. With a sigh, he turned away, leaving the two bullets behind as he passed through the wooden doors.

Stepping outside, the acrid scent of smoke greeted him, choking out his fleeting hope. He pierced his gaze through the smoky haze, his eyes locking on the descending sun, its fiery glow painting the sky in hues of red and orange. He frowned, understanding that even if refuge awaited him, their fight for survival had only just begun. Nightfall loomed, bringing with it the threat of assault from both the Maws and Last Patriots. Clenching his jaw, Jacob hoped against hope that Daemion was dead, and the Maws were weakened, which would offer them a slim chance of survival.

He exited the courtyard and headed south toward a dirt path that wound deeper into Ostria. Soon, he passed a trench filled with water, flakes of ash drifting lazily on the surface. He followed its course, noting that it led back toward the pool where they had rested earlier. His eyebrows lifted, and he shook his head in disbelief. Though he had only glimpsed parts of the settlement, the meticulous detail and thoughtfulness behind its construction were evident. Where Derro boasted impressive buildings, monuments, and advanced technology, Ostria captivated Jacob completely differently. Unlike Derro, which used sophisticated tools and technology, Ostria's builders used limited resources and basic methods.

He wondered which was more remarkable. His upbringing in Derro certainly inclined him toward appreciating Ostria more. Memories flooded back of his youth, walking through a lit-up Tuto with his father, experiencing that same sense of wonder. Perhaps, he considered, those born in Ostria might say the same thing should they ever have the chance to explore Derro's streets. But that was an opportunity that would never come.

Gerrick grunted. "Almost there," he muttered.

Jacob nodded silently, still uncertain whether he could trust the burly man. Eventually, they arrived at another fenced area nestled against the rear of the palisade, snug against the towering mountain. No guards were present, so they entered freely. Jacob's gaze swept ahead, revealing three wooden buildings constructed side by side, stretching along the landscape, their roofs thatched. His eyes narrowed, noticing a flock of owls glaring down at them from the gable of the roof.

There were no dirt paths here, only an expanse of dried-out grass trampled into submission by countless footsteps. Each step Jacob took elicited a soft crunch from the parched blades beneath his feet as they made their way across the open field toward one of the buildings.

Stepping inside, a long, dimly illuminated interior that stretched onward greeted him. Indeed, like one long hallway. Burned rays of sunlight streamed through the glassless windows, providing the only source of light. The lack of flooring struck him immediately. The parched terrain outside seamlessly transitioned into the building, as if the architects had overlooked the need for a solid foundation.

Glancing around, he took in his surroundings. To his left, rows of wooden bunk beds stretched along one side of the space, occupying nearly half of the building. On his right, a series of wooden cages lined the walls, fading into the darkness in the distance.

"What is this place?" Alex asked.

"These three buildings are our Sanctuary Halls," Gerrick said. "They used to serve as temporary housing for new exiles."

Jacob turned around, his eyes finding Gerrick, who ushered in a large group of newcomers—rough men and women in tattered clothing. One of them was missing an arm. Jacob's eyes bulged, his body tensing. These people weren't outside, which meant they must have already been inside, hiding in the darkness. Waiting …

"They are among Ostria's oldest, dating back to its creation," Gerrick said, his eyes steady as he approached. He grinned. "But that was a different time. A time when Ostria was … more welcoming."

The door slammed shut.

"Put them with the others," Gerrick ordered coldly.

Jacob's heart raced, the hairs on his neck prickling with unease as more dark figures emerged from the shadows. He staggered backward, but before he could react, hands from behind seized him. Fingernails dug into his skin as two men forcefully dragged him deeper into the building. Jacob cried out, his bite wound screaming as he struggled against the grip. He dug his heels into the ground, but they overpowered him with ease.

"Don't touch me!" Alex yelled.

A sharp smack pierced the air, snapping Jacob's attention forward. His body went limp, giving into the dragging as he saw Alex strike the man holding her. In retaliation, another man delivered a brutal blow to her stomach, sending her crashing to her knees. Gasping for breath, she was quickly subdued by another, who grabbed her flailing arms and dragged her away in the same direction Jacob was being taken.

Meanwhile, Ammon, fighting against the grip, elbowed one of his captors in the stomach and broke free. He sprinted forward and tackled the man who had assaulted Alex; their bodies skidded across the dirt floor. He landed a fierce punch to the man's face before being overwhelmed by others who intervened, wrenching him away.

In the chaos, Jacob frantically searched for Morgan, but he was nowhere to be found. He panicked, his heart pounding with a newfound sense of adrenaline. He bit the arms of his captors, trying to escape their grip, but unfortunately, it was futile.

Then a sudden force hoisted him to his feet and shoved him forward, making him stumble against the hard ground. He scrambled back in terror, eyes darting wildly, his stomach sinking. He was inside one of the wooden cells.

Ammon and Alex were thrown into neighboring cells, the heavy wooden doors slamming shut, sealing their fates. Jacob flinched, his ears only registering the thud of three closed doors. *Where's Morgan?* He desperately searched beyond the dimly lit cells, glimpsing Gerrick standing with folded arms, watching them with piercing eyes.

"You four just had to try and wreck everything," he sneered. "No worries. Your stay in Ostria will be shorter than expected."

"That … it … will, *dearies.*"

No, it can't be …

Jacob stood petrified as a dark figure emerged from the shadows, head bowed and face partially obscured by a hood. The figure dragged Morgan along, gripping his amber locks tightly. Morgan winced and cried out with every harsh tug.

The figure raised an arm toward their hood, and Jacob's eyes bulged—not at the face slowly revealed, but at the arm itself. Where a hand should have been, there was a knotted sleeve. The figure brushed back their hood. Standing before them, unmistakably alive, was Daemion.

"*No, let him go!*" Jacob yelled, his voice cracking with fear as he rushed to the barred frames.

A sinister laugh escaped Daemion's lips. He yanked Morgan in front of him, wrapping his arms around the boy's chin, his remaining hand still gripping Morgan's hair tightly. One sudden jerk was all it would take … Morgan trembled, eyes bulging, tears falling.

"I told you the boy's death was inevitable," Daemion said.

"No, please—"

Daemion jerked his arms in a brutal motion, snapping Morgan's neck.

Jacob screamed, his body slamming against the barred frames. He gripped them tightly, shaking them with desperate fury as he watched Morgan crumple to the ground. The bars held firm, and Jacob's strength gave out. The weight of his loss, of his failure, crushed him. He slumped to the floor, pressing his face against the weathered wood, desperate to be as close to Morgan as he could.

And then, he wept.

CHAPTER THIRTY-FOUR

THE FINAL DAYS BEFORE EXILE

THE GROUND FELT like a cold stone against Jacob's bottom and back as he huddled in the corner of a dimly lit cell. He shivered, gaze fixed ahead on the holographic cell door, where beyond, he caught the youthful eyes of an armed Culler. The young man wore the same stern expression Jacob saw from their last encounter, when he and Ezra had run into Wes as they exited the elevator.

Right before I beat a man unconscious, Jacob thought, his mind replaying the violent assault.

The fury he had felt lingered, simmering within him like an unresolved tempest. Now he feared he would never have the chance to release it, with true justice slipping from his grasp. All he could do was wait for Ezra to return with the council's verdict. Ezra had said it could take time. Jacob's fate depended on whether the Last Patriot survived. The last thing Ezra had told him before leaving his cell was that Ammon hadn't woken up yet.

Could this really be it for me? Jacob ran a shaky hand through his frazzled hair. *All is time, hunting her killer, only to be exiled before* true *justice could be served?*

He now knew, without a doubt, that Richard was responsible for Charlotte's murder. Why, however, he still wasn't entirely sure. But Richard had hired those men to strike fear into him, to prompt him to want to sell Hoos. And it had worked. Richard had now taken everything of meaning from him.

Charlotte.

Their unborn child.

Hoos.

Myself?

Jacob felt like nothing more than a hollow shell, an empty gun, spent and drained. But one could still reload an empty gun. And Ammon had done just that for him by exposing Richard.

I will have my revenge.

"Culler, do you think the council will exile me?" Jacob asked.

"Yes," the Culler said bluntly. "But your chances dwindle should the Last Patriot survive."

"Dwindle enough to avoid exile?"

"Nah, they'll probably still exile you. Your biggest mistake was assaulting the Seeker and commander."

Jacob expelled a heavy sigh as he bowed his head. *How could I allow myself to lose all control?* The look of disappointment on Ezra's face as he'd ordered Alpha to secure the holographic cell door flashed in his mind. *Hopefully, he'll understand, in the end.*

Outside the cell, the faint sound of footsteps echoed down the corridor. As they drew closer, Jacob's heart quickened as he braced for what was coming. Would the council condemn him to a life of exile, forcing him to survive on one of their treacherous islands? Or would Ezra find a way to spare him such a fate?

"Alpha, open cell number 815," Ezra requested.

The holographic door vanished. Ezra stepped in, his fingers pinching the skin at his throat. *Shit. He doesn't look like he comes bearing good news.*

"Allen, your presence is not needed," Ezra said, glancing back at the Culler. "You're dismissed."

"But Commander Brody—"

"That's an order, Culler."

"Yes, sir," Allen conceded, and then started down the corridor.

"The Last Patriot woke up," Ezra said, turning his gaze to Jacob.

"Will he be okay?"

"He'll live. It's *you* I'm worried about."

"So, I'm being exiled?"

"Not sure," Ezra said with a sigh. "Now that Ammon is awake, the council is deliberating. They don't take acts of violence lightly. However, considering your clean record, social score, Ammon's condition, and the context of your actions, I've recommended they show you leniency."

Jacob's eyes drifted shut, a wave of dread settling in his stomach. "So, you know who the council is?" he asked, opening his eyes.

"No," Ezra said, shaking his head. "No one does."

"Then how did you recommend leniency for me?"

"I wrote a letter and uploaded it to your case file. The council will update it soon with their decision."

Jacob scoffed. "So, even you don't know who you're serving?"

"We all serve them."

"I guess that's the only certainty we have about them."

"Yeah," Ezra said with a soft scoff. "Shouldn't be long before we hear from them."

"Thanks, Ezra."

"Don't thank me just yet."

Jacob frowned. "So, what's going to happen to the Last Patriot?"

"He's slated for exile. Poor guy probably wishes he hadn't woken up. I can't say I'd blame him. Death may have been a relief. The things I've heard of Eremos ..."

"Him coming forward didn't make any difference?"

Ezra shook his head. "Being a Last Patriot sealed his fate with the council. Plus, he didn't tell us much. Unless, that is, you've got something to share?"

Jacob hesitated, letting the awkwardness of the moment hang between them. Ezra was probing him, intent on uncovering the reasons behind his assault. Jacob's mind swirled with conflicting emotions. The Last Patriot had revealed crucial information, helping Jacob piece together Richard's involvement in

Charlotte's death. Sharing this with Ezra might offer Ammon the chance to avoid exile, though that seemed unlikely.

But what truly troubled Jacob was the fear that revealing the truth to Ezra could result in Richard's exile, jeopardizing his chance for revenge.

For some, exile alone isn't enough justice. Ezra's words from earlier crept into Jacob's mind. Now he understood those words more than ever. Knowing that Richard had hired those men, exile felt less like justice and more like a reprieve. *Why should he continue to live after his actions caused the death of my family?*

"He was telling the truth," Ezra said, breaking the silence.

Jacob blinked, snapping himself out of his thoughts. "Who?"

"The Last Patriot. His alibi checked out. I called Bel, the owner of Liberties, and he confirmed Ammon was working that night."

"And you just believe him?"

"Why would Bel vouch for someone he's fired?"

Jacob was quiet.

"I also reviewed the security footage we seized from Bel, and it seems Ammon wasn't involved. He was in the kitchen, just as he claimed, before and after the cameras went down. Street cameras also showed him outside Liberties with the others during the aftermath. The evidence leads me to believe he's not her killer."

Jacob frowned. *It doesn't matter. Whoever pulled that trigger, accident or not, Richard was the one who'd put him there. My wife's blood is on his hands.*

"What's it mean?"

"What's *what* mean?"

"The sicker people get, the longer they survive."

Jacob bowed his head, his face hardening as those words pierced his ears once again. They only stoked the flames of his thirst for revenge.

"I don't know," Jacob lied.

"Then why attack him?" Ezra pressed. "It makes no sense."

Jacob's eyes traced the cracks in the ground as he tried planning a proper response. But he couldn't. Not without revealing the truth about Richard. So, instead, he remained silent.

"What he said triggered you," Ezra continued, gently probing. "You lost all self-control."

"I just got caught up in the moment," Jacob lied again, his words coming out in a rush. "After all this time with no leads on finding her killer, I wanted it to be him. I let my emotions cloud my judgment, and I acted impulsively."

Ezra frowned as he shook his head. "I just feel you're not telling me the truth. There's more. I can feel it."

"I promise there's not."

The sound of footsteps echoing down the corridor alerted Jacob and Ezra. Jacob scrambled to his feet, his heart pounding in his chest. *Please don't be exile.*

Commander Brody appeared at the threshold of Jacob's cell, her footsteps halting as she folded her arms and leaned against the wall. The memory of Jacob throwing her against the wall flashed through his mind. Strangely, he felt no remorse.

"How's it feel, Mr. Hughes?" the commander asked.

"How's *what* feel?"

"To be a criminal."

Jacob scowled.

"Has the council arrived at their verdict?" Ezra asked, pushing away the hostility.

"They have. After a thorough review of the crime and the surrounding circumstances, the council has decided to … *not* exile you. You're free to go."

Jacob breathed an enormous sigh of relief, his tense shoulders relaxing as he absorbed the news. He turned his wide eyes to Ezra, a smile tugging.

"Consider this a warning," Commander Brody said as she sauntered deeper into the cell. "It's extremely rare the council ever shows leniency. I assure you, should there be a next time, you *will* be exiled. And I'll personally ensure it's to Eremos. Just so you can be reunited with the Last Patriot you attacked."

Jacob's smile faltered. He clenched his teeth, struggling to control the urge to lash out at the commander. The feeling was almost overwhelming, but he quickly regained his composure and held his tongue. He had narrowly avoided exile, and he needed to make sure it stayed that way.

For now …

Commander Brody turned away and exited the cell. Before she vanished from view, she threw over her shoulder a final remark. "So, tread carefully, Mr. Hughes. The council will be watching."

"That woman really has it out for me," Jacob grumbled.

"She has it out for any criminal. It's her job. Just be sure not to commit any more crimes, and you'll never have to see her again," Ezra said with a wry grin.

That won't happen.

"Come on," Ezra said, starting toward the exit of the cell. "Let's get you home."

Jacob followed, his eyes growing distant as his mind started to race with plans to enact his revenge.

It was time Richard paid for what he had done.

Jacob's own form of exile.

CHAPTER THIRTY-FIVE
DAY SEVEN OF EXILE

JACOB SQUEEZED HIS eyes shut and turned away as a Maw dragged Morgan by the arms, wishing he could block out the sound of Morgan's feet scraping lifelessly against the dirt. He sniffled, wanting to wipe the tear streaks from his face, but his hands were mucky. So, he left them to soak into his skin instead.

A stinging reminder that he had failed once again.

He turned his head and peered into the cell next to him. Ammon sat on the ground, his back against the side of Jacob's cell. Bowing his head, he veiled his face with his hair. Further down in the cell next to Ammon's, Alex was pacing, her face pale, eyes hollow, and fists clenched at her sides. A stunned silence had engulfed the three of them.

"It's a shame," Daemion said as he approached the cells. "I forgot to ask the boy what he did to get exiled."

"You're a *fucking monster!*" Alex roared.

"I don't suppose he told you, did he?" Daemion asked, completely ignoring Alex's outburst. He strolled down to her cell, nails dragging along the wooden bars, sending shivers through Jacob's core. "Must've been pretty severe for

Derro to exile a child. Probably worse than killing your own husband, don't you think?"

Alex spat, making Jacob's head jerk up. Through the bars, he watched Daemion slowly move his head closer to her cell. His face had recoiled from the impact of her spittle. With a crooked smile, Daemion tilted his head and slowly wiped his face with his single hand.

"I was hoping you'd do that," he said. Then he brought his hand in front of his face and dramatically licked his palm. As he tilted his head back, he let his hand fall limp at his side, savoring Alex's repulsive offering. His shoulders trembled as he shook himself out of the pleasuring experience and then met Alex's disgusted gaze. "Damn, I've missed your taste."

"I'll tell you what the kid did," a voice announced from the other neighboring cell next to Jacob's.

He turned his head around, instantly recognizing that arrogant tone, and there, emerging from a shadowy corner, was Wes. The former Culler's face was battered and bloody, one eye swollen shut, resembling two thick lips pressed tightly together.

"If you let me leave," Wes said, "I'll tell you what the kid did to get exiled."

"Ah, tempting," Daemion said, tapping his temple as if weighing it. Then he smiled. "But no. I rather enjoy not knowing. Whatever I imagine will be worse, and I'd hate to disappoint myself."

"But—"

"Shut it, Culler," Gerrick said. "Or else I'll close that other eye."

Wes grunted, then scowled. Jacob's stunned silence had turned to shock. Wes was here; and in rough shape, his face a testament to Gerrick's handiwork, which explained Gerrick's black eye; Wes had clearly put up a fight, though not a successful one.

From the start, Jacob had sensed there was something off about Gerrick. All this time, he had been working with Daemion, providing him and his Maws shelter after Michael burned down their camp. Did this mean Gerrick was also a Maw, perhaps even the mastermind behind the planned attack? If so, what did that mean for the Last Patriots who were on their way here now? Jacob frowned as he realized their warning to Ostria's council had been rendered meaningless.

Doom seemed inevitable.

"Death and destruction are insatiable," a hoarse voice declared from a cell farther down, shrouded in darkness. "And neither are human *eyes*."

Jacob's stomach plummeted. He had a sinking feeling who had just spoke those cryptic words. His fears rang true as Michael erupted into a fit of coughing. The harsh sound rattled Jacob's bones, evoking vivid memories of their encounter aboard the Screech. He squeezed his eyes shut, trying to black out the haunting image of Michael firing a bullet into Allen's head. Opening his eyes, Jacob forced the memory away, only to have them widen suddenly with horror.

If Michael is here, the gun must be too.

Wes must have captured him, brought him to Ostria intending to use him as leverage for refuge, only to be intercepted by Gerrick at the entrance. The council's questions made one thing unmistakable: they knew nothing of Wes. Which meant they knew nothing of the Maws. The conclusion crept in a fear Jacob wished he could dismiss. Just as Gerrick had let Wes and Michael in, he'd also let *them* in, a group that harbored a Last Patriot. Gerrick's earlier reaction to Ammon's wrist, and that they had still been allowed in, suddenly aligned with unsettling clarity.

Jacob glanced toward Ammon, who shuffled and turned just enough to reveal a face streaked with tears. He sniffed, met Jacob's eyes for a fleeting second, then looked away. Like Jacob, he was grieving Morgan; the weight of that loss pressed visibly on them both. Or perhaps Ammon had known this was coming? He shook his head, forcing the suspicion aside before it could take root. Trust, once questioned, unraveled too easily, and doubt was a luxury he could not afford at the moment.

"I'll tell you what," Daemion said, passing Jacob's cell. "I think this madman might just be crazier than me. 'Death and destruction are insatiable, and neither are human eyes.' Ain't that the truth." He laughed darkly to himself as he came to a halt in front of Wes's cell. "Speaking of satisfaction, I have an idea. One my insatiable eyes are dying to see. *Trigger alert!* It involves death and destruction."

Daemion lifted the thick wooden latch, a struggle with his only hand, and opened Wes's cell. "The Culler wants to go, does he? Then let's allow him that chance."

Jacob stood gingerly, his achy bones protesting as he watched Wes stagger backward, his one open eye darting in every direction.

"Come on out," Daemion said, gesturing for Wes to exit the cell.

Wes remained stock-still.

"No?" Daemion taunted. "That's odd. I thought you wanted to go. Yet you cower in your cell. A pity, really. What a good beating can do to someone. Gerrick, grab the Culler."

"*Okay,*" Wes shrieked, arms shooting up defensively. "I'll come out."

"A wise choice, dearie," Daemion drawled.

Wes dragged his feet out of his cell and stepped into the light. Jacob noted he wasn't wearing his Culler uniform, but tattered clothes that barely fit his massive frame.

"Daemion, what are you doing?" Gerrick asked as he folded his arms.

"You'll see," Daemion said, grinning.

"We don't have time for your games," Gerrick said. "You've had your revenge."

"Oh, hush," Daemion sneered. "My revenge isn't finished until I say it is. Don't go soft on me now."

"We need to stick to the plan," Gerrick pressed. "We need to get back to the council soon—"

"And we will," Daemion cut in. "Trust me, I'm looking forward to that part of my revenge. Now be a good Maw and release the woman."

Jacob snapped his gaze toward Alex's cell, catching swirls of dirt billowing in Ammon's cell as he shot up, clearly having heard what Jacob had.

"*No,*" Ammon yelled.

"Oh, that's right," Daemion drawled. "Ammon here knows all about our pit parties."

Jacob frowned, heart pounding as he watched Gerrick approach Alex's cell. Daemion was going to have Wes and Alex brawl, just like he had Ammon do in the pit. Ammon had killed that man, hoping to earn his freedom, only to find Daemion had been lying all along.

But Wes didn't know that.

"Don't you *fucking* touch her," Ammon roared.

"Calm down, dearie. As much as I'd love to, she's not my type. Can't say the same for the Culler here, though."

"Wes, he's lying," Jacob said. "No matter what happens, no one is getting out of here. Think about it. Do you really believe he'll let you go?"

Daemion scowled, his eyes narrowing into slits as he glared at Jacob. "*You,*" he said, jabbing his finger at Jacob. "Don't think I've forgotten about you. The boy was just the beginning. You'll get what's coming to you."

"I'll fight him instead," Ammon pleaded.

"*Ha,*" Daemion spat. "Do you think I'm stupid? I remember what happened the last time I let one of you volunteer." He raised his knotted sleeve. "And now I live with that mistake. I won't make it again."

"No one will fight for me," Alex said, her chin held high as she willingly stepped out of her cell.

Gerrick ushered her toward Wes, and a group of Maws gathered around them, leaving an open space for Jacob and Ammon to watch. He gripped the cell bars, seeking support as he watched Alex accept her fate with unwavering resolve. She understood that resisting Daemion's commands was futile. By complying, she denied the cannibal the satisfaction of seeing them plead for a different outcome.

Plus, she and Wes had history.

"Alex, what are you doing?" Ammon asked, his wide eyes fixed on her.

Ignoring his question, Alex cracked her neck as she focused on the conflict unfolding in front of her—Wes.

"I win," Wes said, turning his gaze to Daemion. "You let me join whatever this is."

Daemion laughed. "Focus on winning first, dearie," he said, his attention shifting to Alex. "Oh, I knew this would be a good match. Tell me, does he resemble your husband?"

Alex flared her nostrils, her fists trembling as she clenched them tightly. Then she smirked at Wes. "You should see the look on your face."

Wes snarled.

Jacob blinked, his dry eyes in need of moisture as he struggled to tear his gaze away from the impending brawl. There was a raw fury simmering inside him, a desire to stop this from happening, but he knew there was nothing he could do this time. That rage boiled, much like it had that fateful night—the night he killed Charlotte's murderer.

This is, until it begins again. Ellis's remark, in response to Jacob's declaration that his killing days were over, crept unbidden into his mind. *After all, seasons do come and go.*

Jacob scowled. *That they do.*

Then he watched as Alex burst into a sprint, meeting the fight head-on. The Maws erupted in cheers. Wes assumed a defensive stance, fists raised. As Alex closed the distance, Wes swung a sweeping right hook. Alex swiftly leaned back, narrowly evading Wes's fist as it whizzed past her chin.

Wes closed the gap as he launched a left jab. Alex ducked and sidestepped to her right, positioning herself where Wes's swollen eye limited his vision. With bent knees, she unleashed a powerful blow to the back of Wes's ribs. He grunted in pain, staggering as he struggled to regain his balance. Before he could recover, Alex struck again, landing a jab to his ribcage.

Wes crumpled to his knees.

But Alex didn't relent.

She vaulted onto his back, her left hand gripping his neck for leverage as she hammered her right fist relentlessly onto his head. Wes endured only two punches before he slammed backward, crashing onto the ground with an enormous thump, sending clouds of dust swirling into the air. Alex gasped, her breath escaping from her lungs. Wes rolled off of her and crawled away, grunting with the effort.

The Maws' cheers escalated in pitch, their excitement palpable as they exchanged glances, pointing in astonishment at Alex's adept fighting. Jacob mirrored their shock, his mouth agape as he remained rooted to the ground, eyes locked on Alex, waiting for any sign of movement. She gasped again, this time drawing breath back into her lungs. Then gingerly, she turned onto her stomach, using her elbows and knees to help herself rise. The cheers from the Maws grew louder.

A loud thud snapped Jacob's gaze to Ammon's cell, who had just punched the wooden bars and was now pacing, brimming with nervous energy as he, too, understood there was nothing he could do to stop this.

Alex whimpered, pulling Jacob's attention back to the fight. She clutched at her ribs, her face contorted in pain, her nose bloodied. Wes's head must have slammed into it when he fell back. Jacob watched as she took a fighting stance. Wes stood upright, appearing to have recovered as he snarled at Alex. Despite the battering he had taken, it was clear that it would take more than just two strikes to the ribs and face to defeat him.

Alex cautiously sidestepped to her right, aiming to enter Wes's blind spot, however, this time, Wes expected it and countered by stepping to his left, narrowing the distance between them. Alex hesitated. It was clear she'd hoped Wes would step to his right, allowing them to circle each other, but Wes welcomed the proximity.

Alex pivoted left, trying to avoid Wes's advance, and unwittingly moved into his line of sight. This was Wes's objective all along—to keep the fight within his view, ensuring he wouldn't be blindsided again. Alex would need to rethink her strategy.

Wes lunged forward, the heavy thumps of his footsteps drowned out by the rising cacophony of cheers. Alex backed away, her eyes darting as she assessed her next move. As Wes closed the gap between them, she planted her foot in the earth and swiftly kicked up, sending a spray of dirt into Wes's face. He grunted in agony, clawing at his eyes and face, his body swaying as he blindly sought his balance. Seizing the opportunity, Alex didn't hesitate. She darted forward and delivered a powerful kick to his stomach. Wes dropped to his knees once again.

Alex moved in, but before she could act, Wes reacted first. Hearing her approach, he quickly rose to one knee and lunged forward, arms sweeping closed to ensnare Alex in a tight grip. She grunted upon impact but relentlessly struck Wes's head as he charged toward a wall of Maws, who scattered to avoid the collision. In the chaos, a wide hole opened up, revealing a large timber beam firmly embedded in the ground, supporting the building.

Wes crashed through it, Alex's back colliding with the timber. It snapped in half, sending splinters flying. Alex and Wes crashed to the earth, their bodies wracked with pain.

Jacob rushed to the end of his cell, wincing at the sight of Alex's motionless body. "Come on. Come on. Please move," he muttered desperately.

But Alex remained still, appearing lifeless. Jacob prayed she was merely unconscious. Meanwhile, Wes struggled to his feet, crying out with each laborious movement. The noise caught Ammon's attention, causing him to slam against the bars of his cell in alarm. Wide-eyed with terror, he watched as Wes started toward Alex's prone form, each heavy step thumping in rhythm with Jacob's heartbeat.

"*Alex!*" Ammon yelled, trying to wake her.

Jacob joined in, matching Ammon's urgency as they both shouted her name. Daemion's laughter filled the building as he watched Wes closing in. The cheers from the Maws dwindled, all attention fixed on the imminent fatal conclusion.

Wes raised his foot high, looming over Alex's head. Just as he slammed it down, Alex swiftly swung a large piece of timber and smashed it into Wes's face with a heavy thud. Wes spun, disoriented by the blow, and crashed heavily to the ground, sending dirt flying.

The Maws erupted in cheers.

Jacob's head jerked back in shock as he watched Alex gradually rise, her fist still tightly gripping the timber. Despite her visible struggle against the pain, she managed to straighten, her chest heaving with ragged breaths, her lip curling as she stared down at Wes, who was motionless on the ground.

"*Finish him!*" Daemion commanded.

Alex lifted her gaze, her look of disgust transforming into an angry sneer. Her bloodied nostrils flared, fingers tightening around the timber. Then she dropped it, letting the heavy wood fall to the ground next to Wes. She drew a deep breath, her chin lifting defiantly toward Daemion.

"Do it yourself."

Daemion snarled. "Put her back in her cell."

Alex smirked. She had let Daemion revel in the sight of destruction but had denied him the ultimate satisfaction of death that his eyes craved. Gerrick approached her and seized her arm, but Alex wrenched it away.

"I can walk on my own," she snapped, starting toward her cell.

As she passed Jacob and Ammon, her gaze lifted slowly, a small smile tugging at the corner of her lips before faltering abruptly as she winced. Jacob stood stunned. He had always known Alex to have a backbone, always ready to throw the first punch, but he had never expected that.

"Are you okay?" Ammon asked, approaching her side of the cell.

Alex leaned against the cell bars and slid down slowly, grimacing as she settled onto the earth. Eventually, she nodded, then tilted her head back, resting it on the cell bars. Exhausted, beaten, and in pain, the adrenaline coursing through her offered temporary numbness to the agony, but once faded, Jacob knew she would be in a world of hurt.

Jacob's cell door opened, forcing him to yank his gaze away. He hesitated, his heart pounding in his chest as he faced Daemion. Those eyes … up close, he instantly recognized those piercing slits, triggering flashes of that night in the cave.

"You're *next*," Daemion said.

Jacob curled his fingers into his fists. Abe had proven right; Daemion was a thorn in Ostria's side, and all the same, he'd become Jacob's personal tormentor. Since his exile, Daemion had made his life a living hell. And even after escaping, Jacob had unwittingly walked into another trap by coming to Ostria—the very place where the attack was set to happen.

His actions had led to Morgan's death. He had failed his friend. Just as he had failed Charlotte. Once again, he was reminded that he was no hero. And now, it was time to face the consequences of his actions.

He stepped out of his cell willingly.

"Jacob," Ammon said.

Jacob glanced over his shoulder and nodded to Ammon with assurance. "It's okay."

Then he walked toward the center of the building, Daemion creeping close behind him. He noticed a few Maws dragging Wes's massive form into a cell. The rest of the Maws huddled around him, their hostile visages triggering a flood of memories—a blow to the face, followed by a series of relentless kicks, flashing through his mind.

My revenge isn't finished until I say it is. Daemion's words from a moment ago crept into Jacob's head, filling him with dread.

His steps faltered as the Maws dispersed to unveil his opponent—Michael.

Jacob stood stock-still, eyes growing wide with alert. Michael stood tall, his piercing eyes locked intensely on him. Barefoot and clad only in jeans, the madman bore no shirt, exposing a canvas of burned flesh running down the left side of his chest. Gunpowder residue caked his hands black. Matted hair brushed against the taut tendons of his neck. And his face … Jacob gulped as he took in Michael's disfigured features once more.

"Daemion, sunset is nearing," Gerrick said. "The Last Patriots will arrive soon and will be waiting for our signal."

"There won't be anything left for them to arrive to when I'm finished," Daemion said as he sauntered between Jacob and Michael. "But the Firebug knows all about that. He destroyed my home, after all, setting all of Eremos ablaze. *Talk about death and destruction!*

"And don't be mistaken. Psycho to psycho, I commend your efforts. *Hell,* we could've worked together, had my Maws successfully captured you. But you murdered them. Along with others, when you burned down our home. That makes you our enemy."

Michael snarled, his eyes piercing into Daemion, just as they had that day on the Screech with Wes.

"You see, normally we feast on our enemies," Daemion said. "It's more … *personal* than your use of fire. It's our way of saying we're *stronger* than you. We can *consume* you. It's why I didn't kill the woman. Oh, the meal plans I have for her! But you see, she has something you don't … *untainted* skin."

"In the heart of your domain, kin shall turn on kin, feasting on their flesh," Michael said. "I shall mete out retribution, scattering the remnants to the winds in flakes of ash. Only the righteous will be spared."

"Whoa there," Daemion said, laughing to himself as he stepped away from Michael. He threw his arms wide, inviting the madman's words. "Where does he come up with this stuff? I fucking love this guy."

With a sudden whirl, Daemion pivoted on his heel and jabbed his finger toward Jacob. "But this one … I *despise*."

Jacob snarled, his fingers clenching into fists, preparing for action as Daemion sauntered toward him. He mirrored the hate Daemion carried, and strangely, he savored it. He let it consume him, just as it had *that* night.

"Normally, I'd wait to kill you last," Daemion said. "Let you watch as I kill every last one of your friends. Only then would I feel completely *satisfied*. But … seeing that Gerrick has mentioned it twice already, I don't have the luxury of time."

He grinned. "Plus, killing the boy already gave me that satisfaction. So, instead, I'll watch as the pyromaniac delivers his judgment. And boy, do I love to watch. Seems rather fitting, doesn't it? The one who destroyed my hand versus the one who destroyed my home. Next comes *death*."

He leaned in close, coming within reach of Jacob. "Let's see if you can find your way out of this one," he said, stepping aside to reveal Michael waiting. "Now *fight!*"

Jacob remained rooted in place, his heart pounding as he braced for Michael's inevitable fury. The fight would be quick. Jacob had no intention of being a pawn in Daemion's game, choosing instead to accept his fate as a consequence of his own actions.

Judgment served.

But Michael's fury never unleashed.

Michael stood still as well, his gaze fixed on Jacob's eyes, as if he were piercing into his soul. "The eyes of the Lord are upon the righteous," he declared solemnly.

"*Ha*," Daemion spat, chuckling as he pointed at Jacob. "This guy?"

"A wise man scales the city of the mighty and brings down the *stronghold* in which they trust," Michael continued, his words directed at Jacob. Then suddenly, he started to cough, his body folding over as the hacking wracked his fragile frame.

"Oh, fuck this," Daemion said, stepping forward from the wall of Maws.

Jacob's eyes bulged in shock as he watched Daemion reach behind his back and reveal the Talon. The cannibal strode toward Michael, halting mere inches from him, and aimed the gun at the back of his head. Then he pulled the trigger. The shot pierced Jacob's ears, his head flinching back as blood sprayed out from Michael's head before crumbling into the earth. Dust billowed upward.

Daemion watched the swirls of dust with a grim smile, his hands weaving through the air. "From dust you came, and to dust you shall return."

Daemion's aim fell on Jacob.

"*No!*" Ammon yelled.

Jacob closed his eyes, shutting out the cruel cackle of Daemion as he waited for the inevitable gunshot. Strangely, he felt a serene calm descend upon him. The moment had arrived. He had no cunning plan this time. He simply embraced his fate, clinging to that fragile vision he kept seeing. Whatever it was, he just hoped that his sacrifices on Eremos had earned him a reunion with Charlotte.

"You know, I guess I was wrong," Daemion said. "Oddly, there's a certain satisfaction in killing the strongest first. The agony of watching friends witness their hero's demise … it's like indulging in dessert before the main course."

"Daemion don't! I'll fight him!"

Jacob's eyes flew open, his head jerking toward Ammon, who gripped the bars of his cell, gasping for air, beads of sweat streaming down his face. *Or were those tears?*

"I'll make it a show," Ammon said, the words rushing out. *"Quick. Brutal.* And when it's done, you let me join you." He thrust his arm out of the cell, revealing his Last Patriot tattoo. "I'm a Last Patriot. Myla plans to kill you when she arrives. She wants Ostria for herself. I can stop her."

Daemion scowled. "How do you know this?"

"It's been the plan all along. The Last Patriots wanted to take over control in Derro and establish a new nation. When we failed and were exiled here, we shifted our focus to Ostria."

We? Our? Jacob flinched.

"Myla doesn't want to see Ostria destroyed like you do," Ammon continued. "She wants to rule it. And she won't hesitate to kill you to achieve that."

"Not before I kill her first," Daemion sneered.

"She won't let you get close to her. But she'll let me. She sent me here. To lure you to her. But I'll lure her here instead, believing I succeeded. That's when you strike."

"Oh, I like the sound of that," Daemion said, grinning. He strode toward Ammon's cell, swiftly unlocking it and swinging the door open with a flourish. "Spoken like someone who knows what it takes to survive. Consider this fight your application. And no funny games, or I'll end you."

"We don't have time for this," Gerrick interjected. "He's clearly lying. The Last Patriots are waiting for our signal. The council will have finished deliberating. We need to—"

"Shut up," Daemion cut in, snapping his aim at Gerrick. "Or I'll kill you first. The council isn't going anywhere. And I'll signal the Last Patriots when I'm damn ready, and my Maws are in place and ready to ambush them. We talked about this."

"Ammon, what the *hell* are you doing?" Alex asked.

"What I should've done a long time ago," Ammon said.

The Last Patriot stepped out of his cell, head bowed, avoiding Jacob's stunned gaze. His steps faltered as he approached, slowly lifting his head to meet Jacob's eyes. Tears brimmed. Arms trembled. Breath came in rapid gasps.

Fingers curled into fists.

"I'm sorry," Ammon said. "It wasn't supposed to happen like this."

CHAPTER THIRTY-SIX

THE FINAL DAYS BEFORE EXILE

TONIGHT WAS THE NIGHT.

Jacob's heart raced, his pulse echoing the rhythm of his thoughts, which he tempered with a measured sip of whiskey. Just enough to steady his resolve without clouding his senses.

Clarity was paramount for what lay ahead.

He replayed the plan in his mind, each detail ingrained into his consciousness after days of unwavering observation of Richard's every move. Doubt had flickered briefly, a persistent whisper in the back of his mind, but each time he glimpsed Richard's arrogant smile, memories of the pain he inflicted upon Jacob surged back, igniting the fire of vengeance simmering within him.

But in the times he wasn't watching Richard, the doubts of taking his life lingered back.

No! Jacob told himself. *You took my wife and unborn child's life,* he muttered to Richard in the recesses of his mind. He took another sip of whiskey, savoring the burn in his throat. *And now, I'm going to take yours.*

He stood and started toward the staircase, his gaze drifting over the framed photos adorning the walls. Each one reminded him of the life he once shared with Charlotte. As he ascended, he traced the edges of the frames with trembling fingertips, seeking solace in the tangible remnants of their memories. Yet, as he reached the top, the realization dawned upon him. Those frozen moments belonged to a past irretrievably lost, leaving him a stranger, even to himself.

That's not me anymore.

He continued onward, his footsteps faltering as he approached his father's study. Then his progress halted altogether as his eyes glanced at the empty bedroom where he had assembled the crib. The door stood slightly ajar, beckoning him inside. An unspoken invitation. He hesitated, memories flooding back, causing him to snap his eyes shut. He hadn't dared enter that room since that day.

But today felt … different.

Today, Jacob accepted the finality that there would be no tomorrow.

He stepped toward the door, pushed it open, and crossed the threshold. His gaze softened as he took in the crib, its pristine beauty standing in stark contrast to the emptiness that filled the room. Yet, despite its elegance, it served as a painful reminder of the life that never had the chance to be. The life they had painstakingly planned for so long, only to be shattered by Richard's callous actions.

Like Jacob himself, the crib had lost its purpose. *He took everything from me.*

The vengeful flame ignited within him once again, pushing him over the edge. He bent down, his hands trembling as he grabbed the hammer from his tool bag, fingers curling tightly around the handle.

Then, with a primal scream, he swung the hammer down on the crib with relentless force. His heart thundered in his chest, drowning out all other sounds save for a piercing, high-pitched ringing that echoed in his ears with each ferocious swing. Splintered wood shot up at him as the crib succumbed to his violent assault. Sweat soaked his brow, mingling with the tears that blurred his vision. Yet Jacob refused to relinquish the hammer, letting his overwhelming emotions control him until he destroyed the crib.

When his strength had finally waned, he dropped the hammer, his hands trembling as he fought to catch his breath. Through tear-streaked eyes, he gazed upon the wreckage he had wrought. In that moment, all the lingering doubts he had about his plan vanished. He had been reborn. A vessel brimming with anger, ready to enact his revenge.

He left the room, his determined steps propelling him toward his father's study. Driven by his fury, he barged inside and crossed the room, his eyes locked on the glass case he had placed on the shelf. With steady hands, he opened it and grabbed the gun. The same one he had crafted with his father as a kid. The very weapon Mason had coveted, the catalyst for the chaos that had ultimately led to Charlotte's death.

A reminder of the blood on his hands. And now it would serve as Jacob's instrument of vengeance.

I should've shot them. I should've given them the gun. I should've stepped more in front of her.

No! he screamed internally. His time for regrets had passed.

With determined resolve, he checked the magazine, confirmed it was fully loaded, and then pulled back the slide, the satisfying *click* fueling the vengeful flame burning within him. Holstering the gun at the back of his waistline, he turned and left his father's study.

Then he stepped out into the night, leaving his home, knowing he'd never return. Raindrops pattered against his head as he made his way toward his Nervo Pod. The sun dipped below the horizon, casting Tuto into darkness. Jacob welcomed the dark, embracing the path he had chosen—where the dawn of a new day would forever elude him.

Richard Woodwin frowned.

Bel is calling you, Eve alerted. *Would you like me to answer it for you?*

Richard drew a deep breath, his gaze drifting to his phone resting on the table. His fingers hovered over the glossy surface, betraying his inner turmoil as he wrestled with the decision to answer the call.

"I can't help you anymore," he muttered to himself with a heavy sigh.

Bel has been rather persistent, Eve said.

After a moment's hesitation, he finally relented. "Go ahead, Eve, you can answer," he grumbled to his Aux.

The ringing ceased abruptly, replaced by Bel's impatient voice on the other end. "Richard, what the hell, man? I've been trying to reach you all day."

"I told you already," Richard murmured. "I can't help you anymore. My father won't allow any more transactions from you guys."

"And I've told you, you don't have a choice," Bel shot back. "What's the problem? Did your father finally figure out *who* we really are?"

"No, definitely not. He knows nothing."

"Then why does he suddenly care?"

"Because he noticed the same name on all the purchase orders."

"I thought you said he doesn't bother with paperwork."

"He *doesn't,*" Richard said, the words rushing out of his mouth. "But with the increase in business, he grew curious. I managed to divert his attention."

"What did you tell him?"

"I told him I'd received a contract from the council to help them buy businesses within no-go zones."

"Good lie. But that still doesn't explain why he suddenly won't work with us."

Fuck! Richard screamed internally. *What have I gotten myself into?*

"It has to do with the last sale," Richard admitted. "Hoos."

"What about it?"

"When the owner came to sign the paperwork, he said some things. Stuff that really resonated with my father. Now he thinks he's doing more harm by helping the council."

"Harm?"

"*A woman died, Bel!*"

A heavy silence enveloped them.

"That was a mistake," Bel finally said.

"*Your* mistake," Richard fired back. "It was your idea for me to seek out random criminals—"

"Yeah, so that if the crimes went haywire, they couldn't be traced back to the Last Patriots. And if they went well, then we had new recruits. No one works harder for the cause than people who want to be a part of it. And resource acquisition was essential for the destruction of the council's Control Hubs. You know this."

Richard scowled. "I'm well aware of the importance of resource acquisition. And if you recall, I told you Mason wasn't the right man for the jammer. It took us years to allocate the parts and find someone to create it. And now our only one is in *their* hands. You didn't listen to me then, and you didn't listen to me about those two thugs."

"So, *that's* what this is all about?" Bel said, scoffing. "That wasn't on *me*, Richard. Their deaths were on *you*. I told you—"

"They demanded more money. Threatened to go to the Cullers if we didn't pay. They knew we had ulterior motives. You told me to handle it. What else was I supposed to do?"

"Hire someone else to do it for you, just like you did with all the other jobs."

"Yeah, except the other jobs didn't involve killing—"

Bel hung up.

Richard frowned, a heavy weight of apprehension settling in his chest. He drew a deep breath, trying to quell the nervous energy coursing through his veins, but it proved futile. Bel hanging up wasn't a good sign, and Richard had done little to prove he could continue being helpful. He frowned, uncertain of his future.

As moments stretched into minutes of tense silence, he found himself lost in thought. Time slipped away unnoticed until the stiffness in his joints reminded him of his prolonged stillness. With a sigh, he rose from his seat, joints protesting with audible cracks as he gathered his things. Today had taken its toll. He needed respite to gather his thoughts and devise a plan for tomorrow.

Convincing his father to continue with the purchases was paramount. Their safety hung in the balance.

He just hoped it wasn't too late.

He stepped out into the chill of the evening air, a biting gust of wind ruffling his hair and stinging his cheeks. Raindrops pattered his head as he started toward his Nervo Pod.

"Eve, open Nervo Pod."

As Richard approached the open door, a sudden force seized him from behind, powerful arms wrapping around his chest while a hand clamped over his mouth. Startled, he thrashed and struggled against his assailant, but their grip was relentless. He panicked as a strange, sweet scent assaulted his senses. His vision blurred and dizziness overcame him.

With a last, desperate gasp, Richard's consciousness slipped away.

Jacob bit the insides of his cheeks.

His arms trembled as he paced, his gaze fixed on Richard's unconscious body. Bound with his arms behind him, Richard sat slumped in a chair. With the gun gripped tightly, Jacob's palms grew slick with sweat, forcing him to constantly readjust his grip.

Come on, wake up! Waiting had become unbearable. His mind wouldn't stop spinning with tumultuous thoughts, urging him to flee. *It's not too late*, his conscience painfully pleaded.

If Jacob left now, there was still a chance he could escape detection. He could simply tell Ezra what he knew and let Richard face exile.

No! Jacob's inner scream echoed with fierce determination. Leaving now would squander his chance for revenge. Yes, Richard would be exiled, but so would he. *It has to end now.*

A heavy groan shattered the silence, drawing Jacob's attention to Richard as he slowly stirred. Jacob's hand tightened around the gun, his heart quickening. With shaky hands, he slowly slid his owl mask over his face and pointed the firearm at Richard, eyes bulging as Richard lifted his head.

"*What the hell?*" Richard yelled, his panicked breathing coming in quick gasps. "Tell Bel I'm sorry! I'll handle it, *I swear!*"

"*Shut up!*" Jacob shouted as he lunged at Richard. "If you so much as alert your Aux, this will end very badly for you."

Richard nodded, his lips trembling. Jacob smiled, the vengeful rage that had simmered within him rushing back, consuming his insides. He leaned closer to Richard, their faces inches apart—Charlotte's killer's and his own.

"Do you feel that?" he said. "That sense of panic coursing through your bones, urging you to act, but you can't? The fear creeping through your veins as your mind spins with worst-case scenarios? The dread coiling in the pit of your stomach, warning you that something *terrible* is about to happen?"

Richard's eyes widened with each word, the whites around his irises starkly visible. His only response was a suffocating gulp.

"Good. Let it resonate. Because it's the exact feeling my wife and I had. Right before she was murdered."

Richard sat stock-still, his eyes darting around the room, realization hitting him like a punch to the gut as he pieced together where he was—and who was in front of him.

"Jacob?"

Jacob slowly removed his owl mask. He no longer needed it. Its purpose had been served—to make Richard feel, if only for a moment, the same fear that he and Charlotte had endured. Richard's mouth fell open in stunned silence.

"Was it Hoos that gave it away?" Jacob's voice was calm, almost taunting, as he stood and took a few steps back. "I thought it was only fitting. For it to finally end where it all began."

"Jacob, please."

"Or was it the owl mask? 'Cause *that* I'd understand. Were they your choice, or theirs?" He jabbed the gun toward Richard. "Or was it *the reminder of Charlotte's murder?*"

Richard winced. "Please, you don't have to do this. I can—"

"Yes, I do. You have to pay for what you did."

"I didn't kill her. I swear. That wasn't me."

"*Stop!*" Jacob barked. "Accept what you did to *her*. To *me*. Own it. Just like your desire to help the council with their no-go schemes."

Richard frowned as he lowered his head, avoiding Jacob's gaze. A violent silence descended upon them, broken only by the relentless patter of raindrops against the windows. Jacob waited, his eyes fixed on Richard, searching for a confession that never came.

"Did you know she was pregnant? You didn't just murder my wife. You murdered my unborn—"

"*Okay!*" Richard shouted, his frown deepening as he lifted his head. "She wasn't supposed to die. That's not what I hired them for. *They* pulled that trigger. Not *me*."

"*You pulled that trigger!* The moment you hired them." Jacob scoffed, shaking his head. "You're just too blind to see it. But that's indicative of the society we live in, isn't it? We tend to overlook the bigger picture, or in this case, the underlying problem. And that problem is you."

Richard's head dropped, his chin sinking to his chest as he absorbed the familiar words. Jacob started toward the empty glass cases, letting the weight of his words settle in as he stepped behind them. His gaze fell upon the grime ingrained into the glass case, smeared with Charlotte's dried blood. The sight served as a reminder of what Richard had become to him—a permanent stain that couldn't be washed away.

Only destroyed.

"You remember telling me that, don't you?" Jacob said, his gaze lifting. "Right after your *Crimson Hands* sales pitch." He scoffed. "Little did you know, you were talking about yourself the whole damn time."

"Jacob, I'm sorry. I got caught up in things that are *way* bigger than me. I could never have known things would end the way they did. Just please … don't kill me. I'll turn myself in."

"Yeah, so you can still live in exile? That's not enough justice. Why should you live when *they* can't?"

"Killing me won't fix it," Richard pleaded. "Sure, justice would be served, but at what cost? Your exile too? You'd become no different than those thugs I hired—"

"*I'm nothing like them!*"

"I know that. It's why you can't face me. Deep down, you don't want to kill me. Because you're a good man. A better one than me. Even my father could see it. You don't want my blood on your hands."

"*Stop,*" Jacob spat as he pulled back the hammer of his pistol. The sharp *click* filled the room, causing Richard to jerk in his seat. Jacob aimed the gun, pointing it at the back of Richard's head, his knuckles turning white as he squeezed the grip.

"Jacob, please, I beg you," Richard said, his body trembling as he fought against his restraints. "I'll tell you who he is. Just let me go. I'll turn myself in and I'll tell you who he is. The one who got away—"

Suddenly, the jarring sound of a bell caused Jacob's body to tense.

"*Freeze!*"

Standing at the threshold of Hoos, drenched in wet clothes, was Ezra. He held a gun, its barrel trained directly on Jacob.

"Jacob, drop the gun," Ezra calmly commanded.

"Oh, thank God," Richard said. "Please, you have to help—"

"*Stop talking,*" Jacob barked, his pistol gesturing sharply toward Richard. He turned his attention back to Ezra. "How?"

"I've been watching you. Since that day you snapped. I could tell you weren't being honest with me. You'd figured something out."

Jacob scoffed. "Well, isn't that just the best investigative work I've seen out of you yet."

Ezra frowned. "Jacob, it's not too late. You can stop what you're doing. You don't have to do this."

"*Yes, I do.* This man took everything from me. He hired those thugs. He's the reason my wife is *dead.* He destroyed my entire life."

"And I'll make sure he faces exile—"

"Just before you exile me, right?" Jacob cut in bitterly. "*No.* He doesn't get a second chance. And after what I'm going to do, neither will I."

"Jacob, no …"

Ezra's plea fell on deaf ears as Jacob tuned out the surrounding noise. The rain pounding on the windows became distant drums, matching the erratic beat of his heart. His body trembled, causing him to clench and unclench his grip on the pistol, his fingers hovering over the trigger. Conflicting emotions assaulted his mind, but one dominated them all: hate.

He let that hate consume him.

"You know, I finally got around to reading that damn book your family loves so dearly," Jacob finally said, watching Richard jerk in his chair. "And, like you, I learned something."

"Jacob, I need you to drop the gun," Ezra's distant plea sounded in Jacob's ears. "Don't make me do this."

"What are you doing?" Richard shouted. "Shoot him."

"People can hate so damn much," Jacob said, squeezing the grip of the gun, "that they'll rip the world apart."

You're stronger than you think. Charlotte's comforting words seeped into Jacob's darkened mind, a delicate whisper for him not to pull the trigger. He knew deep down she wouldn't want him to.

Not today, Charlotte.

Jacob squeezed the trigger.

The gunshot pierced through the chaos, reverberating like a crack of thunder in Jacob's ears. His eyes bulged as he watched Richard's head jerk from the impact before slumping lifelessly against his chest.

"*Oh, God,*" Ezra gasped.

Jacob's heart hammered against his chest, his body trembling uncontrollably at the sight of what he'd done. Slowly, he turned his gaze, locking eyes with Ezra. They stood frozen, both stunned by the irreversible turn of events.

"Jacob," Ezra said, his gun still trained on him. "I'm going to need you to drop the gun now."

Jacob's gaze flickered to the gun he still clenched in his hand. It hurt to look at; its blue finish a haunting reminder of his father. A reminder of what his father had done. That same act whispered from the darkest corner of his mind, urging him to follow in his father's footsteps.

After what he had just done, it seemed like the only way forward. The only path that offered even the slightest chance, however slim or improbable, of being with her.

The distant sound of sirens broke through his contemplation. Cullers would arrive any moment, but he refused to leave his fate in the hands of the council.

"I don't believe I ever told you how my father died," Jacob muttered. "Although I'm sure you already know."

Ezra shook his head, eyes widening. "Jacob, please listen to my words—"

"After all, it mirrors the very same fate as your brother."

"Don't do this," Ezra pleaded, taking slow steps toward Jacob, his gun shaking in his grip.

"You remember what you told me about him?"

Ezra frowned. "Damn it, Jacob, please don't do this!"

"You told me he'd chosen his own form of exile."

Jacob slowly, as if his body was fighting back, raised the gun upward inch by agonizing inch, his hand shaking vigorously as he pushed through the resistance.

"No!"

"I can't live another minute without her," Jacob cried, his finger hovering over the trigger. "I have nothing else to live for—"

A gunshot shattered the air.

Jacob's shoulder jerked, and he stumbled into the shelves as a searing pain pierced his chest. His gun slipped from his grasp as he clutched at his shoulder. With wide eyes, he looked down at the blood pooling in his palm, realization crashing over him like a tidal wave.

Ezra had shot him.

He lifted his gaze to find Ezra frowning. Then he felt his legs give way, and he collapsed to the ground, the world around him spinning. The metallic taste of blood filled his throat, triggering a fit of coughing. Through the suffocating haze, Ezra kneeled before him, his frown deepening as he applied firm pressure to Jacob's shoulder. The searing pain was unbearable, stealing his breath.

"You're going to be okay," Ezra said.

A wave of exhaustion crashed over Jacob; the agony of his bullet wound and the weight of what he had just done overwhelmed him. His eyelids grew heavy, and his body felt as though it had reached its limit. Unable to resist any longer, his eyes finally succumbed to the darkness as he lost consciousness.

Outside, the rain continued to pelt the glass, its soothing melody calming Jacob's fading awareness. In that fleeting moment, he clung to the fragile hope that maybe, just maybe, there was a future for him beyond the existence of exile.

CHAPTER THIRTY-SEVEN

DAY SEVEN OF EXILE

JACOB SHOOK HIS head in utter disbelief. "Ammon ..." he murmured.

He was stunned. Speechless. He couldn't believe his eyes. The reality hit him hard, bringing forth the nightmare he'd had nights ago. In it, Ammon had betrayed them. Just like he was doing now. But this time, it wasn't just a nightmare.

It was real.

"I should've known better than to trust you," Jacob said.

"I can't just watch us all die without telling you the truth," Ammon said as he approached, stopping just beyond Jacob's reach. "I lied to you, Jacob. I took that job. I'm the one who killed Charlotte. I'm—"

Jacob's mind went blank as his nostrils flared, and his eyes narrowed into menacing slits. He felt his fingers curling into fists, arms tightening as a raw fury pulsed in his veins, his mind only seeing red. The rage simmered inside him, threatening to boil over.

He let it.

"My, my, my," Daemion said as he neared them both. "Who is this Charlotte? She sounds *delightful.*"

Jacob flew his fist forward, slamming it into the center of Ammon's face with a sickening crunch. The Last Patriot's head snapped back as he stumbled backward, his hands reaching at his nose, which gushed blood.

Jacob roared as he rushed toward Ammon and tackled him around the waist, driving him to the earth with a massive thud, clouds of dust billowing. He rose, legs pinning Ammon down as he straddled him, preparing to unleash a flurry of punches.

Time seemed to slow as memories assaulted his mind, a devastating onslaught of images.

The first punch landed with ferocity, shaking his core, catapulting his mind back to that night; the night Ammon killed Charlotte. His gun firing, face hidden behind an owl mask. Charlotte crumbling to the ground, blood pouring through her fingers as she clutched her stomach.

The second blow landed with a dull thud, triggering a rush of anger as Jacob recalled the morning at the Culler station. Ammon's voice echoed in his ears, quoting Richard's favorite line from his favorite book … *The sicker people get, the longer they survive.*

The third punch splattered, blood spraying up at Jacob's face, taking him deeper into that memory. He'd yanked Ammon by his hair, his arms bound by holocuffs, defenseless to the fury of blows Jacob rained down on him.

Just as he did now.

Ammon didn't resist or raise a hand in defense. He simply absorbed each blow, one after another, as if resigned to his fate. Blood mixed with tears, streaking his battered face.

Jacob's fist flew through the air again, ready to deliver another punishing strike, but before it could land, firm arms encircled his waist, yanking him back. He fought against the grip, his arms flailing forward, his vision slowly returning.

"*Let me go!*" he roared.

But the arms held firm. They dragged him away from Ammon's motionless body until Jacob fell onto the ground, his back hitting the earth. He scrambled backward, eyes locked on Ammon, his mouth slackening with shock as he realized what he had done.

Daemion stepped into his view, snarling as he reached for the Talon holstered at the back of his waist. "I should've known better than to trust the Last Patriot." He aimed the gun at Jacob, the hollow barrel glaring down at him. "He made it quick, all right. For *himself*. I don't know who this Charlotte is, but it's apparent she's important to you. About time you were finally reunited."

Jacob's heart jolted as he braced himself for the gunshot. Then suddenly, he saw two large hands wrapping around Daemion's face and *twist*, erupting in a sickening crack. Daemion's head wobbled, face slackening as his life escaped him. His knees buckled, and he crumbled to the ground, revealing a standing Gerrick.

Gerrick bent down and grabbed the gun from Daemion's hand. Then, asserting his dominance, he planted his foot on Daemion's back and swung the gun toward the approaching wall of Maws who'd advanced toward him.

"Don't even think about it," Gerrick roared, sweeping his aim across them. "Go. Get the hell out of here."

The remaining Maws exchanged stunned glances, the gravity of their situation slowly sinking in. Their leader was dead. *Finally.* A few of them exchanged terse nods before scattering in a frantic rush, hastening toward the opposite end of the Sanctuary Halls.

Was that how Gerrick had gotten them in undetected? Jacob wondered, remembering the building they were in was nestled against the rear of the palisade, snug against the towering mountain.

"Damn imbeciles," Gerrick muttered, drawing Jacob's attention from the fleeing Maws. Gerrick released the Talon's magazine, checking the remaining rounds. "I said Daemion was too manic to be trusted."

"What the hell is going on?" Jacob finally asked, still reeling from Gerrick's sudden actions. His gaze flickered to Daemion, his neck sinking deeper into his shoulder under the weight of Gerrick's foot.

"It's a shame, really," Gerrick said, slamming the Talon's magazine back into the grip. "I was really looking forward to seeing the council's faces as Daemion shot each of them. There's nothing like witnessing someone reap what they've sown." He holstered the gun behind his back. "But it seems I'll have to handle it myself. A new reign is coming, and I'll make sure of it."

The Last Patriots, Jacob realized. Gerrick must have been collaborating with them all this time. Had Myla turned him, recruiting him as her inside man in Ostria? It was the exact tactic they'd used in Derro.

"You're a Last Patriot," Alex said, connecting the dots herself, her arms clenching the bars of her cell. "You've been working for Myla all this time."

"Not quite," Gerrick said, lifting his foot from Daemion and straightening his posture. "My original loyalty was with Ostria, but that's recently changed. You see, unlike your friend here, I wasn't exiled for being a Last Patriot. I'm just aligning with the winning side."

Jacob snarled. "Just like *he* tried doing," he said, gesturing toward Ammon with a nod.

Gerrick raised an eyebrow. "*Is* that what he tried doing? Because, as I heard it, he told Daemion he was going to fight you. And what I saw was not that. Instead, he confessed, and you sought revenge. Hell, he didn't even defend himself. If I had to guess his intentions, I'd say he was about to ask for your forgiveness before Daemion killed you all. But your thirst for vengeance blinded you to that."

"He murdered my wife!"

Gerrick's head jerked back. "This happen in Derro?"

Jacob nodded.

"Damn," Gerrick said, shaking his head. "Now, *that's* a twist. And you just happened to find each other during exile? Or is that why you're here? You get exiled so you could hunt him down? Avenge your wife?"

Jacob shook his head. "I killed the man who hired him."

"That right? Wow! Talk about fate. You murder the man responsible for your wife's death, get exiled, only to find the man who actually—"

A pained groan interrupted Gerrick. Jacob jerked his head to the right, peeking around Gerrick to see Ammon gaining consciousness.

"Well, well, would you look at that?" Gerrick drawled, grinning as he watched Ammon struggle to roll onto his stomach. "It seems fate has spoken once again. And who am I to stay in its way?" He stepped out of Jacob's line of sight and started toward the exit, brushing past Jacob. "I suggest you do the same and stay out of my way. Fate, after all, has left me low on bullets. And I have more pressing matters to attend to. Consider this our farewell, Jacob."

Jacob watched Gerrick leave, knowing he was on his way to assassinate the councilors. They wouldn't even see it coming. Jacob wasn't sure how low Gerrick was on ammo, but he knew there were two bullets waiting in the Council Tower. He patted his pocket, feeling the weight of the one bullet he still had. He still didn't know why he kept it, but it offered him a strange comfort.

Perhaps even a fighting chance.

Just as Jaci had felt, risking her life to guide them all here, hoping to prevent the attack. A fighting chance to protect the ones she loved. Even if it meant never being reunited.

I can't just let them die.

Even if it meant risking how own life. That risk didn't deter him. Instead, like the bullet in his pocket, it offered a strange comfort—whether delusion or truth—that if death came for him, Charlotte would be there to greet him.

"You've got that look on your face," Alex said. "You're not *actually* considering—"

"We have to stop him," Jacob said.

He rose to his feet and headed toward Alex's cell. Out of the corner of his eye he noticed Ammon now sitting upright, spitting blood out of his mouth. Jacob ignored him and focused on lifting the thick wooden hatch of Alex's cell, catching blood on his knuckles. He swung the door open.

"No," Alex said, her hands resting on her hips. "You heard Gerrick. The Last Patriots are waiting for his signal. They're probably already nearby, waiting."

"I won't just let them die, Alex. Ellis and Abe are Jaci's son and husband. She told me their names before we left her."

"That could be any—"

"Do you remember what Ellis shouted to his father before storming out of the tower? He said, 'How are *they* any different from *Mother?*' He was talking about Jaci. He didn't want to grant us refuge because he believed it wasn't fair to her. He saw us no different from her or any other exile."

Alex remained silent, her lips pressed together as she considered Jacob's words.

"That's *them,*" Jacob said. "I'm sure of it."

"Okay, let's say you're right," Alex said, dropping her hands to her sides, "and that's Jaci's son and husband. What are you going to do to stop Gerrick? He has a gun. Myla and her Last Patriots will storm Ostria at his signal. You're just one man."

Unfortunately, she was right. Yet the urge to try was something he couldn't dismiss. He owed it to Jaci. He owed it to Morgan.

But most importantly, he owed it to himself.

"We should leave while we still can," Alex said.

"No," Jacob said, his resolve solidifying. "You can go. I'm going to try and stop this."

He turned to leave, but Alex grabbed his arm. "This is because of Morgan, isn't it? You want to prevent the same from happening to Ellis—"

Jacob yanked his arm away, his head bowing as the painful memory of Morgan's death entered his mind. He fought the urge to find the kid's body, knowing it was in here somewhere. He didn't have time. Instead, he pushed aside the emotions threatening to come forth.

"His death wasn't your fault, Jacob," Alex said gently.

"*Yes,* it was," Jacob said, jabbing his finger into his chest. "Coming to Ostria was *my* idea. The very place where the attack was planned, right into Daemion's trap. Morgan's blood is on *my* hands. It was foolish to come here, thinking our warning would make a difference—"

"But it *did.* Ellis evacuated Ostria. Women and children are safe because of you. You convinced the council to act."

Jacob shook his head. "They may be safe now, but they won't be if I don't stop Gerrick. I won't let him destroy their home."

He turned and started purposefully toward the exit.

"*Jacob!*" Alex shouted as she hurried alongside him.

"You're not going to stop me, Alex."

"Can we at least talk about this more?"

"There's nothing more to talk about. I've made my decision."

Alex grabbed his arm again, halting his stride. "Just wait a second," she urged, taking a deep breath. She winced, no doubt still in pain from her fight with Wes.

"What now?"

"What happened earlier with Ammon ... Was that ... true? Did all that really happen?"

Jacob briefly lowered his gaze before glancing over his shoulder at Ammon. He was slowly getting to his feet, visibly battered. Their eyes met, and Ammon frowned, his face a mess of blood and bruises—much like when Jacob had found him in the pit. Back then, he hadn't seen him as Charlotte's killer.

Unlike now.

"Ask him," Jacob replied tersely.

Without waiting for Alex's response, Jacob turned away from Ammon and Alex and ran out of the Sanctuary Halls.

He burst out into a gloomy, red sky and sprinted across the open, parched field. The warm, humid air clung to his face, making it difficult to breathe. He coughed, the acrid smog searing his lungs and throat as he exited through the fence, swirling dust trailing his feet on the dirt path that led deeper into Ostria. The sound of flowing water reached his ears, accompanied by the distant roar of the waterfall.

And then, in the distance, swirls of gray smoke rose into the crimson sky. *The Council Tower!*

Michael's last words crept into his mind, finding purpose. *A wise man scales the city of the mighty and brings down the stronghold in which they trust.*

Gerrick was burning down Ostria's tower, the very symbol of the council's power and a beacon of hope for other exiles. *That's the signal!* The Last Patriots were undoubtedly on their way.

Jacob pushed himself to run faster than he ever had before, his heart threatening to burst, lungs screaming for air. He raced past the now desolate market, the familiar path to the waterfall, and then finally saw the courtyard in the distance.

Screams tore through the air.

Jacob skidded to a halt, chest heaving, aghast at the scene unfolding before him. There, in the distance, people fought in a deadly battle at the entrance of Ostria, their forms barely visible through the smoky haze. The Last Patriots were already here. Ostria was fighting to defend their home.

He bowed his head, summoning his breath as he prepared to sprint, when suddenly his gaze fell to the ground below. Sprawled in the dirt was a dead owl, its glassy, lifeless eyes catching the flickering of flames.

A chill ran through Jacob. The owl felt like a harbinger of death, a reminder of life's relentless cycle. He refused that fate for the council.

He burst into a sprint once again, desperation lending wings to his feet as he neared the courtyard entrance. *Please*, he thought, hoping there was still time to stop Gerrick. To save them.

He entered the courtyard, boots skidding across the cobblestone. In the distance, he saw the councilors scrambling out of the burning tower, their faces twisting in horror as they turned back to watch the flames consume their beacon of hope.

He wasn't too late. They were still alive.

Then suddenly, Gerrick emerged from the tower. Jacob's pulse quickened as he watched the brute round the council, unaware of Jacob's approach. Gerrick reached for the Talon.

"*No!*" Jacob shouted.

The councilors whipped around, their heads snapping toward Jacob as he made his way toward them. Gerrick froze mid-action, his hand hovering near the gun, a snarl twisting his face as he turned to face him. Jacob moved quickly, closing the distance in a few determined strides. When he reached Ellis, his body doubled over as he gasped for air, the searing heat of the flames licking at his back.

"*You*," Monique roared. "This is all your fault. Ellis was right. You and your friends came to initiate the attack!"

"You've got it all wrong," Jacob said, his words rushing out between breaths. He pointed urgently at Gerrick. "It's him! He's been colluding with the Maws and Last Patriots all along. Burning down the tower was his signal to the Last Patriots. They're coming!"

Monique's eyes grew wide as she turned to Gerrick. "Is this true?"

"He has the *gun*," Jacob said.

Gerrick bared his teeth in a menacing sneer. "I thought you'd be more concerned with the Last Patriot," he said, reaching for the Talon behind his back. "But no. I guess you had to interfere with fate."

Monique gasped, retreating unsteadily as Gerrick leveled the gun at them. Jacob inched closer to Ellis.

"How *dare you*," Abe roared. "After everything we've done—"

"*Enough!*" Gerrick shouted. "All you've done is incorporate the same punishment as Derro, which, if you can't see by now, only makes the outside factions stronger. *The Maws. The Last Patriots.* That's all on *you*."

Jacob's attention was yanked away as he noticed shadows moving behind Gerrick. There, in the distance, a figure was sprinting toward the courtyard. *Is that …*

"Now you must face the consequences," Gerrick said.

Jacob's attention shifted back to Gerrick, muscles tensing as he watched Gerrick take aim, the barrel pointing directly at Ellis.

No!

Jacob thew himself in front of Ellis.

The gunshot cracked through the air, and a searing pain erupted in his gut, knocking the breath from his lungs. He crumpled to the cobblestones, the impact jarring through his body. His eyes flew open, wide with shock, as a warm, wet sensation began spreading beneath his shirt.

"You fool!" Gerrick shouted. "You don't even know who you're protecting."

The world around Jacob blurred and distorted, the ringing in his ears muffling the shouts of panic. Each shallow breath came in sharper than the last, pain radiating with every movement. His mind spun, teetering on the edge of consciousness, but his gaze found Ellis—frozen, unharmed, and staring down the barrel of the Talon gripped in Gerrick's hand.

"No matter," Gerrick said. "I have more bullets now."

"Don't …" Jacob managed to rasp.

Just as Gerrick pulled the trigger, a figure tackled him from behind. Gerrick crashed to the ground, the Talon flying out of his hand and skidding across the cobblestones, coming to a stop in front of Ellis.

Despite the agony, Jacob watched as Gerrick struggled against the assailant grappling on top of him. It was Ammon! Ammon swung a hard punch, landing it squarely on Gerrick's face, but Gerrick retaliated with brutal force, throwing Ammon off effortlessly, sending him tumbling across the pavement.

Jacob grimaced, eyes squeezing shut as he clutched at his bloodied stomach, each breath a battle against the searing pain. And then he saw her—Charlotte.

No! his mind screamed, jolting him back. He wasn't ready for her. Not yet.

Gritting his teeth, he forced his body to respond. Pain lanced through him as he tried to rise but collapsed again; the agony was unbearable. Lying there, his gaze darted around for the gun. It was gone. His blurred vision drifted to Ellis, who now stood over Gerrick, the Talon gripped tightly in his hand.

He aimed it directly at Gerrick's head.

"You—"

Ellis pulled the trigger, the shot silencing Gerrick.

Jacob's mouth fell open, his body freezing in shock as his heart hammered wildly against his chest. Every shallow breath felt like a battle, and he clung desperately to the remnants of his strength. The world around him seemed to crumble. He searched for his fellow exiles and found Alex helping Ammon to his feet.

They were here. They had come. They had helped save the council.

Jacob now gave himself over to the pain and relaxed ever so slightly.

"Ellis …" Abe's voice trembled, stunned by his son's actions.

Then Ellis turned sharply, aiming the Talon directly at his father.

Jacob's eyes bulged as he watched Abe's steps falter, his hands rising slowly in front of him. Monique gasped and moved closer to Abe, her arms outstretched in caution. Jacob couldn't fathom what was happening.

"Son, whatever you're thinking, please; you don't have to do this," Abe said, his voice steady, imploring.

"Gerrick's right, you know," Ellis said, scowling. "Exile is futile. Derro sends their miscreants here to fester, while we do the same to our own, allowing them to gather strength and form alliances. An attack was inevitable. I warned you countless times, but you ignored me."

Abe frowned. "Son—"

"But *this one*," Ellis said, his voice rising as he pointed the gun at Jacob. "An exile from Derro!" He pointed the Talon back at Abe. "He spins some heroic tale about escaping the Maws, and suddenly you believe his warning about an attack. But not your own son!"

Jacob's eyes pulled away from the rising tension as he caught Ammon starting toward Ellis. The young man snapped his aim at Ammon, causing him to halt.

"Don't even think about it," Ellis said. "Unless you want to end up like *them*."

"Son, I'm sorry," Abe murmured.

"*Are you?*" Ellis roared, snapping the Talon's barrel back on Abe. "Are you sorry for ignoring my warnings, or are you sorry for exiling your own wife? *My mother!*"

"You don't understand—"

"*Don't!*" Ellis cut in. "I know what *you did*, Father. You had Mother exiled for the death of her former husband—a man who exiled himself, hoping to reunite with his love. And when he found her with you, you couldn't stand the thought of losing her. So, you had Gerrick kill him. Mother suspected you, and when you realized she knew, you framed her and had her exiled."

Abe's frown deepened. "How … did you—"

"Gerrick told me. The day I *hired* him to approach the Maws and the Last Patriots for the attack."

Hired? Jacob's dying heart plummeted. He had just taken a bullet for Ellis—the mastermind all along—Jaci's son. The one he'd vowed himself to protect. For her.

"It was *you*," Monique cried. "*You're* the reason for the attack?"

"You had to pay for what you did," Ellis said, stalking closer, the Talon still leveled at his father. "Gerrick found it easy to convince them. They were already planning to strike. They just needed a nudge; a false promise that Ostria could be theirs in the end. I just never expected Gerrick to betray me."

Screams erupted from the entrance of Ostria, cutting through the tense air.

Monique frowned. "But the Last Patriots—"

"—Are being handled," Ellis interjected calmly. "I followed your orders. A team escorted the vulnerable to safety in the caves. Then I had our forces plan for the attack. I've had them primed for this moment, prepared daily under the guise of defense. Those screams? That's my men repelling the Last Patriots."

Ellis brandished the Talon. "Even if Myla manages to slip through, I have this to stop her. And when it's all over, when my forces bring everyone back, they'll find me—the lone survivor, the councilor who weathered the storm started by these three refugees you allowed in."

Ellis laughed darkly, his gaze sweeping over Jacob, Ammon, and Alex. "Oh, and by the way … they were going to grant you refuge. A split vote—two to three—once again, my vote unheeded."

He glared at Abe and Monique. "But no more. I will rule Ostria alone, and my people will embrace me—the one who issued warning after warning, only to be constantly ignored. I will usher in a new era, welcoming every exile Derro banishes here. We will build a proper nation. And those who refuse to abide by my laws, they will perish. Just like you."

Ellis fired the gun twice.

The sharp cracks pierced the air, each shot followed by horrified screams as the bullets found their mark. Abe and Monique's heads jerked back, their bodies collapsing onto the unforgiving cobblestones.

The courtyard fell into a stunned silence, interrupted only by the distant echoes of battle raging beyond the walls. Jacob couldn't believe his eyes. He squeezed them shut, trying to avoid the sight of Abe and Monique's tragic demise. A groan escaped his lips as his mind and body grew weaker by the second. Footsteps drew nearer, and reluctantly he forced his eyes open, spots of light dancing in his vision.

He saw Ellis approaching.

Jacob's pounding heart sank deeper as he watched Ellis stride forward, his footsteps heavy and purposeful. He locked his eyes on the young man's face, a mask of determination and ruthlessness. There was no trace of the innocent son Jaci once knew. Only a cold, calculated killer. Wincing, Jacob braced himself for his inevitable demise.

"Go," he rasped, urging Ammon and Alex to run.

Ellis aimed the Talon downward, flames dancing off its chrome finish. The barrel hovered directly above Jacob's head, swaying amid his blurred vision, a deadly threat that made his eyes bulge. But he didn't flinch. He couldn't. He was already dying; the blood seeping from his wound made it hard to focus. His vision was fading.

He had failed. In so many ways.

His mind flashed to Charlotte, her face twisted in agony as she lost her life. He should have done more to protect her. And Morgan, his loyal friend, whom he'd brought here only to die. He couldn't save him either. The council. Jaci. He had let them all down.

"It's crazy," Ellis said, his voice muffled and distant. "The sheer power a single gun wields. The length it drives people to. One squeeze, one bullet, and lives are forever altered." He laughed darkly. "You never truly knew who you were shielding."

The gunshot rang through the air, the sound deafening in Jacob's ears. His body jerked violently, breath stolen from his lungs as a searing pain exploded in his chest where the bullet tore through. It wasn't his head, as he'd braced for, but the pain still left him reeling.

Ells grunted, his knees slamming onto the ground as he continued pulling the trigger. *Click. Click. Click.* The gun was now spent.

Then Jacob's eyes grew wide as Ellis's pale face fell onto the cobblestones, coming into view just inches from Jacob's gaze. Looking down, he saw the Talon now lying near Ellis's limp hand. His focus shifted when he noticed an arrow lodged in the cobblestone, its stone tip stained with blood. Tracing the shaft, he saw the other end protruding from Ellis's back, pointing toward the crimson sky.

The reality of the events unfolding before him was too much to comprehend amid his dying state. He could barely hold on as it was, but he grasped onto what little he could hear. The sound of burning wood snapping, stone crumbling, and distant roars reverberated through his ears, reaching him in a hollow, muted way, as if coming from a great distance.

He was fading away.

To his left, the Council Tower burned, radiating oppressive waves of heat that clawed at him and threatened to consume him. He followed the trail of destruction, head rising, and watched as the flames raced upward, their fiery tongues determined to bring the tower crashing down.

Ostria's last beacon of hope was crumbling before his eyes.

All because of a gun in the wrong hands.

The bullet! Jacob screamed internally.

He couldn't let anyone find the bullet in his pocket. The risk of it being used to kill was a burden he wouldn't allow. He had seen too many lives lost because of guns.

Wincing amid the pain, Jacob somehow managed to reach into his pocket, each movement sending a spear of agony through his chest as he retrieved the bullet. He crawled upward, crying out as he pushed through the pain and grabbed the Talon in his other hand. Releasing the magazine, he glanced to his right, piercing through the haze, and saw many figures approaching, led by a woman. His heart sank as he spotted Ammon and Alex among the crowd, their faces grim as a figure stood on each of their sides, restraining them.

He had little time.

He slid the bullet into the magazine, slammed it back into the grip, and pulled the slide back. Then he raised the Talon and pointed his swaying arm toward the advancing group.

"Stay back," he managed to rasp.

The figures halted.

Jacob's chest heaved as he struggled to keep focus, forcing his body to stay present despite the overwhelming agony. With a strenuous effort, he somehow forced himself to his feet, the Talon still trained ahead. He wobbled, his shirt heavy, soaked in his own blood. He could feel his knees wanting to buckle under his own weight.

"Jacob ..." a voice called.

It was Ammon.

Jacob saw him break away from the men holding his arms and step forward, arms raised in surrender. Blood still seeped from his battered face; a grim reminder of the brutal punishment Jacob had inflicted upon him.

Punishment for killing Charlotte.

Jacob would have killed Ammon. The rage and hatred that had built up inside of him exploded in a fury of blows, relentless until he could no longer lift his arms. Until Ammon was nothing more than a lifeless shell.

Vengeance for Charlotte served.

But Daemion had stopped him. Another failure. One he still had time to make up for.

The thought flashed through Jacob's fragile mind as he watched Ammon approach. The temptation to pull the trigger, to end it all, gnawed at him. His finger twitched on the trigger. Vision fading, he stepped forward, shaky aim trained on Ammon. He adjusted his grip on the Talon, fingers turning white as he prepared to fire a single bullet in the chamber.

It was fate.

"You . . . killed my . . . wife," Jacob cried.

He coughed, blood filling his mouth, the taste metallic and bitter. His world darkened, fading in and out, but the Talon in his hand remained solid. *Real.* He pulled the hammer back, the click of the mechanism echoing in his ears, a sound both satisfying and damning. It fueled him, that vengeful flame rising within him once again.

Ammon flinched, bracing for the gunshot, but his eyes never left Jacob's. "I know," he cried. "And I've lived with that mistake for over a year. I wanted to tell you before, but ... I didn't know how. I'm sorry. It wasn't supposed to happen like this."

Jacob frowned. *Those words ...* They echoed in his head. *I'm sorry. It wasn't supposed to happen like this.* They were the same words Ammon had said earlier tonight. Jacob had misunderstood them before, believing the apology was a prelude to Ammon's betrayal.

But he had been wrong.

Ammon wasn't going to betray them. He wanted to make sure he had told Jacob the truth, realizing their last moments were imminent. Just as Jacob's was now. The moment replayed in his mind. Ammon's bowed head. His apology. The quiet acceptance of blows.

Jacob's mind dug deeper, stirring more memories.

Ammon's haphazard gunshot that killed Charlotte. A fatal mistake that had come only in response to Mason's gunshot. Jacob had known that then, but he'd been so consumed by his desire for revenge that he chose to ignore it. Ammon had even betrayed his closest friend, choosing to save Jacob's life when he shot Mason, preventing him from delivering the fatal shot. He had said those words then too.

I'm sorry. It wasn't supposed to happen like this.

His mind flashed, revealing a hazy image of Ammon towering over him, clutching a large rock in his hand—the very moment he had ended Twig's life, opting to save Jacob then too. Just as he had done when Wes snatched him. And just like he had tried doing tonight by stopping Gerrick.

You're stronger than you think. Jacob's grip on the Talon wavered as Charlotte's voice whispered in his mind, urging him to make the right decision. He frowned, the lines between right and wrong blurring in the face of a truth he had refused to see.

Her words had reached him on a night much like this one. He had failed to listen to them when he murdered Richard. He had been too weak then, consumed by revenge and hate. And now, as his life slipped further away, he felt even weaker than before.

But unlike that night, he welcomed her words, letting them comfort him, infusing him with strength. He felt them seep into his core, igniting a revelation.

True power didn't lie in the weapon, but in the strength to resist using it.

I'm strong enough today, Charlotte. Because of you.

"Ammon ... you're ... forgiven."

Jacob's vision blurred further, the edges darkening. It was time. With a last surge of strength, he redirected his aim toward the bloody sky and fired. The sound of the bullet echoed through the night.

A symbol of release, of choosing mercy over vengeance.

Jacob's knees buckled and slammed onto the cobblestones with a dull thud. His strength ebbed away, and the world around him grew dim, Ammon fading before him. A sense of peace washed over him as all the hatred he'd bottled up finally released.

And then he saw her—Charlotte.

She was sitting on a peaceful beach. *Their* beach. She fixed her gaze on the endless expanse of the ocean, the soft breeze gently dancing in her hair. It was peaceful. It was—

Hello, Jacob.

"Sid!" Jacob blurted, his eyes widening at the sudden voice in his head. "Is that really you?"

Well, of course it's me, Sid said. *Did you expect someone else?*

"No, I just …" His words faltered. "Sid, how are you … *here?*"

I am always here, Jacob.

But you weren't. And how are you now? And where even is here—

"Come on, *you,*" Charlotte called, waving him toward her.

Jacob's heart fluttered. Her face … was so beautiful. Drawn by the pull of her presence, he started toward her. He could feel the warmth of the sun on his skin and the soft sand between his toes. It felt … almost … real. *Is it really her?*

With cautious steps, he approached her, his heart thundering in his chest. As he drew closer, her form became clearer, her presence almost tangible. A smile broke across his face, tears of joy welling in his eyes as he reached out a trembling hand to touch her. To feel her once again.

Charlotte smiled, her hand meeting his on her shoulder. Her touch. It felt soft. *Real.*

"We've been waiting for you," Charlotte said, her other hand resting on her stomach.

Jacob's heart swelled as he gazed into her eyes, those familiar, loving eyes, and felt the weight of the world lift from his shoulders.

All the pain, all the loss, faded away in her presence.

The scent of the sea. The warmth of her hand. It was all so real, so beautifully *real.*

But how?

"Charlotte," Jacob began. "This place … Am I—"

"Home," Charlotte warmly interjected. "You're home, Jake."

Jacob smiled, a deep, contented smile. He was where he belonged. *Finally.*

Home, at last.

EPILOGUE

JACOB HUGHES IS DEAD.

Ammon Curran stood stock-still and frowned as he watched Jacob, his friend, crumble to his knees and collapse onto the earth.

The gun slipped from Jacob's grasp, hopping and then skidding across the cobblestones until it came to a stop near Ammon. He kneeled, listening to Alex cry out from behind him. Others present gasped and whispered, unsure of what they had just witnessed.

Jacob had tried saving Ostria.

He had failed.

Ammon picked up the gun and cradled it in his hands. His frown deepened, understanding how much damage the firearm had caused in its temporary life on Eremos. The people it had changed. The innocence it had stolen. The lives it had taken.

Ammon sadly knew the damage all too well.

He shook his head slightly, his mind still in disbelief. Ells—Jaci's son—had been the mastermind behind the attack on Ostria all along. And Jacob had lost his life trying to protect him.

I've failed.

Ever since that morning in the pit, the morning Ammon was convinced he was dead—because, how else could he explain seeing Jacob Hughes exiled—he'd vowed to himself to protect him.

After all, Jacob would never have been exiled had it not been for Ammon. He owed it to Charlotte Hughes to protect Jacob, a hollow attempt to redeem his actions that had led to her death. That dreadful night continued to haunt him, and he knew it always would. Now, however, he faced another terrible night to remember.

Ammon sniffled, tears streaming down his face, stinging as they mingled with his open wounds; a painful reminder of the punishment he had endured. He felt he deserved worse. *More.* Although Jacob had chosen to forgive him in the end, his last words still echoing in Ammon's mind; Ammon still struggled to forgive himself. The notion seemed simple, yet extremely difficult at the same time.

He understood now why some believed exile to not be enough justice. Sure, his exile had been a living hell, wrought with cannibals, madmen, and arduous treks, where every day felt like it might be his last. Yet he still lived. Unlike Jacob and Charlotte Hughes. If Ammon could have chosen, he would have taken Jacob's place, trading his life for Jacob's without hesitation.

The world needed more people like Jacob Hughes.

He hadn't pulled the trigger on Ammon tonight. He had changed his aim. *If only I had done the same … Better yet, if only I had the strength not to pull the trigger at all.* If only everyone in Derro could find that strength. Maybe then the country might finally have a chance at being something better.

Ammon stood, eyes lifting to the flames that consumed the Council Tower. Wood snapped and stone crumbled, echoing final cries as the tower clung to its last moments. It was only a matter of time before it collapsed entirely.

He heard footsteps approaching from behind. He didn't turn. Even if he wanted to, he couldn't. Someone stopped next to him and rested their head on his shoulder. He glanced over to find Alex. She frowned, tears cutting through the dust caked on her face. The bridge of her nose was bruising, blood still trickling.

And yet, Ammon still found her beautiful.

"He died for nothing," Alex cried.

Ammon frowned. "It does feel that way," he said. "But I refuse to let myself believe it. He died for something. Even if we can't see it yet."

A raindrop splattered on Ammon's head. Followed by another. Then another. His eyes grew wide as he snapped his head upward, staring into the crimson sky. He had expected rain, a divine blessing from God for the fire consuming Eremos.

He was wrong.

Instead, he faced a different kind of gift—one from another god.

High in the blood-red sky, like an obsidian orb, a Screech hovered. Neon lights traced its form as torrents of water, and plumes of red powder streamed from its sides. It looked as if the sky was bleeding.

"What is *that?*" Alex asked.

"It's fire retardant," a voice said from behind, scoffing. "It was only a matter of time before Derro intervened."

Ammon turned to see a woman approaching, a bow clutched in her hand, ready for use. Her braided ponytail swayed over her shoulder as she neared, bouncing against her fitted tank top. She had been the one who had killed Ellis, firing a single arrow into his chest. Ammon had a strong suspicion of who she was.

"I take it he was a friend of yours," the woman asked, nodding toward Jacob as she came to a stop within Ammon's reach.

From this close, the woman appeared to be middle-aged, her brown, sinewy skin showing mild wrinkles. Strands of her hair had fallen loose, trailing down her rough face and brushing against her lips. Ammon also noticed cuts along the bridge of her nose and on the top of her forehead. She had clearly battled her way into Ostria.

"I'd like to think so," Ammon finally said.

"Ah, so it's complicated."

Ammon nodded.

"That's life; a series of complications. We handle each one as it comes." The woman turned her head, locking eyes with Ammon. "Speaking of complications … I'm still deciding what to do about you and your friend here."

"You're Myla," Alex said.

"Indeed. And you two must be part of the group that kidnapped one of my Healers. That didn't sit well with me. Especially after I discovered one of them was a Last Patriot." Myla glanced down at Ammon's wrist, then slowly raised her gaze, eyes narrowing. "There's nothing worse than being betrayed by one of your own."

Ammon scowled. "I did what I thought was *right*. What I thought would give me the best chance to survive."

"How noble of you," Myla said. "And I understand. Sometimes, to survive, we must change, become someone else. We both certainly weren't born a Last Patriot, now, were we?"

She smiled. "Nonetheless, I'm willing to turn a blind eye. After all, you did fail, and I lost many people. Those losses will need to be replaced as we begin our new reign on Eremos. If you're willing to do the same and support me as president, then you're welcome to join us. It may just offer you the best chance of survival."

Ammon's gaze wavered as thoughts raced in his mind. Myla's offer hung in the air, a lifeline or a noose—he couldn't tell which. He glanced at Alex, her expression hopeful yet uncertain.

"You don't have to decide now," Myla said, her voice dropping to a whisper as she stepped closer, her eyes piercing. "But do choose wisely."

Ammon's fingers curled into a fist as Myla turned and started toward her forces. The weight of his decision pressed down on him, heavier and more suffocating than the surrounding smoke. It didn't feel much like a choice. Just as it hadn't on his first day of exile, when Wes had ordered him to jump out of the Screech.

It's an unfortunate way of life. Jacob's words entered his mind. *We chose the path with the highest chance of success. Or, in our case, survival.*

That day, he had chosen the clearest path.

Just as he always had, in order to survive.

ACKNOWLEDGMENTS

THERE HAVE BEEN many people, knowingly or unknowingly, who helped me along this tough, sometimes crazy, but mostly amazing journey of writing *The Exiled.*

First and foremost is my beautiful wife, Kayla. Thank you for always urging me to "Keep going" during my times of doubt (which, as you know, were frequent). Your unwavering support goes beyond words. Thank you for listening to my countless rants when I needed to get the writing out of my head and spoken aloud, without always needing feedback. Those rants were necessary, and when you did offer insight, it was always invaluable. I owe Jacob's arc to you. Thank you for your love, your constant encouragement, and for keeping me sane through it all. Most of all, thank you for being the amazing mother you are to our Rylee.

I also want to express my deepest gratitude to my beautiful daughter. Rylee, thank you for filling my heart with joy every single day through your silliness and unconditional love. There is no greater joy than being your father. You've breathed new life into me and taken me on a journey I never could have imagined. Thank you for your incredible superpower of always bringing me back to the present. It's natural for me to get lost in my head, sometimes too deep, but you always pull me back. And most of all, thank you for simply being you. As you continue to grow, never stop being yourself. Find your own voice; and find it early.

And to the rest of my family: my twin brother in crime, Jared; my mother, Crystal; and my father, Douglas. Each of you, in your own unique way, encouraged and inspired me throughout the journey of *The Exiled*. Thank you.

Two editors played a crucial role in shaping *The Exiled*. Thank you to Erin Young, who saw the rawest version of my manuscript and helped me transform it into what it is today. Your edits and suggestions, especially in the realm of world-building, were invaluable. And to Joe Pierson, who took the most complete version and polished it into its final form. I'm deeply grateful to both of you.

And as much as the words inside the book matter, the presentation matters equally, including the book's cover. I'm incredibly grateful to Christian Storm for bringing *The Exiled* to life through the cover and interior formatting. Your creativity and attention to detail have truly brought my vision to reality. Thank you for your exceptional work.

I also want to express my gratitude to my incredible friends who offered their input, tirelessly read and re-read chapters, and encouraged me to finish. Thank you to Bravo, Deb, Megan, Ian, Maranda, and Chef.

And finally, to you, the reader. Whether this book found its way to you by chance or intention, thank you for giving it a shot. If you've made it this far, I'm forever grateful and hope you truly enjoyed *The Exiled*.

ABOUT THE AUTHOR

JORDAN LOWERY is a husband, father, and, when he can carve out the time, a writer living in Oregon. *The Exiled* is his debut novel. Growing up, Jordan loved getting lost in books. So much so, he spent over a decade getting lost in his own. As a lifelong book and movie nerd, he is always in search of anything that challenges him to question his existence—including why he can never remember where he left his keys.

Learn more at: **WWW.JORDANLOWERYAUTHOR.COM**